Ain't Misbehaving

Dallas Duets 1

Marji Laine

Write Integrity Press

Ain't Misbehaving

© 2018 Marji Laine

ISBN-13: 978-1-944120-57-3

Published by Write Integrity Press
PO Box 702852
Dallas, TX 75370
Find out more about the author: Marji Laine
Or email her at AuthorMarjiLaine@gmail.com
www.WriteIntegrity.com
Printed in the United States of America.

Table of Contents

Dedication

Setting this story in my hometown has made it all the more special to me. Not only were both my mom and dad born in Dallas, but most of my family has stayed in or near the Dallas/Fort Worth metroplex.

And my family means so much to me!

I dedicate this, my seventh published book, to the seventh member of my family, my precious daughter-in-love, Amy. I'm so grateful to my son for bringing her into our family. And I'm so grateful to her for bringing out the best in my boy. Your love and encouragement and outstanding hugs bring such joy to my life!

Chapter 1

Her future wasn't the only thing at stake.

Annalee Chambers slipped into the bare consultation room with her mother, father, and attorney. Reporters filled the hallway and shouted questions as the door closed.

She tugged at a stray blond curl the August breeze had pulled from her hair clip and sank into the wooden chair. If only invisibility were possible—a desire initiated when they'd arrived at the Frank Crowley Court Buildings, and cameras started flashing.

Leaning against the high back of the seat, she stared at a ceiling fan making a slow rotation. For a solid minute, she matched her breathing to the fan's rhythm.

"The judge has to toss away this whole fabrication." Her mother paced the same path as the shadows from the circling blades. "Can't she identify the real victim in this case?"

Annalee bristled at the insinuation. "Mr. Madison was the victim. He and his family are the ones impacted by the accident." Accident. She hadn't even realized she'd hit anyone.

"It's clear the district attorney is only trying to hurt my

campaign." Father lifted a slat from the blinds hanging over the only window in the room. The sunlight made him squint. "He's been a fan of Mayor Ellis since the beginning. Now, since I'm a real threat, he's doing everything he can to make me look bad."

And Annalee had aided in the destruction of her father's mayoral campaign when she traveled to club-row to pick up her tipsy friend.

"We don't have too much time to plan this defense." Mr. Walbright bent his balding head over his briefcase. He unearthed a stack of legal-sized documents and came up for air.

She caught her father's disgusted glance. Poor Walbright. He probably hoped that his representing Annalee would pave the way for him to work at her father's firm, but his lack of organization and planning for this case destroyed that dream in its infancy.

The man thumbed through the stack until his forehead relaxed, and he pulled a page from the chaos. "As I understand the events of the night, the officers didn't actually see you driving the car. Is that correct, Miss Chambers?"

"Yes, but what does it matter?"

"That is the whole point. Can't you see?" Mother took another lap around the room. "There are no witnesses. Not even Mr. Madison saw your face because you had something white covering it."

"Giselle's napkin." She eyed her Versace bag, tempted to pull out her sketch pad and let this conversation fade from her mind.

"Whatever." Her mother halted. "If no one can place you in front of the bar, there is no case."

"But her car was at the scene." Mr. Walbright pointed to another report he'd extracted from the mess. "Circumstantial, yet it does place her at the accident."

"Except she wasn't in her car when the police joined her in the parking lot." Her father swung around, his blue eyes bright under his tawny hair. "She was helping her friend get in the backseat."

Friend. A Strange term to use for Giselle. The woman claimed she remembered nothing of her trip home—not blocking Annalee's view or hysterical giggling or even slamming her foot on the gas pedal. And she hadn't so much as called to wish Annalee luck in court.

"If only you hadn't gone to that club." Mother stared at the ceiling.

"I told Giselle to call me. She needed a safe trip home." And the ride would have been safe if her friend had stayed on the passenger side of Annalee's Mustang. The moment she crawled across the seat, Annalee should have pulled over.

"I assume she didn't appreciate having to sober up at the jail."

Better than being in the hospital if she'd attempted to drive herself home. Annalee focused on the heavy table in front of her. What unpronounceable combination of elements made up the super industrial-strength material? And where could she get some to help her through this next hour?

Sharp heel clicks resounded in the hallway. The low rumble of voices gave way to a few raised ones, maybe questions being shouted but not distinguishable. The door opened. Annalee shielded her eyes against camera flashes. Several of the reporters called out, but she ignored them.

Her tall, elegant sister shut the door and tugged sunglasses from her face. "The people are crazy out there." As a well-known model, Ramona Chambers knew what crazy looked like.

"Another reason why the judge will throw this whole thing out." Her mother stood as tall as her daughter, though her hair was short-cut and silvery instead of the perfect long waves that Ramona enjoyed.

Annalee examined her French manicure against the smooth gray of the sturdy table. How many fists had pounded on it yet not affected its steady balance? The temptation to do a little pounding crossed her mind, but instead, she refocused on Mother's comment. "If the judge throws out the case, what will happen to Mr. Madison and his family?"

"You'd better worry about what happens to your father and his campaign if Judge Vaught doesn't." Mother withdrew a lipstick from her purse and applied the pinkish tone.

"But the man works two jobs." She lifted her gaze to the quad. Each of them stared down at her like her nose had gone missing. "His family will be on the streets."

"Where did you get all of that hogwash?" Her sister pulled the wispy scarf from around her head and tucked it into her bag.

She stood. "It's not hogwash. The story has been on the news and all over the Internet."

"Well, you've got me there. Must be true." Ramona chuckled.

"None of that matters, Annalee." Mr. Walbright packed his things back in his case. "The judge will decide."

"But if there is a case …" Father stood.

"If Judge Vaught accepts the DA's charges, which she won't, I'll make sure the delays extend well past the election. After November, DA Barrett may lose interest when his man is no longer in office." Walbright chuckled and led Mother to a back door leading to the courtroom.

Father patted Annalee's hand. "See, Sunshine? Things are going to be fine."

Fine? Maybe for her family, but the Madisons would see

nothing fine about Mr. Walbright's scenario.

He ushered her in front of him through the door. She followed her attorney to a small table on one side of a wooden rail while the rest of her family sat behind the divider.

The slender judge climbed to her place as everyone stood. She took her seat in a cascade of black robes.

In this heat? No wonder the woman's gray-brown bangs stuck to her forehead.

"Be seated." She proceeded to read the formal case title and all of the details of the accusation. "Defendant, please stand."

Annalee rose, every eye watching like an audience at an open-heart surgery. She lowered her chin but glanced at the judge. The robed woman there gave her a lingering perusal.

"Straighten up." Her mother's whisper brought reality to the situation.

Annalee relaxed her shoulders and lifted her face.

"You stand accused of the crime of Leaving the Scene of an Accident Involving Injuries, a Class A misdemeanor carrying up to one year in county jail, a fine not to exceed $5,000, and restitution to the victim in this case …" The judge flipped a page in her file and continued in a robotic tone. "… a Mr. Robert Madison."

She hadn't considered the possibility of jail time. The thought chilled her. Maybe Walbright's ideas were best after all.

"How do you plea?"

Annalee stole a look at her attorney. Why didn't he say anything?

"Just say not guilty," he whispered.

What? She had to talk in front of this whole roomful of people? Wait … *she* was the one to declare her plea?

A low rumble resonated over the room. The judge tapped her pen against a wood block. "Quiet, please." She arched her unibrow in Annalee's direction. "Miss Chambers?" The jerk of her head made her wispy bouffant teeter.

"Guilty." Annalee's answer came out in a conversational tone, as though she commented on the weather.

The room erupted with urgent voices. Annalee clamped her jaw tight. Her announcement would have repercussions of storm-like proportions.

Mother exclaimed and leaned over the bar, hissing instructions. Ramona joined her, though slightly more composed. Mr. Walbright called for the judge to give him a few minutes alone with his client. Father stared at his hands on his knees.

Annalee hated betraying him, but the mayoral race wasn't life or death.

The judge tapped on the block again and raised her voice to gain order. "Mr. Walbright, you just came from a conference with your client. Didn't you discuss this?"

"No, your honor. I mean yes, but …" He ran his fingers through what little hair decorated his bare scalp. "She's confused."

"Are you confused, Miss Chambers?"

Annalee shook her head and lifted her chin higher. "No, I'm not." She dug her nails into her palms but kept her voice steady and strong.

"She seems coherent to me, Mr. Walbright." The judge narrowed her eyes. "Perhaps you're the one who's confused."

He nodded, adjusting his rimless bifocals. "A minute, please?"

"You have five while I consider the matter." The judge held up her hand as Walbright shoved Annalee back through the side door and shut it behind him. "What were you thinking, Annalee?"

The man mouthed her mother's words like a ventriloquist dummy.

The thought caught her off guard for a moment, but she clasped her hands in front of her and straightened her shoulders. "I told you I didn't want the Madison family to bear the financial burden of the accident. Then you and Mother and Father decided their needs didn't matter." She turned toward the window.

"So, you took it all on yourself?"

She whirled on him. "Who else should?" If her father's money was the only valuable thing about her, then at the very least, she could support those poor people.

"But I could have gotten you off. You would have walked away." He lifted both fists and turned toward the doorway, probably plotting his escape?

"Mr. Madison can't walk. At least not for a couple of months while he heals." Surely, Mr. Walbright could tell the difference between winning and stepping on people.

He spun in her direction. "Don't you realize you can go to jail for this?"

Not until the judge mentioned it, but by then, Annalee had already made her decision. She crossed her arms. "It's your job to see I don't. Your magical defense?" She eased the sarcasm out of her voice. No need to further rile the man.

"The only thing I had was their lack of evidence. With your guilty plea, my defense is null and void."

She hadn't thought through the details but didn't regret her action. "This was the right thing to do, Mr. Walbright."

"Maybe yes, maybe no." He took her arm and led her back toward the courtroom door. "But you put your future in the hands of a perfect stranger." He paused as he pushed the door open. "And she was appointed by Mayor Ellis."

Oops.

Summoned to Camelot.

CJ Whelan approached the expansive doors of the Preston Park Country Club. Hand-carved wood, wrought-iron handles, and lead-crystal insets proclaimed their value in a dignified tone. He jerked one of them opened and passed through the portal from normal life to luxury.

"May I help you?" The host's tuxedo seemed too formal for such an early hour and way too hot for the Texas heat wave going on outside.

"I'm here to see Scott Whelan." His dad had insisted he attend the Intercede Foundation's board meeting. Everything in CJ wanted to rebel or at least, find a plausible excuse. But when he'd blown off last month's meeting, they'd cut some of the funding for the program he directed.

This time, he'd spent almost an hour talking to God about the situation before he arrived. Dad didn't understand the importance of the program.

Or maybe he only cared about getting his way.

The man behind the concierge counter dipped his gaze toward CJ's sneakers and back up across his blue jeans and shirt. "I beg your pardon. Mr. Whelan is in the formal dining room." He emphasized *formal.*

What was his problem? CJ wore a button-down shirt over his tee. In this August blast, that took effort and dedication. "And?"

He lifted his chin and nailed the host with steady eyes.

The man didn't meet the challenge. Instead, he dug through a drawer on his left. "The Preston Park Country Club has certain standards for our formal areas." He pulled a folded, navy tie from the drawer. "This should satisfy the membership."

Next time his dad forced him to come here, he'd not bother covering his Casting Crowns tee shirt. He ground his molars together and snatched the silk dog collar. Knotting it around his neck, he left it loose. The maître d' attempted to tighten it, but CJ swatted his hands away. "I can see myself in."

"No, no, no." The man leaped to bar his way. "I must see your identification, sir. Mr. Whelan has given me a list of his guests, and I must check off your name."

Of course. We mustn't color outside of the lines, must we? He whipped out his license and dropped it on the host station. "There. We good now?"

"Mr. Whelan?" The host's eyes widened. "I'm so sorry, sir. I had no idea."

"So, I'm not on dear Daddy's list?" CJ collected the card and stuffed his wallet into his back pocket.

"No need to be on his guest list. As Mr. Whelan's son, that is, your father's son, I mean of course you are, but your entrance is automatic, or at least it should be. I'm terribly sorry for all of—"

CJ raised his palms. "Look, if you'll tell me where to find my dad …"

"This way." The man's face had reddened from his ears forward.

He probably expected CJ to raise a fuss or make an official complaint. Fishing a dollar out of his front pocket, CJ stuffed it in his hand. Not the amount of tip the man normally received, but it would have to do. "It's all right. Really."

The worker slunk away and left CJ scanning the six faces around the table. His dad had his head buried in a deep discussion with two men on his left. Leon sat beside him with Davis one seat down. On his right, Mr. Simons had his arms crossed and lips pressed together. Next to him, the only woman in the group, Delfia Moncrief, matched his body language, only adding furrowed eyebrows. A large balding man, Arthur Bench completed the circle. The grimace he wore, along with his hand on his swollen belly, looked more like gas than disagreement.

"Ah. Carlton." Dad's toothy smile didn't reach his eyes. "You decided to come."

"After you cut funding during your last meeting, I didn't have much of a choice."

"And I didn't agree with that motion, either." The woman pointed a slender finger toward Dad.

With every seat occupied, CJ pulled a chair over from a neighboring table. Dear old dad hadn't truly expected him. Fancy that.

"So, what is it you don't agree with Mrs. Moncrief?"

"Selling that beautiful old house where the center is. I'd rather see it become some sort of monument than another parking lot."

Sell the center? A thousand tiny scorpions stung the back of his neck and began traveling down his spine. "The center is kinda still using the building right now."

Dad straightened. "We can't expect you to come in mid-discussion and understand what all is going on." He tapped the table in front of Leon.

Alton Leon cleared his throat. "I move this discussion be

postponed until we can discuss details more fully."

"I second." Charles Davis puffed out his chest with the announcement.

"Well, I don't. I want to discuss this now." Mrs. Moncrief patted the surface of the shiny wooden table.

You go, Mrs. M. CJ studied his father. The man's lips curled up a bit, and he acknowledged Mrs. Moncrief through half-closed eyes. He held the influence, and he knew it.

"Let's keep moving." Arthur Bench popped a couple of Tums from a small bottle and leaned on his elbows.

How had this group ever made any decisions? "Where are you planning to move the center if you end up selling the Haskell house?" He didn't care what Davis and Leon declared. Dad was the puppet master, again attempting to direct CJ's life for him.

"That's a discussion for another time." Dad pointed to Mr. Bench. "Didn't you have a—"

"But I'm here. And moving the center will make drastic transitions for me and my team, not to mention the families we serve. If you move to a building too far away, those who walk to their homes, almost thirty percent of our children, won't be able to use our services at all."

"My thoughts exactly." Dean Simons slapped his palms on the table. "Moving isn't necessary. We can add on where it is right now."

Add on? This was a discussion CJ could embrace. "Absolutely. The side lot goes virtually unused, except for the bus drive-through. We could move the lane further over and have enough room to make two more buildings, both as big as the first."

Mrs. Moncrief smiled at him. "You are so like your mother, CJ. So singular in your purpose for those children."

Dad stiffened at the mention of Mom.

"I love the idea." Simons tapped the table.

"You're getting ahead of yourself, Carlton." Dad's gaze, no longer under the comfortable half-lids, pierced him with warning. The others chimed in and a rumble of discussion overwhelmed the table.

CJ gave his dad a side-long look. "I'm not the one selling a building that's still in use."

Dad's composure slipped. "No one said we were selling." A red blotch grew above his proper business shirt.

"I second the motion." Mr. Simons slapped the table again.

"That wasn't a motion." His dad pulled at his collar.

"All in favor." Mrs. Moncrief's wide smile overwhelmed her tiny mouse-like face, but she raised her hand and called out "Aye" along with Simons and Bench. "Opposed?"

"Now just a minute." Dad's graying hair, normally smoothed to perfection, had a few fraying edges. His eyebrows mimicked the look as he attempted to regain the control he'd lost. "This isn't a real—"

"None opposed. The ayes have it." Mrs. Moncrief let out a tiny giggle, girlish despite her sixty-some-odd years. Bench and Simons joined in her laughter. Davis and Leon looked confused.

Dad took an audible breath. "Very well. We won't be selling the center … this year." He drew a hand across his hair from front to back and lowered his tone. "But we have received a serious complaint from one of the surrounding businesses."

Surrounding businesses? "There's only one, and the owner and I are good friends."

"I'm not speaking of the adjacent body shop. I'm referring to The Glan-Sec offices on the east side of the property. They insist the loud noises of the children while they play interrupt their business dealings."

"What business dealings? One's a dentist and the other's a day-trader." And neither of them could claim quiet offices if CJ's visits were any indication.

"Nevertheless, the children may not play within fifty feet of their building from here on in."

"That's ridiculous. They can't stop children from playing in their own yard during the middle of the day."

"But it's not their yard." Dad's volume rose and conversation at nearby tables silenced for a moment. His Adam's apple dipped. "The center's in a business district and had to earn the acceptance of the surrounding owners before we could move in."

"And the owners of the Glan-Sec building approved. They can't go back on their agreement now." CJ leaned forward. "Besides, Glan-Sec are only lessees. They don't have any say."

"But they can complain to the city planning and zoning committee." Leon agreed with Dad. Small wonder there.

"Yes, and the committee can remove the center's license, making the entire foundation look bad." Davis's comment only confirmed CJ's opinion that he was indeed a shadow of Leon and not a separate man at all.

"Still, you can't force the children to stay indoors all day. That's not healthy." Mrs. Moncrief's argument brought mumbles of agreement from the other two men.

"You seem to have a standoff, Dad." CJ gripped the edge of the table. "Maybe you should postpone this discussion, too, until someone actually makes a formal complaint against the center." Which would never come.

Dad squinted.

"Seems fair, Whelan." Mr. Bench rocked forward. "I suggest we call this meeting complete."

"Second." Simons raised his hand as the rest of the attendees mumbled. "I think we're on the right course, Scott." Mr. Simons shoved against the table to stand. Bench engaged him in conversation as they walked out together.

"Well, if we're done here, I have an appointment." Leon didn't look at Dad. "Good-bye, all." Davis followed him out without a word.

What sort of invisible adhesive did those men use to be so synchronized?

"You've got a good man in charge over there." Mrs. Moncrief smiled in CJ's direction and patted his dad's shoulder. "The afterschool center is in good hands."

Dad's eyes hadn't strayed from CJ's face.

CJ ignored the stare-down, drumming his thumbs on the polished wood. "Don't you all eat at these meetings?"

"We ate before the meeting began. And you were late."

"Better check with your secretary, Dad. I was here five minutes early according to her e-mail."

He broke his choking glare and scooted his chair back. "I'll do that. Next month, be here at eight." He waved a finger at CJ's neck. "And wear your own tie."

Dad exited the dining room without a backward glance.

CJ resisted the smile wanting to spread.

This win was only round one.

Chapter 2

Annalee's hair slapped her face as the wind whipped, matching the storm inside her that spun out of control. She darted around the corner of the Brimming Café and almost mowed down a young potted tree. Losing her grip on the sides of her flaring yellow skirt, the wind caught hold of it. Someone whistled, and her cheeks heated before she secured the hem around her thighs.

"Pay attention, Annalee." Ramona grasped her scarf with both hands. Her column-style Kate Spade skirt couldn't blow up if she wanted it to. No wonder her sister always came across with calm elegance.

Annalee side-stepped the tree, wondering how it withstood the gale. With hair stuck to her lip gloss and partially blocking her view, she made it to the door and pushed her way inside.

"Go find a spot for us. I'll get your frappe."

Her sister might as well have said *I don't want to be seen with you when you're such a mess.* Annalee finger-combed her curls. Spotting an empty corner, she set her purse on a low table. The vinyl cooled her legs, even though it groaned a bit under her settling.

She glanced out the window where the little tree wavered and shook against the battering. A lady chased down a slip of paper across the parking lot. She had no chance until a worker in an orange vest stepped on the page and waited for her to catch up.

Her sister rounded the frosted glass barrier separating the homey couches from the diner-feel of the barstools and ordering counter. She set two large cups on the table.

"Looks like orange is going to be my new color." Annalee pointed out the window at the man's vest. "I can see myself picking up trash along Interstate 35."

Her sister's low chuckle perfectly matched the rest of her, calm, ordered, controlled. "Don't be silly. Only convicts wear orange jumpsuits. They'll put you in a yellow vest with reflector tape."

Peachy. Annalee withdrew her sketch pad from her purse and opened it to the picture she'd started while waiting to leave the court building.

"Community service won't be that bad. You'll probably get random jobs to do at some county clerk's office." Ramona smoothed her skirt. "At least you aren't stuck with that guilty plea."

And why was that? Why had the judge questioned her about the whole thing? "That still completely confuses me."

Ramona expelled a sharp exhale and glared at Annalee. "It's really simple, Annalee, though I have no idea why she would make the offer to you. It's not like she's a fan of Father."

For all of her sister's puffing and posturing, she hadn't explained anything. "So?"

"So, it's the difference between being convicted of a crime and just making up for the problem. You have all of the requirements of a guilty plea, but it doesn't go on your record. Nolo contendere—no contest." She took a deep drink from her cup. "Don't look a gift horse in the mouth." She chuckled. "And I do mean horse. Did you see the nose on that woman?"

Her sister's jab at the judge didn't engage Annalee. She had nothing to laugh about with months of random work hanging over her head. Why did the judge think she needed to waste her time doing … whatever it was, especially after slapping her with a huge fine and extensive restitution? She sipped from her cup and let the chocolate chill seep in. "I just hope I don't mess up. You heard what the judge said about jail time if I'm not successful in my work."

"The key will be to make a good impression on your probation officer so he'll give you a simple task."

Annalee shut her eyes for a moment then focused on her drawing. She wanted to get the judge's nose right. "I make good impressions, Ramona. I don't have to be five-foot-thirty with a perfect cat-walk style to do that."

"You need to keep your mouth closed."

What? Surely, Ramona of the C-average wasn't insinuating A+ Annalee wasn't very bright. "Say again?" Annalee paused her pencil-scratch and looked up.

"Guilty? Really? What were you thinking, Annalee?"

Ugh. That phrase. Only a few years older than Annalee, Ramona had picked it up during her pre-teen years from their mother.

"You already know what I was thinking. Must we rehash this?"

Ramona sipped her frothy drink. "Sure made a great impression in the media. Everyone in that courtroom thinks you're a bonafide idiot for accepting responsibility for the man's injuries."

"Except Judge Vaught."

"Yes." Her sister lifted her gaze to the ceiling. "Except for the one person who could have declared you crazy and released you."

"I'm not crazy." Annalee shaded-in the face of the district attorney. Shame she didn't have her colored pencils. He'd turned a lovely shade of mauve when the judge reprimanded him for pushing a guilty verdict.

"What is it, then? Did you get religion? Or simply a misplaced need to be a martyr?"

"Look." She laid her pencil down and took another drink from her cup. "I've already explained what happened. You don't get it. Let's move on."

"It is you." A man with a silvery mustache and wispy, gray hair that surrounding a ball cap approached from the other side of the pseudo-wall.

Annalee didn't recognize him, but Mother had friends all over Dallas. Not usually ones who wore over-sized, untucked, plaid shirts, but … "Do I know you, Mister …" She held up her hand.

"McDermott." He eyed her hand and sniffed as he looked away. "No, and you don't know the hardworking man you mowed down a few weeks back."

Oh. Annalee let her hand drop to the table.

"People like you should be locked away in them little boxes, what you call, isolation rooms."

"Now you wait one minute." Ramona stood, towering over the man. "You may know your friend, but you have no idea to whom you are speaking."

Annalee almost glowed at her sister's defense.

"My family has lived in this county for over a hundred years, and my father is running for mayor. If anyone is hardworking, he is."

And there went the warm-fuzzy. *Splat.* Ramona couldn't help her attitude. Her ancestry and the social circles in which she ran meant everything to her, as they did to Mother.

"Yeah? And that makes you think you gots the right to run over innocent folks in the street?"

"If he hadn't been in the street, she wouldn't have run him down."

Oh, yes, that was much better. Annalee stood. "Ramona, thanks, but let's go."

Her request went unheard. The wind kicked up again, spinning a wave of dead leaves against the glass pane. With a crash, the tree collapsed. Clumps of dirt and pottery shards blended with broken branches and litter.

The Brimming Cafe had become a sanctuary for CJ. From the first moment he'd come upon this place, the comfortable chairs, the coffee aroma, and familiar faces gave him a place to be in the real world with real people.

CJ picked at his blueberry muffin, mulling over the call he'd received on his way here. Christina Vaught had been Dad's friend for years. But that wasn't why he'd agreed to help her. Her threat to contact his dad about the matter had turned that corner. The ever-present tension in their familial relationship needed no extra fuel, even from a well-meaning old friend.

Tony, the owner/barista, swiped at his spotless counter then popped his rag against the register. "And that's what I think o' the woman on trial today."

Along with most of Dallas. At least those who ever noticed local news reports.

"Something about her—up there on the news." Tony twisted his rag around his finger and pointed to the large flat-screen in the corner.

The text flashed across the screen with the name of Annalee Chambers—a name that had become almost infamous in the last several weeks. A pudgy man with a dark comb-over was speaking to a reporter. Probably her lawyer. He looked the type.

More text showed up announcing the judge's verdict. He already knew that, and most of the why behind it, though he still didn't buy the judge's assumptions about the woman's character.

Then she was on the screen. The girl, in a yellow, sleeveless dress, had incredible blue eyes and perfect curves over some serious high heels. Her legs went on forever.

He eyed the beautiful woman making her way down a cascade of steps as the wind tossed her curly hair about her shoulders. CJ kept his eyes glued to the TV until a commercial broke the feed. "Wow."

"Wow, nothing." Tony whistled. "That girl is hot. And richer than your wildest dreams, my friend." He laughed. "Well, richer than mine anyway."

CJ smirked. Tony was one guy who knew riches didn't impress him. "Say's she pleaded guilty."

"Yeah. But the judge didn't accept her verdict. Something political, I bet."

"But she's paying all the medical expenses." CJ kept watch on the news crawl at the bottom of the screen.

"At least that helps." Tony sponged down the sink. "Isn't Mr. Madison the dad that Miz … that Margo told me about? Has some kids in your center?"

CJ stifled a smile at the mention of his assistant's name. Tony stuttered over it every time he mentioned Margo. "He's the guy." What a sad day after the accident. The two Madison boys had whimpered all afternoon, sure they'd never be allowed to come to the after-school program again. CJ took another swig of coffee. "At least with the restitution, the family won't have to worry about being thrown out of their apartment."

An aged voice rose on the other side of the glass wall. "That poor man gots three kids to take care of, and you couldn't care less to see them all on the street." The older man approached and eyed Tony. "You need to be more careful of the thugs you serve in this joint. Gives the place a bad name."

Tony stiffened. "Settle down, now." He pasted a half-smile. "Why don't I get you a muffin? On the house."

The man, CJ only knew him as McDermott, snorted in Tony's direction, but leaned closer to the glass counter to eye the pastries.

A fashion-model type with a dark bob trailed the man. "Wait a minute. He strikes up a fight, insults my family, slanders us in public, and gets a free muffin for his trouble? You have a unique way of doing business."

Another woman, CJ could only see her shoes behind the taller lady, followed her. "Let's go, Ramona."

"Hey, I'll give you a muffin, too." Tony raised his voice. "Free muffin day. While they last."

CJ looked around. Cheap announcement. Only one other table had someone sitting at it and he had earbuds in.

The model tossed her cup into the trashcan but leveled a haughty expression toward CJ. "And no one said she actually hit the man. Not even him."

He tucked his chin and shrugged. She hit someone? Funny, he couldn't picture her even curling those sculpted nails into a fist.

"Ramona, please." The other woman spoke low, glancing in CJ's direction with long blond curls and brilliant blue eyes under thick black eyelashes.

The knockout from the TV. She still wore the same outfit. CJ straightened. Maybe he could warm up to a fiery war of words after all.

"Hey, that's you." Tony folded his towel over the rack behind the counter. "That's you on the TV, there, Anna-Whats-it."

She was even more beautiful in person and possessed a wide-eyed innocence he seldom found in women of his father's social group.

The Ramona-woman hissed. "And she's late for an appointment."

The blonde cleared her throat and held out her hand to Tony. "I'm Annalee Chambers. Do you know Mr. Madison?"

"You don't have to be polite to him. He works here." The brunette's appeal fell flat.

Tony stared at Annalee's hand for a moment then shook it as if the tiny thing might be infected with cooties. "Yeah. Nice guy. Hard worker. Three kids."

"I've heard, though I haven't met him."

"That's right, you knocked him over and kept going."

McDermott stretched to his full height, at least a half-foot less than either woman, and fisted his waist. "A woman like this doesn't deserve your free muffins."

Her pleasant expression stiffened but remained on her face. "I only came for coffee, anyway." She tossed her cup in the trash.

Little lines appeared between her sculpted brows as McDermott continued his rant. Despite her composure, the man hit a nerve. She probably didn't get such obvious dislike from men very often.

Ramona turned and placed a graceful hand on her hip. "We wouldn't have even entered this hole if we hadn't had to stay downtown so my sister could meet with her probation officer."

"Not helping." Annalee's sing-song made little effect in the verbal attack.

"No self-respecting person in our circles would be caught dead in this roach trap." She whirled and stormed out.

CJ clamped his jaw against the laughter which threatened. The woman's anger warped her words to insult herself more than Tony. Despite her appearance, the dark-haired model was easy to dislike.

Annalee's cheeks had reddened. She glanced at Tony. "I'm sorry about all of that."

He chuckled. "I'm sorry her rant caught you up in unintentional slights."

Her practiced smile broadened slightly into the real thing. "I'm used to it." She turned toward McDermott, opened her mouth, but shut it again.

He fidgeted under her stare. "What, you gonna run me down, too?"

"That's enough, Myles." Tony reclaimed the towel and wiped at his spotless counter. "She ain't done nothing to deserve you talking that way to her."

CJ's cheeks heated. Why hadn't he taken up for her? Said something to calm the man down.

McDermott turned away but paused when Annalee touched his arm. "Sometimes things aren't always what they seem."

"That a threat?"

McDermott was an idiot.

CJ found his voice and stood. "No, it's not a threat. She's saying the awful things you believe about her aren't as true as you think they are. Like you stealing all the sound equipment missing from the church."

McDermott stepped back. "What is this? I didn't steal any sound equipment."

"No, but if enough people were to say you did, then someone would believe it and think you're a horrible person."

"Yeah, but this ain't no gossip. This lady mowed down a very nice man."

"I know." CJ laid a calm hand on the man's shoulder. "But I think there might be more to the story than the reporters are sharing."

"And how many times does that happen, eh?" Tony laughed, putting the finishing touches on calming the atmosphere.

"Hey, Tony, get Mr. McDermott here another of his usuals on me." CJ turned to the older man. "You like that? We good?"

He lifted his chin. "Hokay." His face dropped into a scowl as he passed Annalee. Turning, he took his new coffee and exited.

"That was very nice of you. May I please pay for the coffee?" Annalee reached behind her.

"No need."

She looked down and spun. "Oh, no." She quick-stepped in

skinny spikes around the glass wall. CJ followed.

"My purse." She sighed as she reached the table. "I was a little distracted." She recovered the large tan bag hanging on the back of a chair.

"So, you're meeting with your probation officer?" Of the few he knew, Hankins would do the best job with her case. Nice. Fair-minded.

"That sounds so convict-like. I confess the whole meeting has me a little nervous." She looped the strap of her bag over her shoulder, and a paper fluttered to the floor.

CJ reached for it. A courtroom scene spread across a sheet of plain notebook paper. So much detail, the dark paneling, the faces. "This is really good."

"Oh. It's only a doodle."

"Are you an artist?" If this doodle was any indication, she was.

"No, no. Nothing like that. I like to paint and draw, and I've taken classes."

He looked into her eyes. "Then you are an artist."

She avoided his gaze and shook her head. "Artists actually have finished works. Whether they sell them or not, at least they have them. I just have a basement filled with ideas."

CJ held out the drawing. "Could've fooled me."

"Keep it if you like. Since you won't let me pay for the man's coffee. And thanks for speaking up for me."

She hesitated like she wanted to say something else, but Ramona opened the door. "Would you come on? You're going to be late."

"Mm-mm-mm-mm-mm." Tony practically hummed as Annalee darted out. "Wait 'til I tell your ... Margo about this little tête-à-tête of yours with Evil Rich Woman."

"You saw her. She's not evil." Though he wasn't sure his assistant would feel the same way.

"I saw her Versace bag."

"You know Versace?" CJ stifled a chuckle.

"Are you kidding? I have three teenage nieces, kid." Tony snapped the towel in his direction.

"Wearing designer clothes doesn't make you evil."

"Really? Then what *does* it make you?"

CJ's mind flitted back to the fights of his parents as his mom flew off to Milan or Paris. "It makes you have a whole 'nuther set of problems."

"Kinda like you'll have when that assistant of your … um, Margo finds out you played nice with Annalee Chambers." Tony popped the towel again and turned his back, laughing outright.

Probably so. "*If* she finds out." He lifted an eyebrow in Tony's directions, and the man laughed again.

CJ glanced at the ceiling. "Still, her fit would be nothing compared to my dad's."

"What's the great Scott Whelan got against a cute little number like her?"

"Not her, her father Todd Chambers. I don't know what started the animosity, but Dad doesn't have a kind word for that man."

"Well, your dad sure won't hear nothing from me." Tony headed for a recently vacated table and rubbed it down.

At least Dad's dislike didn't have to do with the size of the family's bank account.

Margo was a different story. Her wealth-hating had escalated. CJ had been procrastinating, but he would have to say something about it, now. Especially after that phone call from Judge Vaught.

And hopefully, he could figure out a way to save his own hide from Margo's sharp attack.

Marji Laine

Chapter 3

The glare outside blinded. Annalee slipped on a pair of Oakley sunglasses, but they did nothing for the nerves wiggling their way into her core.

Her treatment at the café offered little comfort. The one guy was nice enough. And the barista was hospitable, of course, he had to be. But the adamant hatred exhibited by a perfect stranger? She hadn't counted on such behavior or attention. The composure training her mother drilled into her had come in handy.

If only she had a little privacy to let out the wrapped-up emotions. But no. She had to go meet her new probation officer. The coffee soured her stomach. Her precarious position weighed on her.

Ramona had pulled her car to a fire hydrant on the one-way street. She rolled down the window. "Hurry up before I get a ticket."

Annalee looked past Ramona's Jaguar to the high-rise construction down the street. Hard-hatted workers moved along

37

the narrow beams like circus performers.

She hesitated, sure she would witness one stumble and plummet. Her heart crept up her throat, blocking out all of the downtown Dallas traffic noises. She couldn't breathe, and her gaze riveted to the construction site.

"Come on." Ramona honked as Annalee lingered for another second. "You're going to start off probation by being late? That's going to make you look really good."

Jolted out of her nightmare, Annalee forced unsteady legs to move forward. She climbed into the passenger-side of the car. While she appreciated Ramona's support, she'd rather have the family chauffeur driving her. Parker knew how to calm her and improve her spirits.

Ramona merged into traffic. "Don't worry. Your officer is going to take one look at you and drool, like those wannabes in the coffee shop were."

"No one was drooling." Annalee tugged her notepad and pencil from her purse and started sketching the construction she'd seen. Surely, the men had some sort of safety tethers.

"Yes, they were. And so will your PO. He'll be so smitten, he'll likely want to shorten your time so he can date you."

"Don't be ridiculous. He can't do that." Annalee framed the building site on the small page and started to add shading and details.

"You're right. He'll probably extend it so he can see you more often." Ramona laughed. "But don't open your mouth. No telling what will come out."

She paused in her drawing and glanced at her sister. No reason to revisit the topic. She took a deep breath of the new car smell. Not as fresh as real country smells but more pleasant than the exhaust and dust of the streets.

"This is as far as I go." Ramona stopped outside the grand building. "You think you can make it from here?"

Why was everybody treating her like a child? "I'm twenty-five years old. I can find my way into an office."

"Touch-y." Ramona pointed to a parking garage across the street. "I'll find a spot and check my e-mails. Give me a call when you're done." She pulled back onto the wide thoroughfare.

The silence, without Ramona's constant instructions and comments, lifted Annalee's spirits until she turned around. The court building loomed in front of her like a giant bear cave. As much as she determined to push through this, she would have relished her sister's continued presence.

She glanced at the drawing she'd been working on. Mother complained about her art as a childish pursuit. Annalee knew better, but dropping into the escape of more doodling would be childish indeed. She crumpled the picture in her fist.

Her probation officer had ultimate power over her right now. She could live with that, but getting on the man's good side would be helpful. It was worth a try anyway.

She punched the elevator button for the third floor. The panel slid open, and a frosted glass with the words Dallas County Probation stood closed directly across the hall. Perfect. She pushed through the door into a small waiting room with a counter barring access to two desks and windows beyond.

"May I help you?" A heavyset woman with tanned skin poked a pencil behind her ear, her voice decorated with Spanish overtones.

"I'm... I'm..." Annalee scanned the room. No bears, no dragons, no narrow beams. She could do this. "I'm Annalee

Chambers. I'm supposed to report to my probation officer."

"Yes, Miss Chambers." She pointed down a hallway behind a swinging panel. "First door on the right. She's been expecting you."

Annalee turned down the hallway and stutter-stepped. Her heels clattered on the tile floor. Did the receptionist say *she*?

She advanced a few more steps before knocking on the door, convinced of a miscommunication. Her hope vanished when a feminine voice called out, "Come."

Her stomach twisted. The floor beneath her seemed to wobble, and she grasped the doorknob to steady herself. She nudged open the door and peeked inside.

The tall, unsmiling woman stood. Her brunette waves quivered in a messy bun. She extended a slender arm. "Laurel Stewart, Miss Chambers."

"Please call me Annalee." She flashed a grin and accepted the handshake. The tight squeeze made Annalee's amethyst ring cut into the flesh of her pinky, but she refused to flinch.

Laurel Stewart released her hand and motioned to a chair.

As Annalee sat, prickles rose in her stomach. She could swear she teetered on one of those beams she'd seen across from the cafe. "Exactly what is community service?" She clasped her hands and rubbed her thumbnail across her palm.

The probation officer sat and flipped through an open file on her desk. "Usually, merely a matter of doing odd jobs for the court system. Tasks too menial or tedious to assign to an administrative assistant."

"Like road work?"

The woman chuckled without mirth. "No, no. Often random filing for different departments or officers of the court. However, in your case, I've had to adjust my initial plan."

Plan? "Which was?"

"Originally, I was going to have you work for Judge Vaught herself. She recently lost her clerk. Though she has temps to work in the actual hearings, she needs someone to complete tasks of typing and copying in her office."

"I could do that." Maybe this community service wasn't the scary beast she'd imagined.

"Yes, and the job was something I thought you'd be suited for."

"Thought?" As in past tense? Just when Annalee had started feeling comfortable with the possibility.

"The judge had other ideas." The brunette turned over another sheet in the file.

That's right. "She mentioned such in court." Something about logical consequences and direct interaction modification, whatever those were.

"Yes, she called me as soon as your hearing ended." Ms. Stewart came around the desk with a legal-sized document stapled at the top. "This details your expected behavior during her probation. I suggest you read it thoroughly before you try to make an appointment with the center's supervisor. Contact me with any questions."

What center? Prickles climbed higher up Annalee's spine. She signed and dated the last sheet on duplicate copies.

"Judge Vaught thinks you would be better served working at an afterschool program."

"After-school?" As in kids? How was it that Annalee could still hear the judge's pen tapping against the wood block as though Her Honor sat in the next room?

"Yes. It's supported by the Intercede Foundation, but it works in cooperation with the county to provide childcare to people in the neighborhood who can't afford it."

"Childcare doesn't sound too bad." She strained to keep her calm demeanor while her insides crumbled. *What do I know about children?*

The woman's green eyes flickered fully open to stare at Annalee without her head moving. She snorted. "You haven't been around intercity kids very often, have you?"

Annalee rubbed her palm harder. "No... but, I mean, they aren't going to tie me up in a chair like in silly old movies." She smiled. At least she thought it was a smile, though almost impossible to squeeze past the knot in her throat.

The officer returned to her side of the desk. "Probably not." She scribbled something on a notepad, tore off the sheet, and held it out.

Obviously, the interview was over. Annalee stood and took the note from her outstretched hand.

"This is the address of the center. You're due there Monday afternoon at two thirty to get a feel for the place and work out your schedule." She leaned over to write on another sheet which she then handed to Annalee. "You'll need to give them this form." She straightened. "You might as well know, the judge put in a call to the center's director to request your placement there. While they reached an agreement, it was with deep reservations. You should consider yourself warned."

She blinked, while her insides went into full tilt. Then why had the judge assigned her there? She focused on maintaining her mask. *Steady. Calm.*

"The leadership at the center doesn't tolerate affluent people who take advantage of their social status." Laurel Stewart reseated herself at her desk in silent dismissal.

Was that an accusation? If anything, Annalee had resisted using Father's influence. How much more could she do than accept full responsibility for the whole accident?

She squeezed one hand with the other and sucked back the barbs she wanted to hurl at the ice queen. "Thank you for the warning. I'll be on guard."

Making her way back outside, her heel clicks on the linoleum held a strange metallic sound. An image crept into her head of a condemned pirate walking the plank.

Late again.

CJ braced his left hand between the points of the wrought-iron fence and swung his legs to the other side. Tony had brought up the Yankee/Ranger game coming up this weekend. Never a short conversation since they both held strong opinions of the other's home team. They'd likely pick it right back up tomorrow.

But with the children due soon, his delay likely stressed out his assistant. He dashed toward the front porch and leaped onto it.

"'Bout time you got here." Margo Pritchard barely looked up from her computer screen when he stepped into the cool, dim interior of the center.

"Don't you want any lights on in here?"

"Huh-uh. Too warm with the lights on. Besides, I can see fine." The reflection of a Facebook page showed in the glass of her readers.

"I can see you're working hard … ly."

"None of your sass, boss-man." Her short, salt and pepper hair bobbed as she spoke. "I suppose you've already seen the news about the rich woman's day in court?"

"It was only a hearing." He hung his keys on the board behind his assistant's head and leaned against her desk.

"What did Tony say about it?"

Bother. Why didn't she visit the café on her own instead of making him spill about the man? "He said..." He'd said Annalee was hot, but CJ sure wasn't willing to convey that thought. "...she hadn't done anything to deserve ugly gossip." Or something along those lines.

"Really? Are you sure Tony was talking?"

CJ smirked. The comment might have been a little out of character for the king of covert conversations but not so strange for him to come to a lady's defense. And Annalee Chambers was definitely a lady. "I think he was assessing the fact that she pleaded guilty."

"She better have, after what she did to poor Mr. Madison then taking off like nothing happened." She tsked. "It's a good thing they nabbed her, or she'd have bolted and looked back laughing."

"If she'd wanted to escape her responsibility, why didn't she fight the accusation?" Where did Margo get such crazy pictures? The woman he'd met was nothing like the one she described. "What happened to love thy neighbor?"

"I'm not from her side of the tracks."

"Seriously, Margo. Show a little of the compassion you pour out on the families here."

"They need the care and comfort. They don't have anything

else." She crossed her arms. "That girl owns the world."

"And I know firsthand how empty a high-society life can be."

Margo huffed. "Are you really taking her side?"

"How can she have a side if she already gave in?" CJ shrugged. "Besides, I can't hold automatic disgust for anyone because they happen to have money."

"Of course not. You'd have to hate yourself." The woman's eyebrows rose.

How well he remembered. And he knew the prejudice going along with wealth. Or the lack of it. "And you already did enough of that for both of us." He moved to his desk and sorted through the junk mail.

Almost two years had passed before Margo stopped assuming his every decision was rooted in dollars and cents or profit for his father's company. But with her background, he couldn't fault her too much for having a dislike of the elite crowd. Especially when some of them exuded entitled attitudes.

Besides, telling her the same attitude showed up across socioeconomic ranks wouldn't break a chip off of her stubborn prejudice.

"True enough. But as for Annalee Chambers, I'm convinced you're taking up for her simply because she's pretty." She clicked away at her keyboard.

He pulled on his work gloves. "I'm not taking up for her." Even though she was drop-dead gorgeous. Her wide, blue eyes flitted across his memory. But he'd better play her looks down if he wanted to make it through the conversation unscathed. "And what makes you think I'd say she's attractive?"

She turned the laptop to face him. "There. As if you haven't already seen pictures of her. But I'll play along."

The screen showed her dressed as she'd been at the cafe', likely taken right outside the Frank Crowley Courts Building. She looked distressed and rather helpless. Add to that the gentleness he'd witnessed with Myles McDermott, and she seemed irresistible … to someone who sought a relationship—which he did not. How could he be so attracted to a woman he'd barely met? He tore his eyes away. "She's okay, I guess."

"Okay? She's a Texas Princess."

"Since when do we have a royal family?" He pushed the computer back around and strolled into the kitchen.

"That beauty pageant thing." She followed, her rubber-soled shoes squeaking on the linoleum. "And she won it, so your fake *okay* doesn't fly with me."

"Whatever." Best to not linger and give the busybody more fuel. He wished he hadn't seen the picture. Something stirred in him making him want to run a Google search of his own. "I'm working on the back fence before the kids get here. You should—"

"I best get snack started." She pursed her lips and began pulling pots and bowls out of the cabinet. "I get it. Leave the boss alone."

"I don't want your wealth-hate to seep out to the kids. That goes especially for Tyrone and Hayden Madison." He paused at the screen door. Those boys didn't need any other excuses to be angry at Annalee, especially since she would likely be working with them. But he wasn't about to spill that information to Margo. Not yet.

Her shoulders slumped a little, and she stared at the counter. "Give me a little credit. I wasn't born yesterday." She picked up a wooden spatula and whacked the soup pot for punctuation.

CJ chuckled. "Not by a long shot."

"I heard that."

He darted off the porch in case the older woman decided to fling the utensil in his direction.

Annalee erased a stray line from the canvas and eyed one of the scenes she'd doodled that afternoon.

Mother insisted the family take on an appearance of mourning through the weekend. "The media would love to click pictures of us smiling and laughing with our friends in the face of this tragedy."

Annalee resisted commenting on her melodramatic reaction but didn't argue. After all, Mother's decision meant free, uninterrupted time in her studio. Though she did have to disappoint Boyd by missing their weekly date at the country club. She'd grabbed a sandwich and descended to her happy place.

Forgoing her golf game with some friends on Saturday wouldn't be a big deal. And giving away her tickets for the Bass Performance Hall's production of West Side Story, while annoying, was doable, even if the tickets only went to one of Father's more influential clients.

The creamy fall colors of her private domain comforted her. And she needed the peace, especially after the man yelled at her in the coffee shop. Crazy how his harsh rant bothered her more than the uncomfortable meeting with her new probation officer. Something must be wrong with her to care more about her interaction with a man who likely slept in an alley than someone who could put her in jail.

Cool in the bright lights of her basement studio, she laid her pencil down and took a bite from the edge of the croissant, eyeing the new picture. Maybe this was one she could actually finish. Taking another, larger bite, she set the snack down and reclaimed her pencil, focusing on Judge Vaught's nose. This time she'd get it right. She'd lightly sketched in the shape when Boyd's guitar strummed ringtone sounded from her phone.

"Why guilty?" The whine in his voice didn't impress her. He could be as bad as Mother.

"Because it was the right thing to do." She was getting tired of saying it over and over. "For Mr. Madison and for Father."

"I get that it was good for Madison. A winning lottery ticket worth of good. I wish your father had allowed me to lead your defense." He obviously wasn't convinced.

"Father said letting anyone from his firm defend me might stir up accusations of foul play."

Boyd snorted. "Yes, but that was before you pleaded guilty. What was Walbright thinking?"

"I didn't tell him."

Silence played across the connection. As it lengthened, she wondered if she'd lost the call.

"Boyd?"

A heavy sigh roared into her earpiece. "I never thought of you as a fool, Annalee."

Enduring a full-body wax would have hurt less. Her stomach coiled into a knot around her bite of turkey and provolone.

"I don't understand how your father benefits from any of this."

"The district attorney milked the whole accident to dress up the injured man as pathetic. He expected us to fight the accusation, making Father and I look heartless. But my pleading guilty, especially in the face of flimsy and non-existent evidence, destroyed his plan. I came off looking honest and making Father into a benefactor trying to help the poor and downtrodden."

Though not the prime reason for her action, at least this was a concept Boyd and even her mother might be able to embrace.

He remained silent as she explained. Did her excuse sound as icy to Boyd as it did to her?

"I stand by my opinion." His response sounded like an attorney.

"That I'm a fool?" Even if she had convinced him, he'd never admit such.

"I know you're a little different, and your artistic phase is rather amusing, but to invite such scorn into your family and on top of your father's election …"

Amusing? Puppies were amusing. Clowns. Puns. Her neck stiffened. The man didn't understand her passion to create.

She could picture him shaking his head. He wouldn't finish his thought. He never did when he was worked up. Just as well. "Perhaps we should talk again, later this weekend." She focused on keeping her voice even.

"I'll call you when I can." He hung up, leaving her stinging from his rebuke.

I never thought of you as a fool. She tossed her phone onto her bed. How dare he?

Staring in her oval mirror, she let her thoughts drift through the day. Had she been foolish? If she'd been able to cover the man's medical bills and support his family from her own allowance, she would have. Then pleading innocent wouldn't have been a problem for her. But her monthly supplement wasn't nearly enough, and she didn't have any savings of her own. Pleading guilty had been the only way to help the man and his family—with Father's money to pay the ordered, and greatly needed, restitution. Why couldn't Boyd see that?

And Mom. And Ramona. And Mr. Walbright. And Father.

Maybe she *was* the idiot and everyone else was right.

Funny how Boyd could suck the creativity out of her like a helium thief. She abandoned her project and stacked it in the corner with all of the other unfinished canvases.

The following two days, she couldn't even bring herself to descend into her studio. No inspiration. No creativity. Certainly, no peace. Mother hardly spoke to her. Father burrowed in his office.

She swam a bit, hit a bucket of tennis balls, read through a magazine, and Internet-surfed until she was bored out of her mind.

Finally, on Sunday night, she called Boyd, hoping they could go to dinner. When he didn't answer, she tried Giselle, but the call went directly to voicemail. No surprise there. Her friend had insisted she had no memory of the accident she'd caused, and then she'd never contacted Annalee again.

That blister still burned.

Even Ramona abandoned her, though she'd at least answered.

"I'm bored out of my mind."

"What did you expect?" Her sister almost sounded like the family had purposely distanced themselves.

"Certainly not solitary confinement." The tiny gray box that man at the coffee shop talked about came to mind.

"Did it occur to you that from the moment you uttered guilty, certain assumptions took over? You have to act like you're sorry for the man."

What was she talking about? "I am sorry for him. And his family. It's why I …"

"I know. I know. But you can't go about regular life. Not if you want to save face. You have to act sorry."

The words made a loose circle in her brain. "Then this weekend is a self-imposed punishment to convince people I'm remorseful."

"Exactly. And completely unnecessary if you had engaged your brain before using your mouth." Her sister never left slights unspoken.

Annalee pursed her lips as she said good-bye. Surely, her mourning didn't have to continue. She straightened. Of course not. Annalee wasn't helpless, and she didn't have anything to prove.

Marji Laine

Chapter 4

CJ relished the grilled beef smell drifting into the parking lot as he opened the heavy wooden door to M's Restaurant. Given the choice of where to meet his father and the Intercede Foundation's financial officer, he decided he might as well choose a place he liked.

He signed in with the hostess and looked around. Football on the mounted television screens drew as rowdy a crowd as the exclusive north Dallas address allowed. The nearest TV showed the silver and blue star of the AT&T Center. When was the last time he'd gone to a Cowboy game? How strange to think football had been his whole life not so very long ago. Now the thought of wasting three hours to watch a game made him a little sick.

Maybe he should have chosen the Mexican place across the parking lot. Except Dad hated the spices. And this was all about keeping the Chairman of the Intercede Foundation Board happy. Okay, happy was a stretch. At least complacent enough to leave CJ in charge of the center for another year.

His phone vibrated, and he slipped it from his pocket and mashed the button before the ringtone started. Having the theme to Jaws play in a steak and seafood place might not be the best idea. "Hey, Dad. It's not like you to be late."

"I'm not coming. Burton couldn't make it at the last minute. No need to come out there at this point."

Of course, there wasn't. Dad's time meant money, business, and deals. Why waste the evening and a perfectly good dinner with nobody-important like his son? "All right then."

The call ended. Had he expected anything else? At least this postponement likely bought him another year as the center's director.

The Cowboys made some great play, and the restaurant exploded with cheers. He scanned the room, looking for a corner where he could enjoy his solitude and nurse the re-emerging wounds coming from years of trying to impress his dad.

A curly, golden head faced away from him near a back corner, avoiding most of the craziness. He swore the hair looked familiar. Then Annalee Chambers turned to speak to a server. He'd been right.

This might be a perfect timing type of blessing. He could discuss the phone call he'd gotten from Judge Vaught and make initial arrangements for Annalee's work at the center before Margo even knew about her coming. He moved to the hostess and canceled his table. "Can you tell me if the woman over there is waiting for anyone?" He pointed. "This sounds crazy, but since my appointment isn't coming, I thought I'd join her. She's an acquaintance."

It wasn't a lie. She was an acquaintance, even though he'd never formally introduced himself.

The woman at the stand gave him a knowing look. "She's on her own as far as I know, but she's already eaten."

Bummer. Before he could contemplate whether to join her or not, she slid out of her booth, dressed much more relaxed than last time in a sleeveless sweater and white shorts covered in lace. He approved.

She turned his direction.

Whoa. He spun and strode to the door. *Crazy stalker.* She had every right to think so if she recognized him even though it wasn't true. Maybe he could make it to his truck without her notice. He pushed open the outer door into a blinding camera light.

A man holding a television camera and a woman with a microphone stood at the bottom of the steps. The woman barked out orders. "Make sure your vantage point is looking up at her to give her a heavier appearance. Dawson, go see if you can get her receipt or any ticket with high dollar items. We'll highlight her celebratory dinner while the man she hit is only just out of the hospital."

CJ stiffened. Poor girl. She didn't deserve this. Though he'd taken a step outside, he retreated, shouting through the opening, "Backdoor." Then he let the heavy wood fall back into place before turning.

He caught the shocked look in Annalee's eyes as he barred her way.

"What are you doing?" She tried to push past him. "I need to leave."

"Wait a second." He peeked through the crack in the door to see the cameraman trotting. His own weight and that of his camera and light kept him slow. "A reporter was outside ready to ambush." He opened the door a crack. "I think you're good to go, now, but you better hurry."

"Thanks." She stepped out and halted. "There's another team out by my car. Looks like I'm going to have to pay twice for going out to eat."

"Not necessarily. I'll take you home. You can have someone come for your car later."

Her eyebrow lifted as she lowered her chin and crossed her arms. "I don't think so."

"Fine. But you wait and this lot will be full in a few minutes."

A crease showed up between her sculpted brows. "I don't even know you."

"CJ." He held out his hand. "We met at Brimming Café last week, sort of." He eyed the group gathered by the Mustang. "We better hurry."

He dashed down the steps hoping Annalee followed. He had to pause to unlock and open the passenger door of his beat-up Chevy truck, but she climbed in and reached across to open his door, as though she'd grown up in such a vehicle. The group near her Mustang noticed them.

"Put your head down."

She obeyed, squatting in the floorboard as he calmly coasted past the crew. "We're clear." She resumed her seat after he accelerated onto the street. Another television van passed them on the road, headed toward the restaurant.

"You were right about the reporters."

"They swim in schools." He shifted and smiled. "Where to?"

"I live near Forest and Midway."

His peripheral vision caught her studying his profile.

"Lucky you happened along, CJ."

"Yes. I had an appointment, but it got canceled at the last

minute."

"Are you a reporter?" She didn't sound angry.

He cut his eyes toward her. The light was dim, but she didn't look angry either. Didn't look anything. She held the same calm expression he'd seen at the café. "Not me."

A moment of silence wrapped around the car. "You happened to be going out as I was, and recognized the group of reporters there?"

He let out a hard exhale. This explanation didn't even sound good in his head. Pulling to a stop at the left turn light at Midway, he faced her. "I was actually coming in, but I recognized you. Thought you might think I was a crazy stalker." He explained how his intention to drive away before she saw him halted when he recognized the Channel Eight news team at the bottom of the stairs.

The signal changed to a green arrow, and he proceeded.

"If they had seen me, it could have looked bad for my father." She pointed to a side street. "Turn there."

CJ complied. "Why? What do they care where you eat?"

"Not where I eat. *That* I eat. Remember, I'm the heartless socialite who tried to run after hitting a poor man and leaving his family destitute." She neither smiled nor laughed at her statement.

"You pleaded guilty though. They're not going to be destitute."

"Yes, but the reporters in this town, at least some of them, are paid to vilify me, especially if it can reflect on my father."

Not such a stretch considering the way they had treated others reaching for a political stronghold in this city.

"Take the next left."

He turned into a neighborhood making the change from large old homes to huge upscale ones.

"You'll take a left when you reach the dead end."

A brick wall interrupted by a wooden gate and cluttered with enormous trees loomed. The road jigged to the right again. They entered an area that looked like a park flanking both sides of narrow Valley Ridge Road. A large planter filled with something yellow stood on one side while a lane lined with old-fashioned gas lights adorned the other. He drove a hundred yards and followed her directions to turn into the lane and then left onto a driveway, which had been completely hidden.

A security car was parked next to the driveway. As CJ made the turn, the vehicle powered up and rolled a few feet forward, blocking access to the drive.

Annalee rolled down her window and waved to them. "It's just me, Trent."

The window on the security unit rolled down and a hand waved them on as the car reversed back into its place.

How rich was this Chambers family? To be on Dad's radar, Todd Chambers had to have money, but how much? CJ couldn't even see the house, but old sturdy trees completely covered the cement drive. A break in the trees on his left exposed the house. Akin to a French chateau, it had been just on the other side of the thick tree line.

"This is fine." She unlatched her seat belt. "If you keep going straight, you'll reach the wooden gate. The dead-end where we turned? I'll have security open it for you."

Security? He jumped out and ran around the front of the truck, but she'd already climbed from the cab.

"Thanks for helping me. I don't know what I would have done if you hadn't been there." She pulled out a bill.

"I don't want your money." He held up his hands.

Passing him, she tossed the Franklin through his open door. "Go have the dinner you missed out on." She waved and released a semblance of a smile before turning and disappearing behind a hedge.

He'd never been so thankful his dad canceled on him. Annalee Chambers was special.

But for the next several months, she was only a volunteer at the center and he needed to treat her as such. After that, the chances of him even seeing her again were slim and none. Unless he agreed to his dad's demands for his future and rejoin the entitled lifestyle he'd left behind.

And he had no intention of ever doing that.

Annalee drove down Haskell Avenue twice before finding the correct building and then a third time to figure out where to park. She finally settled on the gravel driveway, which ran alongside the two-story, red-brick building. The old house looked like it had been built in the 1930s. Inspiration billowed from the empty hanging baskets lining the second-floor balcony. A large, green tree draped massive limbs over the wrought-iron fence around the front of the house. She shook her head. Sketching had to wait.

Straightening the belt on her designer sheath dress, she eyed her shoes. Maybe a little overkill? But she wanted to make an impact on the director. She was serious about doing a good job here. Besides, dressing nice made him know she wanted to impress him and showed her respect for his position.

Besides, the narrow cut of the skirt would keep it down regardless of the wind. She dug the address from her handbag then checked the black numbers above the door. They matched, but the home contradicted her impression of an afterschool center.

A worker in gray coveralls knelt on the opposite side of the enclosed yard. A dirty Texas Ranger ball cap shaded his face. Maybe she should ask him about the center.

Walking around to the front gate, she glanced at the building, black letters barely contrasted against the backdrop of a brown door. The foundation should have used white or at least a cream color. No one from the street would see the name on the glass storm door, but at least now she was sure.

The confirmation didn't ease the bugs crawling through her insides, though. So much depended on her good impression with this director. A man who already had issues with her working here and disliked affluent people. Like she could help that.

She pushed through the gate. Avoiding broken places of cement, she hobbled toward the steps. Maybe she could be of some help to this place after all? Give it a makeover. While she wasn't great at yard work, she knew some experts. And she did have talent and experience in what looked good and what didn't. The bird-droppings that covered the stair rail fell into the latter group. She avoided it altogether and trotted across the porch.

She opened the door and stepped inside, startling a woman who sat at one of the two desks crammed into the small front room.

"May I help you?" The older woman appeared slight. Her hair wound in a wavy frizz around her freckled face.

Undoubtedly the director whose good side Annalee needed to find. Again, female. She hesitated, her throat suddenly dry. She wiped her sweaty palm against her thigh and dug the paper she'd received from Laurel Stewart out of her purse. She held it toward the director.

"Can you speak at all, or do I need to learn charades?" The woman frowned, her joke more of a challenge than a friendly comment. She ignored the paper and stood, crossing her arms.

"I can speak." Annalee forced the words out then coughed. "May I have some water, please?"

"But of course. I'm happy to serve you, milady." The woman disappeared through a doorway.

Annalee chose to ignore her sarcasm. Should she follow the woman? "I've been told I'm supposed to let you know the days I can work." She raised her voice to make sure she was heard.

The woman came back around the corner with a paper cone half-filled with water. "Won't that be peachy."

Taking the cone, Annalee handed the woman the paper. "I'm sorry. I should have introduced myself. I'm Annalee Chambers. Thank you for the water."

The director scanned the page. "You have got to be kidding me." She muttered something else.

Annalee turned to once again glimpse the business name on the door. Yes, like she'd first seen. *Intercede Foundation Children's Afterschool Center.* Why was the director acting so surprised? "Is there a problem with the paperwork?"

The director flashed a furious look at her before spreading her lips into a wide grin. "So, you've been assigned here for your hours of community service?"

"Yes, ma'am. Tuesdays will be best for me, but I can also work on Thursdays. Occasionally, I could work on a Monday or a Wednesday, though I have regular art classes on those days."

The plastic smile grew. Annalee's attempt to prove that she

was simply a normal person with a normal life seemed to backfire. Though why, she couldn't fathom.

"You teach art?"

"Oh, no, ma'am. I study it. I usually spend both days in my studio after my tutoring sessions. I also play tennis on those mornings, but I can adjust that schedule if need be."

"Well, now. This will be a lovely arrangement, won't it? You can squeeze in work on Tuesdays and Thursdays and it should only take you a couple of years to whip out those pesky hours." She showed her teeth and scrunched her nose, looking a little like a squirrel.

Annalee had never seen this woman before. Yet her overaction was unmistakable. Irritation oozed. But maybe it had nothing to do with Annalee. How could it?

"I thought so." A couple of years seemed excessive, but then the judge hadn't been forced to assign her so many hours.

"So why don't you scurry home to enjoy your art programs and work hard in your studio today, and I'll see you back here at two o'clock sharp, tomorrow afternoon." The woman ducked her head toward Annalee like a squirrel wanting a treat. "Will that work for you?"

Maybe the over-the-top sweetness was just the director's way, though she needed a glass of milk to wash down the syrupy tones. "That will be wonderful. Thank you."

She didn't need to be so judgmental about the director. Her hours worked out perfectly. This job would be great. She practically danced to her car. Mother and Boyd didn't believe in her, but she was going to succeed in this assignment. She'd make her father look good.

And she'd stay out of jail.

CJ had been watching for Annalee, but a call from Paula Zane, their general cook, sent him running to the back door near the time of her appointment. The stove was having trouble again. The thing was worn out, probably forty or fifty years old. But the foundation hadn't set aside funding for new balls, let alone a new stove.

Thankfully, the chore didn't take too long. He hustled out the back and picked up the dolly he'd been working on from the shed. He'd wait in the side lot and catch Annalee before she went inside.

He finished adjusting the castors on the dolly and tapped each with a hammer before sliding off his work gloves and checking his phone. Annalee was late. Almost twenty minutes late. The kids would be arriving anytime now.

He returned the dolly to the shed. The front door shut as he locked up the small building. He rounded the corner of the house and removed his teardrop shades. A red 1967 Mustang backed out of the bus loading zone and drove down Haskell Avenue. The car was unmistakable, but he'd missed it on the other side of the house.

Great.

He swung over the fence and trotted up the steps to the front door. Bracing himself for the tirade, he pushed his way inside.

He laid his hammer and screwdriver on his desk in the corner. Of course, he hadn't used his office space in almost a year, but at least he had one in case he had the chance or the need.

"I suppose you saw Princess Annalee Chambers, in the flesh." Margo arched her eyebrow. "Was there some reason why you didn't bother telling me she was coming?"

He laid his work gloves on the hammer and shrugged. "I knew you would yell."

"Darn right I'm gonna yell."

"And then you'd yell again after she came, so I thought if I didn't warn you, I'd only have to hear you yell once."

Margo pressed her lips together. "And when …" Her tone had lowered significantly. "… pray-tell did you learn of our inestimable honor?"

"Friday morning. I got the call just before I saw her at the coffee shop." Oh, wait. He wasn't going to share that detail.

"Coffee shop? Tony's place?"

He was digging himself a deeper hole. How was it he always stuck himself firmly between Margo and Tony in their undefined relationship?

"Are you telling me both you and Tony actually met the woman and didn't tell me anything about the encounter?"

CJ ran his fingers through his hair. If Tony kept the matter from her, his silence was his business. "We saw her about the time she was leaving. And she spoke with McDermott. You know the bald guy with the gray mustache." Better to inform on him than Tony.

"He talked to her?"

"Mostly fussed at her, once he realized who she was." All true. *Now let the matter drop.*

"And why hasn't Tony mentioned this to me?"

"Ask Tony." Margo's relationship with the café owner was complicated, to say the least. But her gruff exterior concealed deep wounds that needed soothing. "She wasn't there more than five minutes. At least not that we noticed. And why are you all upset anyway? She doesn't threaten you. Here, she's a small fish in our established community."

"Well, she's one that's going right back into the lake where we found her. Maybe she'll grow up someday to be a real human being."

"That's harsh." If she'd be working here, Margo's attitude needed his attention. "Remember what I said the other day."

"I know what you said, but this gal's a bonafide prima donna." She held out a report from the Dallas County Probation Office. "She's got it into her head she'll only have to work two days a week."

"She'll be working through next year at that rate." He scanned the sheet. Her paperwork seemed straightforward. He noted the officer in charge. No wonder everything was in order. Laurel Stewart was nothing if not efficient.

"And she's the type who can't see past her own nose. On the other days, she's busy. Get this. She has a private art tutor and spends the afternoon in her studio."

He studied the form, remembering the paper she called a doodle. "An artist?"

"She thinks she is." Margo wandered toward the kitchen entrance. "Whose cockamamie idea was this? I know it wasn't Laurel's."

That seemed a strange assertion. Of course, Judge Vaught had made the arrangement with him, but it could very well have come through the probation office. It had before. "Laurel is her officer. She might have assigned it."

"Ha." Margo lifted her chin and turned back toward CJ. "Not if she got a look at the woman she didn't."

"What's wrong with the way she looks?" Especially today,

though her designer dress looked more like something for a New York office than the craziness of the center.

"Nothing." She paused. "And right there is the best reason for Laurel to keep her working in some dark hole someplace where no one, especially you, can see her."

He let his gaze stroke the low ceiling. "You're crazy. There's nothing between Laurel and me. We've never even dated."

"What about the banquet?"

They always attended together. So what? Only out of convenience. "That's not a date. We happen to be going in the same direction. After bumping into each other the first year, we keep going together to avoid the awkwardness of the event."

"That's not why she keeps going, but you tell yourself whatever you want."

He tapped his knuckles on the wood. Blast the woman and her stupid matchmaking. "Either way, it has nothing to do with Annalee Chambers working here."

Margo fisted her hips. "You know as well as I that a big donation by rich-girl's daddy would erase every single one of those service hours."

"Maybe she doesn't realize that." And he was as sure as Margo that Judge Vaught would accept a donation in place of the service. The woman seemed to have a plan of her own in mind.

"You mean we're stuck with her for the duration?" She pressed her lips into a thin line. "Hmph. I'm not fielding the trouble with this royal pain by myself, CJ. We're getting rid of her as fast as physically possible. To start with, she's gonna take on the same schedule the rest of the workers have. If she doesn't like it, she can go to jail for all I care."

He shook his head. "Don't push her too hard. A woman like

Annalee isn't used to this type of work. She might really like it eventually, but move slowly."

He usually allowed Margo to arrange things with the workers while he dealt with his father and the foundation board, but feeding Annalee to the snarky mountain lion in front of him could be construed as abusive.

"You going soft on me?" She glared at him. "Just because she's got a pretty face and figure, you're throwing all of your standards out the window?"

"I don't want to be too hard on her when it isn't necessary. Let's let her ease into the job." He dug his paintbrush out of the cardboard box of tools on the floor.

"You've trusted me for these last many years to help you run this center, right?"

"Yes." He knew what was coming. She'd laid it on him before when he didn't agree with her method of doing things. More often than not, with her decades of experience, she'd been right. But this time a woman's freedom was at stake.

"Let me take care of Annalee Chambers."

He straightened. "You think you've got this lady all figured out. You think she's heartless and entitled. But I'm telling you, I've seen how she interacts with people. So what if she's wealthy and has a father in politics? That doesn't mean she's not worth giving a chance."

"I'll give her a chance, all right. But I expect her to accept the same treatment as anyone else."

"On one condition." He held up his finger and took a step toward her. "You treat her like you do all of the other workers."

She returned to her well-worn ergonomic chair. "The others are volunteers who give willingly of their time."

"Yeah, and I want you to be as friendly to her as you are to Bertie, Paula, or Dee. It's that or no deal.

"What do you mean *no deal*?"

"I'll take on her training myself if I can't trust you to do things right." He placed his hands, paint brush and all, on her desk and leaned toward her.

"Why do you care about some girl you barely met at a coffee shop?" She narrowed her eyes.

"I recognize pain when I see it." He kept his gaze steady. "She's experienced quite a lot." If McDermott's scowling face and the reporter's insinuations were any indications.

"And I've seen the reality deep in your own eyes, Carlton James Whelan. You've had your head turned by a pretty face." She tsked.

"But you'll do as I ask." He lifted his eyebrows.

"Hmph." She rose and stomped into the kitchen.

He could count on her.

And as for Annalee's pretty face, he'd seen lots of those in the last few years and could have possessed any one of them if he'd been so inclined.

But he hadn't. Even though Annalee Chambers piqued his interest, the likelihood of her holding his attention was slim.

Chapter 5

Annalee couldn't remember the last time she looked forward to dinner. Mom had finally rescinded the period of mourning and they planned to dine at the country club.

Boyd would be joining them, which really was a good thing considering she hadn't seen her supposed boyfriend since his announcement of her foolishness.

If only Mother would be as excited as she was about her community service.

Hee. Almost like a real job. The giddiness threw electric volts up and down Annalee's spine. Did everyone feel this way when they secured a working position?

She could hardly contain herself in the car but maintained the composure her mother always insisted upon. Even as a child, she'd been expected to remain still and quiet until she was engaged in conversation or released to the care of her nanny.

Once seated at their regular table, the buzz traveled across her shoulders. She couldn't hold onto the news any longer. "I had a meeting today with my new boss."

"That's fine, dear." Her mother scanned the room. "I see Tamara Hathaway. I must speak to her about next week's garden club." She crossed the empty dance floor toward her friend.

Annalee really only cared to share with her father anyway. "I don't think I told you my probation officer assigned me to work at an afterschool center."

"That's wonderful, sweetheart. Childcare. Sounds... interesting."

"Isn't it? My probation officer said something about typing and copying. I have a schedule and everything."

"I'm glad you're excited about this prospect." He waved to a group and rose. "Hold your thought. I need to greet some people."

He strolled to the entrance and shook hands or gave half-hugs to everyone he passed then engaged a couple of men by the bar for at least a half hour.

By then, Boyd had arrived. But he joined Father at the bar, laughing and chatting with the three men like a golf buddy.

When had they become so chummy? Even though he worked for Father's firm, the business was huge. And Annalee hadn't seen them together before, not without her between them. Pulling a slip of paper from her bag, she began to draw Father, Boyd, and the three men they spoke with. The room filled with color and noise, but she had a good vantage point at the raised table. The men alternately tilted their heads together then pulled back in laughter. One of them eyed the behind of a passing female, and the others laughed again.

Then Boyd watched the backside of a woman as she leaned over and whispered to someone at a table.

Great. Here she sat while his mind filled with the thought of other girls.

He glanced in her direction, and she focused on her drawing as though she hadn't noticed him at all. But she had and quickly changed the details of his face to give him fishy eyes, a flat nose, and gills.

Finally, her father returned. "Now tell me more about this job, sweetheart."

Boyd, moving in his wake, reached down for a kiss, but she made him settle for her forehead.

"I'm excited about a new opportunity." She didn't look at Boyd. "Variety is the spice of life, and I feel I've been in a rut long enough."

Boyd cleared his throat.

Annalee smiled internally. Yes, he'd felt the pointed end of her arrow.

Mother had joined them as Annalee spoke. Her mother sat next to her father. "Todd, you can't let your youngest child waste away with the dregs of society in such a place. If you're not going to stop all of this nonsense, you'll deserve the ruined reputation you'll get when Annalee blows her chances and finally gives up."

"Mother." The woman didn't believe in her, but did she have to voice her thoughts in public?

"Don't be silly. I'm not blaming you, dear. You can't help the way you are."

Annalee inwardly winced but kept her face stoic.

"I have to agree with your mom, Annalee," Boyd chimed in as though he had some right. "How would it look for your father's daughter to be working in a low station such as you describe?"

His opinion meant rather little at the moment, as did his choice to condemn a huge group of people merely for living beneath his own means. She lifted her chin. "Forgive me. I hadn't realized I'd stepped out of my American royalty and into the peasantry."

"Well, you are a princess." Her mother tittered and lifted her chin.

The mention of the ridiculous contest brought back sour memories. One judge did nothing but leer at her, and another constantly glared in her direction. The third hardly glanced at her at all. She was shocked to learn that the final judge had awarded her perfect scores.

"Seriously, though, Boyd makes a fine statement." Mother opened her compact and rubbed a finger across the bottom of her lower lip. "If someone wants to be offended by what he said, they should step up and prove him wrong."

Annalee would get nowhere championing the poor and downtrodden, so she tried an altruistic approach. "I'm actually thinking of how good all of this will make Father look." She held up an invisible headline. "Mayor's Daughter Makes an Impact on the Poor, or Mayoral Candidate Proves His Desire to Help the Little Guy as His Daughter Works with Impoverished Children."

Boyd did an about-face. "I like the second one. This could be highly beneficial to the campaign."

Of course, he'd give such consideration to the mayoral campaign. *Hello. You're dating me, not Todd Chambers.* Though she would be hard-pressed to prove the fact with his actions and attention tonight.

At least her ideas set Boyd and Mother on the exciting topic of future headline possibilities and let Annalee get through the meal without their increasing disapproval. Maybe this job of hers would prove valuable to them as well.

Why here, Lord? Why her?

CJ sloshed paint thinner in the metal bucket with a temporarily yellow brush. He glanced along the fence line. The wood begged for a second coat, but he'd likely have to dig into his savings to add one. Still, the yellow looked bright, cheerful, kid-like.

And those kids were the most important thing. Like Mr. Madison's boys. Did the judge know they came here? Had she assigned Annalee Chambers to the center for a specific reason? Maybe to give the wealthy, careless girl something more to think about. More to regret.

But he'd seen her face. She didn't need help in the regret area. And from the looks of the news stories, she'd received all sorts of backlash about her plea.

Then there was Margo's personal vendetta against Annalee. She had to curb her anger. *Help me know what to say, Lord.* And how he should speak. He'd worked hard to gain Margo's trust, and her work was vital to the center. The place simply wouldn't run without her. The woman wasn't naturally mean-spirited, but she felt responsible for these families. They depended on the center for a lot more than simple afterschool care. Advice. Counseling. Christian exposure and all the expectations that included.

The first bus unloaded a handful of children. Their laughter and chatter echoed as they circled the wrought-iron fence and clomped across the porch. How many more were in the vehicle, watching these kids leave. Kids who wanted to get off, but because of socioeconomic limits, were forced to go to an empty house. The wait list held almost a hundred names. The center needed more help. More room. More funding. A person with Annalee's connections could enable huge improvements.

His jaw tightened. He was agenda-thinking. "God, I'm trusting You instead of myself. No money, no connections, can outdo Your power to move as You wish." He finished cleaning the brushes and washed his hands in the sink near the back door.

Inside, he made for the office through the kitchen. He didn't glance at Margo or Paula. They'd been chatting about something but stopped abruptly when he entered. He hoped Margo wasn't spreading poison about Annalee but feared she probably was.

He sat down at his desk for the first time in months and picked up the old-fashioned office phone. Dialing Laurel's number from memory, he waited for her to answer.

"Stewart."

"Laurel, I'm glad I caught you."

"CJ?" Her tone changed. He could picture the smile she must have donned as the sound flattened. Her Texas accent deepened. "So good of you to call me. But it's not time for the annual banquet."

"No. I'm calling about Annalee Chambers."

"Already? Hm ..."

Okay, now she was toying with him. "I take it you've already heard from Margo."

Laurel laughed. "Margo called me last night. I heard she made a terrible first impression, and Margo is determined to shoo her away like a fly."

Actually, he thought she made a nice first impression. Dressed to impress. Polite. He shook the image from his head. "Yeah. I know the Judge asked to have her here, but I'm wondering if my agreement was such a good idea."

"I knew you'd hate her, but the judge assigned the position. All I do is document the success and failure. But if she's not going to work out, I can save you the trouble and go ahead and report that to Judge Vaught."

Was there a lilt to her voice? "Wouldn't that get you into trouble? I mean, you're supposed to prepare the probationers for their positions. That would make you look bad."

"Oh, thank you for your concern, CJ. That's really touching."

It wasn't so much concern as curiosity about the delight she seemed to have with the prospect of explaining the center's refusal to Judge Vaught.

"It won't be such a big deal for me, though. I would have put Annalee Chambers in the judge's own office, a place where her attitude wouldn't be tolerated and her mistakes wouldn't hurt innocent people."

"Sounds like you don't hold out much hope for the woman."

"No more than you do. After all, you're the one giving her the boot, right?"

Not yet, he wasn't. "It's not because she's done anything wrong, though." Something about her phrase about the boot stuck with him. "If I did change my mind about her working here, would you find her another position for community service?"

"I thought you'd already made that decision." Laurel's tone sharpened.

"I'm just asking, feeling my options if Annalee doesn't work out." And with every second, he was beginning to feel the need to protect the girl from Laurel as much as from Margo.

"Well, I'm sorry, but you did accept the placement. There isn't another option for her. It's up to the judge as to whether she avoids her jail sentence. Probably her father can pay her way out of the penalty of jail time, so you shouldn't worry about it."

"I see. Well, you're right about one thing." Her explanation cleared his mind on the issue.

"Good." She sounded positively bouncy. "I'll put a call into Judge Vaught right now."

"That's fine. And when you do, tell her from me that Annalee Chambers is going to work out perfectly for the center." That should take a little bounce away from her.

Laurel was silent for a second and then stuttered a bit. "Wa... I … bu … I thought you said I was right?"

"About one thing. I did accept the placement. Miss Chambers shouldn't be punished for me changing my mind. All she needed was a clean background check to work at the center, and she got that thanks to Judge Vaught's deferred adjudication." Even with the misdemeanor and the jail time hanging over her head, she had a clean slate.

"Very well." Laurel's voice returned to the honey-like tone she'd had before. "I'd be happy to discuss options for dealing with her. Are you free Friday night?"

He'd rather make a plan for working with Annalee right away before she started tomorrow. "How about tonight? Can you meet me here at the center at eight?"

"It's a date." She ended the call

Good. Annalee was going to need his help to … *Wait. What date?*

Annalee drifted to her studio as soon as she reached the house. Not that she planned to work there. But she sought calm.

However, even the comfort of her little kingdom didn't still the tempest building in her stomach. Could she succeed? She'd never had to work before. Not more than helping with Mother's many charity events. Certainly, nothing she had to complete on her own.

Footfalls on the carpeted steps caught her attention. "What are you doing down here?"

Father paused on the bottom step. "I can go away if you'd like to be alone."

Her chin lowered. "No. Please come in. I was thinking about the work I'm supposed to start tomorrow."

He wandered toward her and picked up a wax apple from a model display. "I wondered how you were feeling about your new prospect. The thought has occurred to me, you don't really need to be down in such a dangerous environment. Especially because of who you are. The crime element itself is enough to stay away."

"You'd rather me go to jail?" She cocked her head at him. "I look nasty in orange."

He snorted. "No, sweetheart. I think with the right approach, I can persuade Judge Vaught or one of her superiors to consider this matter closed."

Persuade. Bought off. His proposition would make things much easier. No concern about possible jail time. No scheduling to organize or free time to give up.

And Mom and Boyd would be right about her. Again. Unable to stand on her own. Incapable of completing a task. Always depending on her parents to fix her little issues. Not like there had been so many. A banquet she tried to throw. A vacation she planned, which went awry. Then there was the horrible Texas Princess pageant. What a humiliation that fraud had been.

"I don't want you to fix this." She pushed up from the couch. "I'm so sorry if my plea hurts your business or your campaign, but I know I did the right thing, even if my actions did land me in community service. I need to do this." She put her hands against his chest. "And I can do this, Father."

"Never had a doubt in the world. That doesn't mean I want to see you hurt, though."

She kissed his cheek. "I'll be careful."

He nodded and planted a kiss on her forehead. He returned the apple to the bowl. "By the way …" After taking a couple of steps up, he turned toward her. "… I understand your guilty plea. And I admire the strength it took for you to make it."

He retreated, but his words settled deep in Annalee's heart. He believed in her. Now all she had to do was prove him right.

CJ glanced out the front window as headlights danced across the wall. A brown compact pulled into the driveway. Looked like Laurel had arrived. He lowered into his almost forgotten desk chair for the second time that day. He'd hate for office work to become a habit.

"I guess I better scoot." Margo hustled out of the kitchen, wiping her hands on her jeans.

"Not on your life. You are not abandoning me." He leaped to his feet. "This is business."

"I know better than to be a third wheel." She picked up her purse and draped it over her arm.

As she passed, CJ snagged the strap and halted her forward motion. "We have to deal with Annalee Chambers tomorrow. You need to work this out more than I do. You're staying, and we leave together."

"Laurel's not coming to see me." The woman eyed him over the top of her rimless glasses.

"I'm the one who called this meeting. You're staying. Frankly, Margo, you're part of the problem."

She slunk to her desk and stuffed her purse into the bottom drawer. "I know how to deal with this woman. If you'll let me."

"I don't think you do." Finally, she seemed to be listening. "You've put her in a little box and decided you know all about her. I think you're wrong."

"Wrong about what?" Laurel pushed open the front door and shut it behind her. "Why hello, Margo. I thought you'd be done for the day."

"I thought so, too." Margo glanced at CJ, her eyebrows lifted. He scowled at her.

Laurel tossed a shock of straight brown hair over her shoulder. "CJ and I can work all of this out. I know you have things you want to do."

Without moving his head, he lifted one eyebrow. She had better not make a noise about leaving.

She sighed. "No. I'm the one who works with the new volunteers. I'll stick around and hear what you have to suggest."

Good. He tugged a seat over from the corner and set it in front of Margo's desk. Then he returned to his chair.

Laurel pursed her lips. She drifted past CJ, leaving a wave of rose scent in her wake. "Very well. I don't really have so much I can offer, though." She pulled a file from her oversized purse and perched on the edge of CJ's desk. "She's the daughter of Todd Chambers, who's a senior partner of Layton, Deeson, Chambers, and Pierce Law Firm, and a candidate for mayor. High society for Dallas, he and his wife are regulars at most of the charity events featuring local celebs. And her sister, Ramona Chambers, is a sought-after fashion model." She closed the file.

He waited. Surely her short monologue didn't include all the information she had. "And?"

"I have some of the specific events in which Mr. and Mrs. Chambers attended. Some of their main charities, alumni associations and such."

"You don't know anything about her? About Annalee, not her family?"

Margo shifted. "We know she grew up in luxury."

"Maybe her parents have money, but you don't know how they raised her."

"Did you see the red Mustang convertible she was driving this afternoon? If that's not a hey-look-me-over car, I don't know what is." Margo bobbed her head as punctuation.

"She has to be careless. Otherwise, she wouldn't have been drinking and driving." Laurel reopened the file.

Wait. He hadn't seen anything about her being drunk. "I read an article about the case. They didn't attach a DWI. I know I saw something saying she passed a Breathalyzer." Though why she'd be in the club district escaped him.

"Hm. I didn't hear." Laurel scanned another sheet. "I suppose she hit the man without any excuse then."

Great logic. If she was drinking, she's entitled and careless. If she wasn't, she's completely heartless. "I think there must be something we're missing."

"And I think it doesn't matter beans about why she's here." Margo leaned forward. "What matters is, we're stuck with her, and we have to figure out how to get rid of her."

CJ stared at Margo. The depth of the woman's hatred twisted his gut. He'd always been able to count on her counsel, her impressions.

Not after this outburst.

She dropped her gaze and slumped in the seat.

He had to get Annalee reassigned. Placing her here meant certain failure. "Maybe, I was right in the first place. I'm not sure this will work."

"Then simply let her go." Lauren's face was an innocent mask.

"But this doesn't have anything to do with her work or her behavior. You can explain that the change wasn't the fault of the probationer, right?"

She clicked her tongue. "I can include what I know in my report, but most probationers that don't complete their community service hours have to serve their full term in jail. That's entirely up to Judge Vaught."

Who hand-picked the center as the place she wanted Annalee to serve her term. Great. He shouldn't have hoped for Laurel to carve out a different option. She'd basically shared the doom and gloom earlier that day.

Laurel snapped fingers of both hands. "Hey, you know that's actually a good idea."

"Good idea? To send the lady to jail?" Was she really sliding over to Margo's crew of wealth-haters?

She leaned toward CJ and tapped a fingernail on his desk. "It would serve her right and get her out of your hair at the same time."

"I thought you were supposed to be on her side. Want to see her succeed." CJ pushed back in his seat. His neck heated. Didn't Annalee have anyone in her corner?

"Realistically speaking, she has precious little chance of getting through her probation." She shrugged, glanced at Margo, then examined her fingertips. "Sounds like you'll have to endure the grueling few months, then she'll still go to jail."

"Hmph." Margo's reaction was hardly heard, but her grimace spoke at a high volume. "I'll give her three days before she quits."

"She'll go to jail for quitting, too." Laurel sidled over to the chair by Margo's desk and perched on it crossing her lean legs.

"Then let's get one thing straight." He glanced at Laurel before returning to Margo. "I'm not firing Annalee Chambers. And we're not pushing her to quit. Her failure here will be an obvious mark on your record, Laurel."

She shrugged. "Not so much. Probationers blow it sometimes. I'm not held responsible."

He cocked his eyebrow. "You can bet you would be this time. Don't forget the media surrounds this woman and her family. Your whole career could be in danger."

She stiffened. "You don't really think so."

"I do. And I know my father and the board will be most displeased if her failure has anything to do with the center …" He eyed Margo. "… or any of our staff." Chances are, his dad would be smack-dab in their corner cheering on her jail time, but he wouldn't let either of these women know that.

"Understood." Margo set her chin in her palm, elbow on the desk. "So how do you propose we coddle this princess?"

"I don't. But I don't want to make her run screaming into the street either. Ease her in like you do with all of the staff. Like I said before."

"Cleaning?" Margo raised her brows.

"To start." He had her attention. "If we find out she's really the brat you think she is, then we'll talk again. Get Laurel to put some pressure on Judge Vaught. Or maybe contact her father with the threat of failure and jail time."

"I'm not so sure we shouldn't talk to Mr. Chambers right now." Laurel uncrossed her legs and leaned toward Margo. "Avoid all of this unpleasantness." She tilted her head as she eyed CJ with her thick-lashed doe-eyes.

Margo's prejudices blazed like a neon sign, but that didn't explain Laurel's animosity. Unless she really had joined Margo's unofficial club. But if she truly hated wealthy people, she covered it well at the annual banquet. "Never knew you to be a quitter, Laurel."

She gasped, and her hand flew to her collar. "I'm no quitter. You all are the ones who are dealing with this prima donna."

"When you met her, she had a diva attitude?"

"It was a brief encounter." She lifted her chin.

"If she didn't display self-absorption …" He leaned back and crossed his arms. "… then why did you call her a prima donna?"

"This discussion isn't getting us anywhere." She stood and stuffed her file back into her bag. "If you all insist on staying the course, then fine. If you decide Annalee Chambers needs to go, you can call me, and I'll have her fanny in the county jail so fast her Mustang won't be able to catch up."

She strutted across the room, tripping on the doorframe into the hall but catching herself and slamming the door behind her.

"I think I might have gotten on her bad side."

Margo straightened. "Momentarily. She'll get over it." She stood and pulled her purse from the drawer once more. "You really think this woman is worth the time and trouble of us learning to work with her?"

He nodded. "I think there's a lot more to her than the media photos show." He pushed to standing against the desk.

"Well, I can't make any promises." She pivoted and stuck her finger in CJ's face. "And I won't let her disrupt our harmony here or endanger the children."

"Naturally." He turned his palms toward her.

"I'll do my best with her then, like I would with any other worker." She lifted her chin as she stepped onto the porch.

Funny how the hollow thumps of her footsteps held more substance than her promise.

Chapter 6

Sometime while she slept, Annalee's worries faded. As the morning progressed, a giddy bubble inside her swelled. *Work to do*. The thought made her bounce.

Father called right before lunch. "Hi, honey. Are you ready for today?"

He'd found time in his crazy schedule to check on her. Just for her. The bubble grew. "I am. Is it ridiculous that I'm excited about this new prospect?"

"No. I'm glad you have a positive outlook. You'll find difficulty soon enough. Don't let it break you. You're equipped to do the tasks set before you."

Her? Equipped? Not for much more than shopping and assigning color combinations. At least not for the last several years. "Do you really think so?"

"Of course. I've always thought so, even with your mother's doubts."

Mother's doubts? The woman would question that Wednesday was Wednesday unless someone had a calendar to prove it. And she'd spent all of Annalee's adult life questioning her every decision. Enough to convince Annalee to stop making them altogether. Well, until poor Mr. Madison entered the picture.

"Do your best, sweetheart. You'll be glad you stuck with this program."

Hanging up her phone, Annalee mulled her father's words. Why hadn't she gotten a job or volunteered before now?

Keep a smile on your face, and make your father look good. Mother had always kept Father's reputation in mind. Annalee dared not attempt anything that wasn't an automatic success because failure would reflect on Father. No wonder Mother hated the idea of her working, even simple volunteer work.

But she determined to succeed. And on her own.

From her visit to the place, Annalee decided that dresses were too fancy, even for office work. She pulled on deep plum jeans with a matching peasant blouse and fringed ankle boots. A vivid color the kids would like, though she wasn't sure she was ready to actually meet any of them. Not yet. Not until she had a clue about children in general.

Reaching the center, she parked in the same empty driveway where she parked before. The director with whom she'd spoken stood at the doorway, frowning. "You're late."

Was she? Seemed like she got here the same time as the day before. Annalee navigated through the side gate and offered her hand. "I didn't hear your name yesterday."

"Miss Pritchard." The woman looked at her watch. "Thirty minutes late. You'll make up for that."

"Was I supposed to be here earlier than yesterday?"

"Hmph. I suppose you weren't listening very well." She turned and held the door open for Annalee to follow. "The children will be here in roughly fifteen minutes. You must be here at two o'clock every day."

A minor setback. Not enough to stifle her enthusiasm. What was an extra half hour? She could make that up anytime.

Wait. Did she say *every day?* "I thought I was only working Tuesdays and some Thursdays." She followed her into the same dim office room.

"You'll work Monday through Friday just like everyone else here. If you had a real job or academic classes, I'd adjust, but your cut, paste, and crayon time doesn't count. Also, you'll work every other Saturday beginning next week. Until seven thirty on weekdays and nine o'clock to five o'clock on Saturdays. For every fifteen minutes you're late, you get to work another half hour. Today you're thirty minutes late, so you get an extra hour tacked on. You'll be on the clock until nine." She pointed to the entrance. "If that's too much for you, there's the door."

Annalee's bubble disintegrated into atoms. The center's time element didn't seem fair, but it was Miss Pritchard's center. She could do whatever she wanted. "Um, you said I work an extra hour tonight. Wouldn't the ending time be eight thirty?"

"I added another half hour to get a head start on all the other days when I'm sure you'll be late." She stepped into the room beyond, leaving Annalee in the shadows.

Now, she understood Laurel Stewart's warning about this woman. She expected Annalee to fail as completely as did Mother and Boyd. All the more reason to prove herself capable.

She sidestepped where Miss Pritchard sat the day before and scooted behind the other desk. This one covered with boxes of scrap paper, files, tools, and craft items. She hung her purse on the back of the chair and began straightening her workspace. She piled the extraneous items into the closest box and set it on the floor behind her. Tools went into the next one which also held used copy paper. She assumed they reused the scraps. That box stacked on top of the first.

She noticed Miss Pritchard leaning against the doorframe with her arms crossed.

"Did you need something?" Annalee set a third box full of glue, scissors, ribbon, and feathers on top of the others and wiped her hands on her jeans. Whatever Miss Pritchard needed, she stood poised and ready to provide.

"I need you to move away from Mr. Whelan's desk." She pointed to a nameplate Annalee hadn't noticed under all of the paraphernalia. "Or didn't they teach you to read in the fancy boarding school where you spent your childhood?"

A jolt of adrenaline shot through Annalee as she picked up the placard. Carlton Whelan was carved into the other side. "Oh, I'm so sorry." She returned it and picked up her purse. "Where shall I work, then?"

"This way." Miss Pritchard turned without waiting, and Annalee hopped over tools and scattered supplies to catch up with her.

She led Annalee into a large room full of rectangular tables, each with chairs lining both sides. "This is where we bring the kids for snack and rainy-day activities. Nursery is through there." She pointed to a closed doorway. "Upstairs are six classrooms. The center can hold up to sixty children, aged four to twelve, a dozen or so toddlers, and eight babies. Right now, we are full to capacity and have a significant waiting list of children who wish to be included."

Miss Pritchard stopped outside two doors labeled with stick

figures, one wearing a dress. She handed Annalee a clipboard. "This is your office for today. You'll find all of the needed supplies in the closet behind the girls' door. Complete the checklist in both bathrooms. Then come see me for your next task.

Bathrooms? She glanced at her clothes. Feeling the woman's skeptical gaze, she gave a thumbs-up and a half smile. "No problem."

She slipped through the door and hung her purse on the corner of one of the stall doors, wincing over the urine-tainted breeze.

Big problem. Where did she even begin with this task? She opened the closet and found an assortment of spray bottles, powders, and other cleaners. Several pairs of rubber gloves and an unmated one lay on a shelf. A large bucket sat underneath, and a mop and broom with some sort of attachment leaned into the corner.

She heard an intense clatter in the large room. Squeals, laughter, and running feet. Much of it faded as quickly as it rose. A few girls entered and eyed her. She snatched down her purse, clutching it and smiling. When they left, she shoved it into the closet.

First things first. Mop and bucket. She could certainly grasp that concept. Donning one pair of gloves, she extracted the bucket and tried to fit any part of it into one of the two sinks. Total failure.

She carried it into the kitchen, but Miss Pritchard stomped her foot. "Don't bring that filthy thing in here. What were you thinking, Annalee?"

She flinched at her mother's favorite phrase. *Here, too?*

On her way back to the bathroom, she snatched a paper cone. It took a while, but she finally filled up the bucket one cup at a time.

While she filled the bucket, noise outside grew. Several girls came into the bathroom and stared at her as she poured the tiny servings into the huge bucket.

"You know there's an easier way to do that, right?" One of the girls dallied after the others left.

"Well, the bucket won't fit into the sink."

The girl couldn't have been more than eight or nine. She probably didn't understand the concept.

The child opened the cleaning closet and pulled the attachment from the broom. "It ain't gonna help much now that you're almost done." She turned off the water and laid the flat pan under the faucet. She turned the water back on and let it pour through the hollow handle into the bucket like it had been made for such a reason.

"Oh, that's wonderful. How did you ever learn to do that?"

The girl turned the faucet back off. "Been helping my momma clean rich people houses since I could walk. Just takes the sense God gave you." She handed Annalee the pan with the hollow handle and exited.

The center grew quieter again. Kids were probably playing in the adjacent field. But the girl's words stuck with her. *The sense God gave you.* Obviously, Annalee had missed out on her free sample.

She needed cleaner to put into the water. Something to take the stench out of the air. Most of the bottles in the closet had labels long ago torn away. But one had a bluish liquid in it and smelled like her bathroom at home before the automatic fragrance took over.

That was the clean aroma she sought. Not knowing how much to use, she poured until the water turned a little blue then swished it around with the mop until it foamed up good and frothy.

She pulled the mop out and started to shove it back and forth on the floor. The wet stringy strands picked up several sheets of toilet paper and a couple of rubber bands.

Okay, first lesson learned. Sweep first. Check.

She grabbed the yellow broom. As she manipulated it around toilets and under sinks, other girls came and went. She stopped sweeping and smiled at each of them, handing them paper towels like attendants in some of the finer restaurants and hotels did for her. By the time she actually got to the mopping stage, the noise in the outer room had grown again. Playtime must've ended early.

She glanced at her watch and gasped. So much time had passed. She hadn't even finished the first item on her list. The mopping took even longer with kids coming in and out. Every time someone walked across the wet floor, she had to mop away their footprints. Finally, they gave her enough of a gap to let the clean floor dry while Annalee waited in a corner for the shiny blue tiles to dull back to normal.

The floor looked pretty good. Especially for a first-timer. But she needed to hurry or she'd have to finish the cleaning tomorrow. Spotting a squirt bottle, she spritzed the glass and much of the wall. The paper towels disintegrated into little chunks on the rough surface and littered her clean floor.

Great. Lesson number two.

Out came the broom again. At least it didn't require re-mopping.

The spritz worked in the sink as well, helping her finish both jobs in only a little over a half-hour. She felt like cheering.

See, I can do this. She drew a huge check mark in the air.

With her stomach growling, she set to make the toilets sparkle.

A can of powder showed a picture of one. That had to be the cleaner to use for this job. She sprinkled it all over, dirtying her floor once again. Lesson three: sweep and mop last.

Getting on her knees to ensure a good clean, she wiped the seat down and swished the powder all over with a brush she found. The smell made her eyes water, but the stuff sure did the trick. The toilets practically shined by the time she finished. With a wet paper towel, she even cleaned the excess powder on the floor.

A knock on the door startled her. A male voice called out. "You still in there?"

"Yes. I just finished." She stood and wiped her gloves on her pants then slipped them from her hands. She'd finished. Without help. *I'm king of the world!* Victory scenes from a half-dozen movies crossed her mind. *Titanic, Rocky, Seabiscuit.* She deserved a victory lap with arms raised.

The door opened, and she spun, coming face to face with the same guy who helped her with the reporters—CJ. Was he really stalking her? "I thought I'd better get started on the boy's bathroom."

"You? What are you doing here?"

"I work here." His eyes traveled from her toes to her hair. She'd had men eye her before, but never with a look of bizarre horror.

"What's wrong?" She turned toward the mirror and gasped. Her frizzed hair was the first thing she noticed, but the smallest detail. Sharp black points of mascara from where the fumes made her eyes water adorned her cheeks and her exposed skin was full of red blotches and welts.

"You must be allergic to something in one of the cleaners." CJ took one elbow and led her toward the door. "You better sit down, and I'll get you some water."

The big room was empty of the tables and chairs which had filled it earlier. He pulled her into the closed room Miss Pritchard had identified as the nursery and seated her in a rocking chair. "I'll be right back."

Whatever had made her react was starting to make her face itch. She resisted the urge to scratch her neck and cheeks. CJ returned with a cone of water and flicked on the light. Annalee drank the water down. She'd feel better after she got a shower.

She glanced down at her watch. Almost nine o'clock. Her gaze drifted to her pants. The deep purple had streaks of lighter shades and even a little white blended into what had been an eggplant color. Her black, suede boots also had white toes and streaks on the side and through the fringe.

"What happened to my clothes?" She stretched her legs out.

"I can only guess, but I bet you used one of the cleaners with bleach for mopping the floor." He lifted her chin with a gentle touch. "At least your face is returning to its normal color."

She swallowed hard and took another sip. *Hold it together, Annalee.*

CJ scowled. Why had he allowed Margo free rein? Annalee's first experience was like a bad onion in his stomach. She sat stone-faced in the rocker.

Margo paused at the open doorway. "Well, now. How was the first day?"

He could imagine the words that really ran through her head. *How is the princess after the first day of big-girl school?*

Annalee's controlled expression didn't vary. "It's been enlightening, to say the least. I hope to improve the next time I'm here."

Margo fisted her hips. "Which is tomorrow. And on time."

"I understand." Annalee stood, dropping the decimated remains of the water cone in the trash.

So, Margo's comment had affected her. Intensely, by the look of the mutilated cup.

"Well, good night, then." Margo preceded them to the front and made her way out.

Annalee repeated the phrase at a mumble. She set her eyes on the entrance with the look of a caged animal receiving a glimpse of freedom.

CJ followed her to the porch. "Do you need a ride?" He tried to lighten the tension with a chuckle. "I can take you home, especially since I know where it is."

Annalee shook her head. "Thank you for the offer, but I drove myself." She stepped down the stairs before turning back. "But you can answer a question for me. You didn't seem surprised at seeing me cleaning the bathroom. Why?" She tilted her head.

"I saw you yesterday as you were leaving. I was working in the yard over there." He pointed toward the shed on his left.

"I see. What is it you do here?"

He hesitated as his gaze drifted from her ruined clothes to the pain in her blackened eyes. "Clean up messes mostly. Odd jobs. Handyman stuff." And he would do his best to clean up this mess. "And I work with the kids whenever I can." Since she already thought Margo was the boss, he saw no reason to correct her. Not at this point anyway. Why make the awkwardness even worse?

She nodded and turned down the stone path to the side gate. "Then I guess I'll see you tomor … my car." She straightened and spun toward him.

He hadn't seen the tow truck, but he should have suspected as much.

"My car was right here." She pointed.

"That's a towing zone. Bus lane." He pointed at the sign. If only he had checked on her car earlier. Especially when he saw where she parked yesterday.

Oh, yes. Margo was certainly treating her like she treated everyone else. He gritted his teeth.

"You had my car towed?"

"I didn't have it towed." But he might as well have since he let Margo have her way.

She turned her back on him and pulled out her phone. She gave the address to someone on the other end, keeping her back to him.

"I don't mind taking you home."

"I appreciate your offer, but you must admit this all seems too weird. A few days ago, you happen to be at a restaurant at the exact moment I needed a ride home. Now today, my car is towed, and you are again offering to rescue me." She sniffed.

"Coincidence. I assure you."

"Maybe, but it's not such a stretch to believe you called the reporters a few days ago and you had my car towed today."

Surely, she didn't really believe such, but he couldn't counter her logic.

"This all leads me to ask: are you stalking me?" She leaned her phone against her mouth.

He shut his eyes. He'd believe she was stalking him if he'd been in her place. "I don't blame you for your conclusions, but the fact is I've worked here for the past seven years."

She looked at him then. "Seven years as a janitor?"

"Whatever needs doing." He held his palms up. "You can verify with Margo or the Intercede Foundation office."

She slouched. "I'll take your word for it." Returning to the steps, she sat on the top one. "But I do have a ride coming."

"Gonna take a while to get here, won't it?"

"Not so long." She straightened and eyed the darkening street.

"I can at least wait with you." He sure wouldn't leave her alone in this neighborhood.

Running her finger across the end of her nose, she sniffed. "No, thank you. I'll be fine."

He paused. Should he go back inside? He could take care of paperwork while she waited. "I really don't like leaving you here like this. It's not a good area of town."

"Yes, but regardless of what Miss Pritchard thinks of me, I've been a grown woman for some time, and I know how to take care of myself."

Thanks to Margo, Annalee felt she had something to prove. And she had a stubborn streak to boot.

"Good night, then."

Turning away from her response, he walked down the bus lane a few yards, far enough to be out of her hearing then sprinted to his truck in the paid lot beyond the play yard. Shoving the truck into gear he backed up and churned toward the exit, flashed his pass at the laser release button, and rounded the block. He parked at the body shop building next door to the center and jogged to the corner where he'd have a view of his building's porch. At least she wouldn't be sitting there completely without defense.

Annalee had pulled her knees up and laid her head on them. He could imagine her sobbing but heard nothing. His gut tightened. She didn't seem to be the overly emotional type. Still, adding strain to exhaustion and a few harsh sprinkles of insult would test anyone's composure. And his lack of action in controlling Margo had been the source of her pain.

While he watched, she pulled something from her purse, unwrapped it, and took a bite.

What a heartless dolt he was. Everyone ate together at snack time. He shouldn't have relied on Margo to draw her into the group.

How ridiculous to be hiding there in the dark. Now, he'd truly become the creepiest of stalkers. But he refused to leave her unguarded in such an area. Better to let her know he was there and wasn't going to leave until she'd gotten into her car. Decision made, he stepped around the corner of the building, but the long shadow of a limo came into view.

Annalee stood and descended the steps.

In the beam of the headlights, CJ retreated into the shadows behind the corner. He could still see her through the tinted glass of the body shop. Her driver climbed from the vehicle and wrapped her in an intimate embrace.

Ah. So that's why she didn't need a ride home.

Marji Laine

Chapter 7

Wednesday morning, Annalee snagged a biscuit from the platter in the kitchen. Better than having to listen to her mother and sister complain about her demeaning job over a formal meal in the dining room.

Parker leaned against the counter. "Your father asked about the Mustang." He adjusted the collar of the uniform her mother demanded he always wear.

"You didn't tell him, did you?" She set down the rest of the bread.

He sipped from a mug. "How long have we been friends?" A glint sparkled in his brown eyes.

She nodded with a smirk. "Forever and a day." They recited their pet phrase in unison.

"I sidestepped." He set his coffee down, having adapted a serious tone. "But I won't lie to him if it comes up again."

Maybe Father's early morning at the office and his campaign fundraising could keep her missing car off the radar for a bit.

Parker's compliance, however, failed to eliminate her bigger problem of being totally inept in her new job. She went upstairs while Mother and Ramona were diverted over breakfast to see if she could correct that issue.

Corlia still worked on the bed when she entered her room. "I'm sorry, miss. I'll finish after you leave."

"No need. I'd like to watch you work. If that's all right."

The woman, only a little older than Annalee, paused in picking up her cleaning clutter. Her smooth, tanned face clouded with suspicion. "I'm only straightening up your room."

"Actually, I'm more interested in the bathroom."

Her eyebrows twisted together, and her chin tucked down. "You don't like the way I clean your bathroom?"

"No. I mean yes." She shook her head. "I mean, I need to learn what you do."

"You going to fire me, miss?"

This conversation had spiraled. "No." She took a breath. She always communicated better when she slowed down and thought through what she planned to say. "I'm supposed to clean a bathroom today at the place where I'm volunteering. But I don't know how."

"Ah." The woman giggled, probably more from relief than from teasing. "It is not so hard. I can show you what to do." She led the way into the large bathroom and displayed the cleaners used for each of the tasks. These bottles all had clean labels–easy to see and read about their purpose. Corlia led her step by step through all of her checklist items, offering at least a half-dozen aha-moments for Annalee. She used her phone to take a photo of each bottle. If only she could recreate the experience without labels once she reached the center.

Parker dropped her off at the curb with a promise to scout out her best parking option. She thanked him. "Since I'm on time, I should be able to leave at seven thirty."

"You want me to come in for you? That could give a little motivation for them to let you leave."

How nice to have a confidant defending her. But he would only serve to confirm her inability to act on her own behalf. "No." She stared at him. "I'm doing all of this on my own. You'll see. I can."

"I've never doubted that, Annalee." He winked and saluted as she turned to the house.

Like her father, Parker knew her better than anyone. And he believed in her, too.

She faced the red-brick building, looming like a frowning giant in front of her. Not at all like the pleasant scene she'd imagined the day before. With two banks of windows on either side of the door and a porch sagging on either end, she could picture the whole house disgusted with her. What possible benefit could she offer?

Was Mother right? Was Annalee doomed to calamity and utter humiliation for her and for her father? Why had she ever pled guilty? Ramona had a good point. Who was Mr. Madison to her? Annalee had been a fool to put herself into the position where a prejudicial judge could slap her in county jail for several months for the specific purpose of making her family look bad.

Annalee's resolve sprinted away. She stared down the street at the retreating limo. Father's money could get the judge's opinion turned around. Why should she even try?

"You going inside?" CJ emerged from the empty field next to the center.

She startled and faced him. She had no answer. In truth, the battle to stay or go raged in silence. And still, she didn't move forward.

He paused when he came through the side gate. "You look different." He smiled.

Whether from the smile or the hint of approval, his attitude warmed her. She clasped onto it like a lost child and fell into step beside him. "I went with a distressed look. These clothes will actually look better with bleach stains." And her sneakers needed whitening as well.

"Smart lady." He trotted up the steps and opened the door for her. "After you."

Had he called her smart? Even through her A-plus years, she couldn't remember anyone saying such about her, ever. None of her teachers. Not even her father. Pleasant, pretty, agreeable. Those were words people used around her, but never smart.

She climbed the steps and preceded CJ into the center, better equipped for the task she anticipated, but still expecting failure.

CJ's grin started somewhere around his toes. *Wow.* Not only had Annalee returned, but she looked focused and prepared this time. Margo had to appreciate her perseverance. He'd make sure she did.

He found the woman in the kitchen with Paula. "Well, she's back."

She slumped and hung a rag on the refrigerator handle. "I was sure I'd be hearing from Laurel today about a reassignment."

CJ gritted his teeth. Not the place to adjust her lousy attitude. Not with Paula there anyway.

"I'm still surprised her daddy hasn't pulled the strings to get the matter thrown out." Paula rolled miniature meatballs in her dark hands.

Great, the cancer was spreading.

Margo snorted. "Probably a political ploy."

That's it. CJ scowled. "You'd say the same thing if she had been moved. This is ridiculous, Margo. Where's the mind of Christ you seem to have with everyone else you encounter? You have to hand it to the lady. She's worn appropriate clothes, tucked her hair into a ponytail. Not to mention the fact she returned in the first place." Would she give Annalee any credit?

"I don't have to hand her anything. She's required to be here." She wiped her hands on her jeans. "I guess I better go see to the prima donna."

She stomped toward the exit, but CJ blocked her way. "You're taking a leave of absence today unless your attitude changes."

"You're outta your cotton-pickin' mind. You can't run this place without me, and you know it."

"The kids'll suffer. That's a fact. And I'll have a terrible time trying to do all you do, but I'm not letting you stay with this mammoth hatred building."

She pressed her lips together and glared at him. Exhaling, she dropped her gaze. "Fine. I'll give her instructions and leave her alone. That make you happy?"

"I'd be happier if you'd let the hate you've got stop silencing the Spirit I know is inside you." Why couldn't she see the bitter seeds she was planting?

Head down, she walked across the great room. At least she didn't look like she was riding into battle. He glanced at the older woman who had been the cook in the center since the program started. "Why do you suppose Margo has such a hard time accepting Annalee Chambers might turn out to be a nice person?"

Paula shook her head. "She has a lot of hurt, that woman. Surprises me she's not a bitter, old nag."

"She's starting to take on those qualities." CJ peeled an orange and popped a wedge into his mouth.

The woman chuckled. "No. This is only temporary. She'll be all right once she believes Annalee isn't out to manipulate you."

"Me? I hardly know her. Why would she think Annalee is trying that?"

She shrugged. "I didn't say she would, and I don't think she will. But Margo has trust issues. Especially where people with money are involved. You know about her mom's abandoning their family for some rich fella."

Margo had told him a little about how her mom left them all behind when she found interest from a wealthy man.

"She's been burned too deep to forget." Paula dug into the bowl of raw hamburger. "And she cares too much about you and this center to see either of you get hurt."

A harder, more dedicated worker he'd never met. "I know she was hurt, but that's no excuse to target some innocent person with her resentment."

"Give her a chance. She'll warm up." Paula wiped her hands on a towel and shoved a sheet full of meatballs into the oven. "If that friend of hers'll let her, that is."

"Friend?"

"That woman. You know who I'm talking about. I'll think of

her name in a minute. But she's had some pretty nasty things to say about the girl. I don't take to gossip."

Paula usually spoke her mind, though she didn't always live by her statement about gossip. CJ carried his orange into the great room. Was there someone else at the center spreading the verbal poison about Annalee? He'd have to keep his ears open.

Margo came from the bathrooms. "And by the way, you are supposed to do the boys' room as well. Let's see if you can get to both of them tonight?" She let the door close behind her.

He veered to match her trail through the tables. "Quite the encourager."

"Don't nitpick. I know my job."

She sure sounded like she had a lot of bitterness. Paula had to be wrong about her assessment, unless … "Have you ever met Annalee Chambers before?"

"Are you psychoanalyzing me now?" She pushed past him and settled behind her desk.

He turned to face her and bit into another wedge. "I'm trying to unearth the source of this anger you have toward a woman you've never met."

"You've made your point, CJ. Now give me a chance to adjust."

He tossed the peel. *Okay. For now.*

Annalee ended up calling Parker for a ride home after all. What had she thought—she'd take the bus? Mother would have thrown a fit.

She climbed into the back of the limousine and settled in the seat nearest the open window to the driver's cab. "I didn't fail."

"Happy Humpday! You're almost through the week." Kendra, Parker's wife, sat in the front passenger seat, having accompanied her husband on the drive into town.

"Yes. I expected misery and devastating shame."

"I thought you were only cleaning a couple of bathrooms."

Obviously, Kendra had been well taught in cleaning practices. "Next time you're seated beside an energetic senator who wants to discuss the nuclear program of China, let me see how comfortable you feel." Annalee moved to the seat closer to the front and twisted in it to chat through the gaping panel.

The petite, Hispanic lady smiled. Her thick black hair bounced as she nodded. "Point taken. Things went well?"

"I finished." Such a small thing, but so huge when no one believed in her, including herself. "Four bathrooms. Two large ones downstairs and two smaller ones upstairs."

"Was the director pleased?" Parker kept his eyes focused through the windshield.

"I think she was disappointed."

"That's odd." He merged into after-hours traffic on the Dallas North Tollway.

Annalee didn't think so after Miss Pritchard made her opinions known. "I get the feeling she doesn't care for people who have money. She seems to want me to fail."

"Sometimes people need the failure of others to feel better about themselves." Kendra rubbed her hand over her extended belly. "Don't let it get you down."

"How is the little one?" Being the youngest in a small family,

Annalee looked forward to her first experience with a baby around.

"He is destined for World Cup Fame." Kendra arched her back.

"He?" She had been hoping for a girl to play dress-up with.

"He. She. All I know is Little One has really big elbows, knees, and feet."

Annalee eyed her belly as it gave a bounce. She gasped.

"Yeah. Perfect example. How'd you like to have that waking you up at all hours?" She giggled. Kendra's voice gave her away. She was having a blast with this baby inside her. Only a few more months until they got to welcome Little One into the world.

Parker and Kendra's encouragement gave way to funny stories about Kendra's failures with her first job as a sales clerk at a mall clothing store. Too quickly, they arrived at home.

The levity strengthened Annalee's resolve. Good thing, too, when Mother met her at the front door. "Exactly what kind of torture do you want to put us through?"

Annalee's mind blanked. Torture? She resisted the snarky retort poised on her tongue and waited for her mother to complain further. Her mother had taught her the game of composure, though, and was much better at a stare down when she chose to play that way.

Silence grew until Annalee stepped away. She might as well sit in her mother's morning room instead of stand in the entry hall.

"Not in there. That room is for the morning only. If I wanted to use it in the afternoon and evening as well, I'd call it an office or a study. Maybe a sitting room."

Her mother's rantings became more scattered with every year. Annalee turned and quickened her pace into the formal living room. Not her favorite with dark paneling and heavy furniture, but at least Mother couldn't discard it because of its name.

"I hate this room. Far too oppressive."

Mother was manipulating her. For the simple reason that she could. If Annalee hadn't hated the room as well, she'd have planted herself smack in the middle of it, for stubbornness's sake. Instead, she stepped through the dining room into the side of the house which looked out onto the pool. This was a room she enjoyed and where she intended to settle.

"No. Upstairs. The staff in the kitchen will hear us if we talk here."

Annalee sat on the leather recliner and pulled the knob to put up her feet. Rebellion didn't usually color her personality, but her mother had pushed a little too much this week.

"Very well. You obviously prefer to air our problems to the world. Why not invite the staff to the intimate details of our family?"

Still, without a clue as to what Mother spoke of, Annalee kept her gaze steady and crossed her arms.

"Well? What were you thinking, Annalee?"

For years, she'd dreamed up clever answers to this particular loaded question. She toyed with a couple of snide ones but took a page from her mother's instruction book and simply stared at the woman instead.

Father walked into the room. "There you are, Annalee. How was today?"

She shoved her feet down and slid to the edge of the chair. "Not bad. I had a little trouble at first and thought I'd fail terribly like I did yesterday. But I didn't. I did okay. Even the sour director grudged an approval for my work."

"Excellent. I knew you had it in you, sweetheart." He stooped to kiss her forehead then continued through the room to his office beyond.

Mother crossed her arms. "Hmph. While you consider a victory in the hovel of your so-called work, you're happy to spread shame over your entire family."

"Mother, you know I have no idea what you're talking about. I wish you would cease your drama and tell me why you're unhappy. Again." *As usual.*

Mother glared. "Well, if I must tell you, that means you are completely out of touch with your family. A further shame to you, Annalee Michelle."

She leaned against the back of the recliner. "Still waiting."

"It's that horrible maid of yours, whatever her name is."

"Corlia. And she's quite good, Mother."

"Well, she's also quite gone. I caught her chatting with Cook and my maid about your cleaning lesson. They laughed at you. At us. They believe themselves to be better because they know which way to rub toilets." Mother fisted her hips.

"What do you mean she's gone?"

"I fired her, of course. You don't think I'd allow her to stay after making fun of her superiors, do you? Next thing you know, she'd be spreading her gossip to all of the maids in the neighborhood, who would share the greatly exaggerated story with the families of the houses. That would make your father a laughingstock. I wonder you didn't think through the repercussions before you had the audacity of asking that foul woman for advice on something so menial as cleaning a bathroom?"

How did Mother sleep at night with the entire world searching for a way to make her look foolish? "That's quite a concept. I would never have thought of it in a million years."

"Shows how little you consider your family. Luckily you have me for a mother. I keep all of the details in mind. Like your maid. A new one will arrive tomorrow morning."

"I'll hire my own maid, thank you." She wasn't sure how that all worked, but her ability to complete her task at the center made her feel like she could accomplish much. Especially something as small as rehiring Corlia.

"You've never hired anyone before. That's another ludicrous statement."

"She'll be my maid. I want to do the choosing." Annalee lifted her chin, insistent that she would not be coerced or bullied into backing down. *Calm. Steady.*

Mother's face turned into an icy broil, if something could be both frigid and fiery at the same time. Her features froze and hardened, yet a flaming color swept up from the high neckline of her tailored suit. "Very well. But I warn you, Annalee. Your father will hear of your poor attitude. There will be consequences for your flagrant disrespect."

Father would probably applaud.

Chapter 8

CJ watched the blond ponytail bounce out of the girls' bathroom door and head for the stairs. Faster today than yesterday. He couldn't keep the smile from his face. What a fighter. She'd withstood Margo's insults without retort and used the rudeness as incentive to keep improving.

Or at least that's how he saw it.

He glanced at Margo who glared back at him. Yep, that's how she saw it, too, if he was any type of judge. And after so many years of working with the woman, he'd become a pretty good interpreter of her silent communications.

He sauntered toward her, keeping an eye on the charges surrounding him. "She's finishing her first week. Four days. Looks like she's starting to get the hang of things."

"Only days, CJ. Not weeks or months or years. Nothing special here. Might as well be a purple shirt at Mardi Gras. I give her another week, tops."

"You know, I don't get you. She's stuck with it and figured out how to do your chores. She's even doing a decent job of it. Is it so hard to give her credit?"

"You are so blind. Tell me, if she weren't the beautiful blond, blue-eyed girl she is, would you give a flip about how well she does her job? Or what jobs I give her. Or how she gets home at night." She tsked. "Face it, boss-man. You're as smitten as I've ever seen."

"That's ridiculous. I'm impressed she's persevered this far is all. Can't I admire someone without being infatuated with them?"

"Someone, yes. Annalee Chambers, no. You're a goner. And she's nothing but trouble ready to break your heart."

"You need therapy." He laughed. "And my heart is quite content to be nowhere near Annalee Chambers."

"What about Annalee Chambers?" The question caught him off-guard, and he whirled, his cheeks warming. But Annalee didn't stand behind him. Laurel Stewart did.

Margo rushed forward, her face breaking into lines as a smile seldom seen the last few days spread wide across her mouth. "Laurel, so good to see you." She half-hugged the woman. "It's been too long."

He cocked a brow in Margo's direction. "She was only here Monday" Why did he feel set up? He nodded at Laurel. "I didn't know you still did on-site visitation."

She fluttered dark lashes at him. "I don't as a rule. But you know the potential consequences of this case. Someone's leaked that Annalee Chambers is completing her community service here. I'm surprised the deluge hasn't already started. Besides, I can visit some of my favorite people on the county's dime." She reached to hug his neck.

He should have been flattered. Laurel Stewart was beautiful, smart, and worked hard trying to make a difference with people.

But in listing his favorite people, she wouldn't be anywhere near the top twenty, maybe fifty.

"Are we still on for the City Service Banquet next month? I wouldn't want to keep telling other guys no if I don't have a confirmed escort." She rested her hand on his forearm.

"If you'd rather go with someone else, please don't tell him no on my account."

He glanced at a couple of boys who carried on an animated conversation to his right. "You fellows need to use your mouth for eating while you can. Then, you can talk some more."

They gave a chorus of "Yes, sirs." The distraction helped him refocus. Part of him hoped Laurel would let him off the hook. Her attitude wasn't quite as laid-back as it had been with the buddy-dates of the last few years.

And without her in tow, maybe he'd ask someone else? Blond? Artistic? The image of Annalee on his arm brought a smile until the *I told you so* in Margo's voice crossed his mind.

"Don't be silly." She brushed something off his shoulder. "I can't think of anyone else I'd rather be with. Just make sure you don't back out on me."

Wait, that didn't sound good. Too possessive. Too much like a real date.

Before he could respond, or run away, she flipped some sort of internal switch. "Now …" Her Southern accent eased, her charm disappeared, and she turned all business. She quick-stepped toward the office with Margo in her wake. "We've got a situation. How are we going to handle the media?"

"Wait." He followed the two women. "What do you mean a situation, and what does that have to do with Annalee?"

"You obviously weren't listening." She winked. "I'm

flattered." She lifted a slat in the blinds.

CJ raised his eyes to the ceiling.

"Ah, they've arrived."

He joined her at the window. Two news vans had parked across the street along with a few other vehicles. About a half-dozen in all. "What do they want?"

Laurel rubbed her finger under her nose then lifted the slat again. "Dope on Annalee. Most of them want to hear something bad about her. Something they can use against her father and his campaign. Like if he can't raise a daughter, do you really trust him to lead our fair city?"

Margo tittered. "You should be a campaigner."

Laurel joined in and flipped her hair over her shoulder. "So, what can I give the wolves?"

CJ straightened. "Nothing. You're to tell them nothing. Not a word. I'll talk to Annalee. If she wants to make a statement, fine. But not a hint about her is to come out of this center. Not even from you, Laurel."

"Do I need to remind you I don't work here?"

He didn't want this to get ugly, but backing down wasn't an option this time. "I can't help but think about the black mark you'd receive if you violated the privacy of one of your clients."

"Is that a threat?" She stiffened and glared at him. No flirtation this time.

"Simple observation." He held her gaze until she looked away.

"Very well. Still, I need data for my file on her since I've come all this way."

CJ returned to the main room. Let Margo give that information, what there was of it. Annalee's fine. Job's fine. Center's fine. End of report.

He needed detachment from any connection with the girl, yet he sought her out due to the gathering throng outside. He found her in the upstairs hallway.

"Done already?"

She lugged the rolling mop bucket over the door facing. "Yes." Her eyes met his. A slight smile lit her face.

"You're getting fast."

The smile broadened.

"But we might have a problem." He walked her into one of the darkened classrooms, empty with all of the children having snack downstairs. "Seems your working here was leaked to the media, and they all want a piece of you." He gestured out the window, free of blinds or drapes.

Her countenance fell. "I'm so sorry. I'm used to this attention, but I know it won't be good for the center or the children."

"I'm willing to make a statement and ask them to leave, but I didn't want to act without your say so."

She regarded him. "You're asking my permission?"

"Yeah. If you'd rather say something, I don't mind." Living in her own private fishbowl, she likely made statements to the press all the time.

"Oh, no." She shook her head and stepped backward. "But I'll call Father. He'll send someone to deal with them." She practically fled from the room.

Her? Speak to the press? Mother would disown her. Annalee

had stuttered the only time she'd spoken up to a reporter. Even though she'd been a young teen, Mother never forgot.

Annalee wasn't even supposed to say *no comment.* She made the call and let Father work his magic. After having a bite of the full meal they called *snack,* she checked the front windows again. Only one of Father's bodyguards stood near the gate. He was ominous. No wonder the reporters left.

Though his appearance served as confirmation of her working there. He couldn't keep them away every day. She let that concern slide and made a call to Corlia. The phone rang only once before it was picked up. "*Hola.*"

"Corlia?" She hoped it was Corlia. Her own Spanish wasn't very good. "This is Annalee Chambers."

"Yes, Miss? Did I leave something behind?"

"No. My mother acted in haste. I'd like it very much if you would return to your position." There. That sounded formal, yet genuine. Professional.

"But your mother fired me."

"I need a maid. I'd like to hire you. Would you accept?" She didn't blame the woman for her reticence. Mother had always done the hiring and firing, but since this maid would be doing Annalee's rooms and taking care of her needs, she might as well be her choice.

"I would like to return. Would the job and pay be the same as before?"

"Exactly the same as before." She'd need to investigate exactly what agreement stood in place. Surely Father's accountant would know the details of the arrangement.

"I will come in tomorrow. And thank you."

Annalee smiled. Well done. That was two completed tasks on

the day. What other great things could she do?

She hauled her cleaning supplies back to the closet in the girls' bathroom downstairs when she happened upon a child sitting on the sink, looking in the mirror up close.

"Hi, um … where you're sitting is rather dangerous, isn't it?"

The girl turned her head and glared at Annalee. She looked to be about eight or nine.

"Why don't I help you down?" She moved closer.

"You ain't allowed to touch me. Jes go-own." She pointed a tiny finger toward the door.

"Why do you need to be right up on the mirror?"

"So, I can see what I'm doing, of course." She pulled her eyelid down and drew a long line with a thick black lining pencil.

"Oh, sweetie, you're not old enough to use that." Annalee chuckled. "Heavy makeup will steal away your childhood."

"Don't laugh at me." The child's voice rose.

"I'm sorry. I wasn't laughing at you. I remember feeling the same way, wanting to look older."

"You better leave before I call Miss Pritchard. She'll get you good."

Even without the girl's complaint, Miss Pritchard had no trouble getting Annalee. Fine. Let the child look like a cartoon character. What did she care? She nodded and exited without another word. She had something else to do anyway. For the first time, she needed to ask for her next task.

She scanned the room. CJ lifted his chin in her direction. She nodded and made her way toward the office. He puzzled her, and she didn't need another distraction. Not now.

Miss Pritchard was at her desk. Another woman sat next to her, their heads bent in deep discussion. "She's been a complete disaster, but he's blind to the entire situation."

"That will never do."

"This is your territory and you must act or sound retreat." Miss Pritchard sounded like a general rallying the troops. Then she chuckled.

Annalee had never heard Miss Pritchard giggle. The sound was disturbing.

She cleared her throat. "Excuse me, Miss Pritchard, but I've finished with both sets of bathrooms. What is my next task?"

The guest peered from the other side of Miss Pritchard. Her probation officer, Laurel Stewart. Her mind reviewed the conversation she'd overheard. Had they been talking about her?

"Annalee. I understand you've had some difficulty adapting." Laurel rose without greeting.

"Hello. It's so nice to see you." Social grace and manners had been drilled into Annalee. She wasn't about to discard them. "I'm quite happy here."

Laurel's left eyebrow arched into her forehead. "Really. I'm surprised, considering your inability to finish any project given to you."

Annalee didn't understand the hostility, but she didn't shrink from it either. She'd been taught to match aggression with composure and grace. She straightened. "I've come for my next assignment. Miss Pritchard, what would you like me to do now?"

The director sniffed. "Help Paula clean up the kitchen."

"And after that, I'd like to speak with you." Laurel crossed her arms. "I don't think this is working out at all."

CJ spotted Annalee coming out of the office. Despite her calm demeanor, he could tell something bugged her. Maybe it was the lift of her chin or the way she took such long strides.

He stacked the chair he'd been carrying, left the remaining kids to the rest of the workers and followed Annalee into the kitchen.

"Are you Paula?" She stepped up beside lady at the sink and extended her hand. "I'm Annalee, and I'm supposed to help you."

The tall, gray-haired woman set her soup pot back into the soapy water. "Ha, I don't do the handshake thing." She wrapped her beefy arms around Annalee's slender neck. "An acquaintance is just another member of the family."

Annalee stiffened and her eyes grew larger. CJ suppressed a chuckle. She maintained calm and stood solid through all sorts of rudeness, aggression, and attacks, yet the uninhibited love of an older woman moved her.

"Why don't you start over there? Take out the pallet of dishes, dry them off a bit, and put 'em back on the racks behind you with other dishes of their kind."

CJ took over the automatic washer, loading up dirty dishes on the empty pallets. "Everything okay?"

"Dandy." Paula gave him a wicked smile and a wink. "How about with you, Annalee."

"Oh, I'm quite all right, thank you." She wiped off one plate at a time and stacked them on the shelf. "I said as much to Laurel Stewart, but she didn't seem to believe me."

"She thought you were lying?" Not good. Laurel seemed intent to make trouble for this girl.

"Not exactly. I got the feeling she'd gotten complaints. But I shouldn't be talking about this. I know Miss Pritchard knows what she's doing."

"Pritchard?" Paula stabbed the air with a wooden spoon. "Anything she says can be erased with a word from the boss. Right, CJ?"

CJ froze for an instant. He dropped the lid of the soup pot. Silence followed the loud clanging, jarring the topic away from dangerous revelations.

"Are we under storm warnings or are you skittish over an odd draft?" Paula, despite her age, missed little.

He glanced at Annalee, but she concentrated on her task. The identification of him as the boss seemed to miss her. Good thing. He should have admitted who he was when they first met. At least when they met here at the center. But he liked being a mere worker. Not Scott Whelan's son and heir to his fortune. Not an equal in Annalee's eyes.

Maybe he had a test of his own that he wanted to see if she could pass?

He found a reprieve from troubled thoughts when one of his students, Jamaysia Watson, poked her head in the kitchen. "That's the girl." She pointed at Annalee.

Margo and Laurel followed her.

"Well?" Margo crossed her arms and glared at Annalee.

Annalee's neck reddened, but the calm mask on her face deepened as she glanced at Margo. "Well, what?"

Margo stared hard at CJ like she wanted him to do something. But what?

Jamaysia distracted Annalee, her complaint announcing to the room. "She cain't tell me what to do."

Technically she could. Why was Margo letting the child disrespect a worker? "Lower your voice, Jamaysia."

"She ain't nothing but a janitor, done tellin' me how to put on my makeup."

Well, someone should instruct the child. She looked like she'd used a set of inked up binoculars.

"Big, old, plain-faced cow don't know nothing 'bout me. Tryin' to pawn off her beliefs or religion or something."

"Behave. You don't speak to the assistants here like that." If Margo wouldn't reprimand the girl, he would. "You apologize."

"I'm gonna tell my momma, and she gonna make a formal complaint." The little girl spun around and ran from the room.

Jamaysia being the diva again. Try as he might, he hadn't succeeded in reaching through that child's thick barriers.

"What do you have to say, Annalee?" Victory seemed to emanate from Margo. Great. Her bitterness earned a little more fuel, thanks to raccoon-eyes.

"The child was sitting on the sink. I worried she could be hurt. A sink certainly isn't made for sitting. I distracted her with the talk of her makeup hoping she would come down. It didn't work." Annalee spoke with assurance and didn't waver her gaze from Margo's face.

Laurel scoffed. "Well, why didn't you take the girl off of the sink? You're the adult, Annalee. You can't expect the child to know what is or is not dangerous."

Pink tinged Annalee's cheeks. Hardly noticeable, but CJ picked up on it. "I started to, but she said I wasn't allowed to touch her. I'm afraid I haven't been made aware of any rules for dealing with anything. Especially not the children. I didn't want to act in haste and get the center into any trouble."

Touchdown. CJ stifled a grin. Margo reddened, and Laurel looked uncomfortable.

"And I'm sure Miss Pritchard is grateful." CJ crossed his arms. The battle was over, and the hostile attitude Margo continued to layer on Annalee better disappear.

"Indeed." Margo must have read his expectations. She'd told him before he was transparent to her. That played in his favor right now. "I hadn't realized you'd gone without full instruction on the workings of the center. My mistake entirely."

"Ugh." Laurel's scoff sounded like a verbal exhale. "I hardly think—"

CJ turned his back on Annalee and faced Laurel. "That's obvious." His voice lowered to a whispered growl and his eyes became slits.

She matched his tone. "I still need to have a private word with my client."

"Not tonight. You've had enough public ones already." He nodded at Margo.

"Annalee, you're dismissed whenever you and Paula finish the dishes." Margo glanced at him.

Yes, there was more she needed to say. He raised his eyebrows.

She cleared her throat. "Thank you for the hard work you've put in this week. I know it wasn't easy."

Laurel wheeled around, her gaze on the ceiling and another *Ugh* escaping from the depths of her throat. If she did that much more, CJ would be tempted to suggest a cough drop for her drainage problems.

Annalee turned to the side and eyed her turquoise dress with a critical eye. She didn't like wearing strapless after Labor Day, but with temperatures in the high nineties, it would keep her cool and show off the remains of her tan.

With Boyd's indifference since the trial, an evening together might recapture his interest and light a fire under her own. Kindle a relationship which had never quite ignited. That would have been hard as the double date originally scheduled, but thankfully Giselle's betrayal reduced their party to two.

News had gotten back to Annalee that her so-called friend remembered everything from the accident but didn't want to share in any of the blame. Even though she deserved most of it.

Annalee hadn't heard from her since a day or so after the accident. At this point, the separation and silence were probably a good thing. With the bashing of Annalee's calm composure all week long, she'd likely explode if Giselle showed her ugly, fat face.

She pouted at her reflection in the mirror and wondered how the kids at the center got along so well. She'd never been much for kids. Ever. Ev-er. But somewhere deep down, she hoped to get the chance to spend some time with them. Maybe rock some of the babies or help with the crafts?

Someone knocked on her door. "Come." She expected to find Corlia checking on her, but Kendra came through.

"Is that what you're wearing tonight? Boyd's eyes are going

to pop."

"Do you think so?" She turned toward the mirror once again.

"Absolutely." The woman picked up an empty hanger and filled it with one of the many dresses adorning Annalee's bed.

"Is there something you wanted?" Annalee selected a beaded necklace and matching earrings, which drew out the color of the dress.

"No. Not really. Parker and I were talking and … well, we thought you might need a friend about now."

"What has Parker been telling you?" She couldn't fault her friend for speaking with his wife, even if she didn't know Kendra very well.

"Everything. Married folks do that, you know. And enough about you to make me think you're bundling a lot of pain and anger down deep. That sort of thing can make real trouble if you don't find a way to deal with it."

"Parker's worried?"

She nodded. "You know he reads you better than anyone else. He can tell you're troubled about something. Thought I might convince you to let it out."

Annalee sat on the lounge chair. "Well, I don't know much about suppressing things, but I am a little frustrated about my work at the center. I think I'm doing a pretty good job, but the lady who's in charge keeps griping at me. Accusing me of things I didn't do or didn't intend and basically treating me like I'm stupid."

"What can you do about it?"

"Nothing. I need to complete my hours there, or I go to jail." What else could she do? Her earlobe stung, and she tugged at one of her earrings.

"Hard spot to be in." Kendra smiled and sat opposite her. "I'm glad you're going out tonight. You need to let off a little steam, I think."

Annalee's phone chimed with Boyd's ringtone. She leaped and made a dash for the phone. "I'm getting ready as we speak. What time will you pick me up?"

"Well, about that. See, I'm having some trouble getting away." Boyd's voice wiggled slightly.

"Getting away from what? You don't work on Saturdays."

"You know how it is, Annalee. I mean your father is a politician. Sometimes you're just on."

But his father was no politician. "I don't understand."

"I can't make it tonight. We'll try again some other time, k?"

Not okay. Nothing was okay. "Sure. Will you call—?"

A click sounded in her ear.

"… me?" She discarded the question since he was no longer listening. This week kept getting better.

Marji Laine

Chapter 9

As much as CJ enjoyed letting Annalee show up Margo and Laurel the night before, he was pleased to not have her around as a distraction on Saturday. He parked his truck in the paid lot and jogged across the playfield, a spring in his steps that hadn't been there at all the last several days.

In truth, he'd rather have Annalee at the center than Margo, but his right-hand assistant was the glue that held the place together. A shame she had this current blindness. He was tired of playing permanent peacekeeper.

He hopped onto the porch. Margo sat inside, her desk chair next to the opened front window. "Thought you'd take the day off since Annalee won't be here."

"You thought wrong. But then, you've been wrong an awful lot this week." Seemed like the beautiful blonde made waves even when absent.

That easy feeling he'd had before he walked in disappeared. Time to have this out and put an end to the drama. He pushed open the doorway. "Look, I think we need to talk for a moment. You're getting the wrong ideas, and I'm getting tired of coming to a workplace full of hostility."

"Is that what you think? That I'm angry at you?"

"Not toward me, Margo. I feel like I'm having to protect a child against a mountain lion all the time. You've had it out for Annalee Chambers since first sight of her."

"And you've become her little puppy."

He'd had all of such talk he could listen to. "She's already in a relationship with somebody, one, and two, I'm not interested. I wouldn't pay her the slightest attention if you didn't attack her without provocation. You have to admit you've been wrong about her since the beginning."

"She's a spoiled child who has never grown up."

"Why? Because she didn't know how to clean bathrooms? Neither did I, or have you forgotten?" Couldn't she see the poison she'd been spreading?

"How can you defend her, CJ? She and her family represent everything you hate."

"I don't hate. I don't trust wealthy people as a rule." He shook his head. "But she's not acting like the typical wealthy. She's been submissive to you in the face of glaring and undeserved insults. She's maintained her composure during all sorts of difficulty, or have you forgotten how you had her car towed?"

"Parking right there ..." She pointed at the bus lane. "... showed her attitude of entitlement better than anything."

"Have you noticed it cropping up anywhere else? Has she once complained about her nails or the work or the hours or you or me or anything else? No." He crossed his arms. "Can't you admit she's a person like anyone else and let her be?"

"Is that an order?"

"I'd hope you would do it because it's the right thing to do. I'd hoped the Spirit you claim is living in you would convict you for the judgment you've been harboring. Undeserved judgment. I might add. You give this girl any other name, and I bet you'd already be good friends."

"And I hoped you could see the kind of fool she's making of you. How she's manipulating you."

Ugh. Hadn't the topic been closing? Final argument? But no. The door flung open again. "Yeah? And how is that, since I've hardly even spoken to her? She thinks I'm a creepy stalker. Have you seen her laughing or making faces at me behind my back?" He knew better.

"It's all an act. I've seen her kind before." Margo pinched her lips closed.

CJ sighed. If she didn't release her misplaced bitterness, he'd have to take a stronger action. Maybe a leave of absence would be necessary after all, though having Margo miss even one day threw the center onto the edges of chaos. "You do realize she thinks I'm only the janitor. What benefit does she get from tooling me?"

"You haven't told her who you are?" She lifted her head. A wrinkle appeared between her eyebrows.

"No. And you better not let it slip either." He drew in a deep breath and paced. "I swear, I'm starting to hate coming here."

"See? She's added all sorts of stress."

He stopped and planted his hands on her desk. "She's not adding it. You. You're the problem."

Margo's lips pinched together. "And she's already winning. Turning you against me. After all these years."

He lifted his gaze to the ceiling. *God, please help her see with*

Your eyes what's really going on. Leveling a stare on her, he tried again. "I've never seen you act so contrary to the faith. Don't you think she deserves the same love Christ offers to people?"

She turned her back on him and opened her laptop. Great. The wall of solitude.

This topic wasn't over, though.

Annalee stared at the silent phone. The change of plans jolted her, but Boyd's apathy ... she clamped her jaw tight and swallowed hard.

"Don't move." Kendra waddled toward the door as fast as her soon-to-be newborn and the waterbed he/she rode around in allowed. She turned and pointed her finger at Annalee. "And don't change out of that dress."

Annalee wandered to the chair next to her window. Not that there was much to see. No breeze worried the trees on yet another hazy blue-sky. A hot, September day.

A car passed on the road running near the side of the property. She could barely see the flash of chrome through her father's security system. He'd chosen to leave the large trees and bushes on the edge of the property when he had the house built. Even then, he had his heart set on public office. The overgrowth eliminated gawkers and made it impossible for the media to intrude on their private lives.

The security officer tucked in beside their driveway helped, as well.

Right now, Annalee could do with a little intrusion. Anything to get her mind off of the phone conversation. Odd how she and Boyd could have been so close only a couple of weeks ago. As her court appearance neared, he distanced himself, but she justified it in her own mind. His business schedule had been more active than in the past. After she pleaded guilty, though, she couldn't fool herself any longer. He stopped calling, only saw her during the previously scheduled dates and brunch at the club when her parents were around.

Now he'd even broken one of those dates. He couldn't even be bothered to come up with a decent reason.

And she had to postpone visiting a new restaurant downtown, *Elumtude*. The place shouldn't matter, but it did. Her disappointment revealed a lot. If she was truly honest, she was more upset about skipping the fine dinner she expected than missing out on an evening with him. Her mouth flattened. How shallow.

Two taps at the door were followed by Kendra peeking around the corner. "Parker's waiting downstairs." She bobbled in and took Annalee by the hands, urging her to her feet.

She'd changed into a baby doll dress with a red bodice and a black skirt of frilly tulle landing right above her knees. It almost hid her bulging belly. Almost. But it still looked cute, and she accented it with a matching red band tied around her head like a crown.

"We're taking you to *Elumtude*. Parker and me. Won't that be fun?" She pulled her toward the doorway.

With any other couple, the word fun wouldn't have entered the description of a third-wheel date. But Parker always had an inclusive way about him. And Kendra had become very protective of her as well. Made a point to talk with her and really listened to what she had to say. Hard friends to find nowadays.

"I'm game."

This time, Parker drove her father's BMW. They chatted all the way to the restaurant near the arts district of downtown. He helped them from the car, leaving the keys with a valet.

The restaurant was decorated in teak and tan marble in the less-is-more vein. Mediterranean dishes were prepared by a brilliant, award-winning chef. But the real draw of the place was its popularity. Everyone and his brother wanted to see and be seen there. Boyd had asked Annalee to make the reservations over a month ago. He had explained her name had more pull in the Dallas social set.

Good thing she'd reserved for a double date. She had to maneuver her way to the reservation stand. Cigarette breath and heavy perfume combined with smoked chicken and baked fish aromas. She faced a dark-haired hostess who had half-lidded eyes and an unimpressed air. "I have a reservation for Annalee Chambers."

She didn't stand staring over the hostess but turned back to Kendra who had followed her trail-blaze. "Not exactly the quiet, exclusive place I pictured."

"No. This place is crazy." Parker joined his wife.

"I'm sorry, Miss Chambers," The hostess's voice caught her attention, "but your reservation was for four diners."

"Oh, we had a change of plans. There will only be three of us. That shouldn't be a problem, though, right?" She couldn't think of how one less person in this mass of confusion could be a bad thing.

The hostess checked her clipboard. "Well, two in your party have already been seated."

What? "There aren't any others in my party." The woman must have had her reservation mixed up somehow.

"I can show you to the table, but we have no room to add another chair."

"There are only three of us. We don't need an extra chair." Wasn't the hostess listening?

The woman led her into the dining room, also bustling, but not quite as loud. Kendra and Parker followed. They probably hadn't been able to hear any of the discussion between Annalee and the hostess.

She spotted the table long before she reached it and knew the back of Boyd's head immediately. She certainly recognized Giselle's painted face across the table from him.

The nerve. Fire flared in Annalee's chest. Breaking a date with her was bad enough, but using her name to steal the reservation and enjoy it with her ex-best-friend? She clamped her molars together. No composure training was going to help this time.

The hostess said something to Boyd, but he must not have heard her because his eyes popped when he caught sight of Annalee. "Annalee. You're able to make it after all."

"I'm able to make it?" She fisted her hips.

He raised his hand like he was a counselor speaking to a child. "Now don't make a scene, Annalee."

"She won't do anything, Boyd." Giselle fingered the heavy gloss on her lips. "It isn't in her to act on her feelings. Like you said. The Ice Queen."

His eyes grew wider, and he glared at Giselle. "Shut up."

Ice Queen? Annalee picked up his wine glass and flung the burgundy liquid in his face.

Boyd shouted. Whether from shock or the burn of the alcohol

in his eyes, Annalee didn't care.

The room had quieted. Parker put his hand on Annalee's arm. "We should go."

"In a minute." She collected Giselle's glass and showered her as well. "That enough emotion for you?"

She set the glass down as Giselle burst into heated expletives, but her bulk didn't let her move out of her chair or around the table with any speed at all.

Annalee paused. "Don't let her make a scene, Boyd."

Kendra had already gone to the door, and Parker pulled Annalee along. She passed the hostess who giggled under her hand.

At least Annalee's outburst had made someone's night. The lack of control burdened her conscience. She could only hope no reporters had been there.

Sunday mornings always lifted CJ's spirit. Especially when he got to transport children to and from his church for worship. There was nothing elegant about the Rosewood Housing Facility, rough-textured buildings painted in light colors, treeless parking lots, and a small, brightly-colored playground. Like any other apartment complex in the city. But the area had come a long way from the filthy tenements that had speckled the downtown area and parts southward as CJ grew up.

These newer apartments gave families a true chance at breaking out of the bondage of poverty. They provided a place with a real home feel to it. Light and new. Filling the area with an atmosphere of a neighborhood. Like any other complex.

And some of his kids from the center actually enjoyed going to his church on Sunday mornings. That fact made him grin.

CJ's phone began to buzz as he dropped off the Callender kids at their apartment. He glanced at the screen and grimaced.

While he never minded center business on Sunday, he didn't particularly feel like speaking to Margo again after her frosty superiority lasted through yesterday.

"Hi, Margo. What's up?"

"I've been trying to call you for hours. There's been a development you should take action on."

"Hours? What happened to going to your church on Sundays?" Might as well tweak her a little before biting into her newest conspiracy.

"Where do you think I found out about this? How embarrassing to be snickering at a little phone screen only to have my minister's wife identify the subject of the embarrassment as an employee of the center.

"I'm sure you're overreacting. We've got good people working for us."

"Huh. Yeah right. You won't think so when you see the unmitigated attack." She spouted off some YouTube address.

"Wait. I'm driving here. Text it to me, and I'll look at it when I drop the bus off at the church."

"Promise me you'll look at it and take appropriate action."

CJ sighed, sucking in the exhaust fumes of the clunker in front of him. This had to be about Annalee. Margo didn't get as excited about anything else nowadays. "I'll look at it. But keep in mind, my appropriate action might not be the same as yours."

"Make sure you're being fair and objective, CJ. If we can't trust you to make the right decisions, maybe someone else should be director of the center."

Yep, this was about Annalee all right. His neck burned. If only Margo would stop pushing. "I don't like your insinuations. And, frankly, I'm getting tired of your prejudicial attitude. I'll look at your video and take action as I deem necessary. But I suggest you look at it again as well and this time put yourself as the subject of the event. I'll bet your desire for blood would lessen somewhat." He didn't wait for a response but clicked his off button.

Maybe he *should* send Annalee packing? He'd had no peace since she arrived at the center. Even though she hadn't caused any of the problems. He'd trusted Margo's opinion for years. And Laurel had always been one of the best in her field. Could he really be blind to something about Annalee Chambers? Unwilling to see what everyone else saw?

He reviewed the week. Her tears. She hadn't known he watched. And he admired her for facing the challenge and conquering what must have been very hard for her. She'd not displayed a poor attitude, disrespect, not even complaints.

No. He wasn't wrong about this. If anyone was in danger of losing her job, it was Margo.

He pulled into the fairly empty parking lot of Rosewood Baptist Church and settled his bus in its accustomed place at the northwest corner.

The phone chimed a text message, and he took a deep breath. The smell of rain with a slight chill in the air encouraged him. *Lord, let this whatever-it-is clearly break one of our rules of conduct, or let it be clearly a waste of my time.*

He hit the link and found a paused picture of a nightclub or a restaurant. The video, shot through several tables, centered on a woman he didn't recognize. She seemed to be attempting to jump up from her table. The lights were pretty dim, but he felt pretty sure he'd never seen her before. Didn't know the guy standing across from her either.

Play. Might as well get this over with. Pushing the button started the video in another spot. He recognized the silhouette of Annalee. A slight smile warmed his face. She looked gorgeous in her dress, though he couldn't make out the color.

A very pregnant woman stood behind her, and as the scene progressed, a man moved between them, directing the pregnant woman to leave and tugging on Annalee. Her date, maybe? CJ couldn't hear any of the words being said, but the camera wiggled a little and then the view cleared with a more up-close view. He could make out the back of Annalee's head and didn't miss it when she picked up a wine glass and flung the liquid into the face of the man who sat at the table. He jumped up but didn't go into attack mode.

A laugh escaped from CJ. The guy probably deserved it, though he wasn't sure he'd want to know the circumstances. Then Annalee did the same thing to the woman who sat across from him.

She was a different story altogether, shoving out of her seat. The man standing beside Annalee grabbed her by the arm and rushed her out off the screen before the scene froze.

This was what got Margo all riled up? He shook his head. His assistant didn't automatically hate people and try to get them fired. Even when there was an infraction, he usually had to fight with her to let him correct a worker at the center.

What he saw on the video was nothing but a prank. And who's to say the two people hadn't threatened her or mistreated the pregnant woman?

No, if Margo thought he should take a drastic action for nothing more than a forty-five-second silent video of a wine wash, she was sadly mistaken.

On second thought, she was probably right.

Chapter 10

What Annalee wouldn't give for invisibility.

The Reids had encouraged and supported her the night before. Annalee had painted on a friendly expression and laughed at silly jokes through dinner at a local Taco Cabana. But doom neared. When and where it attacked was still a mystery, but not for long.

Parker had seen through her. "This really will be okay." His parting words gave her a glimmer of hope. He tapped the bottom of her chin with his fingertip. "Keep it up, little girl."

"I'm not a little girl." Though she'd given the same response to his particular comment since she was seven years old.

The positives he planted wilted the next morning upon her arrival at the country club for brunch with her parents. She headed for her mother's customary table, near the window in the formal dining room. Two steps inside the large space, Bridgette Montevideo blocked her way. "Nice shot last night, Annalee."

"I'm sorry?"

"In fact, two good ones. I thought Giselle would pop out of her Spanx."

Her stomach twisted. Surely this was simply a rumor. "Were you at *Elumtude* last night?" *Say yes.* Nothing more than a direct witness who happened to be there.

"Not last night."

Like a brick wall awaiting the crash, Annalee froze.

Bridgette shook her salon-blackened hair. "But the video someone posted on YouTube has gone viral. You must feel pretty popular about now."

YouTube? Ice struck Annalee's spine. "My name? Is my name on the video?"

"No. Sorry."

Her heart began to beat again. If her name wasn't mentioned, then what harm was there?

"But your father's is. The headline reads something like Mayoral Candidate Chamber's Little Girl Goes Ballistic." She shrugged. "I don't think that's the label exactly, but your father's name is a tag. That's how I found the show. First thing popping up on Google."

Annalee turned and shut her eyes. This was bad. This was very bad. She should crawl into a hole and stay there until after the election.

"Hello, Annalee." Mrs. Tankerton's greeting made Annalee's eyes pop open and her smile flash. "How is your father?" The woman passed without waiting for a reply.

She braced herself. She still had to deal with her mother. She glanced at her family's regular table and headed in that direction. Mother sat chatting across to table with Boyd.

With Boyd? Was he out of his mind?

Her mother set down her cup and picked up a partially folded section of a newspaper. "About time you arrived. You're almost ten minutes late. The waiter has already brought me my coffee." Her mother couldn't start the day without a strong dose of caffeine and something to nag about.

"Good morning, Mother." Annalee ordered a vanilla cappuccino from the waiter standing nearby. "And a small glass of orange juice, please." She avoided her regular spot, which would put her next to the man of her nightmares, opting for her father's place at the head of the table. If only she could choose a different table. A different room. A different building.

The waiter brought her drinks, and Annalee sipped her orange juice, willing the sugar to invigorate her with the energy to deal with this situation.

Mother set down the paper. "Where are your manners, Annalee? Or are you given to ignoring your intended."

The declaration almost made her choke. "Boyd's not—"

"Hi, all." Ramona entered from the patio. Her manicured hand casually graced the arm of a dark-haired man in a tailored gray jacket over a striped Henley shirt. "This is Thomas Sabatino. My mother, Abigail Chambers."

The tall man bowed over Mother's fingers, making the woman giggle.

"My sister, Annalee and her fiancé, Boyd Tennyson."

He nodded.

Wait. Did she say, fiancé? "Boyd and I aren't—"

"I spoke to your father last night." Boyd stood to shake the man's hand then rounded Annalee's chair. "After our little tiff. The situation gave me a wake-up." He laid his hands on her shoulders and kissed the top of her head.

Ramona and Thomas sat across from Mother and began talking about the coming Milan shoot.

Boyd settled in the empty chair beside her and pulled her close.

But she wasn't buying his pitch. "So, we're now engaged? Is that it?"

"I'll make an announcement if you want." He chuckled. "But I know you don't usually appreciate the center of attention." He snuggled against her neck. "You set the date. Whenever you'd like."

The insincere leech. The chat over Tex-Mex fast food had opened her eyes. With Parker and Kendra's help, she could see how he'd been twisting her around his finger. She wasn't about to get sucked back into his machine.

"How about never?" She pushed against his chest, shoving him against her mother's chair.

"Annalee, compose yourself."

"Yes, please." Boyd looked around and pulled at the collar of his golf shirt. He leaned in close. "Sweetheart, I know you were miffed but not enough to throw away all we have."

She leveled a direct gaze on him and waited for his description of *all we have*.

"Really. Last night's error made me realize how important you are to me." He reached for her again, but she stood and moved behind her chair.

"You mean you realized Giselle's family doesn't have the clout and connections mine does."

"Don't be that way, sweetheart." He turned smoldering eyes on her, but all she saw was a two-dimensional cartoon character.

"I'm not your sweetheart, Boyd." She lifted her chin, maintaining her conversational tone. "I'm not your anything."

Father approached and cleared his throat. "I'm sorry, honey. I was under the impression you and Boyd had some sort of understanding."

"Oh, we have an understanding, all right." She nodded, suppressing her emotions. She lowered her tone another notch to keep the conflict within the confines of the table. "I understand he's a liar and a two-timer, only using the benefits of your connections to build his clientele and your name to enjoy a life he can't afford for himself."

Boyd scooted his chair back and stood. "Sit down, Annalee. You're embarrassing your family." He took a step toward her, but Father blocked his way. "I'm sorry, sir. The last thing you need is another scene caused by your daughter."

Father moved to Annalee's side and put his arm around her waist. "I'm afraid your unwelcome presence has caused this unpleasantness, Boyd."

"And I didn't cause last night's scene, either." Annalee lowered her voice if only for her father's sake. "I made the reservations. You broke the date. The fact you used my name to go out with someone else was your idea, and a sorry one at that."

"Let me get this straight …" Father's neck had reddened. He didn't bother adjusting his volume. The room quieted with the altercation.

"Todd, please." Mother insisted.

Father ignored her and pointed at Boyd. "You came to me last night, claiming love for my daughter, saying she'd accepted your proposal. But what really happened was you cheated on her, and she caught you."

Someone from another table began to giggle.

"Please, Mr. Chambers."

"Had I known, I would have decked you."

"Todd." Mother jumped to her feet and pushed Father away from the table.

More giggles erupted around them.

Annalee dipped her finger in her cappuccino. "This is a little hot." Boyd should have learned from his mistake the night before not to chide her like a toddler. She flung her orange juice in his face, as she'd done with the wine. "Be thankful I cared enough to check so you wouldn't have anything you could sue me over."

"That's it, Annalee. I'm through trying." Boyd spun.

"Brilliant. Finally. Thank you." Annalee called after him, ignoring the laughter and applause sprinkled through the room.

He walked toward the entrance with his head up and orange liquid dripping from his blond hair. The room settled into its normal rumble as excited voices gossiped about what they'd witnessed.

"Well, that display should fuel conversations for several weeks while I'm in Milan." Ramona ran her hand over the side of her coif.

Thomas chuckled. "I know things are different in Texas ..." his thick Italian accent caressed a low tone, "... but I did not expect a floor show with my breakfast."

Annalee reclaimed her seat and asked the amused waiter for another orange juice. "And maybe some extra napkins or a towel?"

She glanced at her sister and pointed toward the door Boyd had utilized. "You know, I think he ought to consider a permanent dye job. Orange is the new black, I'm told."

Ramona tittered as her father and mother rejoined them. "You'd better go revoke his privileges here as your guest before he starts adding up a tab for you to pay."

"Good thinking." Father strode toward the club's management

offices.

Mother sat rigid. "Did we have to do this here?"

"Look at it this way, Mother. You'll be the topic of every household in the north Dallas corridor until next Sunday." Ramona laughed again. "By then, you and Annalee will be able to come up with something equally as dramatic."

Horrors. Annalee summoned a giggle she didn't feel. "After all, we have a whole week."

"That's not funny, Annalee." Mother sipped her coffee.

She shrugged. "It can be. If you care to laugh a little. Think of how much worse our lives would have been if we didn't realize what a creep Boyd was until after I married him."

Thomas snorted. "Terrifying. Even I can see that, and I do not know the man."

"Hmph. I suppose that would have been bad." Mother gave a half-smile.

Maybe there was hope for her after all.

CJ began the workweek sitting in the Brimming Café. Honking horns, traffic, and construction sounds matched the chaos roiling in his stomach.

Lord, would You show me what to say and how to say it? He had to break through the shell of hatred Margo exhibited for Annalee. True, his assistant would insist the whole problem stemmed from his admiration of the wealthy blonde, but she was wrong.

Not that he wasn't attracted to her. What wasn't there to appreciate? Except the money. His own inheritance was enough of a shame.

But his feelings toward Annalee weren't the point. Margo had an unhealthy dislike for her. Was the animosity between them from a personal encounter? If so, did he need to facilitate, rectifying the breach? Or was there something else?

The more he'd thought through the events of the week before, the more he wondered if Margo's friendship with Laurel Stewart had anything to do with her prejudice. She'd tried to play matchmaker between them several months before, but CJ resisted. And Laurel hadn't seemed interested either. He decided Margo was mothering him.

He blew across his mocha.

"You look like you're praying for an ice storm." Tony slid a cranberry muffin toward him.

"In this heat?"

"Or something equally as impossible."

CJ ducked his head. He'd resisted this discussion. Especially while Tony and Margo were … not exactly dating, but seeing one another. In the broadest sense of the term–like little kids staring at each other across the playground.

"Spill. What's eating you, man?" Tony had been his confidant for so long. He'd carried CJ through some of his lowest moments and even led him to the Lord. And he didn't hold his dad's social status or wealth against CJ. Nor did he expect anything from the connection. But this subject called for taking sides.

No, he didn't want to go there. "I'm having a slight problem at work." That should be enough to let the matter lie.

"Yeah. Um … Margo told me you got the hots for the

Chambers woman."

"Margo's full of beans. I hope you didn't believe her." But she was actively spreading rumors. It made the coming conversation with her much harder.

"I believe her, all right. Saw your reaction to the woman myself. Tongue-tied, protective, then all defensive about it. Son, you have it bad."

CJ shook his head. "Whatever. That's not the problem. Annalee's been trying really hard. And doing a pretty good job now that she's figured out what she's supposed to do. For some reason, Margo hates her. I can't fathom why. And the situation leaves me as chief referee of a one-sided wrestling match."

"I tried to talk to her, uh, Margo about her issues. Unreasonable." Tony shoved a hand over his short-cropped black hair. "She needs something to jerk her back into the reality of who this woman is and not the fantasy she has of Annalee's wickedness."

"But how?"

Tony made suggestions, but they troubled CJ. He still mulled over the issue an hour later as he sat in the dimly lit office. The forms he'd completed sat in the center of his desk. *God, give wisdom. And mold Margo's heart.*

The scruff of a tennis shoe on the uneven pavement outside interrupted his troubled thoughts. Clomps of those same shoes sounded on the hollow wooden steps and the porch. He glanced through the window, catching the edge of Margo's curly graying head before she neared the door and it squeaked open.

"CJ?"

"In the office." He braced himself. But he knew what he had to do.

She bounded into the room with the faint appearance of a hunting dog catching a scent. "Well, what action are you planning to take with our little convict?" He pictured her throwing her head back and howling.

Okay, Lord. You're on.

"I wanted to talk to you about what action to take. I trust you viewed the video again, objectively."

She glanced to the side and sat in one of the chairs, leaning her elbows on his desk. "Of course. Did you notice the video has become the first thing popping up when you Google her father's name? Same thing if you put in her name, now, but for a while, it was only under his name."

He'd noticed and nodded. "And exactly what do you see in the video?"

"Didn't you watch it?"

"Yes, but I want to know your take on what it showed."

She sat against the chair back and crossed her arms. "Well, Annalee gave a diva show, attacking two poor people who were simply trying to enjoy a nice dinner. Gives us a bad name. Not to mention huge anger issues. She needs counseling. I bet that could force the judge to remove her from the center."

Interesting. She'd been all for sticking her in jail when Laurel joined her enthusiasm. CJ opened the Google search and typed in Intercede Foundation. The website showed as well as several news articles. He flicked through four or five pages but didn't see the video show up. "I don't see any connection to the center at all."

Her face fell. "And you don't see a problem with the video."

"I see a problem clearly." *Here goes.* He rose and leaned over the desk. "I see a vindictive, bitter woman who's bent on hurting a perfect stranger for no greater reason than her own twisted imagination and deep-set prejudice."

"Now wait a minute." She grasped the arms of the chair with both hands.

"Do you have a specific instance of Annalee breaking a center rule or showing disrespect to you or to any of the other workers?"

"Well …"

"To the children?"

"She's hardly had any contact—"

"Any dangerous behavior? Any anger shown at any time?"

"She's a boiling pot, CJ. You saw it yourself." She stood and gestured to the computer with one hand.

He'd hoped he wouldn't have to take the discussion this far. "Fine. I give up. You win. I've been under a constant barrage of all the havoc she's caused. I'm sick of dealing with the whole situation." He pulled a sheet from his leather folder and put it on the desk in front of his assistant.

Margo looked down then lowered to her seat. "You're going to release her?"

Her face didn't light up. Good. One of the chains on his gut gave ever so slightly. "I'm ready to, if you can tell me what to put on the line for the reason of her termination from our volunteer program. The judge will need to have a legal standing."

A line formed between her eyebrows. "I thought you'd give her a good chewing out. You know, pressing her to quit."

"She can't quit, or she'll go to jail. Why prolong the agony?"

"But if you release her, the judge will probably send her to jail anyway."

"Isn't this what you want? Don't you want to *stick her skinny behind in a jail cell*? I heard you say as much to Laurel."

"You weren't supposed to hear. I was just mouthing."

He shoved the termination record form toward her. Annalee's name on the top line. "Give me a legal reason. Any reason. I'll write it down, sign it, and get rid of her today."

Margo stared at the page.

Had he actually gotten through to her? Time to press the issue. "What's the first item? She didn't help a student down from the sink? Wait. We can't use that because neither you nor I had given her the volunteer handbook."

She glanced out the window.

"What about her blocking the bus lane and the kids had to walk across the street? Nah. That won't work. You had her car towed before the buses got here."

Her gaze drifted to her lap.

"I suppose I could use that she was the subject of an unflattering video, but since there's no sound, and it doesn't have any link to Intercede Foundation, we'd probably get slapped with a lawsuit on that one."

"So why are you so intent on getting rid of her all of a sudden? Last week you were her PR Agent." She straightened and crossed her arms.

"I'm tired of fighting about this. You want her gone? Tell me what I can write on the line that says Reason for Termination."

"I never said I wanted her gone."

"Then what were last week's fighting and yesterday's phone call all about?" He dropped his pen on the desk and straightened.

"You. You've seemed smitten with that girl since she wandered into this place with her frilly shirt, her bleached hair, and her five-inch spiked heels."

"What? Are you kidding me?"

"Claim you're not interested. I won't believe you." She

pointed her chin forward and rested her two fists on the desk.

CJ shook his head.

"Well?"

"Well, what? You want me to tell you I'm not interested in Annalee Chambers? I'm not. I'm not interested in any woman. Not that it's any of your business. But if you think you're going to match me with Laurel Stewart, think again. I have no interest in her beyond the banquet, and after last week, I'm not too keen on spending even that short amount of time with her."

"So Annalee isn't beautiful and charming and intriguing to you?"

"You're pushing this, Margo." He put his back to the woman and pulled another paper from his folder. "What I think about any woman is none of your concern, and I'll thank you to nose out."

"Or what? You need me, CJ Whelan, even with my nose in your affairs, or lack thereof."

"Yes, I do." He turned toward her. "But your prejudicial treatment of an employee over what seems to be a ridiculous notion of my affections for her has caused turmoil and embarrassment to me, to her, and if left unchecked, to the center."

"What are you saying?"

He shoved the other sheet forward, this one a formal reprimand with Margo's name at the top.

She caught sight of the page, and her eyes widened. Good. This time he really had her attention.

"You'll see I've had no trouble filling out the reasons this time. Disrespect. Disobedience. Hostility. Inability to work with others. I have grounds to fire you right now, but I'm choosing this path instead and hoping you'll grasp the seriousness of your behavior. If you plan to continue to look for ways to fire or coerce

Annalee Chambers into quitting, I think you should consider taking some vacation time until her hours of service are over."

He signed the notice in front of her and sank it into the filing cabinet. "If you won't do that, I'm afraid the next Notice of Termination will have your name on top of it."

"You want me to leave?" Her fists disintegrated into weak, old hands.

He finally exhaled. There was the kind, tenderhearted woman he knew and loved. His gut clenched at how broken she sounded, though.

"No." He circled the desk and sat on the edge closest to her. "Not at all. But I can't have another week like the last one. And the cause of the problems wasn't that new worker. It was you and your desire to see her fail."

She stared past him.

"Margo, I've never seen hatred come out of you before. I don't know what that girl did to you, but you locked your sights on her last week and fired at will trying to bring her to her knees."

"I don't hate her. I don't even know her." The voice came out as a whimper.

"Then let's start fresh. Today. I'll be sure to think of her as only the new worker." He wasn't positive he could do that but determined to try. "And you think of her as a person, like all the others who come here. Someone who needs to learn how to give of themselves. And someone who needs to see Jesus' love."

Tears pooled. "You're right, CJ. I guess I thought of her as the enemy from what Laurel told me before she got here."

"Laurel again?" Why had that woman cooked up such animosity? Not that CJ cared enough to ask her about it.

"She's worked on you a long time, CJ."

His chin drifted forward. "Worked on me? What are you talking about?"

"Whether you realize it or not, you're a sought-after eligible bachelor. Laurel has the perk of knowing where you work when most of the Dallas social scene just sit around hoping for glimpses of you."

Shaking his head, he let his mouth hang open. "Where did you get that ridiculous notion?"

"I can't believe you don't realize it. You're listed in D-Magazine every time you attend any function at all. And when you don't show up to a big affair, the women there always complain."

Great. Even as he thought he'd succeeded in removing himself from that world. "What does that have to do with Laurel?"

"Well, it's obvious. Your money, your status. And she's the only woman you've been out with in the last several years."

Working on me. With Margo's conviction of his interest in Annalee, no wonder Laurel treated her with such animosity. "Laurel's jealous? Shouldn't she hand off Annalee's case to one of the other officers?"

"Probably. But I believed what she said. Especially after my first meeting with Annalee. Everything she did confirmed Laurel's appraisal."

He took a breath and rearranged the tools in the box on his desk. Laurel had no real part in the center or in his life. "You think we can start this over and treat Annalee like any other adult leader here at the center?"

She nodded. "I'm sorry, CJ. Especially if I've been the biggest problem for you this past week. I'll make a copy of the handbook now and give it to her this afternoon."

You did this, Lord. He directed a prayer of thanks for the right words. He leaned over and gave her a one-armed hug. "You have a good heart, Margo Pritchard. Keep it open."

Chapter 11

Annalee drove the length of Haskell instead of pulling into her new parking spot adjacent to the center's property. Sometimes, her father's money and influence worked in her favor, like his arrangement with the body shop owner.

Other times, her family's influence brought on all sorts of complications. Like today. The front of the center looked like some sort of political rally with all of the cameras and lights. Miss Pritchard would want to toss her out now, for sure.

She put a call into Father's office and made him aware of the situation. "This is an afterschool care program. Surely, there are some laws about how close they can be to it, right?"

"I'll look into it, honey."

Annalee had turned left on a side street just past Fair Park and done a circle before returning to Haskell Avenue. She avoided the street directly in front of the center and traveled all the way to the Magnolia Theatre before turning around and retracing her path. Traffic was light and she took the track several times before she noticed some of the news crews retreating to the empty lot across the street from the center.

Bingo. They wouldn't even see her if she went through the kitchen. It wouldn't take long for them to tire of wasting their time.

She alighted at the back door of the body shop, feeling empowered to cast off the frustrations of the weekend and sink her gloved hands into soapy mop water.

The place even had a smell of potential—a mixture of clean floors, sweaty kids, and something baking. She found Margo in the front office. "I'm sorry about the reporters, but they aren't allowed on this side of the street since this is a children's care center." At least she thought that was the rule. And seemed like it from the actions of the reporters.

"I'm not too worried about them. Have a seat." She pushed a thin binder toward her. "I should have given this to you last week. Our procedures manual. Let me know if you have any questions. I'll need you to read through it and sign the last page. Please bring that to me by Friday."

"Certainly. Thank you."

"And I thought perhaps you'd like to do something besides the bathrooms at this point."

"I don't mind. I'm happy to work wherever you need me." Even if she did only clean mirrors and toilets and floors. She was getting pretty good at it.

The older woman fussed with files and papers in one of her desk drawers. "I think the upstairs bathrooms should be fine today. They are hardly used as it is. Once you do the downstairs, you can work in the kitchen with Paula." She paused and gave Annalee a direct look. "If you finish quickly enough, you can help serve the children their snack."

Annalee smiled, covering the gasp that wanted to escape. Her chest tightened. She'd never dealt with children before, beyond the few who visited the bathroom while she cleaned. But maybe she wouldn't finish in time. She started with the boys' restroom, having figured out she needed to finish it as early as possible before anyone needed the facility. Once done there, though, she made slow work of her tasks in the girls' room, using every little issue as a new thing to clean and another chance to delay. She didn't come out until few kids remained in the dining room.

"Hey. I know you." A boy from the nearest table set down a paper airplane made out of a napkin. "I seen you last week."

"You did?" She smiled at his freckles and light red hair. "When?"

"You was pouring out the mop water in the back. My brother and I were playing tetherball."

She didn't remember. "Well, did you win the game?"

"Nah. Tyrone always beats me. He's taller." He pointed to an African-American boy coming toward him. He was indeed taller and probably a couple of years older at least.

"This is your brother?"

"Yeah. We twins. Can't you tell?" At that, both boys burst into giggles.

Annalee chuckled lightly, unsure of how to react beyond matching their humor.

The other boy sobered first. "Aw, lady. We messing with you."

"Well, you could be brothers." Same nose anyway.

"We brothers, all right." Tyrone flashed a broad white smile sparkling against the creamed coffee color of his face. "We just ain't twins."

His brother had another fit of giggles.

"Let me guess. You're the oldest. Tyrone?"

"Yeah. I got almost three years on Hayden. And then there's our sister. She's almost three years older than me."

"Is your sister here?" Annalee glanced around, but no other girls remained.

"Nah. She too old." Hayden's laughter had finally subsided. "She had to drop out the program when she hit high school this year."

"I see. Well, I'm Annalee, and I work here now."

"You ain't Miss Annalee?" Tyrone's eyebrows curled. "Everyone here is a Miss or a Mister. Like Mr. CJ and Miss Paula and Miss Pritchard."

Miss Pritchard *would* go by her last name. It matched her character. "Oh. Then, I guess I'm Miss Annalee." She grinned. "Do I need to call you Mr. Tyrone and Mr. Hayden?"

That sent the boys into another fit of giggles, and Annalee joined them for a moment before moving toward the kitchen. Maybe working with the kids wouldn't be so bad after all?

CJ worked at the power washer as he had on Friday, but tonight he had a grimace across his face.

"Is everything okay?" She picked up a rag, dried, and stacked several platters before moving them to a shelf.

"Why did it take you longer to do your cleaning today than last week? Especially when you only had the two bathrooms to do."

She bristled. His superior attitude annoyed. Like he had a right to criticize. "You've just started on the dishes, right? I didn't add too much to your work, did I?"

"That's not what I meant." He dried his hands on a towel and fisted his hips. "What took you so long?"

She couldn't explain her fear of working with the children. He'd never understand. "Not any one thing. Issues." She forced her tone to stay even. "Why does it matter to you?"

"I went to bat for you. Talked to Margo about giving you a better experience here."

So that's where the director's snide remarks had gone. "I thank you very much, but the next time you're inclined to act on my behalf, please don't."

"I was trying to help you."

"And I appreciate your intention, but I want to succeed at this on my own." Succeed. Simply saying the word made her feel powerful.

"Okay, you don't need my help." He sounded … angry. Why should he be angry?

"Correct."

"Good enough." He tossed the towel on the side of the counter and backed out of the room.

She didn't mean at that moment.

Paula emptied a skillet of dishwater and propped it up on one of the washer racks. "Looks like it's only you and me, tonight, kid." She showed her how to fill the racks, wash the load, and then hoist them onto the other counter where the dishes could be dried and put away.

Annalee's face heated and her shirt stuck to her back after only a few minutes of hoisting the heavy dish racks from the washer onto the counter beside it. At her fastest, she could only dry and store half a rack of dishes before the next load finished. Though she'd probably get faster as time went on. Like she had with the bathrooms.

But the animosity from CJ tore at her.

CJ massaged the back of his neck with one hand as he stalked into the dining room.

"Hayden and Tyrone, your momma's here to walk you home." Margo poked her head into the dining room from the foyer then froze when her gaze fell on CJ.

The boys shouted bye and bolted for the entrance as Margo neared. "What in the world is wrong with you?"

A grilling from Margo was the last thing he needed. Her insinuations about his feelings for Annalee, as if he'd taken a second to even decide if he had feelings for her, forced him to take a more detached manner with her. Which wasn't hard since she'd been invisible all afternoon.

"I'm fine."

"Are not. You're mad as a tabby missing his catnip. What happened?"

"Nothing." She'd never buy that answer, but he had to try. He moved toward the office.

"Oh, no you don't. I can tell you're upset, and I'm going to keep pestering you until you give, so you might as well let it all hang out now."

He focused on the ceiling. Prolonging this would only make it worse in Margo's mind. "I'd hoped Annalee would finish quickly enough to get to serve the kids tonight. I think if she works with them, she'll enjoy the experience."

"You're mad about that?"

"I told you. I'm not mad."

She snorted. "You shouldn't be mad, but you are. Did you fuss at her?"

He glanced back out toward the dining room. "More like she griped at me."

"About what, for pity's sake."

Ugh. Why did he have to go back through this? "I mentioned I'd talked to you about giving her a little leeway so she—"

"Wait a minute. You told her you spoke to me?"

"Yeah, but—"

"And she still thinks I'm the director? Huh. I'd have blistered you if I'd been her." She leaned against the doorframe crossing her arms.

"Why? I told her I wanted her to have a little time with the kids."

"And she said to mind your own business."

"Not in so many words." He crossed to his desk and started packing up his laptop case. "What do you care anyway? I thought you didn't like her."

"You showed me the error of my ways, boss-man. She's not so bad, if she's as genuine as you think she is. Though, I do still have a few doubts."

He folded up his cords. "I think she's sincere. And I realize now, she sure doesn't want me around."

"Ah. That's what's got you so upset. She didn't want your help and didn't like the meddling you did when you spoke with me."

"I told you. I don't have any feelings for her."

"Tell me I'm wrong."

A rant passed through his mind, but before he could form the words, Annalee stepped into the doorway. "I noticed the binder instructed me to sign in and out. I'm not sure where I'm supposed to do that."

Margo pointed to a clipboard on the wall. "I signed in for you today. We'll have to catch up last week's log at some point. But you can do the signing for yourself from here on in."

She only just got the binder. Was that what had taken her time in the bathroom? "You started studying the binder already?"

"A little. I wanted to make sure I was following procedures. And I looked at the front page while I waited for the last load to finish in the power washer."

Her open face blew out the fire of fury that had caused his outburst in the kitchen.

"Walk her to her car, CJ. This is a dangerous neighborhood."

CJ shot Margo a glare. Now, she was playing with him. He had a habit of walking all of the women out at the day's end. But walking Annalee out alone would stretch his objectivity.

"You don't need to do that." Annalee scratched information on the clipboard. "I'm only right outside."

Margo stiffened. "Not in the bus lane."

"Oh, no." She had the grace to laugh. "I got permission to park at the side of the building next door." She pinked. "Daddy worries about me driving down here by myself."

"I worry about me driving down here by myself." Margo shrugged. "I take the bus."

Annalee chuckled and stepped through the kitchen toward the back door. "I'll see you both tomorrow then."

The cocky expression on Margo's face made CJ wince. As much as he wanted to let Annalee walk away without giving her a second look, he couldn't. But convincing himself that he felt nothing for the woman was getting tougher with every moment in her presence.

He stepped out the door a few moments after Annalee and watched her walk the short distance through the side lot to her car and get in. Forget Margo and her crazy ideas.

Annalee climbed into her car and glanced up in time to see CJ step back into the kitchen. Her chest gave a slight lurch. He'd been watching her. Keeping her safe. A warm feeling spread across the back of her shoulders.

Had Miss Pritchard made him watch her after all? Likely so.

A strange ache replaced the comfortable feeling she'd experienced. CJ hadn't kept an eye on her because he cared. He'd been sent to the porch by the director because she still considered Annalee some sort of helpless baby who needed childcare.

At least the reporters had given up and gone away. Her chin lifted. Seemed like her emotions played havoc with her a lot lately.

Pulling out, she determined to be glad Miss Pritchard had shown some acceptance of her. Even if a minor victory made her appear as an irresponsible school girl who needed looking after. And what did she care what a janitor-slash-handyman thought of her anyway?

She made her way down the block, not feeling any better from having altered her thoughts to look down on CJ. He'd never given her reason to despise him. That was more Giselle's game than hers.

And the last person she wanted to imitate was Giselle.

So, at least for the time being, he could probably be a friend of hers. Like Parker was her friend. Only CJ would never be as close a friend as Parker. Too little in common and no history. But he could make a nice acquaintance.

Despite the way he filled her thoughts all the way home, she struggled to keep her mind elsewhere on the trip back to the center the next day.

After speaking with Tyrone and Hayden the night before, she yearned to meet more of the kids, maybe play a game with them or teach them about her painting. But talking with them intrigued and excited her.

CJ wasn't the only enticement at the center. Wow. Enticement? Handsome, yes, but ... his smile flitted across her mind.

Drat. She'd made a focused attempt to keep her brain occupied elsewhere, yet the man had still sneaked his way in. A shame she'd had to ruin things when she had words with him the night before. She'd tried to erase the unpleasant memory the night before, but he'd even trespassed into her dreams.

She sighed. Yeah, the man was definitely an enticement. Arriving at the center, she pulled into a spot at the body shop a half hour early. With no reporter in sight, she buzzed with enthusiasm and took the front walk to the porch. She found Miss Pritchard in the office.

"Well, you're here early. Need to leave before quitting time tonight?" The woman pointed to the sign-in clipboard.

Annalee marked the time in the correct column beside her name. "No, but I'm looking forward to helping today. I met a couple of the kids last night, and I think I'm ready to start working with them, if you're willing." She opened her purse and pulled out the folded, signed sheet she'd taken from the back of the binder. "And here's the form you wanted from me."

"After you read the entire manual, Annalee. This says you understand all of the rules and agree to abide by them. You can't do that if you haven't read them."

"Oh, I did. Last night. I fell asleep a little over halfway through, but I finished the book this morning."

The director took the sheet. "You think you're ready to work with the kids?"

"I don't mean I'm equipped. That's for you to determine, of course. But last night I was rather … nervous with the idea of being around them. I guess I didn't think they'd like me very much."

"What made you think that?"

"The first child. The one in the sink? She didn't seem to like me at all, and I barely spoke with her."

Miss Pritchard nodded. "That's Jamaysia Watson. She's fairly hostile to everyone at first. Huge chip on her shoulder and ready to shout lawsuit for any imagined slight."

"I see." Annalee rested her hand on the small handbag she'd hung across her shoulder. "I feel much more prepared though after speaking to the boys last night. They seemed very nice."

"Most of the kids here are. With at least one parent, but sometimes even two, who care about them as much as yours care about you. Just caught up in difficult circumstances that seem to spiral out of control." Miss Pritchard sniffed. "People can be pleasant and happy, even if they don't have money to burn."

Annalee iced. She wouldn't apologize for her parents, her lifestyle, or her upbringing. She hadn't looked down on the boys last night or even thought about their situation. They made her smile, and she looked forward to talking with them again.

If their financial statement didn't matter to her, why was hers the topic of discussion? "I don't quite know how to respond to that. I didn't notice anything special, whether good or bad, about Tyrone and Hayden. I simply enjoyed speaking with them, and my fears at being around the kids ebbed somewhat."

Miss Pritchard didn't answer right away but stood and crossed to a pair of file cabinets in the corner of the room. Opening one of the drawers, she extracted a manila file folder. She scratched something on the tab and then slipped Annalee's paper inside. "All right. You're now official." Sliding the folder into the top drawer, the slam of the drawer punctuated her declaration.

Annalee watched the woman's abrupt motion, though she didn't seem as irritable as she had the week before. "You didn't think I would stay, did you, Miss Pritchard?"

The woman turned and leveled a gaze on her. One full of … sincerity. That was a surprise. "I think I've misjudged you. At this point, I hope that's true. If it is, I'm happy to have you as part of the team."

Giddiness welled up inside Annalee. *Part of the team* sounded so useful and beneficial. "Maybe I should start on the bathrooms, so I can be done in time to help you serve the snack."

She barely heard the woman's agreement. A new boot shipment at Macy's couldn't have been a better announcement. She finished all four rooms before the kids came inside from their playtime. Washing her hands in the kitchen sink, she took in the room. Huge bowls of spaghetti sat on the metal counter with plates of Italian bread. The kitchen smelled like a bakery.

Miss Pritchard swept into the room. "CJ is calling the kids in. Annalee, I'm glad you've joined us."

Even without a smile, the woman seemed almost nice.

Annalee eyed the bowls. "I've been wondering why you call this a snack."

She chuckled, a lighter sound than the first time Annalee had heard it the week before. "That's the verbiage we have to use for official circles. Most of these kids won't have a hot meal, or any meal, for dinner unless we give it to them. They get lunch and breakfast at school. We take care of dinner for them."

Couldn't they get a sandwich at a market or a convenience store? Annalee had little time to dwell on the question. Forty or fifty kids came rushing in. They lined up along the wall with six or seven going into the bathrooms at a time. She'd been privy to the handwashing games, having learned that she should clean up the mirrors after they left.

But now that she saw how the system worked, it didn't matter if the mirrors got messy. She'd have the rooms cleaned before they needed them tomorrow.

CJ came into the kitchen, dead grass clinging to his shirt and dirt speckling his face and hands. Even with the mess, Annalee's heart did a little leap.

Miss Pritchard snapped him with a towel. "I've told you to clean up outside when you choose to act like an overgrown eight-year-old."

He laughed but scooted out the door he'd come in. Several kids, with clean hands, waited for their food to be served. Miss Pritchard gave Annalee the trays of bread and instructed her about a serving size as she dished out ladles full of saucy noodles onto plates.

Though her part was far from difficult, Annalee enjoyed smiling at the kids and handing a slice of bread to each one. Some of them looked at her with shy, wide eyes. Others had more boldness, talking to her. Especially the few she'd already seen. Tyrone and Hayden and a few of their friends, as far as Annalee could tell, greeted her with wide smiles, though she couldn't remember all of their names if she'd tried.

"Thought you done run off." The smirk of little Jamaysia Watson caught Annalee by surprise.

"Why would you think that?"

"Well, you ain't no cleaner."

Annalee laughed. "I'm not very good at it, but I'm learning."

"I ain't never seen no maid with a Gucci bag before."

She glanced down at the strap crossing her chest from shoulder to hip. "You know Gucci?"

The little girl lifted her chin. "I know all the great designers." She took a piece of bread from Annalee. "I'm gonna be better than all of 'em someday." She flounced away with her plate like she owned the catwalk.

As she watched her go, Annalee filed away the little detail that she was into designer clothing. Talking that topic might get Jamaysia to open up a little more.

She continued serving bread and caught sight of CJ sitting with a table full of older boys. She couldn't hear anything being said, but the boys clearly adored the man. They kept interrupting their own eating to talk to him. One of them showed his arm muscle. That got several of them started. Down went the forks on the table. One bare shoulder after another appeared as the boys slid up their sleeves or shed jackets.

CJ's own muscle bulged at one point. Annalee gasped, but the sweet look on his face when it lit up with laughter resonated. The pageant quickly turned into a competition as the boys began to arm wrestle each other and then drag CJ into the battles.

Miss Pritchard was right. He was an overgrown eight-year-old, but he had the complete attention of over half of the kids without even trying. She noticed when one of the kids got upset after losing a match and started shouting. CJ didn't say a word, merely caught his attention with a glance that soaked the flames of the fight right out of the kid.

After a while, Tyrone and Hayden came back to her with empty plates. "We can have leftovers when everyone's through the line." Hayden's announcement must have reached Miss Pritchard's ears because she gave Annalee a nod.

"Okay. Here are a few more pieces of bread. Do you want some spaghetti?"

"Huh-uh, only more bread." Tyrone snatched the piece and stuffed it into his pocket then held out his plate again.

"You want more?"

"Yes, please." Hayden grinned up at her. His missing front tooth making for an enchanting smile.

"All right." She gave them each several more pieces. Might as well. No one else wanted them. But a few moments later, the boys brought their empty plates to the dish pile.

"How did you eat all of that bread so fast?"

"We didn't eat it." Tyrone lowered his voice to a whisper. "We done stowed it."

Miss Pritchard called out the names of some of the children whose parents had arrived and CJ stopped his game-playing to come into the kitchen and start the dishwashing.

Annalee took a moment to step out into the dining room and chat with the boys a little more. "Why do you stow your bread? Do you like it that much?" It looked like any other sourdough bread she'd ever seen.

"It's okay." Hayden drew out the word. "But it's for Tally."

Was that some type of game? "What's that?"

Hayden burst into hysterical giggles.

"Tally ain't a that. She's a who." Tyrone's broad smile brought to mind thoughts of their last conversation.

"Oh. She's your sister? The one who's too old to come here."

"Yep. But when they give us stuff we can pack in our pockets, we bring her home some dinner."

Half a loaf of bread was dinner? "What about the days when they have soup and salad?"

"We usually can scrounge some cookies or a pack of crackers or something." Hayden had stopped giggling enough to explain things to her. "It don't matter what we bring. Tally's always glad about it."

"Hayden. Tyrone." Miss Pritchard's voice cut through the room.

"That's us." Tyrone shoved his brother aside and dashed to the other end of the room where the backpacks lined one wall.

But their leaving didn't remove the information she'd learned or the feeling she should be doing much more.

Annalee's dreams troubled her through the night. By dawn, she felt she had to act.

And this wasn't something she could talk to her mother or father about. They shared a strong opinion about giving handouts.

I can donate money to a charity I'm sure will spend it responsibly, or I can toss it in a tin can and be reasonably sure the person who gets the money will waste on something he shouldn't. The voice of her father tracked through her head, along with his favorite comment whenever she wanted to give money to someone on the side of the road.

She disliked the thought of going against Father's wishes, though. He'd always been adamant about supporting organizations who knew how to give help to people who really needed the assistance.

However, this wasn't throwing away money. She was giving the boys some food to take home to Tally. Food that wouldn't get crumbled in a filthy pocket. And sustenance having more to it than white flour and flash-carbs.

Using a larger bag than normal, she tucked a box of granola bars into the leather sling and entered the center.

Again, she sped through her cleaning, finishing at about the same time as the day before. Then, she washed up and joined Miss Pritchard and Paula in the kitchen. This time the snack was beef soup and the whole center smelled of bouillon and garlic.

When the kids lined up, Miss Pritchard put her at the head of the line. "One ladle of soup in each bowl. The cornbread is pretty crumbly, so I'll take care of that."

"My cornbread is not crumbly." Paula hissed at her from behind the kitchen island.

"I told you not to put in the extra flour. You never listen to me."

"In matters of recipes, why should I? You limit your cooking to frozen dinners and microwave macaroni."

Miss Pritchard held up a hand, stopping the conversation.

Annalee wanted to laugh but sucked in the amusement. The kids clamored for their snack, and she was quite happy to serve them. Again, she greeted each one, asking for their names. Some of the names were starting to connect with the sweet faces she saw.

As before, Tyrone and Hayden came back up toward the end of the meal, after everyone else had returned for seconds.

"Is there any cornbread left, Miss Annalee?" Tyrone reached her first.

"I was gonna ask." Hayden elbowed his way in front of his brother.

"Too late. I already done did."

Chuckling, Annalee checked the cornbread tray. "I'm sorry boys, but the cornbread is all gone. I guess everyone liked it."

"All of it?" Hayden's smile dropped off. "Ain't there any left at all?"

"No. Miss Paula is washing the pans right now." She held up her finger to make them wait a moment while she collected her bag from the corner. She met them at the door to the kitchen. "If you're worried about your sister going hungry, though, don't be. I brought her some of my Granola bars from home. They're very healthy. And if she runs out, you can let me know, and I'll get her some more."

"Gee, thanks, Miss Annalee." Tyrone's spreading smile warmed her heart.

"Hey, lemme carry 'em." Hayden snatched them from his brother's hand as Miss Pritchard announced their names.

Annalee smiled as they left. Not only because of their cuteness factor but also because she'd been able to make a difference. Albeit a small one.

Chapter 12

CJ had tried not to pay attention to Annalee as she served the kids, but her bright face attracted his attention.

Her eyes lit with each new child. A fresh smile crossed her face, and she handed out the plates and bowls with some words of engagement.

Utterly charming.

In spite of his determination to avoid those charms, they caught him at unexpected times. And serving snack to the kids was definitely one of those. Maybe he should assign her to the baby room to have her out of sight and out of his mind.

She'd need a little more experience before he reassigned her, but he vowed not to put it off for long.

A while later, he noticed her speaking to the Madison boys. No surprise there. They could enchant a troll. But when she took a box out of her purse and handed it to the boys, he felt an icy finger track down his spine.

Great. Now, what would he do?

He stepped into the office and took Margo aside, explaining

what he'd seen.

"Okay, boss-man. What are you going to do about it?"

"You're sure she read the entire binder?" His right hand massaged the back of his neck.

"Doesn't matter. She signed off on the binder. The rules are clear. No gifts. Nothing. Nix. Nil. Nada." She took a breath. "You sure about what you saw?"

Had he been? What else could she have been doing? "I believe when you ask her, she'll tell you the truth."

"What do you mean when I ask her?" She opened the door for another parent. "It's time to take off your mask, Phantom."

Admitting what he was, who he was, would only make matters worse at this point. Margo had to understand. He waited until the last family left. "That will make her mad and embarrassed at the same time. I'd rather do one at a time."

"You're making this way too hard, CJ."

"Probably, but we need to deal with this issue, first. Ask her what she gave the boys. If she doesn't admit to it, then I'll deal with her. But if she does, you explain the rule to her again and put a note in her record."

Margo tsked. "You're making a mistake. Mark me, right now, this day. You're going to regret the actions you're taking."

He sighed. "Fine, so marked. Now go talk to her."

He remained in the office, but once the washer turned off in the kitchen, he could hear every word through the open doorway. She'd read the rules, but gifts to her were expensive presents, not food. And she wasn't giving it to the boys, but to their sister.

Gray area at best.

Margo expounded on giving absolutely nothing to the kids. "Not so much as a ponytail holder."

That should get the message across.

She went further though. "When we're at the center, we're the authority. We can't offer anything to the children for our safety and for theirs. What if those bars you gave away were full of peanuts and you gave them to someone with a peanut allergy. Having given it away from the center, it's not only you helping someone out. It's also the center being liable for action taken by one of its volunteers. Do you understand?"

"I think so." Annalee didn't sound angry. Hurt maybe, and a little confused. "So, while I'm at the center … physically here … I can't hand anything to anyone. But if they came to my house for, say, Halloween, I'd have no problem?"

"I hardly think any of these kids would come to *your* house for trick-or-treating."

"Okay, say I happen to see them at a mall and hand them a perfume sample. That's not an issue?"

"Again, hardly a chance of that." Margo could be insufferable.

"But if it did happen, I'm not bound by the center's rules since I'm not at the center. Isn't that correct?"

"Yes. All right. If you happen to see one of these kids on the street corner, feel free to give them the newest iPhone. There, does that make you happy?" Margo's voice sounded pouty.

"Thank you for letting me know. I'm sorry about the confusion. I didn't consider food as a gift, or I would never have given it to Tyrone and Hayden. It won't happen again." Annalee's tone sure sounded like they'd gotten through to her.

CJ could only hope.

Despite the heavy clouds which sucked the life out of the weekend, Annalee couldn't wait to reach the center on her first Saturday of working there. She knew her own maids did extra cleaning on the weekend, so she might get that sort of job, but a big part of her hoped she'd get to work with the kids a little more than simply serving them food.

With a hooded raincoat covering her purse and more than fifty percent of her body, she climbed from her red Mustang and trotted for the entrance.

"Hey there."

With her head down, she'd have run right into CJ had he not called out. She jerked her gaze up and rewarded herself with a splash of cold droplets across her cheeks. "I'm sorry. I didn't see you."

He pushed the gate open and held it for her. "No harm."

She slowed. "It's supposed to do this all day if you can believe the weatherman."

"I don't usually, but they're right this time. Probably won't stop until after dawn tomorrow morning." He matched her stride and paused when they reached the porch.

"I hadn't heard that much detail." She shed her coat and shook the excess water from it.

"And you won't. The media folks don't want to be wrong, so they only give as many details as they must. If they give too many and make miscalculations, people stop listening to them."

"Are you into weather?"

"Science was my best subject in school, but predicting weather was a passion." He grinned. "And I can be wrong all I want since I'm not into public forecasting."

From the looks of the gray, shredded-cotton sky, she believed his expectation. "I wish the temperatures started matching the precipitation." She folded her coat over her arm and glanced at him. "Falling."

"Was that a joke?" He opened the door for her and stood aside. "Did you crack a joke? Are the daughters of mayoral candidates allowed to do that?"

"Only out of earshot of all reporters and members of the opposition."

She paused as he shut the door. Amusement painted his features. "There's another one. Where have you been keeping yourself, Lucille Ball?"

"Very funny." She signed in.

He took her coat from her and hung it in a closet behind the front door. Hmm. Gallant. The word whisked through her head before she could squash it. But the action was rather thoughtful of him.

"What do you do with the children on a rainy day like this when they can't play outside?"

After hanging up his own windbreaker, he closed the door. "Sometimes we do board games. A couple of times a year we pull out costume bins and set up a theater or make puppets and stage a play."

"Sounds like fun. What are you going to do this time?"

"We, Kemosabe. What are *we* going to do?"

"Oh, no. I can't. I've hardly even met these children, CJ." She paused. Saying his name felt nice. "Or am I supposed to call you

Mr. CJ?"

The light in his eyes faded, and his smile dropped away. Did his cheeks redden? "CJ is fine." He ducked his head and rubbed his neck with his right hand. "Follow me up to the attic, and we can choose an activity for the day."

Attic? She trotted up the steps and followed him down the narrow hallway to another steep set of stairs she'd never noticed before. She hesitated at the bottom. "Um … When I think of attic, I think of cobwebs and rats and spiders."

Halfway up, he turned, a smirk dancing across his lips. "What? No snakes?"

"How would snakes get into an attic?"

"I thought they should go along with the rats and spiders." He shook his head. "Sorry to disappoint you, but this room gets a thorough cleaning every rainy day."

She edged upward.

"Though I don't promise anything about roaches."

Her gaze hit the ceiling. Those disgusting creatures could live anywhere. She'd even seen some in her own home in late summer. Blah.

The door at the top gave him trouble. CJ jiggled the knob as she caught up, standing close behind him.

"Is it locked?"

"No. It sticks in this sort of weather. Trouble is, the only time we normally venture up here is when it's raining. A rumble of thunder punctuated his words.

Annalee shivered and descended a step. "Why don't I wait for you in the dining hall?"

He pivoted. "Are you worried about the storm?"

Was it a storm? It had only been raining when she got to the center. Was it building? She hadn't heard anything about severe weather, but sometimes storms bubbled up with no warning.

CJ must have noticed her silence. "This is only a little thundershower. Lightning here and there and some refreshing rain. That's all."

"You never know around here." Her voice broke, and even to her, the argument sounded terribly weak.

"You can go back downstairs if you're worried."

Worried. The word set her teeth to grind. That's what her mother always did about so many things. No. Annalee would not be the same type of person.

"No. I'm sorry. I let my childhood fears get the better of me." Once again, she climbed the steps and tucked herself into the corner of the landing.

He struggled for a second with the knob but convinced it to unlatch. When it gave, he lurched backward, falling against Annalee.

"Oh." She clawed at the handrail.

CJ's arm went around her waist. "Steady." He stared into her eyes for a moment then released her.

Turning away, he rubbed his fingers across his lips. "Sorry." With her help, he straightened and shoved open the door. "I'm glad you didn't go back downstairs. That might have been a painful trip for me if you hadn't been there to stop my stumble."

She warmed to his appreciation. And to her conquering her silly fears.

He stepped aside and flicked on the light. "Watch your head."

Having never been to an attic except through television and movies, she had expected the stereotypical dark, damp space with a bare light bulb dangling from the center of the roof. She hadn't anticipated painted white walls, neat shelves full of labeled bins and floor lighting. Though with the lower than normal ceiling, that kind of lighting was probably wise.

She stopped a few feet in. "This isn't at all the way I pictured an attic."

He closed the gap and put his hand on her elbow, directing her toward the left. His touch ignited a flicker of excitement through her. Like the bells of Christmas.

"This section is full of games." Still holding her arm, he moved along the wall. "All of these bins contain costumes, material, and makeup."

"Makeup?"

"Face-painting, mostly. Theatrical. And next to that are all types of arts and crafts supplies."

Art?

"Styrofoam, feathers, sequins, and paint. Lots of paint."

The word stimulated her as much as the feeling of CJ's hand on her arm. "Paint?" She glanced back at him. Stooped in the short room, his face was close. Very close.

He smiled. "That's right. You're an artist. I forgot."

"Not an artist. Not really. I do paint, though. And draw and even sculpt a little." She could chat about that topic for hours.

"Then art is what we'll do today." His smile broadened into a grin. "If painting will keep a light in your eyes like you have right now."

She smothered her smile. "You don't have to choose it for my benefit." However, she didn't want him to change his mind. "But thanks." She gave him another smile as they collected the materials from the shelves.

CJ enlisted the help of Allison and Kelli Tigh, two sisters who worked with the elementary group. Between the four of them, after a couple of loads, they were able to stock the dining hall with plenty of art supplies and heavy paper, watercolors, buckets of crayons and pencils, even old shirts for paint smocks.

All the while, he kept sneaking peeks at Annalee's face. She positively glowed. She laid out paper and organized the mediums, separating crayons, markers, and paint. She filled cups with water and set up an easel out of large butterfly clips and an old whiteboard.

"Are you going to paint with them?"

"I thought I would. Unless that's not allowed."

"You're welcome to join them." An ache grew within him to see the creativity moving her to such animation.

She'd already started by the time the kids started arriving. Set up on the end of the room, she received little attention until they bored of their own pictures.

Tyrone was one of the first to wander behind her easel. "Aw man. You did that?"

"Yes, sir."

CJ didn't have the angle to see her artwork but caught her smile.

"Can I?"

"Sure." Without hesitation, Annalee dipped her brush into paint and handed it to Tyrone. She pointed at the picture. "Add a thin line right there."

"Like this?"

Leaving the table, he'd been working with, CJ edged closer.

"Exactly. Now do it the very same way right here." Annalee tapped the easel a second time.

"Man, I ruined it." Tyrone shoved the brush back into her hand.

"No. You didn't ruin anything. You made it art. There aren't any rules. It isn't like a photograph. The picture comes from within you. What you see. Sometimes not even what you see but what you feel."

A group of the older kids had gathered, commenting on the picture. "And what you communicate about those feelings through your art makes other people feel, too." She extended her hand to include those around her.

What was this picture that wowed them all? The crowd grew, blocking CJ out. He'd have to be obvious to get a look at it with more and more kids surrounding the girl and the easel.

"Snack." Margo shot him a knowing look from the door of the kitchen. The kids darted to line up at the bathrooms and opened a path for him to inspect Annalee's artwork.

"It isn't finished." She caught sight of him closing in.

"I wanted to see what all of the fuss was about."

She stepped back. He didn't miss how her gaze settled on him. She seemed anxious for his reaction. He'd have to be careful not to show criticism.

Pressing his lips together, he turned toward the easel.

He gasped. "I didn't expect anything like this."

What had he expected? Flowers? Sunshine and trees and rainbows, maybe. But this?

His own blue eyes looked out at him from the canvas. The

essence of a smile curled the lips as the brown sugar complexion and bright grin of Juan DeMarco hovered over his left shoulder. Amy Glassman's black hair hung in a bob as she sat beside him painting on her paper. CJ noticed his own eyes looked straight ahead. At the camera, as it were. But the kids both looked down, probably at the picture Amy drew of a ladybug on a leaf.

It occurred to him he'd been watching Annalee while she drew. Watching the expression on her face, joy lighting her eyes. She must have noticed.

He felt his cheeks heat. But Annalee still watched him. He stepped back. "That's really amazing."

She released a breath. "I was afraid you'd resent being the subject of my picture, but the grouping was too perfect to resist."

The grouping. All about the artistic attraction. Not really about him at all. He chided himself for letting that fact bother him. "I couldn't be upset. I'm flattered."

"I think I missed something in your eyes though. I'll need to work on them. They're not looking the right direction."

"They look fine to me." Surely, she'd noted he'd been staring at her. Or maybe because he was so far away, she only painted the way the light reflected without realizing why it showed up the way it did.

"Do you need help with the snack?" Though Annalee's voice sounded receptive, she stared at the picture, the clean tip of her paintbrush against her bottom lip.

"No, simple grilled cheese sandwiches. We can take care of it."

She didn't respond but unclipped her paper and laid it on the table nearby before adding a new sheet to the board.

He wandered toward the kitchen. The layers of Annalee

Marji Laine

Chambers kept surprising him.

Chapter 13

Annalee's creative juices bubbled up with enthusiasm after painting with the children all morning.

The kids didn't stick with art in the afternoon, opting instead to stack up the chairs and tables and play some indoor group games. She'd had to pack up her supplies right after starting a sketch of Tyrone and Hayden playing table hockey with a crust of bread. She hoped she captured enough of the moment in time committed to her paper to finish it, but that would have to wait until she could transport her sketches to her studio.

Longing for the solitude of her basement slipped away, though, as she watched the children, along with CJ and the Tigh sisters, play some crazy game with a smashed can and cup towels. Even Miss Pritchard joined in after the dishes were finished. Tyrone and Hayden grabbed Annalee's hand and forced her into the circle.

The play reminded her of field hockey, which she'd stunk at the couple of times she'd played in middle school. She'd always heard of players getting their shins slapped. Only the good players, of course. The only time anyone ever got close to whacking her, she jumped back and let them have control of the ball. She'd stayed on the bench and doodled after that.

This game wasn't nearly so intimidating. Probably because the cup towels held little threat of pain. The kids laughed at her slapping at the can with her towel, but she didn't mind and joined them with her own chuckles. As loudly as they laughed, they cheered when she was able to finally hit it well and send it toward the goal, a table on its side. She'd provided entertainment for the group and became a member of it all in one moment.

Belonging. Not something she had much experience with. Goose pimples broke out across her arms as some of the kids wrapped her in a hug. Others crowded next to her in the circle. And the end of the day gave sharp jabs to her heart with every goodbye.

As much as she loved her quiet studio, the organized chaos of the center delighted her. From Paula's jokes to Hayden and Tyrone clinging to her.

She reflected on the day as she lay in bed the next morning. Especially Hayden and Tyrone. The sketch she had started beckoned along with the picture of CJ and a half-dozen others she'd started.

She slipped on some capris and an oversized shirt when her mother knocked on her door. "We're brunching with Boyd this morning."

"Why?" She thought that episode was over and the chapter closed.

"He called your father and asked for an appointment."

The fresh feeling left by the rain disappeared. Annalee stared out of her window at the wild, overgrown forest and creek that made up the back of their property. She'd always preferred that view to the manicured lawns and well-tended gardens on the front side. Not so much today. Humidity hung over the creek in light gray edges of fog. The weight of the air cast a straitjacket around her, especially with Mother's announcement.

Wait a minute. Boyd hadn't called her for an appointment. She wasn't a minor following along with her parents everywhere.

And there was no way she was meeting him at the club for yet another uncomfortable interlude. "Sorry, Mother." She shrugged on a sleeveless sweater over the white shirt and added a matching Ombre scarf before sliding her feet into her tennis shoes.

"What are you sorry about?"

"I'm not brunching with you this morning. I've got other plans."

"You have to deal with Boyd at some point."

Annalee giggled. "I've already dealt with him, twice, though I preferred the orange juice to the wine. I think it looked better on him. Seems like he'd have learned his lesson by now." She shouldered her bag. "You might want to try cranberry juice."

"I'm not flinging cranberry juice at him." She crossed her arms. "It stains."

"Yes, but he'll feel the permanence of the splash."

"This is a family thing, Annalee. Ramona will be there."

"That's her problem." She kissed her mother's cheek. "Boyd made an appointment with you and Father. I don't have to be part of your portrait. And I really don't want to be included."

"Neither do I, but I'm going." Her mother huffed. "You know you'll be the topic of conversation. Since this is all about you, I'd think you'd want to defend yourself."

"Make no mistake. This appointment is about Boyd. He enjoyed being part of Father's family. Assumed I was so meek and compliant that he didn't need to concern himself with my feelings. Only focused on impressing Father. Getting a partnership in the firm has been his singular purpose since I've known him." Annalee picked up her shoulder bag. "Meeting you for brunch is all about him repairing the unexpected damage he created. Irreparable damage, I might add."

"I suppose you could be right, but the least you can do is attend."

"Probably, but I'm still not going." She followed Mother out of the room. "Nothing forces you to go either, by the way. Stand the guy up. Go somewhere else for brunch today. Maybe he'll get the message without the necessity of another shower."

She turned away from her mother and breezed down the hallway without waiting for a reply.

Annalee ignored the sprinkles tickling her cheeks twenty minutes later when she climbed from her car at the Tom Thumb parking lot. She hadn't lied to her mother when she said she had plans. She did. Only laid out moments before the words left her lips, but plans all the same.

In truth, she'd been toying with ways to help Hayden and Tyrone and their sister without getting into any more trouble at the center. This seemed the best time to take action.

She looked up at the white letters raised from the red brick of the building. She'd been in there before. Of course, she'd ridden in the basket on that occasion, on an outing with her nanny after her loud playing and insistent questions had given Mother a headache.

Pulling out a cart, she wheeled it through the doors that separated the entrance from the rest of the store. Deciding to give the family sacks of groceries was easy. Figuring out what to get for them, not so much. She wandered through the produce department. The center served apples all the time. Maybe some oranges would be nice. She put about ten in a plastic bag and twisted a little green tie around the top. What next?

Their mom worked all day. She didn't have the time to spend cooking. Not that Annalee would know what to get if the woman did cook.

She found the deli counter and ordered a couple of pounds of Black Forest Ham, her personal favorite. She spotted rotisserie chicken and picked up two of those. Might as well offer the family a ready-made meal.

She added a gallon of milk to the cart, hesitated, then pulled out another along with a selection of yogurt. The kids at the center treated the creamy snack like a dessert. Meandering through the store wasn't likely the smartest way to shop, but she felt she had a good balance of food. A lot of pantry items and cereal, eggs, cheese, even a couple of candy bars.

Loading the collection into the trunk of the 'Stang was a challenge, but she wedged it all in and put the carton of eggs in the seat next to her. She'd have to make a few trips to do the unloading, but she'd likely have help once she reached their place.

Which was the next problem. They lived in the Rosewood homes, but that was a huge complex not too far from the center. How in the world would she discover which was theirs?

Merging onto the fairly empty North Dallas Tollway, she mulled over who might be able to help her find the family. To start, she'd try to visit the office. If that failed, maybe she could get information off of the Internet. As the last straw, she'd call her father. He had connections on the Dallas police that would give him an address in a heartbeat, but she wanted to avoid chatting with him about anything not involving the campaign. Especially about something he'd likely disapprove.

And even more so on a morning he'd had to spend with "Boring Boyd."

Annalee pulled into the parking lot a little after twelve o'clock. She stared at a small bus, emblazoned with a red rose graphic along the side and the sign, Rosewood Baptist Church. Obviously, a drop-off of some type.

A number of children stood near the door. She spotted Amy Glassman from the center. Leaning against her car, Annalee struggled to contrive an excuse to approach the girl. Then she spotted the bus driver, high-fiving several kids.

Her mouth fell open. "CJ?"

His eyes widened as they met hers. "What are you doing here?" He climbed down the steps and crossed to her car.

He cleaned up well. Navy button-down, dark jeans, leather boots. Not quite country club apparel, but a good look on him.

"I thought to ask you the same." She pointed to the people-mover. "You moonlight as a bus driver?"

He chuckled. "I take a big group of kids from here to my church on Sunday mornings."

"I see. Working at the center isn't enough for your altruistic nature, huh?" Church? What sort of man carted kids to church?

"So, what's your excuse for visiting the slums on a bright Sunday morning?"

His choice of words caught her attention. "Are these slums?"

"They don't look it, but don't be fooled. If not for this city housing, most of these kids would live on the street. As it is, the apartments only have a stove and refrigerator. Some of the families don't even own a mattress."

"They don't even have a bed? Where do they sleep?"

"When they're tired, they'll sleep anywhere. And the Intercede Foundation makes sure they have plenty of blankets, coats, and shoes."

And CJ helped them.

Her heart ached. "What a terrible sort of life. I can't even imagine."

"Is that why you're here? To get a glimpse of what life is like for some of these kids?" His eyebrows twitched.

"Oh, no." That was no better than the paparazzi who hounded her own family, trying to catch every move, every word. But she hadn't wanted to tell anyone about her plan. Especially not anyone from the center.

"I went shopping." Truth, yet not excessive.

"That's not such an odd behavior for you, is it?"

He had her there. She couldn't lie outright, not in her nature. She extended her answer. "Grocery shopping is not a norm. I barely remember the last time I'd been in a market."

He waited a moment, scanning her face.

Awkward silence. Usually, she had no problem waiting it out, winning the stare-down, even with her mother, once in a while.

But this guy. This amazing man who played with children and transported them to church. He deserved the entire story. "Miss Pritchard made it clear I couldn't give the children anything while we were at the center."

A wrinkle creased his brow. "Not while we're at the center, no."

"So …" Shrugging she opened the trunk. "… we're not at the center, now."

He looked in and sifted through one of the bags. "You went to the grocery store to get food for Tyrone and Hayden?"

"Well, for their family." She eyed him. "Is that breaking a rule?"

"No. You can do whatever you want on your own time. It's why I first brought the church bus over here." He examined another sack.

"I didn't go over the top, did I? I wasn't sure what I should get."

He straightened. "I don't think so. Not too much for the refrigerator or freezer."

Then why did he look so troubled? She scanned his face. Troubled wasn't the right description. He was focused on something. Lost in his own thoughts. "Have I upset you?"

He looked up, and a smile peeked out. "No." He dipped his head. "I feel like I owe you an apology."

"Why would you think that?"

"Never mind. I think you'll like Mrs. Madison."

Madison? Surely not the same family. No reason to think so. *There have to be thousands of Madisons in Dallas.* "Is that their last name?"

"You didn't know? I thought that's why you were talking to them so often." He pulled one of the bags from the trunk and then shut it.

She stiffened. Her feet unable to move. "Then, this is the same family …" She couldn't look at him.

He put a hand on her elbow and turned her toward him. "Didn't you know Mr. Madison's kids attended the center?"

She shook her head, staring at the collar of his blue Oxford shirt. It brought out his eyes.

His hand at her elbow softened and stroked upward on her

arm. "The fact you didn't know makes this gift all the nicer. And they need the help."

"But they'll think I'm acting out of a guilty conscience." She searched his face. "You don't think that, do you? I don't like manipulative people who always have an agenda. I'm not like that."

He relaxed and a slight smile broke out on his face. The look warmed her. "I think you've got a good heart and pure intentions." He walked her toward one of the buildings. "Why don't I introduce you?"

She sighed. That's what she'd come for. Even though butterflies the size of bats flitted through her stomach. She moistened her lips. "Please."

He led her to a left side duplex which looked like every other left side home except for painted pictures of rainbows and crosses taped to the glass of one of the windows.

She followed him toward the sidewalk but hung back as he stepped onto the path leading to the door. "You don't think they'll be insulted, do you? I hadn't really thought this through very much."

"Giving up before you even hit the porch?"

"Force of habit." A curl blew across her eyes, and she tucked it behind her ear. She gripped her stomach, insisting the jitters stop. She could do this. "My mother always complains. I abandon my plans because I fail to consider their consequences ahead of time."

"I think the family will be delighted. Your gift is rather miraculous."

Her exhale came out as a scoffing laugh. "You're making fun of me. There's nothing magical about a trunkful of groceries."

"Not at all. And I didn't say magical. A miracle is completely different." He closed the gap between them and laid his hand on her shoulder. "This morning, Hayden and Tyrone admitted their mom and dad go without meals daily, and their older sister, Tally, only gets to eat what they bring her from the center or save from their lunches at school."

Surely, they exaggerated. "Doesn't she eat lunch and breakfast at the school like most of the rest of the kids?"

"She has some health issues which keep her from going to school regularly. You'll meet her in a second anyway, so I guess there's no harm in me telling you. She was beaten as a young child, by her father."

"That's terrible."

"Worse than you think. Her spinal cord was injured, giving her a permanent limp. The constant pain she endures often keeps her out of school. Every day, she has to measure her need to eat and be in classes against her pain levels.

Annalee swallowed. What a horrible decision for such a young girl. "So, her father, Mr. Madison, was the one who was injured?"

"No. Madison is her stepfather. He's a good man. Tally's father was also Tyrone's father, but he'd been killed in some sort of street fight by the time Tyrone came along."

Annalee couldn't speak. Such tragedy on all sides. And she could never imagine someone living in such pain. Especially not a child. She glanced at her designer sandals and sassy pink toenails. Hardship to her had been going without her weekly manicure and pedicure. Even two weeks' work at the center hadn't prepared her for such a way of living. But she had to follow through. She'd have to meet this little girl in order to give them the food.

And she would complete her objective. Determined more now than before.

CJ focused on keeping his eyes off of Annalee as they reached the porch and rang the bell. Twice, he'd caught himself staring at her, lingering on her smile and awed by her kindness. Both times she'd seen him and blushed, pinker the second time than the first.

He was sure he'd reddened as well, feeling his neck warm.

Mrs. Madison teared up when she saw the grocery bag CJ carried. "I'm just the parcel delivery man." He set it on her scant kitchen counter. The boys had joined him and Annalee to bring in the rest of the load.

The graying woman took to Annalee right away. He knew she would, even without bearing gifts. Mrs. Madison loved everyone. She had the full-of-joy Spirit that spread to anyone who got within sight of her. And she'd welcomed Annalee with a warm bear hug.

Annalee stiffened and patted the woman's back. "It's very nice to meet you. I've been working at the center with your boys. They mentioned Tally doesn't always get to have a complete dinner … That is … I thought I might …"

"Sugar, now, don't you stress yourself about bringing such a blessing. We ain't nothing but delighted."

"I'm glad." The wrinkle between her brows disappeared. "But I do want you to know, I only knew your boys' first names." She paused. "I didn't know you were the Madison family until I got here."

"All the more reason to be grateful for your sweet heart." She bustled into the kitchen. "I wish Robert was here. He'd thank you hisself."

CJ expected the man to be here, homebound as he was. "Where is he?"

"The kids didn't tell you?" She halted the boys as they carried in bags. "What happened to your prayer request for your daddy?"

"We announced it, but you wasn't in the room, CJ," Tyrone answered,

He'd ducked out for a cup of coffee. "Is everything all right?"

"Will be." The woman's smile dropped off for a moment but flashed back into place. "Robert has an infection. Something from the surgeries. An ambulance came for him last night when the pain got too much for him."

"Back at Parkland?" He'd visit in a while. Maybe offer a ride to Mrs. Madison.

"Yes, sir. Room 317."

"Maybe we can go for a visit before your shift tonight." He smiled at her.

"I would like that." Mrs. Madison nodded. "Right nice."

Tyrone and Hayden shouted about every box, can, and package as they emptied the bags and stowed away the food.

Their enthusiasm could've awakened the dead. After a few minutes, their sister limped to the hallway. "What's going on? Sounds like a party." Tyrone ran to help her join the group. Her hair pulled into three ponytails with colorful rubber bands on each, she looked like any other girl. Except for the crooked spine and permanently bent knee. And her thin frame made her look a few years younger than her age.

Annalee kept her eyes on the cans, handing them to Hayden.

"It's Christmas in September?" Tally stopped at the edge of the kitchen and clapped her hands.

"And look at this." Tyrone held out a stack of yogurts. "I'm saving you the strawberry."

"That's my favorite."

"And candy bars!" Hayden's eyes popped. He ran around the table and held the three out to Tally. "Which one you want?"

"Oo. I like 'em all. Why don't you choose first?"

"Okay." Hayden laid them on the table and contemplated.

Her task finished, Annalee came from around the table and smiled at the girl. "You must be Tally. I've heard about you. Mostly how much your brothers love you."

"They're good brothers. You must be Miss Annalee. They done tole me how your hair was white gold, like French vanilla ice cream only shiny like sunlight." She limped into Annalee's arms. "Thanks for the snack bars, too. They're delicious."

No awkwardness in this hug. Annalee wrapped her up. "You're most welcome."

CJ had to walk away. The warmth in his chest continued to grow. His mind screamed at him to cut and run. The last thing he wanted was entangled feelings over a woman. Especially some rich girl from the world he left behind and wanted it to stay that way.

But polite behavior demanded he stay for a few more minutes. He chatted with Mrs. Madison while Tally showed Annalee her room. She was so proud to have her own space. Though little more than a closet, she didn't have to sleep on the living room floor with her brothers.

Not much had changed in the house since the last time CJ had visited. Milk Crates provided stools for the makeshift table. A printed plastic sheet covered something that looked fairly square, listing slightly to the left.

The living room was bare except for a flat-screen TV attached to the wall. How the unit could come furnished with a TV, but no beds, CJ would never understand. The boys had large miss-matched couch pillows and folded blankets lining one wall. CJ had sat on them the last time he'd been there. They used the linens as their couch of a sort.

Mrs. Madison smiled at Annalee when they returned to the kitchen. Tally's mom wrapped Annalee again in a warm hug. "My dear. You no idea how our great God used you."

Annalee's eyes widened. She'd probably never heard anything like that before. "I'm glad I could help."

Mrs. Madison put her dark hands on Annalee's cheeks. "You don't understand. But your Father is patient. He waitin'. You'll understand in time. And then you'll know. Then you'll find what you been looking for."

Annalee's face settled into her customary pleasant appearance for a second, but the intensity of the older woman seemed to get her attention. The crease returned between her perfect brows. All pieces of her mask seemed to vanish, and her eyes grew troubled. "I'm not sure what I'm looking for."

"I know. And you won't know until you find it." Mrs. Madison smiled and nodded. "But don't worry, chile. You'll find it." She released her face. "And you're sure gonna know it when you do."

"That's a fact." Tally grinned big and clapped her hands.

CJ shifted his eyes to the floor as a tear threatened. Annalee had given them enough food for a month. Yet she offered it with humility far beyond what he'd expect from someone with her pedigree. She was certainly different than he'd originally thought.

Confusion and curiosity painted her features as Mrs. Madison released her. The sincerity of her emotion drew him in another direction with his musings. One which required action and might even put him in a precarious position.

But the possibilities outweighed the risk.

Marji Laine

Chapter 14

Leaving the Madison's apartment, Annalee felt more convinced than ever that she'd done the right thing by pleading guilty. At least Mr. Madison could get his medical needs taken care of and still have some sort of salary coming in while he recuperated.

And Mrs. Madison. Her words before they left ... strange. Yet instead of the tightness in her chest and knots in her stomach, which usually accompanied something confusing, Annalee felt as relaxed as she had all week. For no reason at all, she believed the older woman. She would find what she searched for. Even though she hadn't realized she'd been searching.

CJ hung behind saying goodbye to the family.

She reached her car and turned. "Thanks for showing me to their place. I guess I'll see you tomorrow."

"Wait, wait, wait." He jogged toward her. "You took care of their lunch. How about one of your own?"

"Come again?" She gave him her full attention, admiring the

glow in his blue eyes and the way his dark hair curled slightly. The wind caught it and made it shiver.

"I'd like to take you to lunch."

She cleared her throat. "Why?" Did he anticipate trouble about the gift from Miss Pritchard? Or maybe he expected Mr. Whelan himself to get involved? She'd only been working there for a couple of weeks but kept expecting to meet Mr. Whelan any day.

"Why do I want to take you to lunch?" CJ's smile grew. "Because I can."

"I mean, do you think I'll be in trouble with Mr. Whelan because of the groceries?"

His smile dropped. "Of course not. I …" He shrugged. "I'd simply like to have lunch with you." A pink tinge crept over his collar.

Such a possibility hadn't even occurred to her. And now she'd embarrassed him. "Oh, that would be nice." She fell into step beside him, changing course toward the large people-mover.

Her mother's voice kept shouting in her ear. *Are you daft, child?* Funny how the soft tones of Mrs. Madison when she called Annalee *chile* didn't compare with her mother's label. Mother's words came from the low expectation she had about Annalee. Mrs. Madison's came from compassion for her. At least that's how the word had sounded.

The rant continued through Annalee's brain. *He's a janitor, for pity's sake. Think of how socializing with a man like him will look to your father's constituents.*

A man like him. She climbed into the front passenger seat and glanced in his direction. Tingles erupted through her body. Thoughtful, good with kids, kind, helpful, funny.

Desperately handsome, especially cleaned up like he was

now.

"If it's okay, I'll return this bus, and we'll go in my truck." He started the engine and shoved it into gear.

"Fine with me."

Considerate. She could keep the list going without effort. He was so different from any of the men she'd dated. Men to whom her parents or their friends had introduced her. Or worse, men she'd met on one of her jaunts with some of her friends. Everyone she'd met while clubbing failed to meet her smallest expectations.

And yet, because they had money enough to play around and have no worth to show for it, her mother would welcome them to her table. CJ wouldn't be given scraps because of the truck he drove and the job he did and the honorable family name he didn't hold.

"What does CJ stand for?" She waited until switching to his truck before stirring up enough courage to ask him.

He didn't take his eyes off of the road. "Carl … Carl James."

A nice name. She'd have to remember to Facebook him and see if he went to a college that would meet her mother's approval. If he had gone at all. "Do your parents live here in Dallas?"

He nodded slightly. Almost warily. "My father does. My mom passed away when I was younger."

"What does Mr. James do?"

Was it her imagination, or did he relax with the question? He settled in his seat, and a slight smile decorated his lips. "He's sort of a manager. Works with different businesses helping them to keep their details in order."

"Sort of like a freelance bookkeeper?" Hmm. Accountant might be a better word to use, for her mother's sake.

"Something like that."

He parked in a small lot outside an old brick building painted white. She could swear he'd brought her to Al's, the drive-in restaurant from the reruns of Happy Days, right up to the rotating round sign. "What is this place?"

"How long have you lived in Dallas?"

"All my life." She shifted in her seat and studied his profile. Strong jaw with a rough edge of trimmed dark stubble perpetually across his lower cheeks and slightly cleft chin. A straight nose, neither too big nor too small, anchored high cheekbones. His clear blue eyes had a fringe of dark lashes giving his face a sincere look and a natural charm.

But at her response, his mouth dropped open with a look of shock. "And you've never heard of Big D Diner?" He shut off the truck.

She shook her head and eyed the small, run-down building. "Looks like a step back in time." She tried to muster a smile. This was likely the best he could offer her. As he trotted around the truck, she determined to pay for her own meal.

He opened her door and held out his hand. "You've got a treat coming."

Avoiding assistance was plain rude, but the warmth of his touch spread through her. Had he felt the same sensation? Probably not.

He released her hand and locked the truck door before shutting it, ushering her toward the entrance. "Wait until you taste the food here."

The aroma of fries and barbecue filled the air. Neither was a favorite, but she kept her eagerness firmly planted on her face. Besides, the mask helped her keep her distance from him.

He pulled open the glass and chrome door while a man in his

mid-forties greeted them from behind a counter. "Hey there." He waved a handful of menus at Annalee. "Are there two for lunch? Oh, hey, CJ."

"Hey, Dale." CJ stood close to her. Close enough to put his hand at her waist if he'd wanted. But he didn't. "This is my friend, Annalee. Dale's not the owner, but you've been working here for decades, right?"

"Working? I don't work. This is what I do to relax." He chuckled. "Nice to meetcha, Annalee." He pointed toward the tiny dining room. "This way."

Then the very thing she'd thought about actually happened. CJ's hand rested against the small of her back for a moment, sending a dozen little quivering satellites racing to her brain with messages she hadn't heard since her starry-eyed adolescent years.

She expected him to remove his hand after she started moving, but he didn't, keeping pace with her and touching her back. Part of her relished the nearness of him, while her mind screamed at her, sure she'd end up making a fool of herself.

Dale seated her at a table and CJ parted to sit on the other side. Though Dale handed her a menu, he fired off the day's specials. Apparently, each day had its own meals and then sandwiches, burgers, and breakfasts could be had at any time. "I don't think I've ever seen a menu like this before."

"This place is part of a dying breed." Dale slipped a notepad from his apron pocket. "But we're gonna do our dead-level best to keep this baby from going extinct."

Annalee looked over the Sunday offerings. Sure enough, Barbecue was at the top of the list. But so was a turkey breast meal, with all of the trimmings, exactly like Thanksgiving. She ordered it, and Dale left them. An awkward silence grew.

"You know, that was really a nice thing you did back there." CJ rested his forearms on the table.

"I think it's the rebel in me coming out. Being told I couldn't help them made me determined to figure out a way."

Dale brought iced tea to the table, and Annalee fingered the rim of her glass.

"Funny I never thought of you as a rebel spirit." CJ squeezed his lemon and stirred in a pack of sugar. Annalee noticed the laugh in his gaze. And the way his eyes seldom strayed from her face.

"Oh, I am. But I have to keep it under cover. Passive-resistant, not so much about rules, but against the demands other people put on me. That's probably why my mother threw a fit over the community service hours."

"She didn't want you to put another mark on the family name?" His expression hardened, and he took a drink of his tea.

She flinched at the implication. Yes, she'd certainly sullied the Chambers' name, but more from the accident than from trying to make amends for it. "She didn't expect me to do the work and thought I'd end up in jail, making her and my father look horrible."

"Then she must be very proud of you at this point."

A scoffing laugh escaped. "I don't think so." How did this conversation turn this direction? "My mother is a very … capable woman. No matter how high the mountain, she will get to the top, even if it means forcing the base of it to crumble."

"You're saying she's sort of like a charging rhino?"

"Exactly, though I wouldn't use such a description to her face." Annalee chuckled. "She has no respect for people who don't make instant decisions." Her gaze drifted to her hands resting on the table. "Even less for those who have trouble following through with plans and goals."

"Sounds like she's the perfect politician's wife."

"Yes. And she has little patience for me."

He dropped his chin. "I see. You're the true artistic spirit. Jumping into projects until the inspiration fades."

"Exactly. At least that's always been the case. But I won't fade on this job. It's not for very long and the alternative of jail time would kill me."

He smiled at her. "I'm not worried, Annalee. I think you're doing a great job at the center, and I loved the way you worked with the kids yesterday. How did you learn to draw?"

She warmed under his compliments. "Art is my passion. "She flicked her lemon into her tea and drew her forefinger around her glass edge, making it emit a soft, high tone. "But I have to confess, my studio gives my mother ample reasons for believing I won't finish anything I start."

He sipped from his glass again. "I'd like to see your work."

She looked down. "Oh, there's nothing really special to show. And like I said, none of the pieces are even finished." She didn't mention she'd been inspired to revisit the few she'd started the day before. Her plans for Sunday changed on the spur of the moment when she decided to go grocery shopping.

"I'd still be interested. I bet you and Tally would get along great."

What a precious girl. Her love for art needed cultivation and instruction. "She's amazing. When she said she wanted to show me her pictures, I thought she meant the rainbows and crosses in her windows. I had no idea of her raw talent."

"She's quite good. I bet you could help her refine her skill."

Annalee wasn't so sure about that. "I'm in awe of her. Do you know she has full portraits drawn on paper towels? And I saw a gorgeous landscape on a napkin."

CJ nodded. "The family has a hard time with Tally's medical bills. Mrs. Madison works as a custodian at a theater and kitchen worker at the school and takes in ironing from her neighbors and the teachers she works with. Mr. Madison works two jobs himself."

"That much I know. At least he did. I hope they're still there for him when he finishes his recuperation."

Dale approached and set plates down in front of them. "If y'all need anything else, just holler." He set the bill down next to CJ.

Annalee mentally kicked herself for not getting separate checks. CJ didn't need to waste his hard-earned money on her. But saying anything now might embarrass him. No way she'd take a chance of doing that.

"May I pray for us?" The sweet look on CJ's face weakened Annalee's spine. He held his hand across the table, and she laid her own in it. He lowered his chin, and she closed her eyes.

"Father, I'm so grateful I can step to Your throne and speak with You in person. Thank You for allowing Annalee and me to spend some time getting to know one another. I pray both of us would hunger to know You more. And as to hunger, Lord, give Annalee a double blessing for her gift this morning. Please provide the Madison family with everything they need, in the name of Your Son, Jesus. And thank You for letting us feast on this food. Amen."

Who was this man? His kindness and sincere joy with the children had captured her attention last week, but the warm feeling of her hand in his and the earnest words he spoke amazed her.

He held onto her hand for a moment longer and lifted his gaze to her with such a tender look, she could barely keep her own eyes steady. Then he cleared his throat and slid his hand off the table.

He took a bite of his burger and washed it down with a drink of his tea. "I'm glad you came to lunch. I've been feeling the need to apologize to you."

"You said something like that before, but you don't owe me anything."

A rueful laugh escaped his lips. "Yes, I really do. See the first time I saw you, at the coffee shop, remember?"

"After my hearing. My sister wanted to help me calm down before I met my probation officer." The memory sliced through her confidence. Why would he bring that up?

"You'd been insulted and yelled at, yet you were kind in return. I felt bad for not coming to your defense. But I justified it, deciding the only reason you'd been nice was to glean votes for your father."

His accusation cut deep. She didn't know how to respond and trained her focus on slicing through her turkey pieces.

"And then you came to the center on the first day. Margo had me believing you were spoiled and entitled."

"I see." His apology lacked something. The warmth of his compliments faded into a chilling rain. But she couldn't blame him too much for his opinion, especially after her initial visit to Haskell Avenue and her discussion with Miss Pritchard. Her impressions and expectations had been entirely wrong.

"No, you don't, because I'm doing a lousy job of this. The truth is, you've really worked hard, Annalee. I'm surprised. But I shouldn't have been. What you did today for the Madisons, the way you did it, proved to me I was wrong all along. You have a true kindness and sincerity about you I haven't seen in most girls … like you."

The way he said it tickled her. A slight smile edged out. "Like me? Blond?"

He laughed. "I meant of your social standing, the elite of the city."

Like he knew the elite of the city. "I suppose you've had a lot of experience with that type."

"Yes. Too much." He winced and cleared his throat. "I mean with the foundation mingling and such."

Ah, that made sense. "About the foundation. I know Mr. Whelan has a desk at the center. Does he ever actually go there? He doesn't seem the type."

CJ's face clouded over. His Adam's apple bobbed. "The desk is a formality." His whole countenance changed from the teasing charmer of a second before to one of brooding.

Why the sudden change? She wanted to adjust the climate control on him, but couldn't fathom the reason for his moodiness. "Well, he doesn't know what he's missing. Those kids are fantastic."

"You're right about that."

"About which?" She bit her roll with impish delight in her didactic question.

"Both. The board of the Intercede Foundation really doesn't understand what goes on down here."

"Has Miss Pritchard ever invited them to visit?"

He reddened, though Annalee had no idea why. Had she messed up again?

"No." He shook his head and snatched up another fry. "They wouldn't bother coming down. That takes effort, time, and desire."

She let him gather his thoughts.

"The truth is, the center is only a deduction for most of them. A way to escape paying higher income tax. They have to donate a certain amount every year, so they give it to the center and trust us to spend it right."

To assume donations were thoughtless throw-away dollars was rather insulting. "I don't know the board members, but my father donates to different charities. He's very careful where he puts his money and has visited all of the recipients personally."

CJ shut his eyes. His right hand moved to the back of his neck. "I didn't mean offense. And you're right of course. It's been my experience with the center that we've had to constantly beg for basic needs."

"Really?" She tore away another piece of her bread. "I thought it had everything necessary."

"Take the cleaning supplies, for instance. Those bottles came from Margo and Paula and me. Margo or one of the other ladies mixes up huge batches of homemade glass cleaner, toilet cleaner, floor cleaner and refills those bottles every month."

"Because you don't have money for store-bought ones?" She had no idea.

"It's more important to feed the kids, keep them supplied in paper, crayons, chalk, and balls which actually bounce."

"Have you thought about doing a fundraiser to collect the extra funds you need?"

His gaze locked with hers for a second of silence. Like she could see the thought reach his brain and make contact with his gray cells. "That is a great idea. I'll have to talk it over with Margo."

Margo would probably hate the prospect, but Annalee liked the way CJ's eyes lit up when he talked about new ways to help the kids at the center.

A niggling at the base of CJ's neck pestered like an irritating fly. With every laugh and smile, Annalee drew him in. Likely completely unaware of the reel she turned. The image of her with a fishing pole crossed his mind. He covered his smile with another bite of barbecue. Still the wish to take her fishing, give her everyday experiences she'd probably never had, and indulge in gazing at her beautiful face … *Stop it.* No wonder the edge of foreboding continued.

As he returned to her Mustang, they discussed the living conditions of the area, what most of the children dealt with. "Not all of them have as loving a home as Tyrone and Hayden."

"Mrs. Madison seems so nice. How did she get mixed up with someone who could beat a little child?" Annalee's forehead crinkled.

"Before she became a Christian, Mrs. Madison had trouble with drugs and supported her habit with prostitution."

"That dear lady?" Annalee's eyes widened.

"Anyone can make bad choices." His neck heated. He knew well the truth of that. "But when the guy died, she was desperate and went to the church for help. Boy, did they ever help her."

"Got her a job?"

"Not until after they placed her in a rehab unit. It took a while for her to dry out and realize all God was doing for her." Did Annalee even understand that statement?

If she didn't, she let it pass. "What about the kids during all that time?"

Ain't Misbehaving

"It was before my time. I've just heard the stories. I think Margo took in Tally and Tyrone, but she never talks about it." He parked next to the Madison's apartment. "She married a man at the church, and they had Hayden."

"I see."

CJ smiled. "You'd have to see them together. Such true dedication."

"I'm ready when you are, CJ." Mrs. Madison came out of her door waving at him. "I have a few hours before my shift at the theater."

He'd almost forgotten. He nodded at the lady and turned back to Annalee. "You want to meet him?"

She flinched. "Oh. I mean, of course, but I'm not sure … he'd appreciate meeting me. Especially not … I mean."

"Are you coming with us, Miss Annalee?" Mrs. Madison opened the passenger door. "Robert will be so happy to finally get to chat with you face to face."

"Well …" She looked from Mrs. Madison to CJ.

He could almost hear the alarms going off in her head. Naturally, most men would have antagonism toward someone who had hurt them, but not Robert Madison. CJ winked. *Say yes. You know you want to.*

She sighed and scooted closer to him on the bench seat, allowing Mrs. Madison to edge in. "I'd love to meet your husband."

Her arm rested against his, sending a spark through him. Her meeting Mr. Madison was a great idea. But CJ surviving more time with her while still keeping his heart intact seemed a dubious possibility.

Marji Laine

Chapter 15

Annalee couldn't very well lean away from CJ, but his nearness ignited fireworks through her. He brushed her knee when he shifted gears. Electricity shot to her toes. She struggled for composure, yet at every intersection, she begged the light to turn red so he would have to shift again.

Get a grip, Annalee. So adolescent.

Focusing away from CJ, she let Mrs. Madison talk. The woman, despite her hard life, spoke of one blessing after another while laughing at herself in recent crazy situations and recounting funny stories about her family.

She inspired awe. Especially since she was still stuck in difficult circumstances. Annalee stifled a tear. Had her mother ever spoke of her with the pride Mrs. Madison shared over her children? No way. Mother loved her, in a never-satisfied type of affection. The only way she knew how to love.

Upon reaching Parkland, CJ climbed out and reached for Annalee's hand. "We'll meet you upstairs, Mrs. Madison."

The woman gave a wave and headed inside.

"You wanted to speak to me?" She had to concentrate to keep her voice steady as CJ helped her out of his door.

He walked in the opposite direction of the building. "No, I just want to give them a little time alone, first."

His hand, warm in her own, pricked her heart. This wasn't a lover's entwined-fingers clasped. Just a friendly, soft grip. Were workers at the center even allowed to date?

What a stupid thought. This wasn't a date. He was helping her, like he helped everyone.

And she needed to meet Mr. Madison and work through her awkwardness. Apologize. Would the man accept?

CJ led her on a meandering path through a park-like area toward the front of the building. He stopped in a shady place and released her hand. "I hope you don't mind delaying a bit."

She picked a leaf off a nearby bush, her hand suddenly feeling a chill. "No."

"Mr. and Mrs. Madison are pretty special. And they adore one another. But without a vehicle, Mrs. Madison can't visit him very easily."

Adore. What would it be like to have someone feel that way about her? "I don't think I've ever actually seen that word lived out."

"What word?" He moved closer, leaning against the tree trunk.

"Adore. Unfathomable." She tore a chunk off the leaf.

"You've never seen two people who adore one another?"

She shook her head. Why had she made such a comment?

"Cherish?"

"Nope, not that either." Her father loved her. But that was

usually in the form of a kind smile and a kiss on the forehead. And he didn't even go that far with Mother. "Don't get me wrong, I've seen people who love each other." Not like she'd experienced the feeling herself. "I've just never known anyone who took the emotion to the level of sacrifice. At least, that's what I think of when I hear the word adore."

His gaze remained on her, though he stayed silent. Almost like he studied her. She picked off and tore apart more leaves. Why had she put her bruised and battered psyche on display like this?

After several minutes, he pushed off the tree. "I think we've given them enough time." He collected her hand. "Much longer and Mrs. Madison will think we got lost."

Part of her wanted to question his intentional hand-holding. The other part delighted in the feel of her hand in his. The nearness. And the feeling of belonging his attention gave her.

His touch only lasted until he let her step through the revolving door. He didn't reach for her hand again after that. Probably only held it while they walked through the grass so she wouldn't trip in her heels.

And she let her mind and heart run away with her over a polite and protective action that was so utterly CJ.

At least his close proximity had distracted her from the coming meeting with Mr. Madison. Her mind whirled with thoughts of the man beside her until she reached the door of the man she'd injured.

She halted and stepped back. How could she face him? What must he think? But she had no time to hesitate. CJ tapped the hardwood and put his hand at her back as he opened the door for her. Though his touch lit sparks, they were no match for the clammy hand of embarrassment that wrapped her in its grip.

"There you are. 'Bout to think you all got yourselves lost." Mrs. Madison stood near her husband's bedside. The man was raised to sitting, and she had her arm tucked around his shoulders.

"Hey, Mr. Madison." CJ shook hand with the large, red-headed man who inhabited the bed.

"And this here is an angel-girl." Mrs. Madison waved Annalee closer.

She held out her hand. "I'm …" *Might as well admit to it.* "I'm Annalee Chambers."

"I know who you are." Even with a tube running under his nose and wires coming from his elbow, he shifted and sat up straighter. "And I know what you did." Something of an Irish accent came through with his words.

He hated her. He had every right. She braced for the attack.

He took her hand just at the point where she'd almost decided to drop it. "To me. And for me. And to bless my family even when you didn't know who they were." He wrapped his other hand around hers as well. "And I'm so grateful."

Grateful? After the accident and everything? She couldn't speak, but also couldn't close her mouth.

"Are you all right?" CJ laid his hand at her back again.

"I … yes. I mean … grateful? Do you … do you really know who I am?"

"You're the one who pleaded guilty for hitting me with her car. Yes, ma'am. I know you." He leaned his head forward an inch. His blue eyes twinkled. "And yes, ma'am, I'm grateful." With a sigh, he reclined again.

"Don't be exerting yourself." Mrs. Madison patted his shoulder. "The doctor thinks he should be fit to go back home tomorrow."

"That's good news. Does he need a ride?" CJ withdrew a few steps toward the door.

Annalee stared at the weary man closing his eyes. All this pain she'd caused. Yes, she'd had help in causing the man injury, but her hands were still at the wheel. She'd believed she could deal with Giselle's virtual blindfold without having to slam on her brakes in that less-than-comfortable area of town.

How could he feel gratitude for her? Even with the grocery shopping.

Mrs. Madison kissed her husband's forehead and joined them at the open door. "I'm thoroughly grateful to you CJ, but I don't think your truck cab is big enough for you, and him, and that big cast he's wearing."

Annalee hadn't seen a cast, but she turned to Mrs. Madison. "I think I can help him get home."

CJ parked next to the Madison's apartment. Mrs. Madison thanked Annalee again and winked in his direction.

He'd planned to sit with Annalee for a few minutes. *Just to talk.* As though the insistence convinced him his feelings were purely platonic.

But she scooted out of the truck, right behind Mrs. Madison. "Thanks for the ride."

He jumped out and jogged around the bed, slowing to match her pace when he reached her. "Are you glad you went?"

She paused. "I ..." She shook her head. "I don't understand

these people."

"Don't you like them?" How could anyone not adore this family?

"Oh yes. They're … amazing." She scanned the rooftops. "But how …" She huffed and pulled out her keys. "I'll see you tomorrow, I guess."

"Wait, how what?" He stood near her door, mesmerized by the pain and confusion in her eyes. If only he could soothe her troubled spirit.

She cast her face downward, and when she looked back up, tears sparkled in the corners of those beautiful eyes. "He said he was grateful to me. Me. I'm the one who caused all of his pain. All of the worry and frustration to his family. Yet he was so nice. So …"

"Forgiving?"

"Exactly. And he doesn't even know me. A couple of sacks of groceries and arranging for Parker to give him a ride home sure shouldn't buy forgiveness so easily."

CJ smiled. "He's not forgiving you on account of some gifts. I think he's forgiving you because he can see you're truly sorry."

She lifted her eyes heavenward. "Well, that just confuses me more. Everyone told me the family was money-grabbing. Playing on the sympathy of the public to make a quick buck. I didn't care. I believed taking responsibility was the right thing to do even if they were taking advantage of the situation."

She opened her door bringing her quite close to CJ. He reached for her. Instinct. His hands cupped her upper arms. "They aren't taking advantage of anything or anyone."

"I know. I can tell. They're reacting in as opposite a way as any I can imagine. That's why I'm having such trouble. Normal people don't act like this."

He grinned. "You've got me there."

Her gaze softened as her eyes met his. "I do thank you for taking me though." Her hands rested on his chest.

"My pleasure." Was it ever. He scanned her lovely face. Then stepped back. "Guess I'll see you tomorrow."

"Mm-hmm. I'm looking forward to seeing the children again."

He waved as she drove away. An ache settled in his chest at her exuberance about the kids. A good thing, but not as satisfying as her being excited to see him.

Ridiculous. Jealous of a bunch of dirty-faced miniature hoodlums. He chuckled. Of course, she loved them already. They'd captured his heart right off, too.

Still, he wanted to kick himself all the way back to his father's downtown condo. What did he think he was doing with Annalee? They'd practically spent the whole day together. He'd even held her hand.

And he tried not to consider the fact that she didn't resist his touch. Even seemed to like the attention.

But he'd seen her with that other man. Embracing her after driving up in a black limo. Obviously, they were in a relationship. That embrace was way too intimate to be between simple employer-employee. And CJ confirmed the relationship when he got a better look at the restaurant wine-tossing video. Same guy right next to her.

He took the elevator to the eighteenth floor and unlocked the door to his corner apartment. The panoramic view of the downtown area failed to enchant him. He left the lights off and strolled to the huge veranda, letting the wind and the smell of coming rain soothe his senses.

"How am I supposed to work with her when she twists my mind into little knots every time I'm around her?" The afternoon sun struck him full in the face. He turned his back and leaned against the wall, facing the stylish living room. Dad's taste.

Though he'd bought the condo to get CJ out of the dilapidated apartment he'd chosen, his dad insisted his son leave the decorating to him. "If I decide to have a cocktail party before a performance at the Meyerson, I want to know I can bring people up at the spur of the moment."

CJ hated the upscale, exclusive feel, though the windows and the inspiration he got from this view made it worthwhile.

Not so much with this problem. He imagined what Annalee would think of a visit here. Of course, she wouldn't visit here, but he could see her coming through the door, the look of delight at the same view he enjoyed every evening along with spectacular sunsets.

But to get that reaction, he'd have to admit he was Carlton Whelan, son of the CEO of the Whelan Group and Chairman of the Board for the Intercede Foundation.

She'd never forgive him for his deception, even as innocent as it was at the start. How could he have known she had the fight within her to continue working at the center? She had the compassion to catch his attention. Had a spirit to capture his …

His mood blackened over the wasted emotions. His feelings had no hope of being reciprocated if he remained CJ the janitor. But fierce hatred lay in store for him if he revealed himself as the heir to his father's financial empire. No matter how he divulged the secret, there was no possibility of her acceptance.

So why is this longing in my heart, Lord? If no hope existed for a relationship …

The room in front of him peopled itself with a family. Annalee brought in a bowl from the kitchen and called to a tow-headed boy playing a video game at a TV hanging on the wall. Another, who looked like CJ's younger self, drew on a tablet on the coffee table. CJ, an older version, came through from the study and picked up the younger, giggling child. Joining Annalee in the kitchen, he paused and kissed …

Stupid imagination. Waste of time and energy. Staying at the apartment alone would only fester more feelings. He slid the balcony window closed, snatched his keys from the shelf, and took the elevator to the garage basement. About where his heart thudded.

Annalee reminisced about her day with CJ as the sun set over her mother's manicured garden. She collected a bottle of insect spray and gave herself a quick spritz so she could stay out and enjoy the environment a little longer.

Father strolled out with his pipe. Mother hated the smell, but Annalee thought the spicy, woodsy scent to be rather homey. Maybe because it was her father smoking it. "What do you think about church?"

"Is that where you went this morning?" His voice held curiosity only.

"No. I met someone who did, though." She tracked the trail of a snail across the brick at her feet.

"It's not like you've never been to church, sweetheart."

"I know, but I've only gone to weddings and funerals and Christmas and Easter services. Felt like dog and pony shows where everything is a grand performance."

Her father chuckled and drifted toward the edge of the lawn. "I've never quite thought of those services like that."

"Do you believe in God?"

"I suppose." He paused in his words and movement. "I guess I've never stopped long enough to contemplate Him. What do you think?"

She forced out a loud exhale. "I don't know what to believe, but I've met some people who have pretty strong ideas. They act like God is someone they know personally."

"Really?" He puffed his pipe. "An interesting concept. An Almighty Creator who chats with everyday people."

"That's what I thought." She pulled her feet to the bench, resting her chin on her knees. "If there's a God like that, I'd sure like to get to know Him."

"I'm sure He'd like to get to know you, too, sweetheart. Although …" He tapped his pipe over a large urn where Mother kept perennials in the springtime. "If He's really God, He already does know you."

"Would it embarrass you if I visited a church sometime to find out a little more about Him?"

"Gracious, no, my dear." He leaned over and kissed her forehead. "Take notes. I'll want to hear all about Him."

"About who?" Mother crossed paths with Father as she exited her study.

"God." Annalee slipped her feet back to the cement. Mother didn't like her to appear childish, even in the privacy of her own home.

Every word spoken or action taken in privacy will be amplified in public. Her mother's lessons echoed through her mind. She was right, but her expectations made for a difficult childhood of always striving for her approval and never accomplishing the goal.

"Why would you be thinking about something like that?" She paused in her quick steps across the patio.

"I don't know." She didn't want to discuss CJ or the God he spoke to with her mother.

"That's never an acceptable answer, Annalee, and I have instructed you to that end on several occasions. Now, where did you go this morning?"

She skipped spending money on food for the Madison family. Her mother would consider that frivolous. "I went to lunch with a friend."

"Who goes to church?"

As much as she wanted to claim no direct knowledge about that, she couldn't. He'd shown her the church, drove the bus, and shared details of the ministry. "Yes."

"He is not of your station." She lifted her chin.

Annalee sucked back her questions about how her mother could make such assumptions.

"You can put away thinking about the man, Annalee. I forbid you to see him."

That word *forbid* made the little hairs on the back of her neck stand on end. "Mother, you don't even know if the person is a man."

"Of course, he is. I can see it all over your face. I won't have you sullying your father's good name with some zealot who will drag you into the fanatical mire with him."

225

As smart as Mother was, she still hadn't realized the surest way to get Annalee to do something was to tell her she couldn't. *Forbid? Won't have?* She'd about guaranteed Annalee to pursue her path.

She definitely planned to spend more time with CJ and at least learn a little about the God to whom he prayed.

Annalee didn't remember her dreams, but a longing swelled in her heart Monday morning. She dressed and prepared for the day an hour earlier than normal. When her father left for work at the end of breakfast, she mindlessly thumbed through her Twitter feed.

"Stop fidgeting." Mother entered the dining room and caught Annalee bobbing her foot.

She couldn't stay still. Not this morning. And she had no desire to revisit her mother's opinions from the night before. She popped up and placed a kiss atop her mother's head. "Have a nice day, Mother."

Without knowing where to go, she knew she didn't want to stay. Still, almost six hours before she was due at the center. She needed a diversion and headed downtown to the Dallas Museum of Art. Strolling through the hallways full of masterpieces always distracted her with calming inspiration.

A wall full of watercolors piqued her curiosity, and she wandered closer. Several preliminary sketches of renowned artist Edward Hopper hung beside the final piece of his diner portrait entitled *Nighthawks*.

She surveyed the angles and notes he'd made from his initial creations and thought about Tally. Her pictures of her brothers playing football with some of the other boys from the complex easily matched Hoppers first jots. With a little instruction or direction, she'd master that medium in no time.

She shook her head and moved on to an exhibition of a relatively new west coast artist. This one also focused on watercolor and her large paintings of exotic flowers jumped off the canvas in colors intense enough to be oils. Annalee would have to experiment with her own supplies to see if she could work up something like that.

A few hours later, refreshed with the inspiration that had surrounded her, she drove to the center. Her mind reeled as to how she could help Tally hone the talent she so obviously had and pursue the dream she'd shared with Annalee.

I wanna paint God's beauty into people's souls. Tally's earnest words and sincere expression touched Annalee's heart, though she had little understanding of exactly what she meant. The girl acted and spoke much wiser than her thirteen years. And Annalee determined to find a way to help her.

Her allowance might contribute but wouldn't complete the necessary funding for the type of instruction she should have, especially at her age. Maybe she could speak to Randolf Vannater. The school he worked with from time to time might be willing to offer a scholarship to someone so obviously gifted.

Thoughts and possibilities whirled until she signed in on the clipboard at the center.

"I have you doing outdoor duty today. You might want a jacket with the wind kicking up." Miss Pritchard didn't look up from the file of papers she worked on.

Outdoors? That meant free time with the kids. Time to talk with them and get to know them better. She felt a glow. Until she wondered what she would say.

Still, the opportunity seemed too good. She quick-cleaned the bathrooms, leaving mopping for later, then dashed out to her car for a jacket as the buses started pulling into the loop.

Recess duty, the thing she'd feared almost from the moment she received this job, turned out easy enough. And figuring out what to say wasn't an issue. *Engage the kids. Swing a jump rope. Shout* go. *Listen.*

And she learned quickly that listening was key. A group of girls gathered around her, talking about everyone's hair, her hair, her nail color. Why she drove such an old car. Such curious little dolls, but so sweet. Why had she worried about this part of the job?

When a kickball game broke out, most of her groupies left to play, making her promise to watch.

"I promise." A promise she intended to keep … after she spoke to one of the girls who hadn't joined the game.

The child sat alone, scraping a stick across the packed dirt over and over. Jamaysia. The one who got her into trouble for discussing her makeup issues and not pulling her from where she sat on the edge of the sink.

She wandered toward her, noticing none of the other kids had talked to her, at least not very much. "You don't want to play kickball?"

"That's for little kids." The girl turned her large dark eyes toward Annalee. "You aren't playing."

"I will if you will."

Jamaysia fisted her hips. "Right. You're gonna go play

kickball in Max Zephen shoes?"

Annalee looked down at the hot pink bows on her slip-on sneakers. "You really do know your designers."

"I'm gonna be one a'them someday. Gonna have people all over the world wantin' my clothes. See?" She pulled an inked scarf from around her neck. "I done this one."

Three colors crisscrossed a cream linen scarf. A little rough. They muddied in a couple of places, but for the most part, the lines were smooth and intricate. "That's lovely. You did it by yourself?"

"Uh-huh. Ain't nobody helped me. I even bought the supplies by myself with money I got from my birthday last year. Been saving it until I could decide what ink colors to get."

"Have you done any others?"

"Nah." She knotted her scarf around her neck again. "I have to get another scarf. Gonna take a while to save up for that."

"It'll be worth it. You did a beautiful job." She offered the girl a hand. "You ready to go play?"

"You seriously gonna go over there? Do you even know how to play kickball?"

"I think I can figure it out. I'll race you." She jogged several steps before Jamaysia bolted past her.

"You race all ya want. I'm gonna to win."

Marji Laine

Chapter 16

CJ hadn't looked forward to seeing Annalee, if for no other reason that the woman had haunted his dreams and thoughts since he'd last seen her. Still, he did an informal search for her through the main rooms.

Finally, he paused in the office. "Did Annalee go home early today?"

Margo arched an eyebrow. "Noooo."

Paula glanced out the window. "You bess check out the kickball game going on."

Kickball? Really?

He bolted to the back door and looked out. Another layer of Annalee pulled away.

Annalee caught up with her at the field. They split them between the two teams and put Annalee to kick. She didn't feel quite as cocky with the ball rolling toward her as she had when trying to persuade Jamaysia to join the fun.

"She can't kick it. She's too much of a girly girl." One of the older boys shouted at her from third base.

Tyrone mouthed back at him from the line of players making up her team.

She took two steps forward and swung her right leg like she'd seen at soccer games. She connected, but the ball only rolled a few feet. A fast runner though, she was able to run to the first base before the kids scampering to the ball could get to it.

Tyrone came up next and gave the ball a sound punt over the pitcher's head. Annalee darted for second base and rounded it, trying to take third as well. At least, that was the way she'd seen the Texas Rangers do it. The ball hit her heel right before she reached the tree marking the base.

"You're out, Miss Annalee." Jamaysia smiled at her.

Tyrone and a couple of others from the team started arguing the call.

"If I'm out when the ball hits me, then I'm out." She led the way out to the field, though she had no idea what to do in such a position. Still, she had fun. Laughing and getting to know the kids. Jamaysia warmed up to the game, especially after kicking hard enough to make it to third base. Suddenly, she was the team's star player.

The game proved even more fun when CJ joined. By then, Annalee had taken more to cheering than playing. The kids doted on him. An obvious athlete, he had the whole team in hysterics when he rounded first, picked up the baseman, and carried him all the way to third. By the time the game ended, he was hard to see through the boys surrounding and climbing on him.

Though Annalee had her own entourage of huggers and clingers and chatters leading her to the back door.

Oh, she could so get used to this job.

CJ had joined the game near the end but reveled in Annalee's fun and encouraging nature.

She'd even persuaded Jamaysia to play. And when the game was over, the little girl threw her arms around Annalee's waist. "That was the funnest. I wanna play again tomorrow."

"I'd love to, Jamaysia." Annalee stroked the girl's black pigtails. "Let's go get some snack, okay?"

"Can I sit with you?"

Annalee nodded as a half-dozen other girls begged to be included on her table. They darted in to get a spot.

He fell into step beside her. "I'm impressed. Jamaysia never plays any of the games."

"She's very sweet, but she doesn't quite fit in with the others. I can empathize."

"Well, you fit in now. You even have a fan club." CJ couldn't resist her either.

She laughed. "No, I'm simply the newest toy."

He shook his head. "You? You're much better than a new toy."

Silence followed, and her stare fell on him as she slowed. The smile disappeared, but curiosity and questions filled her expression.

Better than a toy? Come on, CJ. The atmosphere needed lightening. "Besides toys break. I'm hoping you don't have that type of problem." He smirked and separated from her as they entered the building.

Internally, he smacked his forehead. What happened to his determination to stop thinking about her? *Stay away from Annalee Chambers.* She churned up his insides, and his sleeplessness last night proved that point. Add to that his dad's attitude about Todd Chambers. Like CJ needed another reason for Dad to gripe at him.

And they could never work out their differences anyway. CJ could never again embrace that world he left. Too purposeless.

Though not all of the people in his father's realm were empty-hearted and self-absorbed. Some were kind and compassionate, like Mrs. Moncrief on the Intercede Foundation Board. Her dedication and commitment to the children of Dallas inspired the afterschool program in the first place.

But that cultured work still wasn't for him. Better to have dirt under his nails than personal agendas filling his mind.

And Annalee could never be part of his world of charity work, which in his heart was more the work of a missionary. She didn't have a relationship with God, so there wasn't a way for her to authentically fit in or embrace the point and purpose of this place. Not her fault, but that didn't alter the truth of the circumstances.

He glanced at her chatting with the girls gathered at her table. Animation vibrated from her face, and they responded with uninhibited delight. The lady was the vision of what he'd vowed not to think of her earlier today. As he gazed into her laughing eyes now or caught the scent of her honeysuckle hair before when she passed him, he realized the folly of his attempt.

She was becoming the girl of his dreams. Regardless of the resolutions he tried to make against her.

Annalee didn't actually eat the snack. The workers were allowed, but she'd rather save the food for seconds for the children and grab a sandwich from MacAllister's on the way home.

Besides, after CJ's remark about her being better than a new toy, her stomach knotted in such a way she'd not have been able to ingest anything anyway.

What had he meant by the statement? Several implications flitted into mind. New toys, like fads, flashed for a moment before becoming boring and replaceable. If she was better than a new toy, he might have meant she'd not be easily replaceable. Her heart skipped at that interpretation.

Or maybe the kids liked her better than they enjoyed new toys. Though she doubted the truth to that one.

Maybe he'd meant something more negative? A new toy can draw attention away from more important issues or things with better substance. Using the term toy could have been a demeaning, purposeful act. Like she was some sort of object. *Hm.* CJ didn't seem the type to be so crude.

He probably meant they would tire of her soon. And he was likely correct. She chided herself for over-analyzing. Turning her gaze to him, she noticed, again, a light in his eyes. The joy and delight he had for the boys around him. His compassion for these kids inspired her anew.

Cleaning off her table as the girls began to leave, she remembered the floors she still needed to clean and headed for the bathrooms.

"Annalee." Miss Pritchard stood at the doorway to the office and beckoned her with a raised hand before she called out the family name of another child.

The bathroom could wait a few more minutes. The dirt wasn't likely going anywhere. Annalee went into the room, expecting to chat about something. The atmosphere between them had eased, thankfully.

Instead, Laurel Stewart sat at Mr. Whelan's abandoned desk with her hands resting on an open file. She indicated the straight-backed chair center in front of the desk.

Annalee lowered into it and noticed Margo had abandoned the entryway where she normally stayed when parents picked up their kids. Instead, she'd stepped fully out to the porch and crossed the hall to the great room with every pick-up. She'd effectively abandoned her.

"Good evening, Miss Chambers." She lifted her hands and intertwined her fingers. "How are you doing?"

Annalee had visions of the grim reaper, but that was ridiculous. Miss Stewart was her advisor and advocate. "Things are good. I'm really enjoying the experience here."

"What is it that you are responsible for?"

"I've done several things. I still clean the bathrooms."

"Are they clean now?" Laurel picked up a pen and opened the file in front of her.

"Uh, well, not exactly."

"The first task you were given, you're already ignoring?"

"I … I was about to do them." She sounded lame, even to her own ears.

"Miss Chambers, I'd hoped, after our last discussion, you would make changes in your behavior and get on board with the work the center does for this part of Dallas."

Annalee winced. The words held the sting of a hard slap. What had she been doing except *getting on board*, to borrow Laurel Stewart's cliché? "I really am on board. The director has even allowed me to work with the kids."

The woman jotted something onto a paper inside a file folder in front of her.

"I was assigned to the playground today, so I decided to clean the floors after I returned inside."

She wrote something else. "I see. Putting it off until the very end of the night."

Arguing solved nothing. Annalee clamped her jaw shut. *Steady. Calm.* She cast her gaze downward.

She changed topics hoping to show her officer the positive aspects of her work at the center. "I've been doing other jobs, too. I worked all of last week in the kitchen. On Saturday, I was able to lead the painting activity, and today, as I said, I had playground duty."

Miss Stewart jotted something else down. "Looks like they are trying to find something you can actually do well."

Misfire. She'd thought the job changes stemmed from her getting better at things, not failing at them.

Laurel Stewart removed her glasses and pinched the brim of her nose. "It is apparent to me that the leaders here are unhappy with your performance. They are trying to place you with chores which will help them but haven't been able to find a good place for you."

This revelation went beyond a slap. Annalee had never been gut-punched, but her breath escaped and her stomach convulsed. "They complained about me?"

"This staff is much too kind to complain, but the very fact you've been moved from responsibility to responsibility implicates difficulty in assigning you. And moving you from a self-paced, independent job, to one of limited supervision, and now one of intense supervision marks you as a high-maintenance worker. Someone making the necessary chores harder instead of easier."

Annalee's mind whirled, trying to grasp the truth of what Laurel Stewart communicated. She'd been doing a lousy job? *Leaders*—plural. Did that include CJ? Why didn't he or Miss Pritchard correct her? The director had shown no trouble doing that when Annalee had given Tyrone and Hayden those granola bars for their sister.

"At this point ..." The officer shifted a piece of paper aside and seemed to scan something beneath it. "There is a strong possibility the leadership will need to release you before month's end. If that happens, I have no alternative but to recommend your probation be revoked. At which point you will go to jail."

"I'll do better." Annalee promised it, but she didn't know how to achieve it. Maybe if she asked Miss Pritchard what continued to displease her, she could get specific items to correct.

"I suggest you do more than that." Laurel Stewart closed the file. "First, don't speak to anyone about the discussion we're having. If they felt comfortable speaking to you, I wouldn't be here to take care of the matter."

Strike getting details from Miss Pritchard, or CJ either. "All right."

"Second, your father has influence. If he asks the correct people in the right way, you can likely be reassigned to an easier job. Maybe working as an assistant in a judge's chambers. With a little effort, he could likely get the community service removed altogether."

"I can't continue to work here?" Her attachment to the center had crept around her heart without her knowledge. Not seeing the kids again, being able to crack jokes with Tyrone and Hayden, or discuss the hot new bands with the group of girls she'd snacked with.

She wouldn't let a tear rise. Showing the affect Laurel Stewart's words had on her was unacceptable. And that went for the disappointment of Miss Pritchard reporting to her officer instead of speaking with her first.

"I'm not in a position to tell you what you can and can't do here at the center. I'm only giving you the benefit of my experience with hundreds of probationers. Both successful and failed. And I think if you attempt to continue your work here, you could find yourself in a four by eight cell for Thanksgiving." The woman stood and tucked the file under her arm. "I'll expect to hear from one of the judges requesting a change in your assignment this week."

Dismissed, Annalee walked from the room, unsure of the next action she should take. Laurel was her advocate, supposed to be in her corner. She obviously saw a problem, a spiral that would likely lead to nothing good.

She stared at the practically empty great room, where CJ paced away from her with a push-broom. His whistle echoed against the walls. If only she could speak to him. Get some idea of how to improve. He turned at the other end, and she glanced away. She veered toward the bathrooms.

Laughter spilled out from the kitchen, Paula's guffaw, giggles from the Tigh sisters, and a titter, which had to belong to Miss Pritchard.

Laurel Stewart's heels clicked onto the linoleum and her voice rose from behind Annalee. "CJ, walk me to my car."

The woman tucked her hand under CJ's elbow. The two of them sauntered across the dining room. Their obvious intimacy spread yet another layer of heaviness on Annalee's heart.

She had spent time with CJ, had thought him intriguing and charming. But obviously, her feelings went unreciprocated. So much so that he made formal complaints about her.

Sucking in a threatening sob, she pushed into the bathroom. She grabbed the bucket and dustpan and turned on the water full-force. What did any of that matter if she was compelled to leave? She filled her bucket and began to slop suds on the floor.

Should she ask Father to insist on a reassignment or keep improving and hope for the best?

If you attempt to continue your work here, you could find yourself in a four by eight cell for Thanksgiving. Laurel Stewart's southern drawl wrapped a noose around her neck and tightened.

I can't go to jail. Her breaths came in short gasps. She needed escape.

No. She needed to finish her job. Straightening, she dragged the bucket and mop next door and made quick work of the boys' room. With her mind and face as blank as she could make them, she emptied the bucket and bid her good night.

Her officer had been right about one thing. She needed her father's input on this situation before the end of the week.

What possessed Laurel to grab his arm, CJ would never figure. As he opened the door for her, he detached himself and then ushered her ahead of him. They hadn't made it off the porch before she glued onto him again, and he went through the same process when he got to the wrought-iron gate.

By then, she'd drawn in her tentacles and began speaking about the ominous yearly banquet they had to attend. Only she used words like *excited, anxious,* and *looking forward.* What had happened to the kindred spirit who hated this must-do task as much as he did? Ugh. He'd rather shave his head and pour rubbing alcohol all over it. At least that would only sting for a moment instead of the three hours of monotonous pain. He'd understood the concept of prison after his first experience. And yet, he'd attended again. Every year. Like the lemmings jumping to their death.

Unless … maybe this year he should invite a real date? He wondered if Annalee might join him. He'd use some of Laurel's words with the prospect of Annalee on his arm.

Depositing the woman in her car relieved him, but her presence also added questions. Had Margo called her in or was this a formality of Annalee's probation. And if that was the case, wasn't speaking to the probationer's supervisor a matter of course.

Maybe this visit had been for an entirely different reason.

He neared the center as Annalee stormed out the front door.

"Hey. Done already?"

She halted and took a step backward, her eyes on the ground. "I assure you, I successfully completed the job."

Okay. "I thought, perhaps ..." He looked to the left and rubbed his hand down the back of his neck. "... maybe you'd like some coffee or a sandwich? I talked straight through the snack tonight and didn't eat anything."

She looked up with something akin to horror on her face. Questions in her eyes. Her mouth opened in an unspoken word. She shut it and gave her head a shake. "No." Without another word, she breezed through the gate and stretched out her stride down the sidewalk in front of the center.

Served him right after resolving to leave her alone. He'd know better next time.

After locking things up, he drove Margo to the bus stop.

"You're awful quiet." The woman leaned against the closed passenger door.

He put the truck in park, planning to stay here until the bus arrived. "I saw you sent Annalee out to yard duty."

"Yeah. She seems to have a real knack with Jamaysia. Did you notice her actually playing today?"

"I noticed." He fidgeted with the steering wheel.

"Something bothering you?"

"Nah." The last thing he wanted to do was admit that she'd been in any way right about him and his interest in Annalee.

"Did Laurel say anything to you?"

He shifted and stared at her for a moment. "Did you know she was coming?"

She shook her head. "I thought you wanted her to see Annalee doing so well."

"So you didn't talk with her?"

"Nothing beyond girl talk. Nothing about Annalee." She lifted her chin. "Bus is here." She opened her door. "I don't think there's anything to worry about. Annalee did a good job today. Laurel had to see it."

She started to climb out then halted. "But then that might not be such a good thing."

"She's her officer. She has to be on her side." The words were empty though. He'd seen the bitterness the woman held.

Margo waved and jogged toward the bus's open doors.

Images of Annalee playing with the kids filled his mind. The woman had kept him awake most of last night. With Laurel's arrival and Annalee's coolness as she left, looked like his dreams would be wrapped up in her again.

Strange to have such conflict inside like the warmth of possibility against his desperation to forget his feelings. Growing feelings. Ach. There, the itch inside him had been defined. Yet all he could pray was *Why, Lord?*

The woman's image haunted his condo, settled on his thoughts, and danced through his dreams. How could he get rid of her? At least the part of her that had adhered to his brain.

After a miserable night of tangled sheets and dreams of stress, betrayal, helplessness, and failure, Annalee bolted out of bed a good thirty minutes later than intended. Her father, he had to still be here. She shrugged on a hoodie over her pajama shirt and slipped on some sweatpants before racing down the stairs to the dining room.

"Morning, sweetheart. Good timing." Her father lifted a cup of coffee in her direction.

Yea. He hadn't left for his rally yet. She took a deep breath, willing her pulse to slow and spooned a clump of scrambled eggs from the buffet onto her *breakfast china* plate. Mother had a special set for all three meals and others for special occasions.

"Would you like to join me at the rally, today, Sweetheart? I could have Parker take you to the center later?"

The center. The place had excited her the day before. Thoughts of the children. Some approval from Miss Pritchard. Well, what she'd thought was approval.

And CJ. Her chest ached from the night of twisting emotions about him. A diversion to Father's rally might be exactly what she needed. Except for the smiling and waving and … gracious, the last thing she needed was to be in a room with reporters and other media. "I think I'll pass, but thanks for the invitation."

She pinched off a bite of toast and popped the tasteless crust into her mouth. "I saw my probation officer yesterday."

"Really? I thought you only reported to her monthly." Her dad lowered the papers in his hand and laid them on the table.

"That's the requirement, but she can show up anytime at my volunteer placement."

"Was there a problem?" He took another sip from his coffee, but his concern poured out from his gaze over the top of the cup.

Problem didn't come close. "She said the center director and other leaders are complaining about me. Wait. Not complaining. She alluded to their discontent, though they hadn't fussed about anything in particular. She can just tell they don't want me there."

"They aren't complaining?"

She shook her head. "She didn't mention anything specific, and I thought they were pleased with my work."

"But your officer can tell, out of the thin air, that they don't like you." His brows furrowed. "I'm not buying that."

"She's my PO. Why would she lie? My failure is her failure, right?" Or was this some sort of test to see Annalee's commitment level?

"That's usually the way it works." He tilted his head. "But you're a pretty good judge of character, Annalee. Do you see anything in their behavior which would make you think they want you gone?"

She lifted her eyebrows. "Not until Laurel Stewart explained it to me. What I thought were greater responsibilities, rewards for getting better at my job, she said were constant movements to try to find something I could do well. The fact they kept switching me meant I couldn't do anything right."

"That's ridiculous."

"You don't believe her?"

He paused. "What does she want you to do?"

"Get you to use your influence to end my community service. Or at least move me away."

"Why?"

"So I won't end up in jail." Couldn't he see that part of the problem for himself?

He tucked his papers inside his folder. "Instead of bringing you and the leadership together to try to work through the difficulty, she wants you to manipulate to get relieved of your responsibility at the center. Is that about right?"

"Exactly."

"Do you want to leave?"

Annalee shut her eyes and lowered her chin. "Not even a little bit." She raised her gaze back to her father's face. "I really love working there."

"Then I can't help but wonder if something else is going on under the surface. Maybe something that doesn't even have to do with you."

Annalee turned his suggestion over in her mind.

"Whatever the undercurrent, you certainly will not go to jail. Not unless you become a monster who puts the children in danger." He chuckled.

She sighed relief. At least for now, she'd stay the course.

Chapter 17

Annalee's aloof attitude during the next several days made it easy for CJ to avoid asking her to go out with him again. While she threw herself into every activity she was assigned, she rarely responded to his comments and ignored his jokes.

Her attitude bordered on the schizophrenic. Playful and full of joy with the children, yet reserved, moody, almost indignant anytime he attempted interaction.

On Sunday, he half-hoped she'd show up at the Rosewood Housing complex, desiring a ride to church. Or maybe she'd visit the church directly since she knew where it was. Stupid fantasies. Of course, she didn't show.

And her red Mustang hadn't appeared in the parking lot when he took the kids home. But Tally came limping out of her apartment when the bus pulled near.

"Mr. CJ. Take a look." She sneezed.

Mrs. Madison came to the doorway. "Tally Simone, you get yourself right back here and under the covers."

"Are you sick?" CJ walked with the boys toward their

apartment.

"Just the sniffles."

"We missed you this morning." He lifted his hand. "Missed you, too, Mrs. Madison."

"Thank ya, CJ. Lord didn't miss me though. We been singing in between nose wipes."

He chuckled.

"But iffen I'd been to church, I wouldna got this gift." Tally held out a thick, leather-bound sketch pad. "And I gots some extra paper to put into it when this pad runs out."

"Where'd you get that?" Tyrone eyed the gift while Hayden ran his fingers over the etched cover.

"Miss Annalee done brought it to me. Said an artist should never be without her supplies. She brought me pencils, too. A whole wad of 'em." Tally rubbed her finger under her nose. "She brung y'all a new soccer ball."

"She did not." Tyrone's eyes glowed. "Where?" He darted into the house with his brother in his wake.

"You better get back inside, Tally. And get to feeling better." He said it regardless of her painful existence, though no one would know of that pain to look at her ever-present smile.

She hobbled to the door, her mother helping. CJ waved them off and turned back toward the bus.

So Annalee had showered her compassion on this family once again. His mind poured over every encounter he'd had with her as he exchanged vehicles at the church and headed north on Central Expressway toward Fitzhugh.

Though he hadn't seen her the day before, his interaction with her all week continued to sting. Her gift to Tally and the boys proved the former impression he'd had of her, the kind and giving

Annalee, seemed to be the true woman. So, what happened last Monday, a full week ago, that initiated this long-lasting deep freeze?

He remembered some offhand comment he'd made, not the exact words, but a compliment. He thought it had been a compliment. Maybe she didn't take it the way he meant. Now that he thought about the encounter, she had been stunned. And then he'd given some sort of wisecrack. Maybe that interchange offended her?

The road ended and CJ zigzagged toward Preston where his father waited for him at the Preston Park Country Club. Naturally, he'd delayed. Talking to his dad was hard enough, and even worse in a place full of pretensions.

Dad sat in his normal seat in the men's grill near the windows overlooking the first tee and one of the cart paths spanning Turtle Creek. "About time you decided to show up."

"Nice to see you, too, Dad."

"Don't be obnoxious." He took a swig from a highball glass.

"I'm delighted you decided to join us today, Mr. Whelan." Marcus stepped closer, the towering top of his head a little grayer than CJ remembered it. But he hadn't visited the men's grill in a while. "What would you like to drink?"

"Water is fine." CJ smiled at the man. "And how's the weather up there?" The old joke never failed to draw a smile from the gentle server who'd worked at the club as long as CJ could remember.

"About as good as it is for you little people." He chuckled. "High today is ninety-one degrees with sixty-two percent humidity. A ten percent chance of rain, but I don't believe you'll actually see any precipitation until next weekend." His forecasts were usually as correct as his manner.

"You ever think of giving those network weathermen a challenge?"

He chuckled again and turned away.

"Sounds like the morning weather baked you, Dad." Getting his father into a discussion of his latest round of golf might pass this necessary get-together a little quicker.

Dad complained about the uneven dry grass on the green at fourteen, the traffic that messed up his putt on seventeen, and the uneven cart path over the creek going to twelve. Then he started in on the other three players.

By the time he finished, CJ had eaten his entire Denver omelet, two slices of Canadian bacon, and half of a Belgium waffle. At least eating at the club gave him one delicious, and international, meal every once in a while.

"Well, I'm glad you got to play." CJ put his napkin on the table.

"Hold on. I have something important to say to you."

Here it comes. Every time his father wanted to meet him for a meal, the food came at a dear price. Usually, the time and grief of listening to him go on about CJ's lack of responsibility, ambition, and business acumen. Total neglect of social standards and disdain for the great name of Whelan. CJ not only had to listen to the same song but had to contrive a new way to wiggle out of the conversation without losing his temper, lying to his dad, or giving up on his principles.

Not an easy task.

"I'll be speaking to the other board members at Intercede Foundation, and by next month, we'll have a consensus to close down the center."

"What?" Not at all what he expected. "You can't close the

center, Dad. People depend on it."

"That's none of my concern."

Great, the chairman of the board didn't care about those his foundation served. "Why would you do this? People ... children are going to be hurt by this decision. Dad, we've got almost eighty kids who'll end up at home alone for hours if we're not there for them."

"Then their parents should have planned better for their children's future. Like I planned for my son's future."

Planned. That was a laugh. Most of the families could barely plan for their next meal or next month's electricity bill.

His father laid a fist on the table. "I drew out your future, Carlton. I paved the way for you to attend the finest schools, purchased rights to add you to prestigious registries, made connections, smiled, and spent time with people I can't stand, all so you could have the best opportunities. All so you could take the Whelan Group to the next level."

CJ only half-listened to him. His mind reeled over the effects closing the center would have on the community and on individual families. And what would Annalee do if she couldn't finish her hours of community service?

"A man is only successful if he leaves this world better than he found it," his father continued. "And for me, that means you earn more, do more, and are more than I have been. That's quite a tall order for you. And let's face it, you're getting started terribly late and from a much lower rung than I."

"What does this all have to do with you wanting to shut down the center?" CJ gripped his napkin. "I still don't understand why you'd want to do such a thing?"

"It's the only way I can guarantee you'll follow the correct path." His father cut into his Eggs Benedict and took a bite. "With the center closed, you have no choice but to work at Whelan group, as it should be."

"You could not be so selfish, so manipulative." Heat rose up CJ's spine, and he slapped the napkin onto the linen-covered tabletop.

"Come to work with me, now, and I won't have to play this card." Dad steepled his long fingers above his plate, elbows resting on the table, and a half-smile arching into his right cheek.

CJ jumped up, knocking over his chair. The clatter silenced the room, but he didn't care. "This is wrong. You know it is." He whirled, kicked the toppled chair out of his way, and marched toward the door.

"The choice is yours."

His father's final words, called as he pushed through the exit, weighed down his chest.

In spite of the heat, CJ parked at his condo and walked all over downtown for hours. He stopped at his church and prayed over his dad's revelation then hiked out to the center and sat outside staring at the building.

So many dreams he'd had for this place. For the children who relied on their program. He'd even drawn rough sketches of additional buildings he wanted to add to eliminate the wait-list altogether. Children shouldn't have to be locked away inside their houses or roaming the streets all alone.

God, how can I abandon everything I believe and go to work for Dad? But CJ had no doubt his father had enough pull to shut the center down with little effort. Not that Dad was trying to be cruel. He had his own agenda and never accepted a negative response to his demands. Never.

Especially not from CJ.

Letting the kids suffer on account of his dreams, or his father's expectations, was out of the question.

By the time he reached his condo, exhaustion set in, and he collapsed on his bed without even changing. Around two o'clock in the morning, he woke sweaty and uncomfortable. He peeled off his dirty clothes and dumped them in the hamper. After a quick shower, he feasted on a bowl of Cheerios on the patio.

The Dallas skyline inspired him. Not for the wealth, power, or social status it indicated, but for the dark places at the bases of the lighted buildings. The crags and crannies where the blaze of pride and power couldn't reach.

Those were the places the Spirit of God could touch, places in utter blindness without realization of their lack. And God used the afterschool center to provide for such a place where the youngest and most innocent of these people lived. That was the reason CJ jumped on board when Mrs. Moncrief suggested the center to his dad in the first place.

Granted, CJ hadn't indicated he'd planned to work there. His father assumed CJ would finally join him in his charitable endeavors and extend his interests into his business world. Instead, CJ bailed on him. He'd chosen to live among the people and work at the center doing whatever jobs needed doing.

His father bought the condo not long after, insisting that CJ move there instead of living in the low-rent district. He complied only because it meant he'd have more money to buy food for the kids' daily snack.

But his father ultimately swayed the board. Always had.

CJ poured his leftover milk into the planter at the edge of the patio and took the bowl back to his dishwasher.

A few more hours of prayer and sleep and maybe he could accept his father's demands without emptying his stomach or selling his soul.

With renewed vigor, Annalee arrived at the center. Laurel Stewart hadn't contacted her after she'd let the deadline go last week. And Father stood behind her, thankfully, without informing Mother of the option.

Determined to prove her worth and her dedication to completing her service to the kids, she signed in a half-hour early and headed toward the girls' bathroom.

"Annalee?" CJ came out of the kitchen with a tool of some sort in one hand and a box with a handle in the other. Dirt and sweat painted his features.

"Did something break?"

"No." He looked at the clock directly center in the main hall. "Do you know what time it is?"

"Yes. I wanted to start early today."

"You need to leave early?"

"No." She swallowed. "I enjoy working here. I don't want to go somewhere else." While she had no intention of bringing up the complaints they'd made against her, Annalee at least wanted them to know how she felt about the center and the people who made it so special.

CJ scowled. He set the box and the tool down and wiped his face on a dish towel lying on a nearby table. "What have you heard?"

"Uh …" Should she tell him about Laurel Stewart's visit? She applied her composure lessons and sought an acceptable reply.

"I don't want anyone to know there's a chance the center will be shut down." He sat and offered her a seat across from him.

Shut down? She let the mask fall. Her chin along with it. "Why …"

"There's no reason to alarm anyone. If I can convince the board to overrule …" He flinched. "… Scott Whelan."

"He wants to close the center?"

CJ's jaw clamped. He turned his head. "If it doesn't meet his expectations." He took a breath and glanced back at Annalee. "The center is a drain on the foundation's accounts. Of course, we've been hearing that particular song for a couple of years now."

"What if the center was able to raise its own money?"

"What's this about money?" Miss Pritchard stepped in from the front entry hall. "Don't you think I should be included in a conversation like this?"

Shoot. Annalee had made her mad again. "I'm terribly sorry, Miss Pritchard. I let my thoughts come out without passing them through my brain first." She still needed the director's approval if she wanted to stay at the center. Though, according to CJ, that was a remote possibility anyway.

"We can't charge enough to raise the money we need. The families we serve would have nannies if they could afford them."

She ignored the remark undoubtedly directed at her childhood. "I wasn't actually anticipating the parents paying for their children. I was thinking about throwing a gala where we could charge for admission, have live entertainment, and maybe even some sort of auction for donated items."

"Good grief, Lady-Di, who do you think we are? No one wants to come out to this area of town at night. And where would we put them if you could lure them out? You think they'd like to eat the spaghetti we're having tomorrow or the stew we're serving tonight?" Miss Pritchard smirked.

CJ had a growing glow to his eyes. "No, but I bet they'd love going to the Whelan Mansion. With live music and celebrities in attendance, people would come from all over, even if we did serve the spaghetti from tomorrow or the beef stew from tonight."

"But I don't know Mr. Whelan." Annalee's insecurities closed in. She'd seen these things thrown but had never been involved in organizing one of them. And while she knew a few people of celebrity status who might attend, she couldn't pull off an event like this.

"I do." CJ smiled at her. "Do you think we can pull this off by the week before Thanksgiving?"

"So soon?" Her voice squeaked.

Miss Pritchard narrowed her eyes. "May I see you in my office, CJ?"

The two left her, and she scurried to the bathroom where she should have been all along. Obviously, Miss Pritchard was fussing at CJ for his crazy plan. While she hated for him to be getting into trouble, at least Annalee would be off the hook for preparing such an extravagant evening.

As she cleaned, her mind began to wander about the possibilities of such an evening. The people who might come and the items that could be auctioned. Her mind's journey finally paused with the sight of CJ, tuxedoed and smiling at her.

Silly fantasy.

She finished up with her task and spent the rest of the

afternoon playing with the kids. This time instead of kickball, it was a rousing game of soccer.

CJ played along, with no hint of his earlier conflict with his superior. When they hit a water break, he jogged toward her. "I think this gala is a great idea, Annalee."

"Miss Pritchard didn't fuss at you about it?" Would Annalee actually have to put this together?

"Heavens no." He laughed. "But we should get started on it right away. Why don't you use the desk and write up some ideas we can talk out?" He wiped his face on his sleeve. "I'll keep an eye on things out here."

Sitting inside on such a gorgeous, albeit warm, day wasn't her favorite notion, but she made some calls and found interest from one of her friends on the cast of a daytime television show. She also discussed possibilities of her neighbor, a highly popular star of film, making an appearance. A good start.

By the time the kids started leaving, she had some things to report. Several pieces of art, exclusive products, and a couple of services had already been donated. Five different people of varying celebrity status planned to come if the date worked out, including her first two contacts, a professional golfer who was a friend of her father's, the author of a recent New York Times bestseller, and a country western singer who had gone to school with her.

She'd even made a preliminary call to a caterer who was a personal friend of her family. He would do all he could to work on the date once it was chosen, donating the food and his own service to the cause. If only they could find a team of cater waiters who would donate their work for the evening.

CJ beamed at her. "This is outstanding. I'll speak with my ... Mr. Whelan, and set a date as soon as possible."

Miss Pritchard stared at her, her jaw hanging slack. "I can't believe you did all of that in a few hours."

"Most people are happy to help in one way or another. These happen to be the type who will give of their time."

"Truly, amazing." The woman shook her head, her gaze lowering to the desk in front of her.

With all of the phone calls, Annalee failed to do part of her job. Memory of it sprang to mind. "Oh, dear. I forgot about the upstairs bathrooms."

"We'll deal with them tomorrow." The director waved off the detail.

"I'm very sorry, Miss Pritchard. I'll do them first thing."

"Call me Margo." A slight smile spread across the woman's face. Actually, a pleasant face. Not nearly so old-looking as when she scowled.

"Thank you for understanding, Margo." Annalee signed out. Collecting her purse, she floated to the front door. She didn't fool herself. She'd have to finalize this gala somehow, but once she did, the threat of jail would be gone. She was sure.

Chapter 18

CJ couldn't get over how Annalee had jumped into planning this gala. Still, something she said troubled the back of his mind. Something about never finishing her projects. If that happened he'd have a disaster on his hands.

But so far, she pressed on. By the end of the night, with several commitments in hand, he stood in awe of how the Lord worked through the catastrophe crashing all around him.

And in the midst of the destruction, the sun shone again, reflecting off of the beautiful face of a blonde with a gentle smile and gorgeous blue eyes drawing him in.

He followed her to the door, a habit he'd developed since that first night to make sure she got to her car all right. Although this night he wanted to somehow express his gratitude. His feelings.

He clung to the porch railing until she opened the gate then turned to switch off the porch light so he could see her. Though the street didn't have any lamps, the body shop next door kept a light burning above her parking place.

She walked past the corner of the center lot when CJ heard

voices. At first, he couldn't understand any words or see any people.

"Hey, pretty lady." A big guy darted from behind a bush near the street and grabbed Annalee.

CJ skipped the steps. Landing on the grass in full sprint, he abandoned the detour through the gate and instead vaulted over the wrought-iron fence.

Annalee's scream was muffled as the man planted his mouth on hers.

A second man joined the first, catching CJ mid-stride with a tackle. They both went down on the gravel lot, but CJ had both weight and training on his side. He shoved the little guy over his head and went for the other man. The second fellow caught him by the shoulder and swung a board at his face. CJ ducked and landed two fists into the thug's gut, finishing him with an uppercut that put him on the stones for a moment before he crawled away.

The first man yelled as Annalee's fingernails found his eye. He backhanded her with a powerful blow, sending her to the ground. CJ leaped at him. The man crashed into the side of the Mustang. CJ used the rebound from the blow to pull back and attack, landing a solid right into his jaw. The little guy flinched but recovered and caught CJ in a smash that loosened some teeth and sent him sprawling back over the gravel.

At least he had drawn attention away from Annalee. Margo came rushing down the sidewalk screaming at the man. "I've called the police."

He didn't seem to care.

CJ tried to get his bearings, but the guy pulled him up by his collar and readied to strike another blow. CJ slammed his forehead into the guy's nose as hard as he could. Gaining a quick release, he sank his foot into the man's abdomen. While he doubled over, CJ did a spinning kick that jerked the man's head backward and landed him on his behind. He rolled over and stumbled away.

Margo dashed to Annalee while CJ went down on one knee, breathing heavy. *Thank You, Jesus.* The words rolled in his mind over and over.

Sharp stones pierced Annalee's cheek and her side hurt from where she landed on the gravel. A scream caught in her throat, strangled when she saw the saw the two men battling above her. Her head swam as she tried to rise, and she listed to one side, falling.

A burn started in her jaw and pulsated through to her cheekbone and eye socket. Her mouth stung from the hit and also from the roughness of the man's kiss, his prickly stubble, and the taste of his foul breath.

"Annalee?" Margo helped her into a sitting position.

"I'm okay. I think … okay." Her own voice drifted in from some distance.

"I'll get ice." Margo leaned her against the Mustang's tire and sprinted for the center.

CJ knelt beside her. He cupped her cheek in one hand and searched her face with an intense stare.

Even with her blurry vision, she spotted blood tracking down his cheek. "You're hurt." She lifted one of her hands toward his cheek, but he caught it in his own and held it.

"Look at me, Annalee." His voice commanded her, but her eyes had teared up, making him a virtual kaleidoscope.

Red and blue lights flashed on the streets. A policeman rushed toward them. She cringed. Not again. Her mother would never forgive her for yet another police report which included her name.

"She needs to go to the ER." CJ didn't sound nearly as injured as he looked. Annalee wanted to argue with him, but her mouth stopped working as the earth tilted to the right.

The next hour or so was a blur. A couple of attendants lifted her from the ground and strapped her onto a gurney. Lights blinded her. She tried to sit up as an ambulance spirited her down the Dallas streets, but belts held her in place.

She tried again when they untied her and moved her to another gurney. This time, a woman in scrubs held her against the pad with a hand on her shoulder. "You're all right. Lie still." The woman jogged along beside her rolling bed. What happened to CJ?

From somewhere Margo gave Annalee's name to someone. Might as well have been announcing it over a loudspeaker with a *ladies and gentlemen* to announce her. She could see the headlines already. At least there had been no one around to YouTube a video of this encounter.

"I don't need all of this fuss." She started with a croak but forced her voice to sound somewhat normal. "I'm feeling better." Although that meant little, considering before, she barely knew her own name.

"Relax. You'll be fine."

Wheeled into a curtained cubicle, Annalee stared at the ceiling for a second until a man's face appeared above her, thin with pinched features and a light brown comb-over. "Do you know where you are, Miss Chambers?"

"A hospital." Memories emerged from the fog and started making sense. "Emergency room. And considering where I was, I would guess Baylor Medical Center."

"Excellent hypothesis. I deduce you have full use of your faculties." He flashed a light into her eyes. "Seems like you've had a couple of nasty blows, but your pupils look fine. Do you remember what happened?"

"A man attacked me. He hit me across the face, and I landed in the gravel."

"Hmm." He covered one of her eyes with his fingers then let the light shine full force. "Your injuries seem to bear that out." He wrote something in the metal book and set it down. "Let me help you sit up."

He reached out his hand and pulled her vertical in ultra-slow-motion. Good thing, too. Her head swam with the first movement.

He paused. "Need a moment?"

She lifted a finger. As though her equilibrium kicked in after being out of whack, the moment passed, and she felt balance return.

"You seem to have a mild concussion. Certainly, no permanent damage. In fact, your thinking has seemed to clear. Do you remember the names of the people who brought you here?"

"Margo and CJ."

He put his penlight into his pocket and wrote something on a paper in a metal flip file. "Good thing we don't have a crowd tonight." He pressed a button that elevated the head of the bed. "I'm going to want you to relax here for a bit." He helped her lean back onto the bed.

"Comfy?"

Was he kidding? "How long?"

"I'll want to check on you again in an hour. Just to make sure I haven't missed anything."

Ugh. But at least it wasn't overnight, and she didn't have to call her parents.

She dozed a bit and someone grabbed her from behind saying, "Hey, pretty lady."

She jerked awake. The curtains were still closed. The lights still bright, and she was still alone. Great, the experience would likely revisit her nightly for a long time.

"Oh, good. You're awake." The same doctor pulled open the curtain and stepped in, advancing with his penlight.

"How long have I been asleep?" She sat up before he reached her and this time had no dizziness whatsoever.

"About two hours." He flicked the beam from one eye to the other and back. "Follow the light with your eyes only. Don't move your head."

No problem. She concentrated on the acrobatics of the little luminous globe for what felt like another hour. "Okay." He put the pen away again. "You will likely have a blistering headache tomorrow. Drink plenty of water. No physical activity, or intense cognitive activity for the next twenty-four hours. Only rest, sleep, and you can color if you want."

"I can't work tomorrow?" She had to work.

He looked at his clipboard. "Unless work consists of nothing more than licking envelopes and pulling out staples, no." He closed it and smiled at her, creating the impression of a jovial pretzel stick. "And no driving."

Tucking the board under his arm, he breezed out of the curtained entrance.

Now what? She'd finally felt her pressure release only to have the intensity resume. This time to excruciating measures.

CJ's fight flitted through her mind. He'd been injured. Had stumbled toward her. His sweet eyes had been so worried. Where was he?

She'd about decided to try her luck at standing and making her way out when a very large nurse waddled through the curtains. Her hips pulled the lightweight fabric along, but she didn't seem to notice. "Doctor says you can leave when you have a ride."

Shoot. Why hadn't she thought of that before she'd fallen asleep? Parker would come for her. And she had no doubt Kendra wouldn't mind driving her Mustang home. "I'll have one, though it will take a bit for them to get here." She started to slip off of the table.

"You wait right there, missy. No walking until tomorrow morning unless you have help. I'll wheel you into the waiting room." Another woman brought a wheelchair through the curtain. The large nurse helped Annalee into the chair and laid her purse in her lap. With everything else happening, she hadn't even thought about her belongings.

Margo jumped up when Annalee rolled into the waiting room. "I thought you might be staying the night."

She shook her head. "No, but the doctor says I need rest. I can't come into work tomorrow. He wants me to sleep as much as possible for the next twenty-four hours."

"Not to worry." Margo patted her arm. "None of this is your doing."

"Has CJ come out yet?"

As though his name called him forth, the doors opened and a nurse wheeled him toward them. He held up a hand. "I'll take it from here." When the chair stopped, he stood and stepped away from it.

She crossed her arms in front of her. "How come you get to walk around? The nurse said I couldn't. Not even when I get home."

"Did they confirm a concussion?"

She nodded. "A mild one. You could tell?"

He shook his head. "Not out there in the dark. But I played football all through school and into college. I've seen dozens of concussions, and I know not to ignore the possibility of one." He took the handles of the wheelchair. "Let's get you home."

"Oh, I meant to call my chauffeur. He and his—"

"I can take you home, Annalee. We'll drop off Margo on the way."

"And I thank you." Margo fell into step beside Annalee.

CJ stopped her chair just outside the door. "I'll get your car." He pulled a sparkling key fob from his pocket. Wait, that was her keychain.

"My car?"

"Your keys were left on the ground." Margo stepped near. "We thought it would be easier for your family if the car was here. Of course, we also thought you'd be there overnight, but I'm glad they didn't need to keep you." She smiled down at her and squeezed her shoulder.

"How will CJ get back to his truck?"

"Oh, that man's got all sorts of friends who will give him a lift. Don't you worry a second about that."

She could certainly believe that. And in truth, she looked forward to the ride home with him.

He pulled the car under the covered driveway, and Margo opened the passenger door. Annalee was fine. Seriously. She didn't need all the fuss. But there he was, jogging around the car. She pulled herself up with the edge of the car door and slipped into her seat before he reached her. He almost looked disappointed but climbed back into the driver's spot.

Margo got into the back seat and began a tour-guide discussion that would rival some of the best docents Annalee had heard. "This city has changed you know. Back when I grew up in this area, the people here knew one another."

Margo rattled on about Dallas history while Annalee stared out the window at the lights.

"My dad would take my brother and me down to White Rock Lake. We'd walk over to Winfrey Point. Sometimes he'd buy us a hot dog when there was a baseball game going on at the field there. Once, we took the whole day and walked all the way around to Flagpole Hill and back. About did old Dad in, but there were always interesting folks out at that lake. Not so much anymore."

Annalee's interest piqued. She'd never heard of these places, though she'd seen the lake many times. They passed the spillway attached to the park and peeled into a neighborhood straight out of the 1940s. "Why not, Margo?"

"I don't think folks care so much as they used to about special places and other people. And that right there is a symptom of the way we've turned our back on God."

What did caring about a tiny lake in the corner of Dallas have to do with God?

"When we stop caring about what the Lord thinks, we're apt to do all sorts of things and never even consider we're in the wrong. And that's only if we care about right and wrong in the first place." Margo must have been listening to Annalee's thoughts.

"Uh-oh, she's on a roll." CJ turned on a side street to stop at a green clapboard house with white shutters. "Sorry to cut you short, Madam Pritchard, but your castle awaits."

Looked like a cozy house, but Annalee wondered if Margo ever became lonely. "Thank you for your help, tonight, Margo."

"We make a pretty good team, the three of us." The woman winked in Annalee's direction.

CJ got out. "Keep the doors locked until I get back." He jogged around to the older woman. Margo swatted his hand as he offered his arm. She sashayed in front of him at double speed and trotted up her steps.

As Annalee watched, the porch light flared. Margo pointed her finger up at CJ's face. He gave a shake of his head and crossed his arms in front of his chest. Margo shut the door with a bob of her head at CJ and a wave at Annalee.

He strode back toward the Mustang, unlocked the door, and climbed in. "Wow. She really likes you."

Annalee lifted her head from the rest. "She does?"

"She included you on our team. I'd say that qualifies as liking you."

Then how come she complained to Laurel Stewart. Annalee wanted to ask him but remembered he, too, had been on the list of the discontented over Annalee's behavior at the center. Maybe the poor reports had occurred when she'd first come?

He turned right onto Garland Road heading west. "Have you ever been up there? Winfrey Point?"

She shook her head. "I think I remember hearing Father mention the area around the lake as a dangerous place, though."

"At night, maybe. But not any more than anyplace else in this city. And it's beautiful, great view of the skyline, the lake. I'd love to show it to you sometime."

That sounded like a request for a date. Annalee rolled her head to the side and studied his profile.

He glanced at her and gave a half-smile. "If you'd like to."

Love to. Her mind had no opportunity to squeeze out a logical or responsible thought before her heart shouted at her. "I'd like that very much."

"Maybe Sunday afternoon?"

"Sunday." She stifled a smile and looked back out her window at the streaks of lights. Sunday couldn't arrive fast enough.

CJ turned west on Northwest Highway and caught a glimpse of Annalee's reflection in her window. A sliver of a smile carved her face. She'd not only agreed to go out with CJ, but her expression made it clear she looked forward to it.

He stifled the whoop begging to emerge and kept driving.

"You've lived in this city a long time?" Annalee turned toward him.

"Most of the time." With boarding school and college, this didn't lead to an easy answer.

"What's your favorite place here? Where do you love to go? Not because you have to be there or because someone else wants you there"

He glanced into her sleepy eyes. Sweet and uninhibited as some of the children he worked with. "The Center."

"No, you can't choose that. You work there."

"Why not. It's where I love to be." There were other special places in Dallas, like Five Sixty at Reunion Tower, his father's box at the American Airlines Center, the terrace of his condominium. But none of those places connected with the CJ she believed him to be.

Once again, he internally kicked himself for not telling her the whole truth about himself. He turned toward her, but her eyes were half-closed. She'd been through enough tonight.

And he did love the center. "I have people there I care about who need me."

Her smile dropped away. Her eyes fixed on the dashboard in front of her.

"Annalee?"

"I don't have any place like that." She didn't move. "Somewhere to belong." She gave a rueful chuckle. "Not even at home. My mother will be ten times happier when I finally move away."

"I'm sure you're wrong." He couldn't imagine someone wanting to get rid of a lady like her.

"I'm not exaggerating. And I'm not feeling sorry for myself. Not too much anyway. It's not like I don't have friends. I could arrive at a party on any given night and be surrounded by a dozen of my closest friends whom I hardly know."

"Am I on that list?" He well understood loneliness in a crowd.

"No. Not on that list." She shifted in her seat and leaned back against the window. "You're someone I do know. And you've been kind to me even when I've been at my worst. And you don't judge me by my pedigree, my financial statements, or my connections."

"And I am your friend, Annalee." Though he'd been a lousy one. A secret keeper. He'd kept silent for too long. She'd be hurt when he did tell her.

He turned onto the lane leading to her driveway. His heart matching the beat of a soundtrack from an old movie. He slowed to a stop before her entrance and put the car into park. "I hope you believe I care about you. That you'll remember."

She pursed her lips. "My reticence has nothing to do with you, CJ." She locked eyes with him. "Recent experience has me doubting every person, every action."

"I get it." He shifted back into gear and entered her drive waved on by the security patrol on site. "But I plan to do all I can to change your mind. At least as far as it concerns me."

He vowed to keep the pledge. Even if it meant enduring her scorn. But this still wasn't the night for that revelation.

He parked at the gap between the tall bushes directly in front of the large entrance. A gas lamp lit the bricks of the path and illuminated a broad circle with warm gold light. He got out and circled the car to help Annalee. She clung to him for a moment.

"I'm not supposed to walk until morning." She put a hand to her head. "I think I understand why."

He didn't let go. Instead, he supported her back, bent, and scooped her legs into his arms.

"Oh, dear. No, this isn't necessary." She flutter-kicked her legs. "Please."

"Doctor's orders." He paused and looked into her eyes. "Besides, you're a featherweight."

She pressed her lips together in a shy smile but stopped fidgeting. "How will you get home?"

"I called a friend to pick me up. He'll probably be here by the time I walk back down to the lane."

"You have friends willing to come out in the middle of the

night to pick you up?"

A whiff of honeysuckle hair filled the air, and he resisted the urge to breath deeper. "Yes. And so do you. Or what have I been doing all night?"

"CJ?"

He paused just before the door and glanced down at her again.

This time, her calm gaze peered directly into his eyes. "I haven't thanked you for what you did when that man …" She flinched. "When he attacked me."

The memory of the man's violation heated his shoulders. He ground his molars for a moment before releasing an exhale. He gently lowered her feet to the porch.

She turned to face him, her hands resting on his chest. "I don't know what I would have done …" Her voice broke.

He reached up and stroked her bruised cheekbone, now only hinting at colors to come. Brushing a strand of hair from her face, he scanned every detail, noting the streaked mascara and the split lip.

She stepped closer, and he allowed his finger to caress her lips, taking care when he moved over the injured area.

Her gaze dropped to his mouth. But to kiss her torn lip would only cause her more pain.

And twist his heart into pieces.

Instead, he planted a soft kiss near the corner of her mouth. Below the bruise from the man's blow and beside the injury caused by the rocky ground onto which she fell.

"Let's get you inside." He reached to lift her into his arms again when he sensed a nearby presence.

"I can help her from here." A male voice spoke from the darkness, and CJ braced himself for another battle.

A man stepped into the illumination from the porch. "I've been worried about you. Kendra heard your car come in and sent me out to check."

"I had a bit of a problem." Annalee introduced CJ to her chauffeur and explained the issue at the center and the hospital.

This was the guy who picked her up that night? The one who met her with such an intimate embrace. CJ stiffened. "The doctor doesn't want her walking."

"A good thing you were there. My wife and I are a little protective of Annalee."

His wife? CJ shook the man's hand and allowed him to take his position helping Annalee.

"Thanks for your help." He lifted Annalee into his arms and opened the front door.

"Yes, thank you, CJ." Her sincere gratitude warmed him.

He turned to walk back down the lane. The intimate embrace he'd witnessed before … was that only her chauffeur's support. Heck, his wife might have been behind the smoky glass, and CJ would never have known.

His grin grew as he departed with a lighter heart and a head full of plans.

Marji Laine

Chapter 19

Annalee rose early the next morning. Corlia helped her to the covered patio beside the pool house and promised to bring her some breakfast when the coast was clear.

Avoiding Mother was going to be a challenge. No amount of makeup would cover Annalee's wounds, though, so avoidance was the only answer. She donned her bug-eyed sunglasses as Father crossed the patio.

His face was beet-ish, and not likely from the weather since it wasn't that warm. "Parker told me there was an altercation last night?"

"I'm okay." And she was, when her dreams gave her some peace. "The doctor just wants me to rest today."

"I won't make you go through the story again. Parker gave me the highlights." Her father went down on one knee and pulled her glasses down. He pressed his lips together in a disgusted line. "Hard to see my baby-girl like this."

"I really am okay." She lifted the glasses back in place. "But

I might need some help keeping Mother away. If she sees me like this, she'll insist that I give up the work at the center."

"I'm not sure that isn't the right choice. I know the chief judge. He has some sway over the probation office. And nobody would profit from something like this stirring up over required community service. After this ... event, there's plenty of evidence that you have no business being down there."

She leaned forward. "But you can't. I've worked so hard."

"Now, now. I didn't say I'd call him. But I could get you reassigned. At least placed in an office with security and ... adults."

She pulled the glasses down again and caught his gaze. "I really love working there. I wouldn't want to go anywhere else. Please don't force me to leave."

He sighed. "You're an adult, Annalee. I'm not in the habit of forcing you to do anything, and I won't start now." He kissed the top of her head. "As for your mother, she's got some club group. She wouldn't come out here even if she was at home. Hates the smell of the water." He turned to go back inside.

Corlia reappeared shortly after he left. "I have breakfast." She arranged a low table with a plate and a tall glass of ice water. "Parker says to drink all of this and a refill before the hour is up."

Sounded like Parker. As if on cue, his better-half ventured from their garage apartment. "You getting her set up, Corlia?"

"Yes, but I'll have to attend to my duties."

"No problem. I've got the invalid."

Annalee glared at her, though her friend couldn't possibly see the look through the dark glasses. "Sitting right here ..."

Kendra chuckled and held out the controller for the flat screen secured under the shelter. "I've already cued up that series I was telling you about last week."

"The historical one from Canada?" It had sounded so good, but Annalee seldom settled down enough to just sit and watch television.

"The very one. Should give you plenty of mindless enjoyment. Between that and the cooler cloud cover, you should be all set." Kendra set her chaise at an angle.

She looked like a plump sentry with a Dallas Child magazine and one eye on the back door at all times.

Thanks to the clouds, they were able to stay on the patio the full day, long past the time when the sunlight would have traipsed into their protection. And the plan worked. Annalee didn't even see her mother the whole day.

Twenty-four hours after the incident, her cheek reached a deep purple shade, and her lip looked like she'd gone a round with a martial arts master.

Her father had checked on her after sharing dinner with Mother. He'd fussed, again threatening to use his influence and pictures of her face to pressure the judge into letting Annalee take an easier position or canceling her probation entirely.

Exactly what Laurel Stewart had instructed her to do. But she couldn't let him do it. "Think of how bad that would reflect on you, Father. The media will spout all over that I received special attention."

"You deserve special attention. The area is monstrous." He struck his determined candidate pose. "And cleaning out the crime will be one of my first priorities when I take office."

"Fine, but for now, I'll be more careful. I'm grateful the incident didn't hit the news. Let's keep it that way."

He tilted his head. "The reporters have been pretty brutal to you, haven't they?"

"Enough to want this whole thing to fade away."

His mouth flattened, and he nodded. "I suppose I understand that. I'm willing to let the matter drop this time, especially since you seem to have a personal bodyguard working with you. I'd like to meet this new man of yours."

"He's not mine, Father." She didn't tell him of the hinted intimacy of their good-bye the night before. She also didn't tell him about the date they'd planned. Father had enough to think about with the election going on. Romance wasn't his thing anyway.

But CJ's invitation remained foremost on Annalee's mind the next afternoon when she arrived at the center. After signing in, she went in search of Margo, but she kept a covert eye out for him as well.

She found neither inside. Paula greeted her with a warm hug. "Missed you yesterday. I'm so sorry for what you had to go through."

"Thank you. I'm feeling better." She'd worked on her makeup to cover the bruises but expected to stay away from the children. She didn't want to explain the assault.

"Good thing CJ was around, though. I'd hate to think what might've happened."

A shudder rippled across her shoulders. Not the first time since the attack. "Do you know where he is? I mean, where Margo is?" Stupid Freudian slip.

Paula eyed her with pursed lips. "Might should look out by the shed. I think I heard them talking about the lock on it a bit ago."

She thanked her and took slow steps across the great room toward the entry. Steady. Calm. If for no other reason than to eliminate the assumptions Annalee could see in the older woman's eyes. Exiting the front, she trotted down the steps and out the gate. A shiver crept across her spine. Why had she come this way?

But the sun shone. Men from the body shop next door called out to one another. Cars sped by and pedestrians waited on the corner of the intersection. Hard to believe this was the same harrowing place from two nights before.

She patted the Mustang as she passed it and skirted the wrought-iron fence on her way to the side lot.

"I don't see anything else missing." CJ's voice as the sounds of metal against metal and wood signified his movements.

Missing? She neared the door. Deep scratches marked where something pried the metal hinge out of the wood. It hung on the face, dangling from the padlock.

A bright beam cut through the interior on the other side of the open door. "Still it adds up."

"Think about a thousand?" Margo stepped outside and clicked off the flashlight.

"More than that." CJ stopped at the entrance, his hands resting against the upper beam of the doorway. "Well, Sunshine. Good to see you back in action."

His sweet nickname warmed her. Or was it the smile? "Looks like someone had a go at the door."

"Just a tad." Margo's flattened lips curved into a smile. "You look better than the last time I saw you." She reached an arm around Annalee and gave a squeeze. "Plan to take today easy."

"I covered the bruises, but I thought I should probably stay away from the children."

"Good thinking. Plan the gala. That's the best way for you to help."

Exactly what she had in mind.

The woman proceeded to the backyard. CJ hadn't moved.

"I heard you mention things missing."

He seemed dazed, but shook it off and drew closer. "Yeah. Sometime last night, someone stole the riding mower, an edger and trimmer, and several pieces of high-dollar tools."

She squinted. "Worth a thousand dollars?"

"Probably more." The words came out as a groan. "Another reason for my … boss to shut this place down."

"Not if we can replace everything missing. Maybe even build a sturdier structure."

"We can't do everything, Annalee." A sad smile spread across his face. "But I thank you for trying." He fingered her bangs.

Her gaze shot to her toes and a grin pressed her cheeks. "I should get to work, out of sight, before the children get here." And she needed to make a call.

She followed Margo's path as CJ stepped back inside the shed. She waited until she reached the corner and pulled out her phone.

Her father's greeting came over the line directly after the first ring. "Are you all right?"

"I'm fine, but someone …" What was she thinking? Her father was already upset at the lack of security in the area.

"Someone? Annalee?"

Pausing was an even worse idea than spitting it out. "I'm here. Someone broke into an old dilapidated shed at the center. They stole some pretty expensive things. Riding mower, other yard … things." What did he call them? "And some tools."

"I'm sorry to hear that."

"Is Mr. Stackard still your client?" She clamped her front teeth together.

"I see where you're going with this."

"I thought he might have some replacements he could donate."

"Like in-store models for display?" Her father understood. "I suppose I can ask him, but it sounds like you need a new shed."

Bingo. "That's a wonderful idea. And maybe even a security light?"

"Why do I get the feeling I've just been conned?"

"It's for a good cause." She didn't want her father to think her insincere. "If you could see these children here. You'd know why I love this place so much."

"Let me see what I can put together." He said good-bye.

Annalee hugged herself. Father would work this out. If only to partly repay the man who saved her life.

She made quick work of the bathrooms then joined Margo in the kitchen to wait for the children to finish their outdoor play.

The swift opening of the front door jarred her. Too early for parents. She leaned into the great room to catch a view of the entry hall through the office. "Father?"

"There you are."

Margo followed her into the large room. Her mouth sagged. "Uh … Mr. …." She furiously rubbed her soapy arms on a tiny cup-towel and threw it into the kitchen. "Mr. Chambers." She advanced with her hand extended. "I'm Margo Pritchard."

He shook her hand. "Very nice to meet you, Miss Pritchard. Annalee tells me you had some trouble last night?"

Annalee kissed her father's cheek. "Yes, but you didn't have to come down here."

"Why not? I have the replacement you suggested."

"The shed?" At his smile, she threw her arms around his neck. "Oh, thank you."

Margo looked stunned. "You brought a shed?"

"State of the art. I don't think you'll be having any more petty-theft troubles." Her father grinned at the woman.

The back-screen door slammed into place and heavy boots stomped through the kitchen. "Margo, can you tell me why several men are hauling my gear onto the back porch?" CJ's voice carried into the great room a full sentence before the rest of him. He glanced at Annalee. She lifted her eyebrows and gave a slight shrug.

He offered his hand. "Mr. Chambers. Nice of you to visit."

Father turned to Annalee. "This the guy?"

At her nod, he accepted the handshake. "Call me Todd."

"CJ."

"Well, CJ, seems I owe you deep gratitude for taking care of my little girl the other night."

Margo elbowed him. "He's giving us a new shed."

"It's the least I could do." He tucked his chin and put his arm around Annalee. "And I mean the very least I could do. I can't hope to repay you for stepping in like you did."

The smile CJ leveled melted her. Good thing Father held her up.

"And tomorrow, a new security light will arrive. During the morning hours so you don't have to worry about the workers getting in the way of the kids." He took a breath and tapped Annalee's nose. "And if you'll get me a list of everything that's missing, I have a good friend who would like to replace it all."

Annalee hopped. A good friend could only be one person. "Mr. Stackard?"

"Stackard?" CJ squinted his blue eyes. "As in Stackard Home and Garden?"

"The same. So, I'm going to need that list."

"Thank you." CJ pumped her father's hand.

Annalee relished the sparkle in his eye.

"You're quite welcome, but I wonder if you all would mind me taking my daughter to an early dinner." He put his arm around her again. "This campaign is straining, as you can probably imagine."

Margo straightened. "By all means. Please. She could use another evening off, anyway. Make sure she's completely restored."

She glanced at her father. What was his purpose in taking her to dinner? She eyed CJ, hating that she had to leave. If only she'd hugged his neck while she'd had the chance.

As much as CJ looked forward to his time with Annalee, he'd acted in haste. He hadn't prayed over the invitation, and he couldn't ignore the negative truth of this encounter. The most important thing in his life, his faith, wasn't something she shared.

But what can I do? How did he add a stipulation of faith at the beginning of their relationship? If she actually did care for him, she'd go through the motions. Besides, manipulation wasn't his thing. And she'd already shared her irritation of being tooled. That and her insistence that she had no real friends probably meant she'd been used before for her money or influence.

CJ could relate. Having people seek him out only for his social standing or wealth only led to deep feelings of inadequacy and insecurity. While Annalee seemed to be a little blind to the devotion that her father, her chauffeur, and apparently his wife, had for her, he couldn't fault her sensitivity to being used.

Like he'd been used. But then, he'd been a great user, too. He'd had everything—skill, fame, money, sex—and still played the game of making the right connections to step up his personal ambition ladder. He had been no better than his father.

And that realization had made him want to throw it all away at the end of a needle.

What an empty life. He'd worn the mask, fooled everyone, even his father was clueless. But he'd been a time bomb.

If only he could find a way to touch Annalee like the misplaced Yankee fan who goaded him into revealing his intentions to end it all when he'd happened into the Brimming Café. What would have happened to him if he hadn't taken Tony's dare to try something different? To try going to church. He'd never have heard of God's love.

Annalee needed to hear about it, too.

This very situation begged his action. If she meant as much to him as … Everyone deserved the chance to know Christ. He called a couple of his friends and asked them to pray for her heart. Then he dialed her number. Hopefully not for the final time.

A banquet? Annalee should have known better than to think her father actually wanted some one-on-one time with her. Not that he wasn't kind and complimentary, but Mother's headache left him needing an escort. With Ramona in Milan, who else could he invite?

Supporting Father was part of life. But three hours of smiling and making small talk with perfect strangers wearied her. She'd rather be playing soccer or kickball. How was it that she had no trouble striking up conversations with the kids, about bugs or clouds or the Cowboys? But listening to businesspeople go on and on about the state of their companies, the things the city should be doing for them, and the way Annalee could invest drained every ounce of interest from her mind. At least her makeup job had kept her injuries from being a topic of conversation.

Her brain hadn't fully returned to functioning when her phone rang on the return trip home. Father had his own pressed to his ear, in conference with his campaign manager. She glanced at the screen and saw CJ's name.

"Church?" The shocked tone of her voice gave him plenty of reason to pause.

But too much was at stake. "Yeah. You can ride with me to do the pickup at Rosewood Homes, visit the service and my fellowship class, and then we can have our picnic after we take the kids back home."

"I don't know too much about church. I'd feel … I mean …"

"I'll be with you the whole time. Nothing fancy. Very informal. And wear comfortable shoes."

"Are you sure?" She paused. "It's not that … I'm used to chatting about politics and social reform. I wouldn't know what to talk about."

He'd pulled her out of her comfort zone. Hopefully not so far she resented him for the action. "Please come. I know it's a challenge, but you've mastered so many challenges this fall."

"You think so?" Her voice warmed.

How could she doubt her accomplishments? "Absolutely. And if you hate it, we can leave. I can get someone else to do my bus drop off."

"I'm not worried about hating it."

No. She probably worried about dealing with something she didn't understand. He related. "I'll pick you up at eight?"

"Okay." An unsure tone returned. "I don't want to embarrass you."

That was it. The truth of her concern. Always worried about shaming her family. Her friends.

"You couldn't do that if you tried." From the sound of her good-bye, he had a feeling she didn't believe him. He hit the red circle and gripped the phone like a lifeline. *God, please don't let me mess this part up. Even if I've already blown any chance with her. She needs You.*

Chapter 20

As interested as she'd been, speaking with Mrs. Madison, Annalee hadn't expected a trip to church in the near future. The few visits she'd made to the church near the club crossed her mind. Formal. Standing and sitting. Reading out loud in chorus and then singing songs in old English.

None of her experiences matched the enthusiasm Tally and her mom had shown. Nor did the relaxed, informality CJ described match the atmosphere during the services she'd sat through.

Sunday morning, her insides rocked with crickets and butterflies. The wings stimulated her. The hopping, sticky feet attacked her courage.

Breakfast wasn't within the realm of possibility. Even if she could have kept something down, she'd not invite her mother's curled lip when she learned Annalee planned to miss their weekly brunch in favor of a church service. While she didn't know of mother's opinion of spiritual things, she tended to disdain anything in which she didn't actively participate.

At the last minute, she remembered instruction to wear

comfortable shoes. She raced upstairs for some slip-ons that matched her chocolate-colored pants and fall layers. Checking the mirror one more time, she proclaimed herself as good as she could get.

For whatever she'd encounter.

She waited for him on the lane. Her heart danced as he pulled the truck toward her. Leaving it running, he climbed out. "You look great."

"Will I blend in?" If she could just avoid wretched humiliation, she'd be thrilled.

He laughed and opened her door. "Not a chance. Face it, Annalee. You could wear rags and turn every head in the room."

With warming cheeks, she suppressed a wide grin and slipped into her seat. CJ's charm and easy manner engaged her into downtown. Much like he did with the children at the center. But he didn't consider her a child. And surely not a project, though he used the same natural engagement with everyone. Wait. Was his invitation to the picnic just a way to get her into his church? The crickets began to swarm.

He'd asked her out. A date. He was interested, right? She hoped that was right. Especially with her affection growing. Even if Mother would never approve of a handyman as a match for her daughter, Annalee's interest in, and respect for, CJ continued to rise.

By the time they took the bus to Rosewood Homes, the crickets in her stomach had diminished to a smattering. Mrs. Madison, Tally, Tyrone, and Hayden climbed aboard.

Tyrone helped his sister up the steps.

"You're here." She wrapped her arms around Annalee. "I'm so glad you came."

The fervor of the girls greeting warmed her heart. "Me, too." Tally settled in beside her.

"I didn't know you was coming." Tyrone gave her a fist bump.

"Me neither." Hayden mimicked his brother then followed him across the aisle where they both tapped CJ on the back of his head.

Mrs. Madison smiled at her. "Time for the blessing to be blessed, I see."

"I don't know much about blessing." But the woman's words each time they'd spoken ignited a deep desire to understand.

"You will, chile. You will."

The boys spent the rest of the ride introducing her to everyone else on the bus whether they wanted to know her or not. Annalee glowed with their enthusiasm. Maybe she was beginning to feel that niche CJ had spoken of?

After the bus emptied, he walked her up two flights of steps and into a room about the size of the great room at the center. The internal hopping bugs returned when he started introducing her to some lovely, vibrant women and kind, engaging men. She smiled and maintained her demeanor as she'd been taught. But the people seemed warm and friendly. Not like her mother's friends or her father's clientele.

One of the ladies, about her age, Chrissy, offered her a cup of coffee and a donut. At first, she only took the coffee, but the more she talked to the people, mostly the other women, the more her stomach settled. She finally wandered toward the box and chose a chocolate muffin.

CJ met her at the box. "Decided you were hungry after all?"

"Starved, but this is too big. Will you split it with me?"

He chuckled and cut it into two pieces with the handle of a

spoon.

"I hate to admit it. I was too nervous to eat."

"People are people." He took a bite of his half. "But I understand insecurity. Especially when you didn't know what to expect."

He did understand. Like he could crawl into her head and examine her thoughts. She finished off her muffin about the time someone flashed the room lights. CJ pointed to seats he'd secured. "What are we doing now?" She leaned toward him and whispered as the room volume lowered to a softer roar.

"The teacher, Mark Carrier, is going to give us some things to think about from God's Word." He laid his Bible across his lap and pointed to a place on the page closest to her.

"What does that mean?"

CJ smiled but didn't answer.

God's Word. The Bible. She got that much. What was there to think about?

Her interest grew during the next forty minutes. The teacher, Mark, talked through a piece from a section near the end of the book. Ephesians. He went sentence by sentence through a prayer that the writer wrote. But this was a letter. Written to some stranger 2,000 years ago. Why did the words feel so important? Like they were meant for her somehow?

Men and women commented, one with tears, about how this chapter touched her life like no other. Another mentioned how he prayed these very words over his brother for years. How his brother had changed his life completely.

She read through the passage again. "... strengthen you with power through His Spirit." The Spirit part seemed unusual, but certainly nothing magical in the words. "… to know this love that surpasses knowledge."

That phrase … drew her. How she wanted to understand love like that. But therein lay the irony. Love to that extreme couldn't be understood. But even without comprehension, maybe she could experience such? This wasn't romance. And as dear as her father was, it certainly went deeper than her family.

How could she experience what the writer expressed?

Faces around the room glowed with inner excitement. Like CJ's when he worked at the center. They had experienced such a love.

She wrote down the chapter and verse from the Bible CJ shared with her—Ephesians chapter three—and determined to read the section again. Maybe if she prayed something like this for herself, God would let her have a glimpse of such a love?

At the end of the hour, they moved into a huge sanctuary. CJ led her to the balcony, joining a row of others who had left the classroom with her and CJ.

"What did you think of the lesson?" Chrissy who had been so welcoming sat on her right while CJ sat on her left.

Should she ask how to experience the love of which the teacher spoke? She hardly knew these people, wanted to fit in, and certainly didn't want to embarrass CJ. She offered a tight smile. "I liked it."

Well, she had. Even if the study left her puzzled and aching. Like a song title she struggled to remember, the verses wouldn't leave her. "… I pray that you, being rooted and established in love, may have power … to grasp how wide and long and high and deep is the love of Christ …" If only she could fathom the meaning of these words. As much as she felt like the 2000-year-old writer spoke directly to her, she echoed the desire. She wanted that love.

Wanted to grasp it. Wanted to be rooted and established in it, whatever that meant.

"You'll like this." Chrissy called Annalee out of her quandary. Then she turned to the man beside her.

CJ leaned close. "What did you really think of the lesson?"

She paused, unsure of how to explain, yearning to understand. "It escaped me. I want to understand what he meant. About …" She couldn't bring herself to mention love, not wanting CJ to get the wrong idea. "Like the term, *God's Word*." She put her hand on his Bible. "I know that's another name for the Bible, but I don't know why."

"The Bible is a love letter to you, Annalee."

There was that word again.

"Even though men wrote it, God's own Spirit told them what to put down. And it shows you all about who He is. Then the story goes on to explain how much He loves you. Finally, the book details what He's planning to do for you."

Love. God loves her? Why would He do that? He didn't even know her. She blinked away the moisture that her thoughts conjured. "Why do you say it's for me?" It sounded too personal. Her logic kicked in. The Bible had been around for so long. God couldn't have written it for her specifically.

CJ shrugged. "Because He adores you."

Music started at that point. Good thing. CJ's reply was like an icy wind that struck Annalee. She reeled. *He adores you.* Compassion to a level of sacrifice. She'd already had a conversation with CJ about that word. And yet it whispered to her. Drawing her in.

The audience stood. The lyrics the band sang showed up on large screens at the front of the room. Annalee followed along but didn't sing. The words inspired her, building up within her like an inflating balloon.

The faces of the people leading the music showed sheer joy, with upturned faces and hands reaching toward the ceiling. They spoke to God, expounding on how He never would let them go no matter what they faced. And the next one had a dance beat. The people on the stage clapped and hopped. Like a party instead of the solemn services she'd seen before. And the lyrics moved her. "I Lay Me Down" had been a prayer her first nanny taught to her. But this song wasn't anything like the prayer. The singers spelled out their devotion to God, giving Him their whole lives, another concept which spun her insides.

That circled back to her concept of adoration. Only this time, it was offered to God. And they didn't look upset or sad about their sacrifice, but they did seem sincere. How did this work?

Following that was a song of the joy they had when they let God have His way. She glanced around. People all over the audience smiled at the ceiling. Even CJ. With his eyes closed and his hands palm up at his sides, he looked like he spoke directly to God.

Peace. Joy. Love. Straight off a Christmas card, but so real here, she could almost touch all three.

Trying not to grill Annalee over her feelings after church commanded most of CJ's self-control. She smiled and thanked several people but avoided his eye. Walking next to her in the parking lot, he wanted to take her hand, touch her back, something. But hesitated lest he break her intense concentration.

She kept her fingers laced together and her face controlled. He'd seen that look before. Her internal switch that maintained composure like she'd used at the Brimming Café with Myles.

The people who rode with him had already assembled. He counted heads as they loaded. Annalee beside him. He stepped her forward, but she resisted. Her calm demeanor cracked.

"I'm not sure …" She stepped backward.

"What's wrong?" He put his hand on her arm. "Are you feeling all right?"

She took a breath. "I don't want to talk right now."

CJ nodded. He'd been in her place. Needing to fathom what he'd learned. "I'll make this a fast trip."

This time, she had reached for his hand as she climbed aboard. Her soft touch and the slight pressure left an impression on his nerve endings. He squeezed his fist tight and released it, insisting his emotions behave.

During the ride to Rosewood Housing Complex, the children chatted with enthusiasm. Tally sat across from Annalee, her face glowing and expounding on the delights of the morning. "Wasn't the music so lit? I jes loved the words o'that one song, all over my story I see Your fingerprints." She twisted in her seat. "I love knowing God's got me in His hands even when I can't see it."

CJ had trouble keeping his eyes on the road and off the mirror which gave him the view of his passengers.

Mrs. Madison chimed in. "Mm-hmm. Especially when you feel like you're surrounded by chaos. You ever feel that way, Miss Annalee?"

"All the time." Her voice responded low, almost whisper-like.

She settled deeper into her seat. Silence smoothed over the bus for an instant.

The others must have noticed her discomfort.

She spoke up again, though. "Do you really believe God can be so concerned with only one person?"

CJ took a sharp intake.

Her innocent question earned a resounding "yes!" from those surrounding her. CJ glanced back to make sure the fervent answer hadn't upset her, but she seemed earnest in her question and accepting of the response.

"Why would He?" Annalee's simple question opened an in-depth discussion of God's love and the way He showed it. CJ had to concentrate on the road and tune out what was going on behind him, but he lifted a prayer for Annalee's heart and her acceptance of God's love.

After dropping off the passengers, they returned to the church in silence and transferred to his truck. He wanted to talk to her about her impression of church and her thoughts about the discussion topic on the way home but decided the better path would be to let her guide the conversation.

"I never thought of God in a personal way."

He hadn't expected anything so abrupt.

"I mean, I know about Jesus, but I've always thought of Him, God, as sort of distant."

"Like the Bette Midler song."

"Exactly. I find it hard to believe that He could be interested in my problems." She turned clear-blue eyes on him.

"He wants to be involved in every part of your life." He laid his hand on hers. "He adores you. You can trust Him with anything. Any problem." The light turned, and CJ withdrew his hand to shift into gear. He hadn't meant to touch her in the first place. It was a simple reaction.

She crossed her legs. "I can give Him any problem? Like my mother? I'd like to give Him my mother." She chuckled.

CJ joined her. "I take it, you and your mother don't get along very well."

"Oh, we get along fine. As long as I agree with her that I'm incompetent and incapable of doing anything on my own."

"You're not either of those things." He stopped at another traffic light.

"Tell her that." She traced her finger along the base of the passenger window. "On second thought, don't bother. Unless you have a Harvard degree or a country club ownership, she won't esteem your opinion anyway." She turned toward him. "I'm sorry. I shouldn't be talking about her. And it's not like she doesn't have a reason to complain. I have a studio filled with partially finished sketches and paintings."

"But that right there is proof of your creativity and skill."

"Oh, no. Painting doesn't count as talent."

"But didn't you win that talent contest? Margo said something about a Texas Princess?"

"Beauty Pageant. But it did have a talent portion." She let her head drop back on the headrest as the light turned green. "Mother had a fit about the talent I chose. I recited a poem about art and how it makes me feel while I painted an eight-foot picture of Michelangelo's Creation."

"Wow. How long did that take you?"

"Don't be too impressed. It was only enough of the picture to identify it, the hand portion. And only in gold and black." She laid her hands in her lap. "But I'd rehearsed it for weeks, and I thought it came off pretty well."

"It must have. You won."

She didn't respond for a few minutes. He resisted the temptation to alter the topic. Something unsaid hung between them for the rest of the journey. He pulled into an open lot for the park.

"About that win." She shifted in her seat to face him but kept her head down. "I thanked one of the judges after the pageant, and she snubbed me. She said my mother's donation sealed my success, and she didn't approve of manipulating contests in such a way."

"You're kidding."

"No. And she wasn't the only one who knew about it. The runner-up was counting on the first-place scholarship for her college tuition. She cursed me out." Annalee shut her eyes. "But I deserved it. I never cared about the scholarship."

"You didn't know."

She looked past him. Her brows ruffled over pain-filled eyes. "No, but I didn't really win anything. Mother bought me the crown. It would never do to have the name of Chambers sullied by a second-place status. Or, horrors, honorable mention. Mother set the whole thing up to lift our family status just a little higher."

Dislike for her mother grew, though he'd never met the woman. They unloaded the area behind his seat. He hauled out the basket he'd packed and followed a path uphill while she carried a large blanket folded over her arms.

He wanted to pursue the conversation. Wanted to see her make a decision to follow Christ, but he hesitated. This wasn't his fight. He would try again to open the door to the conversation and stand ready to encourage and share, but the Spirit had to urge her heart God-ward. He let the silence grow as he led her to the apex of the hill. Clouds kept the sun wrapped, so he veered away from the trees and settled on a spot overlooking White Rock Lake. Annalee laid out the blanket while he anchored the corners with the basket and several stones from a gravel walkway.

She lifted the lid of the basket.

"You asked if God cared to work through the problems of your life. I can tell you He can help you accomplish the tasks you set your hand to. Those things He wants you to do. Like the gala you're working on. And He can heal your relationship with your mother."

"Well, I'm not saying that I don't believe, but … there is a multitude of issues between my mother and me."

CJ smiled. This was something new he could pray for. "Wait and watch."

Chapter 21

How could she have exposed her deepest insecurities like that? Annalee glanced at CJ, while she unpacked the large basket he'd brought. A warm, humid breeze toyed with his hair. He faced the lake with his thumbs tucked into his front jean pockets and his feet planted.

She'd embarrassed herself and left him to try to make the rest of the afternoon tolerable. At the very least, she had to insist on getting lunch ready.

She unearthed deli sandwiches, a bag of tortilla chips and a jar of Picante. At the bottom of the basket, she found an insulated bag of water bottles, plates, and napkins, which she laid out on the yellow blanket that doubled as a tablecloth. "I think that's everything."

He turned. "Looks good. There are some cookies in there somewhere."

She clawed on the other side of the cold bag and found a bakery box of Tollhouse cookies. "Eureka. Mm. My favorite."

"Something else I didn't know about you."

Her cheeks grew warm, as he sat down across from her. Why had she told him all of that about her mom? And how could she turn the conversation to safer and more pleasant discussions?

He held out his hands. "May I pray for us?"

She'd heard grace said before meals many times, even heard him say it at Dallas Diner. Why did this one seem different? She laid her hands in his, relishing his warm caress, and closed her eyes.

"Lord, Annalee has questions. She's searching to understand Your love."

Chills crept across her shoulders. This was supposed to be grace. Why did CJ sound like he was having an everyday conversation? About her?

"Wrap Your arms around her, Father, and reveal Yourself to her. Help me know what to say and when to say it. To answer her questions, calm her fears, and help her know You and accept Your Son as her Savior."

His meaning escaped her, but she couldn't get over the fact that he talked to God about her. Like God knew her by name.

"And thank You for the food You've given us. Amen." He caught her gaze as he lifted his head.

"Thank you." She slipped her hands away, struggling for a new topic. "I can't believe I've lived in this city all my life and never known about this place."

"I only learned about it a few years ago. The church has picnics up here sometimes." He unwrapped a hoagie. "After that, I'd come up here to think and be around normal people for a while."

"Normal people?"

He took a bite in silence.

A couple of families celebrated a birthday party on some wooden tables beside a clapboard house. A small group of teenagers, or close to it, roller-bladed on the cement path below them. Down the hill, a guy flung a Frisbee for his Labrador to catch. If these people were what CJ considered normal, her circle sure didn't fit in.

"Sometimes there's a lot of pressure, you know? Pressure to fit into the molds of expectations."

Was he talking about her?

"I've been in your position, Annalee. The hit and run, I mean. Only I was drunk. And guilty." He bit into his sandwich, his gaze aimed somewhere near the middle of the lake. His eyes matching the gray of the water and the cloud-covered sky.

She dipped a chip in the Picante sauce and let the spices distract her.

"My best friend and I were partying. Hit a minivan on the way home. Totaled my car and hurt a little girl in the backseat of the other car who wasn't wearing her seat belt."

So, he did know what she'd been going through. The trial, the demands. Was he still serving his community hours?

"I couldn't get out of my door, so I crawled over the back seat and climbed out on the passenger side. My buddy wasn't hurt, but he was pretty soused. It took him awhile to get out."

Annalee studied him as he laid down his sandwich. A crevice grew between his brows. The muscle in his jaw tightened through the silence.

"By then, there were people helping the family, so I called my dad. He told me to get sober. I chugged water and started running up and down the blocks to work the alcohol out of my system."

Silence ensued and he stood. "I turned at the end of one block and saw the cops arrive. I started walking, thinking that every second might make a difference between this being a stupid accident or a felony DWI. Halfway down the block, I notice the cops had my buddy handcuffed and were sticking him in the backseat of their car."

"Because he was drunk?" She bit into her sandwich.

He turned toward her like he'd forgotten she'd been there. Unshed tears filled the corners of his eyes. "The driver of the other car only remembered seeing one person in the car. Since my buddy was sitting on the ground, leaning against the tire. He got blamed.

Like what had happened to her. But if Giselle had told the truth, chances were no one would be helping the Madison family at this point. Surely CJ hadn't let his friend take all that blame.

"Dad had arrived by then and wouldn't let me admit to anything. He told my friend the same thing, but it didn't matter because he remembered nothing." He stood and turned toward the lake.

A breeze kicked up, and Annalee caught CJ's plate and shoved it and his sandwich back into the basket.

"I argued with my father, but he kept driving home the need to let matters lie. Even lied about my friend borrowing the car, but I didn't hear about that until weeks later." He paused. "I got pretty low. Dropped out of school and struggled with depression. Driven with guilt, I decided to come clean. I went over to Thornton's house without even talking to my father. I planned to explain everything to him first and then go to the police and turn myself in. But …"

He went silent again.

Annalee repacked the basket. Her thoughts whirled. She wanted to wrap her arms around him and give him her own strength. But she needed to know. Needed to know how CJ made it right with ... wait, what was that name? "Did you say Thornton? Thornton Collier?"

CJ didn't look at her. "Yeah. We played football together at A&M. So, I guess you know what happened."

She knew all right. "He shot himself." Her voice dropped to a whisper.

He hung his head. "That's what I learned when I got to his house. The cops were leaving, and the maid told me when I came up the walk." The muscle in his jaw twitched again, and his hands balled into fists at each pocket. "I couldn't even talk to his parents. Couldn't speak at his funeral. Was barely able to even go to it."

"You can't blame yourself for that."

CJ turned an intense gaze on her. "Yes, I can. My silence..." He dropped to his knees beside her, his face painted with grief. "I did that. As if I pulled the trigger myself, I caused it all. I destroyed my ..." He took a ragged breath. "... my best friend and his whole family. And I'll live with that guilt for the rest of my life."

"CJ."

"I ended up talking to his parents. Telling them what I did. I fully expected them to hate me. To expose my lie to the public. Nothing less than I deserve."

"But they didn't?"

He shook his head and sat back on his heels. "They were believers. Broken-hearted but followers of Christ. And they forgave me."

She shuddered. Losing their only son.... She stood, stretching her legs. "I remember they moved away."

"Yeah, but when they come to visit, they always come see me. And I get e-mails from Mrs. Collier all the time. Encouraging me in the faith. Reminding me of who I am in Christ."

"Oh, my gosh." What an amazing woman.

"I think she started writing to help her continue to forgive me and not get bitter. It's ended up giving us a special friendship. And they've never told anyone else."

She hugged her shoulders as a chilling wind blew in from the other direction. "No one else knows this?"

He stood and moved toward her, covering her hands with his own. "I actually did turn myself in, but the police weren't interested. The case had been closed, the little girl fully recovered, and they had bigger issues to deal with." He clamped his jaw tight for a moment. "I know it wasn't easy for you to tell me about your mother and that Texas Princess contest. I didn't want you to think that you were the only one with a past."

So that's why he'd brought up this awful event. His penetrating gaze warmed her, despite the strengthening wind that whipped her hair.

"The guilt, the mistakes, the shame. That's what Christ saves us from."

She wanted the peace that showed on his face, even after all he'd been through. Wanted to experience the forgiveness, the love.

Cold droplets splattered across her cheeks. The families at the party dashed for the parking lot and the rest of the park-lovers disappeared. She snatched up the blanket, thankful that she'd already repacked the basket.

CJ grabbed the blanket and balled it up. He reached for her hand, and they darted for the truck, finally reaching it after the unexpected rain had thoroughly soaked them.

"That cold front wasn't supposed to make its way through until tonight."

"I don't believe it listened to the meteorologists." She shoved the wet grassy blanket to the floorboard.

CJ cranked up the heat. "Here." He pulled another blanket from behind his seat and tucked it around her shoulders.

"Thanks." The tender look in his eyes warmed her better than the blanket. "I really will think about what you said. About God loving me—."

"Adoring." He smiled.

She nodded, dropping her chin. Such an unfathomable concept. All of it was so confusing, yet intriguing. "Could you … maybe, talk to God more about me? Maybe He could help me understand this better?"

His smile broke into a full out grin. "Every day. You bet I will. And you can talk to Him, too. When you're ready. He's always waiting and looks forward to hearing from you."

Looks forward to hearing from me? The slap of the windshield wipers matched her heartbeat. They drove in silence toward her home.

Everything inside her sang that all CJ had said was true. A truth that she knew nothing about, but longed to know more. *God, are You really hoping to talk with me?* Why would He want to talk with her?

Tears pricked the corners of her eyes. She couldn't do this now. After exposing her deepest shame, she couldn't humiliate herself with tears in front of CJ.

He was like no other man she'd ever met. Not even Parker. Yet she trusted him completely, even though she hadn't known him for long. Despite the gravity of the topics on the hill, or maybe because of them, she'd let down her guard. She'd released her mask. And a connection had grown between them. Surely, he felt it as well.

She looked in his direction. The look of contentment along with a slight upturn of the lips still painted his features. Her heart lurched when he glanced her way.

"You warm enough."

To her toenails and back. "Yes." Warm. Cared for. Incredibly attracted to the man next to her and his message.

She made the conscious effort to silence the echo of her voice in her head. *What are you thinking? What are you thinking?*

Annalee buried herself in her room as soon as she said goodbye to CJ. He hadn't kissed her. Of course not, the rain alone dispelled that prospect. But he hadn't made a move toward kissing her. Why not?

Not that she would have, despite her affection for him and the electricity of his touch. Feelings could be fleeting things. She tried to tell herself that. But these emotions coursing through her core weren't the temporary kind.

She flipped open her laptop and did a search for an online Bible. She found several and chose BibleHub.com. She found the verses from Ephesians. That prayer the writer prayed like he was praying for her. Her thoughts flitted.

CJ was praying for her. Probably at that moment.

The verse said the person who prayed kneeled before the Father. One of Annalee's nannies had kneeled beside her bed at night to pray the *I Lay Me Down to Sleep* prayer. If the writer could be on his knees over her, then she could be on hers as well. She hit the floor next to her window.

"Okay, God. I'm here. I don't know what I'm doing, but I want what Tally Madison has. What CJ found even after such a horrible experience. I want to be released from the guilt and worry I've always carried. I don't want to be in charge of my life anymore, and I sure don't want my mom to be in charge. I want You to take it. All of it." She took a breath. "Even my art." Tears escaped and tracked down her cheeks. "Please help me understand what all of this means." Even without complete comprehension, a strong feeling of peace filled her. She relaxed her head against the glass. This was right. Everything CJ and the church speakers said was true.

And if so … "And help me deal with my mother."

She stayed in that place for a while. Losing track of the time completely, she relished the words of the songs she'd learned that morning. Still not fully understanding them all, she connected with some of them. "I lay me down … hmm, hmm …" *I belong to God.* What a concept.

With the tune still playing through her head, she trotted down the steps to the kitchen. Sunday evening was a potluck meal, though not entirely full of leftovers. Ciera, their cook, always left a fully cooked meal complete with individual servings, ready to reheat in the microwave. But with her time at the center, Annalee had actually learned how to cook pasta. Her mother would be shocked.

She found a box of noodles in the pantry along with the base of the sauce Paula showed her. Before long, she had pots on the stove bubbling and a fresh garlic-tomato smell permeated the kitchen.

"What is that delicious smell?" Mother came from the dining room.

"Ciera left roast beef in the refrigerator. But I have a taste for Italian."

"You're cooking?" She crossed her arms.

"Almost finished. I've got a salad from some leftovers on the counter and a toasted baguette in the warmer. Would you like to join me?"

Mother shifted and dropped her hands to her side. "Is there enough for two?"

"I think we could even get three meals out of this." Annalee transferred the pasta into a colander. "Is Father home?"

"No, he's at a golf game." She leaned over to sniff the sauce pot. Pulling a spoon from the drawer, she helped herself to a taste. "Mmm. This is good. How did you learn to cook spaghetti sauce?"

"I helped with a meal last week at the center. Paula's a fabulous cook. Probably as good as Ciera."

Mom cocked her sculpted brow at Annalee. "I'll set the table."

There was hope. Annalee scurried to complete the meal before her mother's attitude turned. She joined her at the table with her meal elements and a pitcher of iced tea from the night before.

"This is truly lovely." Mother poured tea while Annalee served salad.

When her mother set down the pitcher, Annalee leaned forward. "May I say grace?" She closed her eyes before her mother had the chance to comment. "God, thank You for what I'm learning at the center. For the food we have, and the way You love us. And thank You for Mother and the time we can spend together. Amen."

And please let this be a positive encounter.

Her mother ate a few bites in silence. "You're learning well, Annalee. This is very good."

She smiled. "It's only spaghetti."

"Even so, you've done well."

"Thank you." Her mother's compliment warmed her for a full minute.

"Still, it doesn't compare to the Eggs Benedict or the country omelets at our traditional Sunday brunch at the club."

Calm. Annalee focused on what she said instead of drawing her conclusions. "I do love their omelets." *Redirect.* "Do you suppose the cook would teach me how to make them?"

Mother snorted. "Don't even think of such a thing. How would that look on your father's campaign? I can envision the headlines: Mayoral Candidate Joins Kitchen Staff."

"I'd make the ten o'clock." Annalee tried to crack a joke. Hoping to dissuade Mother from the brewing tirade. "I visited a beautiful place today. You would love it."

"Is that where you went instead of the club? Because your presence was acutely missed this morning. Even Scott Whelan was there, not that he gives us so much as a hint of attention. It was an important day for your father's final push for the election."

She honed in on a diversion. "Scott Whelan doesn't like Father?"

"Heavens, no." Mother wiped her mouth with a cloth napkin. "He and your father are about as far apart, politically, as two people can possibly be. But we get along with many others in the opposing party. For some reason, almighty Whelan believes himself so far superior to your father that he can't even muster a polite comment to him. He refused to even acknowledge us throughout the morning until your father approached him personally. Despicable man."

Annalee decided she liked the hideous beast named Scott Whelan, if for no other than he distracted her mother and became the topic of the evening meal rant. Anything to keep Annalee's neck out of the guillotine was pleasant.

Yet, in the days following, she did feel the pinch of something mother said. This was father's last push for his campaign. She couldn't attend afternoon or early evening functions, but she needed to be available to him at any other times. Until after the campaign ended, she'd have to miss church with CJ. She'd found the church's website, though, and a number of lessons and services were podcasted.

In the meantime, she needed to keep CJ out of her mind. He'd infiltrated her thoughts day and night, but how could she possibly begin seeing the man right now? True, he wasn't the janitor she'd thought when she met him, but he was still only a worker at the center, maybe the assistant director from the way he helped organize and make decisions. Either way, he'd never fit into her parents' world.

For her father's sake, and his election, she needed to remain in that environment and do everything she could to promote him as the best person for Dallas mayor. Maybe after the election …

That made for busy weekdays. She brought extra clothes to the center, changed, and bolted to meet her parents at the local rallies, the Meyerson Center for an orchestra concert, even several jaunts to charity balls.

CJ caught sight of her scampering down the side stairs after changing for one of those and let out a low whistle. "Wow."

Her cheeks heated. The light in his eyes pierced directly into her heart. She'd missed talking with him, keeping her distance to make sure she stayed focused on the kids and on her work.

His gaze drifted from her feet to her face and a smile grew. "You look amazing."

She shrugged on a faux fur stole and snuggled it close around her face to cover the blush she had to be showing. "Thank you, but I'm running late."

"Wait a minute." He stepped in front of her. "You're going out there? Dressed like that?"

"I've left early every day this week. It's barely past sunset." Of course, she hadn't been wearing a Marchesa original gown. She adjusted the short cape over her bare left shoulder.

"I know but not dressed like that." He waved his hand up and down. "Like a worm on a hook at a catfish farm."

"They have farms?" She faked a laugh that she didn't feel. Being compared to a worm fell short of a compliment on so many levels. "Seriously, CJ, the body shop is even still open."

He huffed and stuck his head out the door. "Looks pretty clear." He took her elbow and led her to the porch. "So how come Mr. Wonderful isn't brave enough to pick you up down here?"

Mr. Wonderful? "I'm not dating anyone, CJ. I'm meeting my parents. Charity ball tonight. You know my father is running for mayor. I have to make an appearance." She lifted the long gown as she edged down the steps.

His grip softened and drifted to her hand. He laced his fingers with hers. "You know if you ever need an escort …" He brought her hand to his lips and kissed her fingers.

The breath went right out of her. She stumbled on the bottom stair, tumbling directly into him. His arm went around her waist as her palm caught against his chest. She chanced a glimpse of his eyes, deeper blue in the twilight than the sparkling afternoon by the lake. He was close. Too close. His spicy cologne drifted around her. An airborne net reeling her toward him.

His lips separated in a slight smile, and his gaze drifted to her mouth. Her heart swelled as he looked into her eyes again. He paused, as if making a decision, then cupped her cheek with his hand and moved closer.

Alarms rang in her head. This was the very thing she needed to avoid. She backed away, dropping his hand, and hit the unlock button on her keychain.

She aimed for the gate and practically sprinted, quick-stepping as fast as the five-inch heels would allow. He matched her stride, but the confused and hurt look in his eyes knotted her stomach.

His smile dropped away. Reaching the car, he opened her door. "Have a nice evening."

"I'll try." She smoothed her blue chiffon away from the door. Her chest hurt, but things had to be this way, at least for now.

Chapter 22

All night and even through the next day, CJ smarted from Annalee's rejection.

He stared in the mirror and gelled his hair, chiding himself. The timing had been wrong. But he hadn't anticipated kissing her. It just happened. Her in that gown.

But then, he didn't usually care for women that accepted a kiss so readily anyway. By all rights, he should be glad she stepped away from him. He worked on his tie.

So why did her reaction hurt so much? Bring such confusion?

And had she thought any more about their conversation last Sunday? She'd barely spoken to him this week, though she'd had little time.

He studied his reflection in the full-length bathroom mirror. The tux still fit perfectly. Good thing. He'd lost quite a lot of weight since his college football days when he had the thing made.

If only he'd followed through with his thoughts to invite Annalee to go with him to this banquet a few weeks ago when he first considered the prospect. Although showing up with her, slighting her probation officer, might've resulted in some dangerous repercussions.

After seeing Annalee in all her beauty the night before, he wanted to show himself at his best for a change but couldn't think of an excuse to go to the center before Laurel met him downstairs. Shame. That might have provided the opportunity he needed to tell her who he was.

He should have told her the whole truth on Sunday. He'd planned to. They'd had a moment on the hill. More than a moment, they'd bared their deepest pain.

Maybe she didn't feel for him the way he felt for her. Maybe she considered him too lowly. Another reason he should have explained. Not that she'd ever trust him again once she knew of his deception.

But he'd served up that unappetizing dish all by himself. By the time he cared what she thought, he'd let the masquerade go on for far too long. How could he tell her now? But if he cared, how could he stay silent? Ugh. He clamped his hands to his head. The spiral of disaster had no possible successful outcome.

He stroked his hair again, into a fashionable look he seldom did the work for. The bell rang from the security desk downstairs. He mashed the button on the intercom. "Yes."

"Laurel Stewart to see Carlton Whelan."

She'd been an easy companion the last few years. Other women stayed away because he had a date, but she hadn't been the clingy type. Perfect for an evening that required an escort.

Lately, though, she pouted and appeared moody and entitled. Something had changed.

He checked his watch. Twenty minutes early. Did she actually think he would invite her up? "Have her wait there." The guards had commented more than once about how he never had women in his apartment. He didn't mind that they had bets going on about when he would break his habit of keeping females downstairs. At least they noticed. CJ had been waiting for one of them to bring it up so he could tell them why and share his faith.

Maybe Laurel's coming early could speed up that process. After all, she was pretty and likely dressed to the max. He smiled at the thought that the whole security team would be busy at the desk by the time he got down there, if only so they could enjoy the view.

He hurried through the rest of his dressing and met Laurel in the lobby. "I didn't expect you until …" He fingered his watch. "Almost now."

"And I didn't expect to have to stand around down here. These men wouldn't let me on the elevator."

Sure enough, all three guards pretended to ignore Laurel's fuss while they busied themselves with made-up tasks. "They follow orders."

"Why wouldn't you want me to come up? I've never seen your apartment."

He could have kissed Laurel right then for her flaring anger. "Neither has any other woman. I take my faith seriously, and I don't want to have the appearance of anything inappropriate that will make people question what I believe." He stepped a little closer to the security desk. "Thanks guys for doing what I asked."

Laurel stepped toward the exit. "I think that's very honorable but unnecessary. I'm not worried about anyone thinking less of me for going upstairs."

Had she even heard him? "Yes, well …" How did he make his point clear without offending her? He blew out a heavy exhale, letting the truth evaporate.

She flounced out of the building with her pink dress flapping like a flag behind her.

A small lump of lead formed in CJ's stomach. A few hours. That was all. And the evening would be over.

Annalee emptied her ladle into another bowl and refilled it from the huge pot of soup that still bubbled from the residual heat of the stove.

"Watch what you're doing there, missy." Paula pointed at the drips that painted the counter from where Annalee held the ladle.

"Oh, sorry." She moved the spoon so it would dribble back into the pot.

"What's the matter with you? You've been glazed over like a Christmas ham all day long." Margo took the ladle from her and shooed her toward the pan of cornbread.

"She couldn't even glue a straight line this morning." Paula laughed, her ivory teeth sparkling against the cocoa of her skin.

"I don't know." Though in her defense, the glue point had been stopped up.

"She's in a fella funk, is what she is." Paula laughed again and turned on the water in the sink.

Annalee set her gaze on the ceiling and hoped the topic would dissipate.

"I get it." Margo served the last student and poured a bowl of beef stew for herself. "You're upset because CJ went to that party with Laurel."

Why had Laurel Stewart made such a point of stopping by to show her outfit to Margo? Not to mention her announcing that she and CJ were attending the banquet together. "I'm not upset."

"Discouraged?"

"No." She passed out a few extra pieces to Tyrone and Hayden.

"Tally loves y'all's cornbread," Hayden whispered behind his hand.

"Tell her hi from me." Annalee matched his gesture.

"So, are you discouraged or not?" Margo continued her push for truth from Annalee.

"Maybe." What more could she tell her? *I'm not sure but I might be falling in love with the handyman, but then again, it might be simple nerves?* "How long have they been dating?" Answering a question with a question had been a long-drilled ploy that her mother insisted was necessary to keep others off-kilter and make oneself appear at one's best.

"They aren't dating."

Annalee suppressed a smile. Her mother's technique also served to glean delightful information from time to time.

Margo lifted the pot and set it in Paula's sudsy water. "They started attending this banquet together a few years ago, because they both have to go, and neither of them wants to look for a real date."

"That ain't why that Miss Stewart goes with CJ, and you know it," Paula chimed as she tucked away a few items in the refrigerator.

"Maybe. Maybe not." Margo lifted her chin and scowled at the other woman.

"Maybe what?" As much as Annalee enjoyed not being the topic of conversation, she had to know the extent of which they were speaking.

"Well, she's talked about CJ quite a bit, lately." Margo scrubbed at the pot. "I think she might have developed a little crush."

"Crush nothing. You and she had your heads together all summer trying to figure how to get them married off." She clapped her soapy hands together. "She was the friend of yours I needed to tell CJ about."

"You talk too much." Margo fisted her hips.

"Married?" Laurel Stewart and CJ? The tightness that had developed all day in her chest moved to Annalee's stomach. "I'll be back."

She fled into the crowded dining hall and strolled toward the bathroom. A little cool water on her face would do the trick. Though she doubted the water would solve her pounding heart over the thought of CJ with Laurel Stewart. Dancing with her. Laughing at her chatter. Kissing her.

She shoved open the bathroom door.

This night couldn't end soon enough for CJ. He caught up with Laurel but didn't touch her. "I'll pull my truck around and pick you up."

She halted, teetering slightly, and turned back. "Actually, I thought we could take my Mazda. I know it isn't elite, but it's new and clean and much nicer than that run-down rattle-trap you drive around town. Besides, I'm parked in a tow-away zone, so we might as well take my car. I'll have to move it anyway."

She handed him her key with a flirty smile. What had he gotten himself into?

As soon as she strapped herself into the passenger seat, she started in on his beloved Chevy pickup again. "Why would you settle for driving something like that around town anyway, CJ? It must be a terrible embarrassment for your father to have his son touring in public in such a poor vehicle. You look like a hick from the sticks."

Three hours, that's all. He'd jogged that long before. Cut firewood at one of his dad's pseudo-roughing camps. He could do anything for only three hours, even escort Laurel.

"It's one of the first things I purchased with my own money. Sort of special. And I don't care what it looks like."

"Don't be absurd. You have scads of money. I've seen how much your father's company earns. I even own stock. Did you know that?"

"My father has money, Laurel. I don't. I only use his condo because he bought it and decided to leave it empty most of the time."

"Well, at least for his sake, you can try to act within your station for one night." She huffed. "Pull in there." She pointed to the valet parking. "I want to arrive in style this year."

His gaze shifted heavenward, and he accommodated her. His bow tie took on the feeling of a dog collar. Had she missed out on a special ball somewhere down the line? She even looked like a prom queen with all the layers of crinkly pink fabric.

She claimed his arm before they reached the entrance. Her

tentacle latched on his coat with a dozen or more suction cups. The feeling in his hand faded, and his head hurt from the cackle she used as she greeted each person they passed.

Laurel introduced him by his full name at least ten times and grinned at every impressed response. "Yes, he's the son of Scott Whelan of the Whelan Group."

How many of these banquets had they been to? Four? Five? She'd never acted like this. By the time they finally made their way into the ballroom where the banquet was to be held, CJ felt like he should simply stand behind her chair on some sort of platform and strike a manly pose. She could gesture at him from time to time while she boasted about her conquest.

Yeah, right. He fingered his watch. Two hours and counting. He pulled out her chair and kept a pleasant look on his face. At least with her constant chatter to her friends, he didn't need to engage in conversation.

Until her friends left for the dance floor. No way was he hauling Laurel out there.

"Too bad Annalee Chambers can't dirty her hands with lower class people like these."

Where had that come from? "You don't think so?"

She tossed a handful of her frizzy brunette hair over her shoulder. "It's not personal. Most people of her ilk wouldn't come to one of our banquets. Her kind tend to party at the clubs. They're far too self-absorbed to condescend to the working class. That's what makes you so different." She covered his hand with her own. "Why you're so special."

He cleared his throat and pulled his hand away, struggling for a response that neither encouraged nor offended.

"Of course, that partying is what got Annalee in trouble in the first place. Drunk driving. Even though that part of the accusation was removed. Doubtless her father's influence."

CJ's skin prickled. Did Laurel feel the need to trash Annalee out of some misplaced jealousy?

Her friends returned to the table, but CJ ignored them. He'd hit on the truth. That's why Laurel had been so critical. Why she mentioned trying to get Annalee placed elsewhere.

He'd been the biggest obstacle to Annalee's success all along. How could he have been so blind?

Laurel laughed with her friends. "Self-absorbed and inept. Do you know she threw a fit about not being allowed to park in the middle of the bus lane?"

CJ felt the burn start. This had to stop.

They laughed again and one chimed in, "Why don't you slap her in jail? Show the princess a little peasant action?"

He had to get away from Laurel's lying gossip before he told her off and effectively tossed Annalee into the jail cell they described. He started to excuse himself, but a waiter approached him. "Señor Whelan?" When CJ nodded, the man handed him a note with a slight bow.

The hotel stationery with computer printing gave no hint of the contents, and CJ had to find the right angle to catch enough light in the dim room to read it.

The note was taken by the banquet manager. He'd received a call from Margo Pritchard.

CJ didn't read anymore but leaned close to Laurel so the whole table wouldn't be interrupted. "I have to go."

"What? Why?" Laurel's loud volume collected the attention of their entire table and a couple of others nearby.

"I got a message from Margo." He stood and tossed his napkin into his seat.

"What has that girl done this time?" Laurel followed as he weaved through the roundtables.

"I don't know that she did anything. But I have to leave. It's urgent." Or he assumed that it was. If it wasn't, he'd be free anyway.

"I swear, CJ. That girl is nothing but trouble. Why don't you cut her loose?"

He turned to face her. "Because she'll go to jail." She knew that. As Annalee's probation officer, her successful probation should be her priority.

"So? That's not your problem. And it's where she should be in the first place. Where she would have been if it hadn't been for her daddy's money and reputation."

"Did it ever occur to you that her father's election might have been the reason she got stuck in probation in the first place? The police couldn't even prove she'd been the one driving the car. If she wasn't Annalee Chambers, her case would've been dropped the next day."

"That doesn't make her work at the center any better. I've heard about all of the things she's messed up."

He opened the exit door. "Listen, I'll take a cab." He pulled out his wallet and handed her a twenty. "This will cover the valet."

She stomped her foot and grabbed the bill. "This isn't over."

He let the door close behind him. "Yes, it is." A grin he couldn't suppress spread.

The fact that Laurel and CJ weren't actually dating made little difference with Annalee's dreamed up images of them together. Her chest hurt, and she shoved through the girl's bathroom door, craving a few moments of solitude. Instead, Jamaysia stood in front of one of the sinks. The water poured out at full-blast.

"Jamaysia, I didn't see you come in."

"Just got here. I had to walk." She sniffled.

"What's the matter? Do you have a cold?"

"Huh-uh." She fidgeted and whimpered while tears squeezed from the corners of her eyes.

Annalee reached her and spotted the swollen purple of her arm as it lay in the sink. Her stomach roiled. She'd seen that look before on her friend's arm the one spring she'd played field hockey. Her friend had tripped, landed poorly, and broke her arm. "What happened?"

"I fell. It'll be okay."

Annalee eyed the girl, noticing a darkening mark on her chin. She whipped out her phone and dialed 9-1-1. While she spoke to the operator, she stepped outside to the nearest table and motioned for one of the kids to bring Margo out of the kitchen. Still giving directions, she pulled Margo inside and showed her Jamaysia's arm.

"An ambulance will be here in a moment." She pressed the call-end button.

"Well, done." Margo squatted to the girl's eye-level. "Jamaysia, you're going on a little trip with Annalee. You think that will be okay?"

"Guess so." She eyed the woman. "Will my momma know where to come git me?"

"I'll make sure your momma knows everything."

Annalee startled at her own name. "I don't know how to …"

"You'll be fine." Margo leveled a direct gaze at her. "I'll join you as soon as the children are dispatched."

At least Annalee hadn't had to be alone with Jamaysia in her pain at first. Margo stayed until the paramedics arrived. Then they were with her until the emergency room.

But that was where the attention ended. With the arm stinted, Jamaysia was wheeled into a triage room in the back of the wing, much like the room Annalee had napped in a couple of weeks before. But this night wasn't like the quiet one she'd encountered. The wing was full of injured and sick. Moans and coughs made a base for the occasional cry of pain or shout from a nurse or doctor.

Jamaysia whimpered, and Annalee climbed onto the bed and put her arm around her shoulders and laid her cheek on her head. "I know, sweetheart. I know it hurts. They'll help you as soon as they get the chance."

"But what about my momma."

Annalee had left that detail to Margo. "I know she'll make it here soon."

"No." Her cry turned into a squeal. A passing nurse peeked through the curtain.

"Does it hurt again?" Annalee loosened her gentle grip.

"Huh-uh, but I don't want Momma here. She'll git mad."

Mad? "Why would she be mad at you?"

"I done told you I fell." Tears filled the child's big dark eyes.

Annalee nodded, not trusting her own voice. The nurse's brows furrowed.

Jamaysia took a deep breath, her mouth drooping at the corners. "Only I din't fall. And Momma's gonna be mad."

Annalee clenched her jaw a moment and demanded her

emotions stay in check. "How did it happen?"

"Bruce." The reply squeezed out with a tear that broke away from the others and dripped down her cheek. "He's Momma's boyfriend."

Silence closed in. Annalee hated needing to press her for more information. A sick feeling built up in her stomach. "Did he push you down?"

More tears joined the first. "Huh-uh. I's playing with his phone, and I dropped it. Accident, honest. He chased me into the kitchen, screaming at me." She paused.

"And you fell?"

Jamaysia shook her head. "He swung Momma's cast iron skillet at my head, an' I put up my arm to block it."

Annalee's stomach churned, and her neck heated. How dare that man swing a heavy pan at a child? He could have killed her.

"I ran out the door and went to the center." Her voice broke with a sob. "I din't know where else to go."

With her cheek again resting atop the black braids, Annalee stroked the tears off of the little girl's face. "It's going to be all right. We'll get you the help you need." She caught the eye of the nurse at the curtain. The young brunette pursed her lips and gave Annalee a nod before she dropped the curtain and moved away.

The child's broken breathing eased after a few minutes and steadied into whisper-soft snores. Without jarring her, Annalee clawed through her purse with one hand until she located and extracted her phone.

She dialed Margo.

"I'm on my way, but I had to wait for the kids to get mostly picked up. I'm at the bus stop now."

Annalee sighed. This would be much easier if she had a

partner to help her. "What about her mom?"

"Left a message, but I haven't heard from her. Called in a message to CJ, too."

"Oh, no. I didn't want to interrupt his evening." Or give Laurel Stewart more reason to believe she couldn't do this job well.

Margo tsked. "He needed to know what was going on. That's all. I expect I'll hear back from him before too long."

"She's sleeping now. And we're waiting for someone to see us."

"Plan on a long wait. Another non-life-threatening, indigent case. You'll be behind every sniffle and cough in the place, and anyone else who actually has insurance. And when they do get to you, they'll be asking you hundreds of questions, probably multiples of the same question."

"Well, we're already in the back, but with the busyness of this place, you're probably right about the waiting."

"That's the way the system works."

"But there's more." Annalee told Margo what she'd learned from Jamaysia.

"That's a different issue. I'll get in touch with Child Protective Services. You make contact with a nurse or a doctor on duty and make sure they alert the security team there."

"Security?"

"You aren't listening. I left a message for her mom. She and the goon that hit Jamaysia are probably already headed your direction right now. They'll be prepped to whisk Jamaysia away and glaze over this whole situation so they won't get into trouble."

Annalee recalled the chapter from the training manual. "I got it. Protect the child." The first task.

"You're resourceful, Annalee. I have to go. The bus is here."

She clicked off without another word but left Annalee with much to think about. Resourceful? Another thing she'd never been called before, but she knew how to put it into action.

Careful to keep Jamaysia steady, she leaned forward and pushed the nurse station call button.

Marji Laine

Chapter 23

CJ burst into the emergency room at Parkland Hospital and scanned the crowded waiting room. He made his way to the desk, identified himself and asked about Jamaysia.

"Absolutely, Mr. Whelan. This way." The nurse practically fell over the desk trying to help him to the back. His father donated to the downtown hospitals, giving CJ special treatment that he intended to take full advantage of this time.

He spotted Annalee at the edge of a curtain with a half-asleep Jamaysia in her arms, but he'd never seen this side of her.

Her face and neck bright pink, she whispered loudly at a nurse who was passing by. "What do I have to do to get the attention of a security guard in this place? The man who hurt her might be here any minute."

"You'll need to wait your turn."

"Behind who? That woman you took back there? She came in a solid hour after we arrived, but I suppose she's royalty or something?"

CJ stepped behind her, ready to intervene.

"She has …" The woman lowered her voice. "She has proper identification."

"This is about insurance?"

"When her mother arrives—"

"We can't wait that long!" She stamped her foot and the nurse jumped. "Don't you understand?"

"Ma'am if you don't calm down, I'll have to call security."

"But that's what I'm trying to get you to do. Now. We need this girl protected."

CJ stepped closer and touched her shoulder. "How long have you been waiting?"

She turned her gaze on him and sighed. Moisture rimmed her eyes. "Three hours. Three hours with this poor girl in pain. And for the last one, I've been trying to convince them that if and when her mother shows up, we could have an even bigger problem."

"Margo told me." He opened his wallet and pulled out the platinum card attached to his trust account. This wasn't the way he wanted to tell Annalee who he was, but it couldn't be helped. He held out the card. "I'm …"

"Miss Annalee, I'm cold." Jamaysia squirmed.

"I'm sorry sweet girl." Annalee looked at him. "If you've got this …" She turned and reentered the curtained cubicle.

Indeed, he did. He nodded and lowered his voice. "Nurse …" He glanced at her tag. "Toddleson, charge whatever is necessary to this card to get that child in the care of a physician and in the protection of your security staff within the next five minutes. Do you understand?"

Her eyes grew big when she looked at the card. "Yes, Mr.—"

He cleared his throat loudly. "Like I said. We need security."

The woman darted off in the other direction. Three hours was excessive, but the place was a literal madhouse. And Annalee couldn't know that a security guard was at least present in the waiting room.

He moved into the curtained space and held out his hands. "Let me have her."

She transferred Jamaysia into his arms.

"I hear you had a little accident."

"Something like that." The child's chin drooped, but her large eyes met his. "You look hot. Gotta date?"

Not exactly what he expected from a little kid but not so surprising in her neighborhood. Especially not from Jamaysia. "Thanks. I did, but I'd rather be sticking around here with you." He carried her to the bed and settled her back into it. "Does it hurt much?"

"Not so much anymore. They done give me some stuff to swallow."

He picked up a half-melted ice pack and laid it on the deepest purple spot. "Let's leave this here a few minutes and see if we can get some more swelling down."

She grimaced but accepted the bag. "Seems like Miss Annalee'd be more your speed."

"You think so, huh?" He glanced up at Annalee, but concern etched her face. "I think she's pretty worried about you." He glanced at a bruise on Jamaysia's chin and another slight one on her forehead.

About then, Nurse Toddleson returned and handed him his card. "The doctor will be with you in a few minutes.

CJ cleared his throat. "And security?"

She sighed. "Immediately, sir."

Annalee leveled a tired expression on him. "How did you do that? I've been fighting with that particular woman for the last hour at least."

"The Intercede Foundation has clout."

"At least she took your credit card. I tried that early on, and she would have none of it. She wanted proof that a person like me would actually work at the center. What? Like I'd snag a kid off the street so I could spend money on her?" Her shoulders sagged. "The center will pay you back somehow, won't it?"

"I'll work it out." Touched that she concerned herself about him when she'd been dealing with such frustration, he wished he could at least offer her a seat. "You did a great job keeping her calm." He glanced at Jamaysia who lay in peace with eyes closed and mouth slack.

"Do you think her mother will actually come?"

A loud shout erupted from somewhere in the area. "Not sure. She might even be here."

A stocky man in uniform, a few inches shorter than CJ, but armed with a weapon, pulled the curtain back. "The nurse said you expected trouble?"

"CPS has already been called." Annalee stepped toward them both. "The child was hit by her mother's boyfriend. He could very well have killed her." She glanced at CJ. "Margo thought they both might show up insisting that Jamaysia be released to them."

"A couple did show up, ma'am. Throwing a fit out in the waiting room. Nurse Toddleson is dealing with them." He turned his back to her. "I'll stay here until DPD and CPS arrive."

He let the curtain fall. CJ turned to face a frightened Annalee. "Do you think I did the right thing?" She explained how Jamaysia was injured. "Will Margo add another reprimand to my record over this?"

CJ restrained his urge to touch her face, wipe away the remains of tears. "Over what? You protected her."

"Yes, but I've caused extra trouble for Margo."

He shook his head. "She doesn't think like that. And you did everything exactly right."

Her face clouded. "Will Jamaysia be all right?"

The last came as a whisper. He discarded his attempt to stay distant, stepped closer, and pulled her into his arms. Her ragged breathing heaved against his chest. He relished her nearness. "She's been in good hands, Annalee." He laid his cheek against her soft hair and whispered into her ear. "And she's been in God's hands the whole time, too. Look how He protected her."

Annalee gasped and leaned back, looking into his eyes with her vivid blue ones. "You're right. He did."

Way too close. CJ stepped back as a young doctor pushed aside the curtain.

"I'm Dr. Cantrell. Is there a parent here?"

"We're from the Intercede Foundation. The proper paperwork has already been turned in." He hoped to remain simply CJ to Annalee for a little while longer.

"I have to ask." He checked the screen of his iPad.

"I trust that isn't the A&M football game." CJ chuckled.

The doctor looked up at him with a pan-face. "No."

CJ hoped he'd show a bit more humor with Jamaysia. The girl's fears would return the moment he started adjusting her arm.

Dr. Cantrell turned to Annalee. "You're Miss Chambers? Annalee Chambers?"

"Yes." She nodded.

"Are you the daughter of that mayoral candidate I've heard so much about?"

"Uh …" She took a step to the side as a nurse and an orderly moved in to wheel the bed through the curtain. "Yes. But I don't see what that has to do with anything."

"Just curious. They'll take her to get an X-ray. You may wait here." He glanced at his digital file again. "I have a note that this is a case of abuse. Exactly what did you hit her with?"

"A cast-iron skillet." Her eyes continued to pour out her weariness, but her expression alerted. "Wait. Me? No. I didn't hit her with anything."

The doctor scratched across the screen with a digital pen. "You just said you did."

"No. I meant that she'd been hit with a skillet, not that I did the hitting."

"So, which is it? Was she hit or not?" He jutted out his chin.

"Yes." Annalee spoke the words slowly and straightened.

"With a cast-iron skillet."

"Yes."

"You seem to know quite a lot about this situation, yet you claim innocence?" He scratched some more.

"She told me what happened. I reported it to my superior." Annalee crossed her arms.

The man narrowed his eyes at her. "That's convenient."

CJ had heard enough. "Good thing you're a doctor. You're a lousy detective. I'll make a simple guess that you're not planning to vote for her father, right?"

He stiffened. "My politics are none of your business."

"And her father's occupation is none of yours. Or are you just aching to put her name in your file, so you'll have a sound bite for the media?"

"Her name is already in the file. Possible suspect in this case." His eyes held a challenge.

"There was a nurse who heard her whole story." Annalee fisted her hips. "I had nothing to do with it."

"Doctor…" CJ's patience wore out. "If you report that, I will see to it that your supervising physician gets a notice of disapproval not only from the Intercede Foundation but from Scott Whelan personally."

The man eyed him from his suit coat to his shoes then whirled around and exited the partition.

Annalee sighed heavily and her shoulder's drooped.

CJ hadn't missed the weariness that marked her face. "Sit down."

"On the floor?"

"They haven't offered many options." He sat cross-legged and pulled her down with him without releasing her hand.

"Thanks for standing up for me. That was a good bluff. The bit about having Mr. Whelan himself write a notice on my behalf."

"How do you know it was a bluff?"

"I haven't even met Mr. Whelan, but my father has. Let's just say Scott Whelan isn't a fan."

He stroked the top of her hand with his thumb. "I have my connections."

"I'm sorry about your date. Laurel Stewart is bound to have me fried when she realizes I'm the one who spoiled her night out with you."

"That's wrong on so many levels. First, you didn't spoil anything. I mean that. You reacted exactly as you should have." He gave her a smile. "And second, we weren't really on a date, simply an arrangement that keeps us both from uncomfortable companions." Though he couldn't imagine the night being much more awkward than it had been.

"A woman does not give a man a tuxedo like that when there's nothing serious between them. Trust me. I know Saville Row." She gave him a once-over. "And you look really nice. I'll bet Laurel Stewart was very proud to be with you."

Her confession warmed him. Would she have been so proud? He glanced down at her hand resting on his and covered it with his other one. "Trouble is she was not the lady I wanted to be out with."

His eyes met hers for a moment before she looked down. "I'm sure you would have succeeded with any woman you cared to impress."

Even you? The words hesitated on his tongue.

Then Margo threw open the curtain. Annalee jerked her hand away.

"Well, this is pretty."

CJ winced. He'd have to chat with Margo about her timing inadequacies. "No chairs. But by all means, join us."

She waffled. "I'll pass. Too hyped up anyway. You know they had to haul Jamaysia's mother out of here. Some man with her. I guess the boyfriend. They were threatening and yelling. Dallas PD took control of the matter from what the nurse said."

"The nurse told you that?" Annalee huffed. "I couldn't convince her to tell me the time."

"That's because I'm old and ornery and not a threat to a young working girl. You come in here looking like you stepped out of Vogue, and people automatically create an impression of you."

"I'm not even wearing makeup. And I'm in jeans, for heaven's sake." Annalee stood.

"Designer jeans."

CJ rose. "And you don't need makeup to be beautiful."

Both women turned to stare at him.

"You think I'm beautiful?" A slow smile crept across Annalee's naturally pink lips.

Margo tsked.

"You might as well sit, Margo. You know we'll be here for a while." CJ reached the older woman's hand and gave her a tug about the time the curtain opened again.

A motherly woman with dark skin and expressive eyes looked down on them. "Is there an Annalee Chambers here?"

And so, the questions began. The motherly woman took Annalee out, probably to a side room or office somewhere. Before they returned, another woman, much older and with thinning red hair came calling for him. He followed her to what must have been a broom closet and answered at least a dozen questions twice.

"Look, I know you're only doing your job, but isn't this excessive?" He shouldn't have questioned the woman, but his concern for Annalee grew. He was breaking down, and he hadn't even been at the center. How would she be holding up?

After another half hour of the same questions, he deeply regretted his criticism of the CPS worker. But she finally let him leave. Annalee was in Jamaysia's room, as it were. She climbed onto the side of the bed with her arms around the little girl, whispering to her.

"Has she been questioned?"

Annalee nodded slightly. Looked like it had been hard on the child.

"But they have a very nice lady who has asked that Jamaysia

come stay with her for a few days. That'll be an adventure, won't it, Jamaysia?"

The girl looked up with tears dripping from her mascara stained eyes. "I don't wanna go to some strange person's house."

Annalee looked ready to burst into tears, but she held them in check. "It's only for a few days. Until things get cleared up here."

"No one wants to see you get hurt again, Jamaysia." CJ ran his hand along her pigtails. "And that's one thing this house definitely is, a place where you can be safe."

"And Bruce won't be around?" The girl's eyes held a mixture of hope and doubt.

"He'll be gone." CJ had every confidence that the child would never lay eyes on the man again.

A little while later, Margo rejoined them and the CPS caseworker released them. Well, two of them at least. She asked that one of them stay until Jamaysia was fully released in case she needed comforting before she was taken to her safe house.

Dr. Cantrell returned in time to hear the request. "I guess that leaves you out, Miss Chambers."

"I don't know why it should." She'd moved to stand beside the bed now that Jamaysia had fallen asleep.

"A suspected child abuser shouldn't have a child left in her care."

"I'm not." Annalee stepped toward the man.

But Margo reached him first and stuck her bony finger in his face. "Listen Dr. Pea-brain. Just because you have a bunch of letters after your name don't make you wise enough to judge those in your company. And if you had half the wisdom God handed out to turkeys, you wouldn't be publicly slandering the daughter of a prominent attorney. Especially with her surrounded by sympathetic witnesses.

CJ couldn't have said it better himself. But in the end, Margo stayed with Jamaysia, promising to call him and Annalee tomorrow with any further news.

When CJ had first claimed her hand on the walk through the waiting room, the whole thing felt so natural. But the feeling of his warmth and comfort at that tenuous connection made her spirit soar. The fact that he kept hold of her hand while they waited for the cab rippled excitement through her.

They hadn't spoken much on the way back to the center, but Annalee was prepared when the driver stopped next to the curb.

She extracted her hand from CJ's and tugged a bill from her wallet. "This should cover the whole fare."

"You don't have to do that." CJ reached for the money, but the driver collected it.

"I do. You've already had to pay for one taxi." She pushed open the door.

"Well, at least let me walk you to your car."

She waited for him at her seat. He came around, opening her door and reached for her hand again. Little trickles of anticipation wrapped around her shoulders at his touch.

Remain controlled. Her mother's words reverberated through her head, but she swept them into the corners of her mind and relished his nearness. "I'm so glad you came. I don't want to think of what might have happened to Jamaysia if we had been without a security guard when her mother came with boyfriend-Bruce."

"You did fine. She was in good hands."

"All the same, I appreciate you coming. I wish you hadn't had to leave your event." She unlocked her driver side door.

"Ah, that. No. Leaving was a huge blessing, I assure you." He stepped closer. "The next time I have to attend one of those things, I hope that it can be with someone ..." He drew her hand to his lips and planted a kiss on her knuckles. "... more pleasant."

Her breath caught in her throat, and she swallowed hard as he opened her door for her. Like a graceless zombie, she climbed inside.

He squatted by the door. "I'll see you tomorrow?"

"Yes." Her whisper hardly carried past the opening, but he smiled, stood, and stepped back.

She started the car and gunned the motor much harder than she intended. Her gaze went to the ceiling. How juvenile, love-sick, puppyish.

And yet, she turned to watch him as he made his way back to the taxi. He waved when he climbed inside, leaving her with thoughts of how she could ever deserve the interest of such an amazing man.

Though Annalee had been too busy to attend services on Sunday, the anticipation of seeing her again, and the thrill of their last encounter, carried CJ through.

He heard her footsteps on the porch. Trying to look casual, he rushed into the entry from where he had been working in the kitchen. "Hello ..." He halted and the smile dropped away from his mouth. "... Laurel."

She flung her arms around his neck and planted her mouth firmly on his.

What was she doing?

More steps on the porch sounded as Annalee stepped through the door. CJ untangled himself from Laurel's tentacles, as she pulled smoothly away from him and gave him a final squeeze. "That should hold you until the kids leave for tonight." She walked into the office, her flats shuffling on the hardwood floor.

CJ shook his head. Had he jumped into an alternate reality? He wiped his hand over his mouth, wishing for a disinfectant mouthwash.

He met Annalee's eyes. She dropped her gaze to the floor and closed her mouth. Her brows bunched.

"Don't read anything into that."

She side-stepped him toward the dining hall.

Laurel scanned the sheet hanging from a clipboard on the wall. "She didn't even sign in the whole first week. Is she always so inconsistent?" She fisted her hips, directing the question to Margo, as CJ entered the office.

"Wait." He shifted his eyes to Margo.

"That was my fault." Her shocked expression likely matched his own.

"There are no excuses here. If she doesn't sign-in correctly, she doesn't get credit for the hours. Which is cause for removal. I've been thinking for the past month that this situation is detrimental on several levels."

"Removal?" CJ realized Laurel's intention. A slow burn

started at the base of his neck. Her suggestion reached levels of absurdity that CJ hadn't thought possible of any dimwit. The muscles in his neck stiffened. "So, any excuse to get rid of her."

"I know you want her to leave, darling, but we have to follow the rules." She glanced at something behind him.

He turned.

Annalee, pencil in hand at the sign-in sheet, looked like she'd been slapped.

"Whoops. Seems the cat is out of the bag." A note of triumph pealed from Laurel's voice.

CJ locked eyes with Annalee. Her face held the same expression as before yet with a hint of betrayal. "That's not what I meant." He gave his head a slight shake.

"Yes, but let's not completely humiliate the poor girl." Laurel circled him and put her arm around Annalee's shoulders. "Now that we're all in agreement, let's see if we can work out other arrangements." She turned Annalee toward the front door.

CJ found his voice. "No. I don't want other arrangements." Laurel's progress slowed down long enough for him to grip his own thoughts. His voice turned into a growl and his glare rested and remained on Laurel. "Annalee, please begin your duties. Laurel, I would have a word with you outside."

"Can't this wait for tonight. I've already set up a crock pot of chili in your apartment."

Obviously just announced for show. And she'd gone too far. "Now." He restrained himself from physically shoving her out onto the porch.

Breathing in the polluted air, he exhaled long, blowing out as much anger as he could before facing the woman. "I don't know what made you think you should kiss me and call me darling, but that behavior stops now."

"Of course. I only got carried away. It's nothing less than what you should have gotten on our date Saturday night."

"Ah." He pointed at her. "About that. Not a date. Never has been. And I promise there won't be further confusion because we will never be alone together again. Not if I can help it."

"We're alone now." She slid close to him, her fingers slithering up the sides of his arms.

He stepped back and brushed her away. "Good grief. Stay away from me. And leave Annalee alone."

"Ah, that's how it is. The gallant knight rescuing the damsel in distress." Her eyes hardened. "She bats her eyelashes and schmoozes the boss to get her way. And you fall for her act."

Annalee still didn't know about his being the director of the center. There was so much she didn't know and wouldn't forgive if she found out.

He whirled around, but no one had followed him through the door. Good. He lowered his voice. "Bottom line: you have no control over what goes on in my center."

"She's my probationer."

"Yeah, not your slave or your puppet. You don't do the hiring or the firing and I'll thank you to address any further concerns in writing to me—"

"In writing. You have got to be kidding!"

"And never again arrive on these premises unannounced. Furthermore, I don't know what gave you your crazy idea that there was something between you and me. There's not. And there never will be."

"You can't tell me we haven't shared something special, Carlton." She reached for him.

He pushed past her. "Oh. Yes. I. Can." Moving to the other side of the porch, he took a deep breath and turned back toward her.

She posed against the rail. "I don't understand it. She's a self-absorbed, prom queen. The kind of girl you hate. Why would someone as dedicated to the children as you waste your time on such a worthless character?"

"I'm not wasting my time. And she's not a worthless character."

Straightening, she pointed her finger at CJ and scowled. "I knew you were casting me aside for her. No matter how much you tried to deny it. Know this, CJ Whelan. I'll do whatever I can to get her out of here if I have to have her thrown right into jail."

CJ watched her stomp down the steps. She glared at him as she climbed into her car. Her threat meant little as long as things continued to run smoothly at the center. And he'd have to see that they did.

Chapter 24

The image of CJ kissing Laurel firmly embedded itself on the wall of Annalee's mind like a framed portrait. He'd explained and apologized more than once. Not like he owed her an explanation.

But her heart hurt. How she'd wanted to be in Laurel's shoes at that moment. Even though she wore last year's flats, and a designer knock-off from a thrift store, at that. Hopefully, he wouldn't make such a disgusted face after he kissed Annalee. If he ever kissed her.

Which he would never do if she kept stepping away from him.

But at least for another week, she had to keep her distance. Had to keep her mind focused on her father and his campaign. She could do anything for five days. Even if it meant avoiding interaction with CJ.

Whoosh! A soccer ball flew past Annalee's head, barely missing her ear. "Hey."

"Sorry, Miss Annalee." Hayden and Tyrone smiled at her. They didn't look sorry, but then they had been extra-hyper throughout the week.

"What's up with you boys?" She picked up the ball where it came to rest in a low spot in the lot and tossed it back to them.

"Just excited for Trunker-Treating tomorrow."

She squinted her eyes. Trunker-Treating? She'd heard about Trick-or-Treating all her life. "What's Trunker-Treating?"

"That's where people at the church bring a trunkful of candy and we go from car to car all over the parking lot. Then we have a party with music and some games." Hayden wiped his nose with his sleeve. "'T'sover at the church tomorrow. Everybody's going. CJ even brings over the church buses to pick us up and take us over there."

CJ was in on this?

The boys went back to their game. She found CJ in a deep concentration over a marble game on the bare cement slab they dubbed a patio.

"What's this trunk-or-treating thing I'm hearing about?"

"It's tomorrow." He handed his shooter to a tow-headed youngster and stood. "The bus crew comes and transports all of the kids."

"Can I bring my car? I have a trunk."

His brow knitted in the center of his forehead. "Have you done this before?"

"Trunk-or-treating or Trick-or-treating?"

"Giving out the candy? I'm guessing you don't have many kids making their way to your door very often."

She shrugged. "I've never done any of it. My parents have always attended a masked ball at the country club. Once I went through cotillion training, I attended as well. But I didn't think churches, of all things, would go in for Halloween."

He smiled. "We don't do the Halloween thing, but we take

advantage of the opportunity to give back to the community, share the gospel, and bring people, who wouldn't normally come near a church, onto its very property. And it gives the children a good memory about church that will revisit them when they get older."

"I see." She crossed her arms. "Isn't my trunk good enough?"

"Good enough?" He laughed. "Yours will make the rest of them blush with embarrassment. Knock yourself out. Get a basket or a box filled with whatever candy assortment you want to share and meet me in the lot in back of the church about two fifteen, tomorrow. I'll bring you over in the bus and you can ride back with me and the kids tomorrow night."

"It's a date." The moment the words left her mouth, she wanted to gobble them up and stuff them back inside. Her cheeks heated as she turned away. So much for avoiding interaction with him.

Yet a sparkle of excitement stirred in her chest in anticipation of what the next evening held.

CJ had walked Annalee to her car and waved as she drove away. He'd struggled to keep from taking her hand again. In fact, he stood a little more detached than he usually did. If only to control his reactions to her.

It's a date. Funny how the words out of Laurel's mouth stirred up terror, while the same ones from Annalee flipped his insides.

And the direct look she laid on him as she spoke ignited a fire in his heart. What would she do if he tried to kiss her at this point?

No. Those musings would only bring up too many images. Too many hopes. Good thing he'd kept his distance.

But Annalee never ceased to amaze him.

The next afternoon, decked out in orange and black, she arrived at exactly the right time with a grin spreading across her face. The excitement practically vibrated off of her and consumed him.

"You made it." He spread his arms wide, wishing he could wrap them around her, but let them drop.

"I'm pumped." She unlocked her trunk. "Since I'm leaving the car out in the sun for a couple of hours, I decided against chocolate."

"Good idea." He pinked, eying the bags of Hershey assortment that he'd tucked under the tarp near the cab of the truck. "Wish I'd thought of that." He hopped into the bed and untethered a water cooler that he kept there. It was empty but would keep the chocolate insulated at least.

She lifted the lid of her Mustang's trunk revealing enough bags of candy to please the entire metroplex. "You think this is enough?"

"How many stores did you buy out?" CJ laughed.

"Only one. I wasn't sure how much to bring, so I thought I could donate any leftovers to the center."

He finished filling the cooler with his candy and pushed it into the shade of the tarp. "Skittles, huh?" He jumped down beside her.

"A rainbow of fruit flavors." Her eyes lit up.

"Your favorite?"

"Yes, but not for the reason you might think. I love chocolate the best, but Skittles are all about color." She ripped open a personal pack and poured them out on the roof of her car. "What do you see there?"

"The letter S."

"Mm. Literal, very literal. What else do you see when you let a little daydream in?"

She stood close to him. Close enough that he could smell her citrus scent. Her nearness fogged his brain. Squeezing out a reasonable answer was like crushing out the last wad of toothpaste from the tube. "Okay, a rainbow."

"Oh, dear. You need a creativity makeover." She fingered a few of the candies. "See, here are some orange fish in a pool of blue and purple. A couple of flowers and leaves. There's a face with blue eyes and red lips."

"All that from a bag of candy?" He laughed.

"I used to use Skittles for inspiration. I'd pour out a big bag of them on a table in my studio. They have a Seurat or Monet appearance."

"They look like dots to me."

She lifted her baby blues to the sky and shook her head. With a giggle, she climbed aboard the open bus.

CJ darted to the driver's side. If the prelude was any indication, the night would be exceptional.

Annalee had swallowed hard and taken a deep breath before she stepped out of her car to meet with CJ. The faux pas of calling this evening a date weighed on her. She hoped she hadn't put any excess pressure on CJ.

But he'd acted as he always did, a little sweet, a little joking. Very attentive. Could he consider this a real date?

And if he did, would that be such a bad thing?

He queried her on her art all the way to the center.

She hugged her shoulders. "I've actually finished some pieces. I haven't told anyone. Not even Mother."

"Tell me about them." A light filled his expression. He wasn't simply being polite. He seemed truly interested.

She'd never known anyone interested in her paintings. Except for her instructors who wanted to grade them. But then, they always complained because none of her work had ever been in a finished state. Until now.

Had CJ asked about her projects a couple of months before, she'd have few answers. Various easels with projects in half-completion or worse.

But working at the center gave her a sense of productivity. No matter how tired she felt, she worked for at least three hours after getting home each night. As a result, she had a row of canvases completely done and drying against her studio wall.

"When can I see them?" He backed the bus into the body shop lot and turned it off.

"Uh …" How could she show him? What if he didn't like them?

Her fear must have shown. He climbed from his seat and bent down next to her, taking her hands. "I'm sure I'll love them."

The tender look in his eyes made her melt from the honesty that poured out. A smile she couldn't conceal spread. She never had such comfort from anyone. Not even her father.

He pulled her to her feet and his smile widened. For a moment, he wavered, like he couldn't decide whether to step closer to her or lead her out of the bus.

And Annalee didn't know which she wanted. Though the music of her mother's voice declaring his inadequacy had faded. He stepped toward the entrance, and she entwined her fingers with his.

He glanced at her. A question in his eyes. She smiled her answer and hugged his elbow. He led her down the steps and pushed the button to open the door.

Laurel Stewart stepped onto the center's porch. "Now isn't that sweet."

"You were told not to come back here, Laurel." A scowl sounded as loud in his voice as it showed on his face.

"I'm here on business. I'm afraid that we've had quite a complaint against your little girlfriend, there, resulting in immediate reassignment."

Annalee stiffened. A chilled breeze ratcheted down her spine. *Reassignment?* Who complained against her?

"Unless you have some pretty strong evidence, you can't have her reassigned without a court order." CJ's face didn't register any shock, but his grip tightened. "Unless you can get the director's approval. And you know you won't get that."

How could he be so sure? Margo had been nicer to her, but Laurel might change the woman's mind.

"I've got strong evidence. It seems your blond bombshell took a social shot at the family of a prominent city council member." She paused and watched a car pull into the bus lane and park. "I'll let him have his say."

A tall man climbed out of the driver's side of a Lincoln touring car. Gray peppered his tight black hair and a matching mustache broke the light chocolate of his face. "Is this the woman?" He pointed at Annalee but directed his question at Laurel.

"That's the one." Laurel crossed her arms and lifted her chin. Smug.

CJ released her hand as he stepped forward. "I'm ..." he held out his right hand to shake, but the councilman brushed passed him as though he was invisible.

"Young woman, my sister was cited for disturbing the peace and labeled as an unfit mother because of you. You have no business working with children if you use them to spread unsubstantiated rumors and harmful slander about their parents. I daresay you'll see litigation from the irresponsible actions you took ..."

"Irresponsible?" Annalee's ire rose. She didn't need CJ to stand up for her.

"Irresponsible! Your work at this center is over, and I won't rest until I see that you pay for what you've done to my family. I daresay your father put you up to this to make me look bad before the election."

"You are mistaken." Annalee's tone matched his, though he stood more than a foot taller. She fisted her hips. "How dare you accuse me or my father? I don't even know who you are, but I'm assuming from what you say that you are the uncle of Jamaysia Watson?"

"I am." His eyes slitted. "Like you didn't already know that she was the niece of a councilman."

"I still don't even know your name, though you obviously know mine and are using the tragic battery of your niece to your own political devices. Shame on you for using that precious girl like that."

"What are you talking about?"

"Jamaysia's arm was broken when her mother's boyfriend tried to hit her in the head with a cast iron skillet. It might have killed her had she not dodged and protected herself."

He straightened. "I don't know anything about that. My sister told me Jamaysia was hurt here at the center and that you blamed her for it and had the child taken by CPS."

"She was terrified that the man would come after her again. After hearing her story, I had no choice in the matter but to call in protection for her." She glared at him. "I suggest that you get full information instead of flying off on lies, assumptions, and insinuations." She glanced at Laurel Stewart who darted hate in her direction. "And I believe you owe my father an apology for concluding that this was some sort of political trap. He doesn't know anything about it."

"Is my niece all right?"

CJ had stationed himself at Annalee's side after the man passed him. "I heard from my contact at the CPS office this morning. Jamaysia is progressing. She's shared the event with the counselors there. She doesn't want to see her mother, though. My contact believes some history of abuse might be present in the household."

The man's head rocked backward and came down in a slight nod. "Then my sister tried to use the clout of my office to sweep all of this under the rug. Blaming you and the center to take the heat off of her boyfriend." He sighed. "He's in jail, by the way." He held out his hand. "I'm sorry, young lady."

Annalee shook it. Other words of reprimand poised on her tongue. Like how a councilman should act out of direction instead of flail out of emotion. But she sucked them inside to let the matter go.

He turned toward his car but pointed a finger toward Laurel Stewart. "I don't know how the probation office is run nowadays, Miss Stewart, but it's supposed to partner with the probationers and help them be successful. Your gossip in this allegation was anything but helpful, and your supervisor is going to hear about it."

Laurel Stewart reddened, stiffened her spine, and marched toward them from the porch. Without acknowledgment, she turned her back on them and walked up the street to her car.

Small win. Her probation officer was definitely attempting to destroy her.

CJ watched Laurel drive away. She sucked the life right out of him every time he laid eyes on her.

But Annalee bounced right back into party mode. The kids were hyper, normal for the time of year, dressed in homemade costumes as zombies, nerds, and a variety of objects and foods.

Some of the girls dressed as princesses. Annalee pulled out her makeup kit. She brushed blush on their cheeks and dabbed hundred-dollar perfume on their wrists. Even a few witches waited for the makeover.

He watched her throughout the night. She handed out her candy and chatted with children and even a few of the parents. And she watched him as well. His chest swelled each time she looked his direction.

Buddy, you got it bad.

But there was no going back. No chance of him avoiding the feelings for her that had built out of their work together. December and the end of her community service loomed.

Make the most of every opportunity because the days are evil. This exact situation probably wasn't what the Apostle Paul had in mind in Ephesians 5:16, but the verse fit his situation. What happened in a month, when her required time ended? Would he ever see her again after that? And what about the kids?

That final month of the year, usually so full of joy, would tear her away from him. Well, not tear her away. She'd leave on her own, done with her chore. Though she sure didn't seem to treat it much like a chore.

He'd cross through that threshold later. For now, he relished her glances and enjoyed her playful attitude.

The kids were met by their parents and checked out one by one. The children's pastor made an announcement that the event had officially ended, but a few kids scurried past in a last-ditch effort to grab a little more candy.

"Can I donate all that I have left?" Annalee pointed to her trunk, still half-filled with little red bags.

CJ carried his cooler over. "Sure" He began filling the empty white box. "Did you have fun?"

"A blast. I so wish I didn't have to end this night at the country club."

"I see. I was … well, thinking maybe we could get a bite to eat." Why did he admit that? The answer was obviously *no*.

"I'd rather go to dinner with you." With her chin tilted downward and her crystal-colored eyes peering up at him, she looked almost childlike. Her gaze drooped. "But I have to make an appearance at our ball."

"I understand." He scooped another handful of candy bags out of her trunk.

"Could … would you come with me?" She searched his face.

She invited him? "Yes. I'd really like that." The rush of emotions stuttered his cognitive thoughts. For a moment, he forgot that he was filling the cooler with the Skittles and almost dropped a handful back into the trunk.

"It's a masquerade. You could wear the tuxedo you had on the other night. My father has an old phantom of the opera face plate and opera cape. It would work perfectly."

Her father? He would be there? CJ would meet her mother, too, probably. "Uh. Sure. If that's not an imposition."

"Not at all." She picked up the last few bags of Skittles and dropped them into the cooler. "Give me about a ten-minute head start, and pick me up at my house. The party doesn't start for another half hour, so we shouldn't be too late."

With a wave, she disappeared, leaving CJ holding the filled cooler. He hoisted it into the cab of his truck and raced to his apartment.

A few minutes later, he'd showered and stood in front of the mirror tying his bow tie. He actually smiled at his reflection. This night kept getting better.

Like a battering ram, worry struck his gut. Would people know him at this party? Everyone knew his dad, but he'd kept a low profile since coming back to Dallas for the most part. At least he'd tried to. Hadn't been in the papers much. Not yet, at least.

The memory of another Masquerade at his dad's country club tickled the back of his neck. Couldn't be the same club. Preston Park was exclusive. And while Todd Chambers had money and clout, he wasn't of the same makeup as the members there.

To make sure, he rang his dad.

"What's the trouble now, Carlton?" His father didn't greet him.

"No trouble. Wondering how your night is."

"Hasn't started yet, but the band is warming up. Wish they could use some of the hot air that's being blown out around here."

"Where are you?"

"The masquerade at the club. Would you believe I'm Napoleon this year? Though taller, I think."

CJ had no trouble imagining that.

"If I hadn't brought Angelica Townsend, though, I'd be putting this place behind me. Why the leadership chooses to allow politicians to become members, I'll never know."

Chills rippled across CJ's shoulders. "Politicians?"

"Yes, that mayoral candidate, Todd Chambers. He's shaken every hand in this place at least once. And that biddy of a wife of his is even worse. Somehow, she's got it into her mind that she has an irresistible personality, which she doesn't. She talks incessantly about her husband's plans for the Trinity River project, like I care about that. Which I don't."

He tugged his tie apart and pulled it from the collar. "Well, I hope you get to have a little fun, Dad. Maybe when the music starts."

His dad shared a little more before band sounds covered the words and the call ended. Just as well. He had a more difficult call to make. Mask or no mask, the people at Dad's club knew him well enough. He'd not be able to avoid his last name there. And he needed a little longer to figure out how to tell Annalee the truth without permanently destroying whatever was building between them.

Marji Laine

Chapter 25

CJ's abrupt call to cancel their date started Annalee's night spiraling down a toilet. She still had to make the appearance. She tightened the corset around her eighteenth-century royal ball gown.

"A princess must look like a princess." Her mother insisted on purchasing period royal gowns for every mask.

Her mother didn't have to shove the dress into the driver's side of the Mustang, though. Hoops, yards of tulle, and under-skirting trapped her legs and barred her hands from finding the gear shift and turning the steering wheel very fast, but she made her way into the parking lot at the club.

The band music drifted out on the coolness of the night and she hugged her thin wrap against her bare shoulders. Had CJ come, she'd have enjoyed his warmth and would have looked forward to a night of his company.

But he hadn't come.

She pasted on her tight-lipped smile and entered the ballroom, actually the high-ceilinged restaurant with the tables against the walls. Her parents chatted with someone she didn't recognize, but before she could make her way in that direction, she felt a pull at her elbow.

"M'lady."

Ugh. "Good evening, Boyd."

He pushed the half mask onto the top of his head. "Dear Annalee. And how did you know it was me?"

The stench. She smiled. "I have my ways."

A woman joined him, scowling up at Annalee through wavy, dark ringlets.

Ah, and Giselle. How perfect is this.

"What? No escort? I've heard about your janitor boyfriend."

"He's not a janitor." The boyfriend part tickled her. "Wait, how would you know anything about that?"

Boyd guffawed. "You've been gone far too long, Annalee. You've been on the Gotcha Board for some time."

As much as she wanted to rid herself of the ick-duo, she turned toward the board. They followed as she knew they would. And they got the full desired effect of the horror that Annalee felt when she saw the picture that featured her and CJ.

He wore his overalls and work boots with his back toward the camera, but he held her hand. Her face, with her hair disarranged and a streak of dirt across her cheek, smiled in the direction of the photographer. Must have been after a recent kickball game. She'd had to throw away the filthy yellow sweater.

The picture had the label: Our Favorite Jailbird, Annalee Chambers, Goes Slumming.

Great. That'll get votes for Father.

Giselle tittered behind her hand, and Boyd laughed outright.

Annalee ignored them and spun, bumping into a man she'd not met before.

At twice her age, he gave her the creeps when he looked her up and down. "Well, now, young lady, I'd tell you to watch where you're going, but I'd rather you bump into me anytime."

She cleared her throat. "I beg your pardon."

He stuck his right hand against his chest where the coat covered his fingers. "No begging necessary. I grant your pardon." Removing his hand from his jacket, he held it out to her. "I'm Napoleon, you know."

"Ah."

"And you are?"

"Rather late to meet my parents." She allowed him to bend over her hand controlling her face muscles that yearned to contort.

"Forgive me my little joke. I'm Scott Whelan. Happy to make your acquaintance."

Scott Whelan? All was forgiven. "Oh, I'm so very glad to meet you, Mr. Whelan. I had hoped to meet you at some point. You see, I'm planning a gala to raise funds for the Intercede Foundation."

He kept hold of her hand and covered it with his other one. "You're the lady that all of my assistants are talking about. You've made quite a good impression, my dear."

"I'm so grateful that you agreed to have the gala at your home. That will allow even more of the funds to go to the center."

"It's the least I could do. After all, Intercede Foundation is my charity … uh, the center?"

"The gala will be raising funds for the children's afterschool center on Haskell Avenue to provide the support it needs to stay open for many years to come. I've spoken to all of the members of the board, except for you, of course, and they are most impressed with all of the plans and pleased your lovely home will be part of the event."

"Uh, yes." He released her hand and tugged at his collar. "I didn't realize that the center was the sole beneficiary."

"What better place to pour in our efforts than with the future of Dallas, the children."

"Hmm." His left eyebrow twitched. "I suppose all of this was my son's idea."

"I'm afraid, I'm to blame. I haven't actually met your son." He had a son? Annalee had assumed that the empty desk in the corner belonged to him. "I've been working with Margo Pritchard."

He nodded. "I guess I'll have to accept this blow with grace."

Annalee's mind blanked. What was he talking about?

"At least I can look forward to having you visit my humble home." He reached for her hand again, but Annalee clasped both of them in front of her.

"I've seen pictures of your home, Mr. Whelan. It's far from humble. But I do have an appointment there with the decorator and caterer in a couple of weeks. We'll try to stay out of your way."

He smiled. "As I said before, feel free to bump into me anytime, Miss …"

"Chambers, Annalee Chambers."

Had he grimaced as he walked away?

CJ lingered with Tony at the coffee shop, through the lunch rush and well into the early afternoon. The first day of November had trudged by in a muggy, windy overcast, promising even worse before the weekend arrived. He scowled as he entered the center a half-hour later than normal.

"I guess last night's moonbeams kept you up way past your bedtime." Margo giggled. "Some of the kids overheard you and Annalee planning a date for some ball. I'll bet you were a real Prince Charming."

He faced her, letting her receive the full displeasure of the day, last night's end, and the insinuation her words held.

"Hm. Guess it didn't end so well. Lemme guess. Her daddy doesn't like the Whelan family?"

"I didn't go." He turned away.

"Didn't … why ever not?" She followed him into the kitchen where he poured yet another cup of coffee.

"She doesn't exactly know about … well …" He clenched his teeth. How had he let the charade go on for so long? Taking a sip of the coffee, he hoped to cover his frustration.

"Are you kidding me? You haven't told her who you are, yet? Are you crazy? She's going to hit the roof when she finds out you're über-rich man's bouncing, baby boy."

"I know." His anger blew out with the words. He had to find a way to tell her. Today, if possible. Maybe after work?

Margo's desk phone jingled, and she made a dash for it. He relished the solitary silence for a moment, willing the coffee to ignite enthusiasm or at least a version of it.

"Well, you won't be breaking it to her this weekend." She quick-stepped into the room and filled her own mug. "That was Annalee. Sick as a dog by the sound of her voice."

He straightened. "What's wrong with her?"

"She says it's allergies from the front that's moving through but sounds like a cold to me. Fever and everything."

"Fever? That doesn't sound good."

"I told her to stay home tomorrow, too. You'll get your chance to set the record straight on Monday."

Great.

Missing her work at the center was bad enough. Annalee sneezed into another tissue. "I'll be all right enough to attend the dinner. It's Father's last weekend."

Her mother stayed outside the open door, shaking her head. "Absolutely not. Your face looks like you stayed too long in a tanning bed, and your voice sounds like an old radio program." She stepped inside to snag the doorknob. "You stay right here where you can't make your father sick."

"What about brunch tomorrow?"

"I'll bring you something." Her stoic face gentled for a moment. "Get to feeling better, Annalee." She shut the door.

If she had to miss her father's last few events before the election, she could at least go to church.

But even though she felt better on Sunday morning, she wouldn't show her face or share her germs, just in case. Instead, she indulged in the online experience, scanning the faces for people she knew. She relished in the worship, singing at the top of her croaky voice since no one else was in the house. The sermon left her inspired and eager to see where God would use her.

Once she escaped the confines of the house.

The ringing of the doorbell after lunchtime startled her. Her parents usually lingered at the club until well past two o'clock. And they never rang the doorbell.

She glanced through the beveled glass. CJ stood on the other side.

What was he doing here? She glanced in the mirror. Her unwashed hair looked about as ratty as her father's comfortable, but well-worn, hand-me-down robe. Her nose practically glowed.

The bell chimed again.

She couldn't leave him on the stoop. She cracked the door open an inch. "Hi, um … why are you here?"

He smiled and looked at his boots. The polished cowboy boots she'd seen him in a couple of times along with his regular Sunday attire, dress shirt, and dark jeans. A good look on him.

A shame she couldn't be the least bit attractive in her bedclothes ensemble. She pulled the baggy, plaid robe tighter around her.

"I have some things for you. I thought I'd bring them by." He held up a bouquet of fall-colored flowers and a tote bag.

She eyed the flowers through the crack. No way could she get them into the house without exposing her complete ugliness. Although the tote bag might fit. Politeness wouldn't allow her to suggest he leave them at the door.

With a sigh, she opened the door a little wider. "I'm not exactly at my best."

He shrugged. "Of course not. You're sick." He handed her the bag. "And I don't want to be, so I won't ask to come in. These are from the kids."

"What are they?"

"Our artwork yesterday." He held out the flowers. "And these are from me. My apology for bailing on you Thursday night."

"It's probably a good thing that you didn't come. You might be as sick as me." She sniffed and felt a sneeze coming on. Great. That's all she needed to do in front of him. One of her blast-the-paint-off-the-walls sneezes. "Thanks for all of this, but I better go."

"Okay." His bye was almost swallowed up by the closing of the door and the explosive sneeze that followed. He probably heard that anyway. Her mother swore that her sneezes rattled the china.

She carried her packages to the kitchen. The flowers could wait until the maid got home. She filled the sink with a couple of inches of water and left the flowers leaning against the stainless-steel corner.

Then she emptied the tote bag onto the kitchen table, a large box of copy paper held a stack of papers. Pictures made with glued-on Skittles showed various outdoor scenes.

"Oh." Her eyes moistened. She blamed her fever for the weepiness.

Names were on the backs of each page. The final picture, one of a rainbow, was not made with elementary hands, or only one package of Skittles. A note on the back of it explained. *Not so creative, I know, but like the rainbow gave joy to Noah, so your smile gives me joy. I look forward to your return. CJ.*

The clouds that threatened all weekend finally dumped their

load on Monday. CJ had the buses stop on the street both to avoid getting stuck in the dirt lot and to give the kids a straighter shot into the center.

Margo had towels over every desk and all of the hardwood flooring. Every flat surface that wasn't necessary for walking held a layer of drying slickers, jackets, and raincoats. CJ cranked up the furnace and hoped it stayed strong.

While the kids took sculpting lessons from Annalee. He let his eyes linger on her face a moment. A little puffiness remained around her eyes, and her makeup didn't quite hide the redness underneath her nose, but her voice had lost the nasal quality of the day before. He could barely hear her, but the kids were silent, hanging onto her every word.

He left them to her guidance and joined Paula in preparing a more substantial than normal meal. The kids would need it to fend off the illnesses that typically came during the season of change, spreading through the schools and the center.

The afternoon and evening rushed by faster than normal. Probably due to the close quarters and noisy kids. He barely even saw Annalee before she was wrapped up in her gear and heading for the porch. Something pink and frilly fell midway down her galoshes. "I'm sorry I have to leave early again. Last time, though."

"Let me walk you out."

"Not necessary. Nobody's out in this tonight. Remember to vote tomorrow, and I'll see you on Wednesday."

He reached for her hand, but she'd already opened her umbrella and dashed into the storm.

"I hope your father wins."

She looked back at him and smiled.

His dad would strangle him had he heard his declaration.

Annalee's Election Day started pre-dawn. As she descended the steps, she heard the front door close. Father was already leaving.

Give him peace, God.

How amazing that she could talk to God about her father. About anything. The usual drudge of the election didn't weigh as heavily.

Her mother caught her snacking on a biscuit sandwich in the kitchen. "We've guests."

"I was just leaving."

Her mother's eyebrow shot up and her mouth corners bent downward.

"Or I can greet your guests." Annalee choked down the rest of the biscuit, which took on the texture of concrete. Wiping crumbs from her blouse, she swigged her orange juice and followed her mother into the formal dining room.

"Most of you know my daughter, Annalee," Mother announced. "She's our early bird this morning."

A number of ladies filled the room, including Boyd's mother and Giselle. The latter, chatting with a couple of her friends in the corner, snorted. "More like jailbird."

Several of the women tittered.

Annalee's hostess smile stiffened, but her composure training kicked in. "Yes, welcome to my cell." She led the room in another chuckle. "Seriously, I'm so glad you have come this morning. My father appreciates your support of him, and so do I."

She began to greet the women one at a time, spending a few minutes with each one, asking about the things that were important to them—charitable work, golf handicaps, recent travel. Mrs. Dawson, an older widow with a perpetual smile and an enthusiasm to support charitable projects, laid a wrinkled hand on her arm. "You've changed, Annalee. I can tell. And I've heard about the Intercede Foundation Gala that you're setting up."

A genuine smile plowed through the composure. "The center gives a real chance to children who have very little otherwise. I hope you'll consider supporting the work there."

"Already have. I'll be at the gala." Her green eyes pierced. "What else is different about you?"

Too much to explain. "Working at the center has given me … perspective. And introduced me to …" She wanted to tell about her church experience, but her father's election day wasn't the right time. "… well, to amazing people."

Mrs. Dawson nodded. A conspiratorial look painted her face. "I think you and I should speak again sometime soon."

Exactly Annalee's opinion. She moved around the room, finally reaching the end of the parade. Mrs. Tennyson and Giselle occupied a corner near the kitchen entrance. Annalee eyed her escape. No. She needed to be polite to all of her mother's guests. Even those whose disdain seeped out through squinted dark eyes. The two could have been mother and daughter from their dual expressions.

"It was very nice of you to come, Mrs. Tennyson." She shook her hand.

"Of course, I would be here. I support your father with my

whole heart, and your mother is one of my closest friends. A shame that you have caused her such worry over your poor choices." She stepped away and took a seat at the table.

"Well?" Giselle's lips pressed into a self-satisfied pucker. "You happy to see me, too?" Her eyes glistened with the challenge.

Annalee's composure training cracked around the edges. *God, I need calm.* Suddenly, she didn't see the arrogance of the girl but her fear. Her shallow attempts to claw her way to a higher social status. And even a glimpse of her ultimate goal as the esteemed, and likely lonely, wife of Boyd Tennyson. How sad. Annalee's heart ached. She put her hand on Giselle's and peered directly into her eyes. With sincerity that stemmed all the way from her toenails, she leaned toward the other woman who had been her friend. "I forgive you."

A tear seeped out of the corner of her eye. She meant every word. Leaving Giselle with her mouth hanging open, she made her way through the kitchen to her Mustang. And freedom. How blessed she was to not really be under house arrest.

With a crate full of flyers that expressed the issues at stake and her father's intentions with each one, Annalee campaigned for her father all over the south side. She stopped in every diner, post office, grocery store, barber shop, and salon encouraging people to vote and asking them to vote for her father.

The chill was brutal and her voice almost gone, but that worked to her advantage. People either were impressed that she believed so much in her father or felt sorry for her. Either way, a number of them promised to cast ballots in his direction.

Despite all of her efforts, and the work of the rest of the campaigners, by the end of the after-work news, the current mayor held a marginal advantage. Annalee eyed the list of precincts yet to report. No. Those remaining wouldn't swing the vote her father's way. Dressed in her warmest business suit and fur-lined boots, she tried to pace and stay at peace even while her father's dream broke into a kaleidoscope of jagged pieces.

The news worsened through the hour. Her father's grief and the impending loss weighed on her. She gave him a hug. "I can't stay here anymore. I need to drive around a little."

"Don't be too disappointed, child. The numbers aren't all bad. I might very well have another chance at this in a few more years."

Wow. This was his loss, but he could encourage her. Still, his words didn't release the adrenaline that had accumulated through the hours of walking during the day and waiting throughout the evening.

She pointed the nose of her car north and cranked up the heater. Within moments, though, she wound her way southward and found herself sitting in front of the center as the lights turned out.

Margo followed CJ onto the porch and turned to lock the door.

He jogged down the steps and met her at the gate. "What are you doing here?"

"Let an old woman pass." Margo trudged through. "Sorry about your father, Annalee."

"Wait, I'm walking you to your bus stop." CJ followed her out of the gate.

"Nonsense. I can see it from here." She turned back and gave CJ an odd look. "You just …" She nodded at him and pointed to Annalee.

Strange. But no odder than Annalee showing up on a day when she shouldn't be there. "I'm not sure why I'm here."

"Well don't look at me." He chuckled but sobered. "Hey, I

really am sorry about your father, but some of the proposals that he suggested received good press. I bet he could make another run for mayor or at least city council."

"That's his plan at this point. Who knows?" She leaned against the windshield brace of the Mustang. "I couldn't sit there any longer, watching the returns."

"They're not all in. There's still a chance."

"You don't really believe that." Hope rose, but she dared not let it consume her and lead her crashing to another disappointment.

He shrugged. "It's possible I guess."

"Yeah. I wish he'd go ahead and relent gracefully instead of letting the torture continue."

"I've heard your father speak. He's got a pretty good sense of timing. I think his concession speech will work out when he feels it's the right moment." He closed the gap between them. "I'm glad you came, though."

How could she tell him that she longed for his strong shoulder to brace her, his warm hand to make her feel protected, and his true eyes that showed he cared? She locked onto the sapphire gaze feeling a tear squeeze out and settle on her bottom lashes.

"It's okay." He spread his arms and drew her into them, rubbing her shoulder with one hand and embracing her with the other. He tucked her head under his chin. "Your father is a good man. I believe he can still make a difference." His voice became a whisper against her hair.

She clenched the edges of his blue jean jacket with both hands and snuggled her cheek against the warmth of his flannel-covered chest. Inhaling the aroma of pine and the spices of his cologne she felt contentment that she hadn't experienced in some time.

If only she could stay there.

"And I believe in his daughter. You already make a difference, Annalee. You've made an impact on these kids."

The words drifted above her mind before piercing fog and settling their meaning on her. She leaned back and searched his expression. Flattery looked completely different on a face than sincerity. "I have? Do you mean that?"

He nodded. "You've made an impact on all of us. Margo. Me." He cupped her cheek with his hand and stroked his thumb along her cheekbone. "Especially me."

She ached to believe him. And his eyes remained steady with the promise they held.

You mean so much to me. She wanted to speak the words, but they evaporated on her lips as he brought his down upon them. She responded, curling her hand inside his jacket and around to his back.

His face warmed her and his lips gently kneaded her own with a dozen tender kisses before he lifted his head. "I've wanted to do that for weeks." The words breathed into her mouth ignited a new passion, and he kissed her again. Harder this time.

She tracked her other hand along his chest and wrapped it around his neck. His arms tightened around her waist.

By the time the kiss subsided, his heavy breathing matched hers. She clung to him. Her mouth forming an O that whispered her exhales.

He stroked her hair and kissed her forehead. "I care about you a great deal. I don't want to hear that this will never work. Not tonight. I want to relish having you in my arms for a little while."

Silly man. "I have no intentions of saying this will never work." She snuggled against his chest for a few minutes more then stepped back. "And I care a great deal about you, too." As much as she hated to leave, her choice to come to the center had given results beyond her imagination. Nerve endings all over her body still quivered. She opened her car door. "But I should go."

He smiled and stroked her cheek. "I'll see you tomorrow."

Chapter 26

CJ stared at the mirror and jerked his bowtie. Tonight was the night. Forgiveness or failure, either way, Annalee would know who he was before her grand gala began.

It was only fair.

Though he wished he'd bared his soul to her before now, before last week. Before their kiss.

But no. He'd just had to seal the attraction. Make sure she had the same feelings for him that he had for her. What he had to say now was only going to hurt worse after that. Unfortunately, he'd barely laid eyes on her the rest of the week.

She and Margo had their heads together over the gala the entire next day, arranging volunteers for the waitstaff. And, according to his assistant, she spent Thursday and Friday ironing out details with the caterers and media and helping the decorators at Dad's house.

He looked at his reflection again and brushed a shock of hair into place with his fingertips. "I'm telling her. Now if I can." He'd raced to his dad's home to prepare so he could have some time alone with her before the guests arrived. Surrounded by the opulence of this mansion on Turtle Creek, he'd been watching out the window for the shiny red Mustang but hadn't seen it. Surely, she'd arrived by now.

Someone tapped on his door. His heart swelled for an instant, but it was only one of the maids with his newly polished shoes. What was he thinking anyway? That she'd come up here to find him? Ludicrous.

Though she'd visited Dad's house this week, she'd probably not gotten the hint about CJ. His football trophies and photos lined the walls of the study, but there were no other pictures of him. Nothing more recent for almost a decade.

But during the gala, too many people would know him. Too many would speak to the center's handyman. He had to either avoid everyone, especially her, or find opportunity early on to share his identity with her gently.

Best option wasn't the easiest, though, since she hadn't arrived. He glanced out the window again then checked his Rolex, something he rarely wore, even on occasions like this. One of the gifts his dad had insisted that he needed as a status symbol to stand out from the crowd.

Whatever.

Had she arrived yet? He stepped out of the door and scanned the room. Fall colors hung in festoons all around the great hall. Candles were everywhere. Soft music floated in the air along with the spices of cider and mulled wine. Probably the best from Dad's cellar. Typical for a night like this.

But Annalee was anything but typical.

She crossed the great hall with her back toward him, dressed in a gold, low-backed gown. He recognized her even with her hair in an intricate weave of some sort. He darted down the hallway to the back stairs and trotted into the kitchen. A handyman should enter from the servants' entrance anyway. Although continuing the ruse slammed his conscience once more.

Dad's expert cook raised an eyebrow. "You need someting, Misser Whelan?"

"No, thanks, San-jay. This smells delicious." He could practically hear the little man's internal screaming at him to get out of his kitchen. San-jay had his domain amid Dad's reign over his little kingdom.

He crossed to the dining room door. Annalee worked on covered items in the open living area. A stringed quartet tuned on the balcony overlooking the great room. The dining room table boasted platters of all sorts of delicacies. How had she done all of this?

The bell rang and several people entered. She rushed to greet them. He'd better talk with her now or miss his chance altogether. By the time he reached her, another couple had entered. Annalee smiled, but he could tell in her eyes when she glanced up at him that she had no joy in this arrival.

"Oh, here you are. I'm so glad you made it." She wrapped her hand around his arm.

"Let me guess. This is the janitor." The man laughed.

CJ's jaw twitched. *Jokes on you, buddy.*

"Thank you for the invitation, Annalee." The woman next to him kept her brows raise, but her gaze wandered around the room.

"Ah, yes." He patted CJ's shoulder. "No offense, guy. I guess the politically correct word nowadays is custodian. But then, you don't look all that political."

"Be nice." The woman lowered her voice to a virtual growl.

"I'm always nice." He jutted his dimpled chin toward Annalee. "Did your father tell you I'm on a probationary assignment? I guess we're both on probation." He let loose a single bitter laugh. "But I'd say you've done very well for yourself, Annalee."

"Yes. And you've done a lovely job organizing this gala. I'm impressed." The woman gazed at the festoons on Dad's vaulted ceiling.

"I can't help but wonder how you did it without Mommy's help."

CJ wanted to stick a fist in the arrogant man's jaw.

"Come on, Boyd." The woman tried to turn him away.

"I'm expecting to hear how your mom purchased the crown for Miss Texas Recycling."

"Keep going." His companion gave another shove.

"Or Miss Housemaids Union Number Five."

Annalee squeezed his elbow. "Smile and ignore them."

Leave it to her to speak peace over him. He covered her hand with his own. "I should be saying that to you. Should I know who they are?"

"The ex-boyfriend and ex-best friend that I doused with wine." She pinked but didn't smile.

"Ex-boyfriend, I believe. The woman didn't sound much like an ex-friend, though."

"She didn't, did she?" She brought her thumbnail to her lips.

"And you invited them?"

"I invited his family. Our mothers have been best friends for years. I expect they came to witness my absolute failure."

He took both of her gloved hands in his and locked eyes with her. "You've already succeeded. Your friend was right. This house looks amazing. All of the plans, the food, it all came together. You did this."

She gave him a small smile, but the angle of her brows said she wasn't sure she believed him.

"And there's something else. I'm not a janitor-slash-custodian."

"I know that, CJ. The center wouldn't run without you." A large group came in and claimed her attention.

Ach. He had to speak to her. But once the guest gates opened, the flow continued. Maybe when the dancing began and her other duties stopped.

Annalee still had so much to do. Pressure filled her chest. With every ring of the doorbell, she had to halt and do all of the greeting. If only Mr. Whelan or someone else from the board would take over that task. She should have asked them to arrive a little early.

Her mother sure wouldn't help. Always late, she craved an entrance and felt entitled to the center of attention. Annalee wished she hadn't invited her but couldn't very well leave her off of the invitation list for a myriad of reasons.

She finally secured the attention of one of the board members, Mrs. Moncrief, who agreed to be the greeter long enough for Annalee to uncover the items for the auction.

Aside from specialty items, sporting events, and luxury excursions, many notable artists donated exclusive pieces. She'd even included several of her own paintings of the children playing at the center. One of CJ and some of the boys trying to paint. In fact, CJ showed up in several of the pieces.

She'd been embarrassed about that until Tuesday. But his kiss. The confirmation of his feelings for her stimulated a boldness she'd only recently felt. Even as she uncovered each one, displaying her affection openly on the subject, both the children and the man, courage mounted. "Go get 'em, guys." She wiped away a tiny tear.

God, please let this work.

Her chest swelled that she'd completed so many. And they were truly beautiful. Another tear formed, but she'd steeled herself against the possibility of keeping any of them. Yet, they hadn't been bid upon. Not yet. She might still be humiliated.

Her favorite piece would receive high honor, however. She and Tally had spent every extra minute they had working on the girl's technique. Her self-portrait was the most beautiful thing Annalee had ever seen. Whatever the top bid, she intended to double it in her father's name and dare either of her parents to say a word after all they spent on Dad's campaign.

"There you are, Annalee."

"Mother? I didn't expect you for at least another half hour."

"Don't be foolish, child. This is your first gala. You obviously can't function without me."

Annalee bit the inside of her cheek until she tasted blood though she had been needing a hostess. "I really could use your expertise at greeting people, Mother. The buffet table is to the left and the auction will be in here."

"I'll be happy to help you." She looked around. "My, but these are wonderful. What an amazing collection of art you've brought.

Is it all from a local gallery?"

"No, from several popular artists and local talent. But they are wonderful, aren't they?"

Her mother scanned the room once more, her eyes resting on the picture with CJ and the boys, Annalee's first completion. "I feel like I know them."

Was that approval? And did it count since her mother didn't realize Annalee as the artist?

"Truly exceptional." She turned and reentered the main foyer.

That did it. Annalee bolted for the powder room. With her mother's approval, though unaware, all of the tension reached an apex. Tightening her facial muscles slowed the flood of tears but couldn't stem the tide. Her makeup would require intensive repairs, but *exceptional*. Her mom had used the word. About something Annalee had accomplished.

Without the opportunity to speak to Annalee, CJ kept to the corners, avoiding people he knew and staying away from Annalee altogether.

When the auction began in the great hall, he busied himself with bringing the donations to one of the servers who took it to the mount at the front of the hall for bidding. Chairs had been spread throughout the room so few people milled about. His chances of being exposed lessened, and he allowed himself to enjoy a little of Annalee's triumph.

Many of the artists and donors had come to auction their

donations personally. Annalee's idea. Even this crowd had a harder time of saying no to the face of a creator or famous donor than to an impersonal auctioneer. While the special packages, trips, and tickets to concerts and sporting events were well-received, each of the paintings received stellar purchases. Far above their face value.

He picked up the next painting. A picture he recognized. Annalee had shown him her initial sketches after the first art class she taught, but this finished version held vivid hues in collections of tiny dots no bigger than the head of a pin. How had she done that?

Not able to bid on it himself, he handed it off to the server and found his dad on the back row. "No matter what, purchase this next picture."

"What?" His father had little grace and no patience for spontaneous activity.

"Whatever it takes, buy that picture. Please, Dad. It's important to me."

"How important?" His father squinted his eyes and glanced back at him.

"You win. You purchase that picture, and I'll start working in your offices in January."

He straightened and turned to look him fully in the face, doubt showing in his eyes.

CJ's eyebrow twitched. Could his dad really think him a liar? After all this time? "You have my word."

"Done." Soft and final, his future sealed. Yet, his father made good his promise. And at a hefty price. When Annalee introduced herself as the artist and identified the picture as her first completed work, bids poured in. The crowd knew their art, maybe even continued to bid because Scott Whelan insisted on winning it.

When the next picture proved to be another Annalee Chambers creation, his father surprised him by taking it as well. She'd brought five in all and the Whelan's came away with all but one of them. Todd Chambers, though he couldn't outbid Dad, gained enough sympathy that dad stood down to allow him to go home with one of his daughter's paintings.

"Thanks for that." His dad had come through for him.

"Yours is the first one. I get all of the others." He winked at him. CJ had never seen him wink before. But he'd be spending a lot of time with the man soon enough and would likely see him wink plenty at that point.

Annalee stepped to the podium once more. "Some of you realize there is still one work of art left to auction." This was her favorite with the surprise to go with it, she hoped, would send the bidding over the top.

"The final artist of the night is a local painter. This is entitled Self Portrait." She hazarded a glance at CJ. His eyes widened as the large picture of the ballerina made it to the stand. The perfect extension on pointe, the ruffled tulle of the tutu, didn't hide the clear depiction of beautiful Tally's face.

"I'd like you to meet the artist, Tally Madison."

Tally came out of the dining room where she'd been waiting with her mom. Though Mrs. Madison stayed near the back of the room, tissue in hand, Tally limped up to the mic and took it from

Annalee's offered hand. Lifting her head over her bent back, she smiled at the crowd. "Thanks, Miss Annalee. And thanks to all of you who have come tonight to help raise money for the afterschool center. That's where I first started drawing and painting and the place takes really good care of my little brothers. They didn't come tonight, but that's okay because they're pretty noisy."

A ripple of laughter spread through the room.

"I know I'm not a well-known artist yet, but my dream is to be one someday. Well, besides being a ballerina, which I don't think God has in store for me, but then again you can never tell."

Annalee scanned the room. All the guests smiled and a few of the women wiped under their eyes. Tally was a natural with a crowd. Sincere, earnest, and never backing down.

"So, I guess we better start the bidding. Would anyone be willing to bid a dollar?"

The chuckles spread as several hands went up. Tally worked perfectly, taking each bid in order until the final two. The chairman of the arts board for the Meyerson Center vied against one of the Tate family members who came over from Ft. Worth. The price went higher than any of the other artwork. As much as Annalee wanted to double it, her parents would have fainted. Instead, she tacked on enough to win the portrait and promised the Meyerson chairman that she'd put it on display there.

The man smiled. "I'll take you up on that. Maybe I can persuade that youngster of yours to paint me another one."

Tally whooped with that suggestion, and the long-seated patrons stood to offer ovations. Tally and the other artists made sure that all of the guests opened their checkbooks, even those who hadn't bid.

"I'd say this beat all expectations, but I won't have a total until tomorrow." Margo punched in numbers on a calculator after the final donation was collected. "Suffice it to say that the center will easily stay open for another decade, at least."

"Unless the price of crayons goes up." CJ laughed and gave Annalee's shoulders a squeeze.

Laurel Stewart, wrapped in a sapphire velvet stole, crossed toward where the three had gathered. "Well, I guess you have every right to be proud of yourselves."

"Thank you for coming." Annalee gave a polite smile and wished her away.

"Why did you come? Were you on the invitation list?" CJ startled her with his rudeness, but Laurel Stewart seemed unimpressed.

"Technically, I'm to report on the work of my client. Personally, since you so rudely refused to show me your apartment, I thought I'd take a look at your home. It's really lovely."

His home? Had she heard that right? CJ didn't look at her, and Laurel Stewart ignored her.

"This isn't my home." His chin dropped.

Of course not. What was she getting at?

"Okay, then your father's home. At least he isn't as opposed to wealth as you are." She spun and cat-walked back to the front door.

CJ put his right hand at the back of his neck.

His father … Her mind reeled. His *father?* She gasped. Carlton Whelan. The nameplate. Why hadn't she put that together with Carl James? He'd lied to her. Played her. Realization emptied her chest and threatened to empty her stomach.

She wheeled and headed for the kitchen.

"Wait, Annalee."

She bolted through the door and snatched up her purse and wrap from where she'd laid it by the back door.

"Annalee, please." CJ followed her, but she wouldn't turn around. Couldn't bear to look at him. And she refused to let the tears that burned in her eyes come out.

Someone came in through the back door, and she dashed out of it. CJ lagged, probably having to dodge around the person. She had no chance in her spiked heels to outrun him, but pain pressed her. The need to escape. Was everything a lie? God? The church? No, surely not. *God help me.*

CJ caught up with her and pulled on her arm before she could reach her car.

She whirled around with her palm open and caught him hard across the cheek. "Don't you ever touch me, again."

Total reaction. Her jaw dropped. Had she really? She dashed to her car. In her mirror, he still stood, his cheek red and his fists clenched.

Clamping her teeth, she made it out of the driveway before the tears blurred her vision. She pulled into a grocery parking lot and let them flow.

Her chest ached. Everything she thought was real, a lie. She'd paid for his taxi. Given him money for dinner. *Oh my gosh.*

Sobs rocked her. *He lied to me.* How could he have kept such a secret? When he knew the struggle she'd experienced. He had to know this revelation would hurt her. So why did he wait for someone else to tell her? Especially Laurel Stewart? Surely, he'd have guessed her humiliation. Did he laugh at her? Was this a test to see how low Annalee Chambers would stoop?

Hugging her sides, she let the tears wash her makeup away.

She couldn't tell which was worse, the horrible ending to the lovely night or the fact that she still had to return to the center like her heart hadn't been thoroughly crushed.

Oh, how could she face him again? How could she face any of them? They all had to know her mistake. Stupid, stupid mistake.

Her mother had been right all along.

As the thought crossed her mind, the flow eased.

No. Mother was wrong. Wrong about her and her work at the center. If nothing else, she'd had the confidence to complete artwork. To plan the gala. To stand up for herself. She pulled out of the lot.

Only a few more minutes on the road brought her home. She pulled into the garage. Returning to her life as it had been was no longer possible. She'd made a fool of herself. Even thoughts of spending time hidden away in her basement gave her no comfort.

There were only three more weeks to work besides the break at Thanksgiving. And with all of the extra hours she'd put in preparing for the gala, she might be able to persuade Margo to add hours to her sheet.

Wait. That would be CJ's place. The real director. Of course. Another betrayal bit through her heart.

She'd have to try anyway.

That couldn't have gone worse. But CJ didn't deserve better.

Why had he let it go so far? He drove for hours, touring the streets of the city until he felt somewhat settled down and returned to his apartment. By the time he changed clothes, his nerves had balled up again. He hit the gym downstairs pounding on a punching bag.

Laurel's face floated, superimposed, on that bag. But not for long. The bag was himself. He slammed his fist into the image of his own face again and again until his shoulders burned, and his hands and body ached.

He couldn't blame Laurel for speaking truth. That wasn't the trouble. He'd brought the trouble when he didn't share his identity in the first place.

And why hadn't he? He'd made excuses. Timing. Circumstances. Deep down he'd always questioned the motives of girls he dated. Even of his friends. Maybe this had been a test after all. To be sure that Annalee cared for him despite his background instead of because of it.

And she had. Until this tragic backfire.

Sunday's church and a long nap to recuperate from his late night did nothing to ease his chest from hurting. And not from his punching bag tirade.

He had to find some way to get Annalee to listen, even though her forgiveness was unlikely. How could he expect her to? She wouldn't understand, but he had to try. Intending to drive to her house and talk with her, he instead found himself at the Brimming Café.

Margo and Tony sat at a table discussing the party the night before. Funny how she found the quietest time to visit so Tony could sit down and chat with her.

CJ didn't want to interrupt especially not with the damp towel of his disastrous mistake.

He ducked back toward the front door, but Tony caught him.

"Hey, thought I heard someone coming in. Join us."

CJ sighed and followed him, scooting an easy chair toward their low table.

"Want something?"

He shook his head. "To talk."

"Have you spoken with her?" Margo eyed him. She didn't have to identify the *her*.

"No. Not after she slapped me."

Margo's eyes widened. "I thought your cheeks showed embarrassment."

"You know I deserved it." He leaned onto his knees. "But I don't know what to do now."

"She was the real thing, boss." Margo sipped from a cup. "You saw it right away. Took me longer."

"Then how come I'm the one she hates?"

Tony brought him a cup even though he hadn't asked for one. "I don't think you trusted her very much. You didn't believe in her."

Was that it? He hadn't thought her shallow, but maybe he'd been afraid he was wrong. The reasoning made sense but didn't get him any closer to his next step. There was a next step, right?

Tony's mocha hit the spot. He let his concern drift with Margo's chatter about the money raised, the interest encouraged. His dad had even mentioned feeling better about the center than he had in years. Probably because CJ would no longer be working there, maligning the family name in his dungaree overalls.

But CJ was no closer to deciding on his next course of action with Annalee when she marched into the center on Monday afternoon.

The fact that she never looked at him and gave no response

when he spoke to her didn't leave him many options.

"Annalee, if I could speak to you for a moment." He followed her into the office where she signed in on her sheet.

Margo's eyes flitted between them.

Annalee ignored his request and formally addressed the older woman. "I wonder if I can add the hours in which I worked on last night's paintings, and the ones in which I tutored Tally to my total hours of service?" She laid the clipboard in front of Margo and pointed to some of the dates.

Margo leaned over the paper. "You'd have to get approval from the director." She nodded toward CJ.

"Of course." Annalee turned to face him with challenge painted all over her features and held out the clipboard.

He sighed and took the board and the pen. "How many hours?" He poised to write them in beside his initials.

"Seventy-five."

"Seventy-five?"

She didn't answer him. And he didn't really have a right to question her claim. She wasn't the one who had been living a lie for two and a half months. "Fine. Is that all?"

"This means I'll be done next week."

Next week? "Look, Annalee, can we talk? Please."

She marched into the girls' bathroom without looking back at him.

He turned to Margo. "What can I do now?"

She shook her head. "I can't help you, kid. Beyond telling you to pray."

"Great. Even you can't sympathize."

"Sympathize nothing. I can empathize. Been caught in big lies before. But I never got out of them with the friendships still intact.

Sorry I don't have a magic wand or something." She ambled into the kitchen. "And by the way, Paula's under the weather, today. I thought I might get Annalee to do the snack. It's simple enough, chili. Has to be heated through."

"Fine." He sighed. "If anyone needs me, which clearly won't happen, I'll be outside playing with the kids."

"And working off some of that frustration, I bet."

He wouldn't argue that comment.

Marji Laine

Chapter 27

Avoid CJ as much as physically possible. Annalee's solitary focus broke seconds after entering the bathroom. He'd signed off on her extra work. Her ending date at the center was only a week away.

She should be ecstatic, right?

After making quick work of her accustomed assignment, she took over for Margo in the kitchen. The side window gave a full view of the lot. CJ played football with a group of boys. His smile didn't meet his eyes when he spoke to them. A boy with the ball raced past him, and he stood watching, not even attempting chase.

Was he sorry? Probably not. More likely disappointed that his little game was over. Or upset that he'd been found out to be the lying rat that he was.

No. No one who cared so much for children could be a rat.

And he looked sorry. Her chest convulsed, and she looked away. "Don't be an idiot, Annalee." She dared not give in to her wasted hopes. Look where they had gotten her so far.

She gave her attention to the chili. It wasn't bubbling the way it normally did. With clean hands, she dabbed her finger on the top and stuck it in her mouth. Ew. Ice cold. She lifted the pot and noticed no flames burning. Had Margo really forgotten to turn on the burner? Or maybe the flames hadn't been high enough to stay on.

Grabbing the lighter, Annalee clicked on the gas for a second.

Maybe she should at least talk to CJ. Hear what he has to say.

She leaned toward the furthest burners of the heavy-duty stove and flicked on the lighter.

A flash billowed in front of her and she reeled backward and spun. Trying to catch herself against the island in the center of the kitchen, she banged her head on the cast iron stew pot that was filled with partially frozen chili. Ignoring the pain, she looked behind her. Flames spewed out from the back edge of the stove. The whole wall seemed to be on fire.

The fire alarm screamed into action, waking Annalee from her surreal experience.

The extinguisher. She darted around the island and grabbed the large canister attempting to read the abbreviated directions. Knowing how to work it should probably be part of the volunteer manual. She pulled out the pin and aimed the nozzle at the flames that continued to burst from behind the stove.

Bracing herself, she pressed the trigger. White foam spit out toward the fire but didn't shoot far enough. No matter, the meager offering wouldn't have made much of a dent. A tub of Cool Whip held more.

What else could she do?

Playing football with the boys didn't distract CJ as much as he hoped it would. In fact, his ability suffered from his preoccupation with Annalee.

Her anger. He deserved every bit of it, but could he really give up on the relationship that they had begun? A relationship like none he'd ever had. He had to fight for it.

He turned toward the back door, determined to talk to her, tell her the depth of his feelings and why his fears kept him from admitting his true identity at first.

"Heads up." Tyrone called out the warning. CJ automatically ducked and held up his arms.

The ball missed his hands completely, but bounced against the back of his head, shoving him prone into the dirt.

He sat back on his heels. "Thanks for the warning." He wiped his hands against his blue jeans. *Glad I didn't put on my nice ones like I thought about doing.*

"Sorry, CJ. My foot don't always send the ball where I ask it to." Marcus, a first grader, had a gift for simplistic reasoning of complex matters. Maybe CJ could use something along those lines with Annalee?

"Point yourself away from the center, then. That way, if the foot messes up again, it won't come close to the windows."

"Sure thing." Cute kid. They grew up fast in a neighborhood like this, though. CJ didn't want to think about what would happen to him, Tyrone, Hayden, after the new year. The center would probably put Margo as the director, but they needed a man on the premises. Protection and to be a role model for these boys.

Not like he'd been so great at that.

A buzz from inside the building sounded.

"What is that?" Tyrone tucked the football between his elbow and hip.

CJ turned toward the building and noticed lights flickering in the kitchen window. Reality dawned. "Fire alarm." He kept his voice down and turned back to Tyrone. "Take Marcus and your brother. Get the kids to the lot over there." He pointed toward his truck.

CJ bolted for the back door, yelling at two other workers on the patio. "Get the kids to the parking lot. Keep them together."

He burst through the door. The wall across the room was engulfed, and Annalee stood flinging flour from an open sack at the flames. He reached for her and when she pulled back, he hoisted her over his shoulder and carried her into the play lot.

Margo dashed from the front of the building. "Bertie called 9-1-1. Everybody's out. The babies are next to Annalee's car with the ladies that work with them. I checked the bathrooms on both levels before coming out myself."

Annalee started coughing and tried to sit up.

"No, no, no." Margo knelt and pushed her right back down. "You stay right there."

Guilt piled on CJ. He could hardly look at her laying there, her face already beginning to blister, but nothing like her hands and arms. Her hair still had places that smoked from the singe. Why in the world had she stayed in that room with the fire raging? "Annalee, what were you thinking?"

Annalee slowly turned her head toward him.

A siren screamed followed by another and CJ stood. "Stay

with her. Make sure she doesn't go into shock." Margo had already shed her jacket, covering Annalee with it and moved to hold her feet several inches off the ground.

He jogged around the building, running on automatic with an adrenaline pump. The last thing he needed to do was think.

CJ directed the firefighters to the kitchen and the paramedics to where Annalee lay in the side lot. When he returned to her, the full measure of her burns showed. Her eyelids were the only exposed skin not reddened by the fire. And a deep cut slashed across her forehead like a third eyebrow.

The paramedics dressed it, but she didn't open her eyes, though she winced a couple of times. They wrapped her up and rolled her to the back of the ambulance.

He moved with them. "I want her in Parkland's burn center. But I don't want her to have to wait."

"Got it." The EMT turned to his partner and raised his voice. "She's a first-come."

His assurance that she'd go directly into a trauma unit both encouraged and worried CJ. *God, You have to get her through this.* He glanced at her face. Too red. And way too relaxed for all that she'd endured.

He choked on the sight of her still face as the gurney rolled into the ambulance. He couldn't think, couldn't even pray anymore. Not if he wanted to maintain any control at all. He stomped back toward Margo. "Did you call her parents?"

"The records are in there, CJ." She pointed to the center.

He couldn't leave her alone like that. First, he called the man who taught his Sunday Bible class. Annalee had met his daughter Chrissy. They would go to the hospital right away.

Then, he called his pastor, catching him still at the office. CJ explained a little of what happened and asked if the buses could come collect the children and house them until their parents could pick them up. Especially since sunset closed in.

Margo had the children's parents' numbers in her phone and was busy making calls.

"We'll be moving them all to the church." He walked out to the parking lot where the rest of the kids waited. Margo followed.

The ladies who worked the nursery carried their crib full of little ones across the crumbly surface of the lot. CJ met them halfway, helping them across some of the rougher surfaces.

Reaching the total group, he didn't attempt a smile but used his enthusiastic voice. "Looks like we're going to be moving over to the church where we had your trunker-treat the other night."

Some of the kids whimpered. Tyrone turned a tear-streaked face toward him.

"Don't worry, Tyrone. Miss Pritchard is calling your parents right now. They'll know where to pick you up."

"Ain't worried about that. Miss Annalee. She din't look too good." He sniffed. "She gonna be all right, CJ?" His voice broke.

CJ clamped his jaw tight. *Hold it together.* "She's got a pretty good sunburn, but she'll be all right. We'll have to make some cards for her like we did the weekend when she had that cold."

Only there wouldn't be a place to do that. He gritted his teeth again.

Three church buses wheeled over the curb and drove toward them across the dirt lot. CJ distracted himself by organizing the group into three different sections with adults in charge of each one. The final section had four different workers, including Margo, carrying the babies, toddlers, and infants. The best they could do was sit in the back with the little ones and ask that the bus be driven slowly. The youngest child, not even three months old, CJ carried himself. He braced his head against the seat in front of him and made his body a sort of cocoon around the little man.

Thankfully, the church wasn't far away. But the short trip allowed him time alone with his thoughts. The very thing he'd been trying to avoid all weekend.

And the one most troubling. Had Annalee set that fire on purpose to get back at him? Did he really know her as well as he thought he did?

Like whispers on a stormy night, the questions seeped into his mind. Was there a dark side to Annalee?

The bus slowed to a gentle stop, and he lifted his head. The church lay just ahead. Images of the cars parked with trunks open and festooned with colorful crepe paper and balloons tickled his memory. And Annalee. Full of joy and laughter with the children. Angry and protective with Jamaysia. Vulnerable at the lake.

No. He couldn't believe that about her. Shame from simply entertaining the ideas crept up his neck. This was what happened when left to his pathetic thoughts. He glanced at the infant who had slept through all of the excitement. "Little man, this trip would have been easier on me if you'd have been awake."

The bus pulled to a stop, and he cradled the boy close.

CJ had to keep his wits about him. These kids counted on him to be strong.

Annalee vaguely remembered the ambulance ride. Funny.

She'd never been in a hospital in her life, let alone an ambulance. But in a few short months, she'd been inside both three separate times.

Not a record she wanted to break anytime soon.

Without stopping in the waiting room, the two paramedics wheeled her directly through the trauma unit doors. Every movement created sheer pain across her arms where a rough blanket lay. And the skin under the bands that held oxygen tubes up to her nose rebelled. Screaming through her head with every jarring movement.

Finally, the men stopped and edged back the blanket they'd had on her.

"What do we have?" A tall woman with dark, blunt-cut hair leaned over her and shined a light into her eyes.

"Flashfire. Blew up in her face by the looks of it."

"I tried to …"

"Don't speak, miss." The woman picked at something on her face. "Looks good, fellas. Thanks."

Annalee wanted to thank them as well but stayed obedient to the woman. Another came in, obviously a nurse, so the first was either a supervisor or a doctor. Why a doctor would come in so quick stumped her, though.

"Get a blood pressure hooked up on her ankle. And shoot in another bag of solution."

Another bag? Oh, yeah. The EMTs had poked her arm. Like in the old reruns of *Emergency*.

"Miss, can you hear me?"

Annalee nodded.

"Can you tell me your name?"

"Annalee Chambers."

The nurse tapped away at an iPad screen.

The woman smiled. "Very good. I'm Dr. Artemon. Do you remember what happened to you?"

She nodded.

The nurse said something to the doctor, and her mouth turned down. "Again, in three."

"I tried …"

"Miss Chambers, you've received some bad burns on your arms and your face. Speaking will only make them hurt more, so let's limit that to only what I must know from you for now." She glanced at the screen of the nurse's iPad. "Who can we call about this?"

"Father." News that her face had burned made her stay as still as possible. "Todd on Valley Ridge Road, Dallas." She could give her the phone number, but Todd Chambers was easy to find. He made sure of that and his cell phone rang with great regularity.

The nurse nodded and typed again into her iPad.

"We'll call your father. I'm told you have a visitor, but we'll need to wait a little bit." She typed a couple of keys on the nurse's screen. "Get that BP up."

She turned back to Annalee before she stepped out of the room. "I'll be back, Miss Chambers. And don't worry. I don't see any signs of third-degree at this point, so little chance of scarring from the burns."

"Are you comfortable?" The nurse laid cool material over her face, arms and hands.

Comfortable? Really? Annalee nodded, though she didn't mean it. Her thoughts drifted to who might be waiting to see her. Had CJ come?

Nothing in her believed that. Not after he blamed her for what happened to the center. *What were you thinking?* Would she never escape that question and the scorn that accompanied it?

"There, that blood pressure number is much better. I'll bring back your visitor, now." The nurse stepped out of the room.

In truth, Annalee couldn't think of a thing she'd done to cause the flash. Except igniting it, of course. She'd never be able to convince CJ of that, though. He knew she was upset. Probably thought she'd been careless. Or worse, vindictive.

She discarded the idea. He wasn't that way at all. More likely, he recognized her as a bumbler that could never do things well, at least not with any consistency.

That still didn't answer who waited to see her. She didn't have to wait long. Chrissy Barton stepped into the room. "CJ talked to my dad and asked if I could come over. He wanted me to tell you that all the kids are fine, though a little worried about you. They're all at the church waiting for their parents now, so you don't need to let a concern cross your mind. Has someone called your mother and father?"

Annalee remembered the doctor's warning and nodded slightly.

"It must hurt to talk. Stay silent. Goodness knows I can carry a conversation all by myself without any help, huh."

She suppressed a smile that would doubtless cause a huge measure of pain.

Chrissy laid a soft hand on her shoulder. "Does that hurt at all? Even a little?"

Annalee shook her head.

"Good, then let's chat with our Father for a few minutes, shall we?" She shut her eyes and engaged the Lord in a talk that could hardly be dubbed a prayer. Like she sat on the porch next to Him, she urged His healing and comfort during the painful recuperation. She asked for provision for the kids at the center, a new place to go while repairs were made and that they would be finished with speed.

She prayed for CJ, too. For his courage as he worked with the kids and comfort as he watched someone he cared for go through the valley.

He cared for her? He must have said or done something to make Chrissy believe that.

"And help him as he prepares to leave the work he feels You've called him to. Give him courage to stand in that situation as well."

Wait a minute. He was leaving the center? Why in the world would he do such a thing?

Chrissy's amen only started the conversation.

"CJ's leaving?" Annalee opened her eyes.

"Did I say that?" Her gaze twitched from side to side. "I get caught up in prayer sometimes and talk to God without thinking about who else is listening in. Sorry. I guess I should share the rest, though. CJ and his dad made some type of deal. I don't know all the details, but CJ's part of the agreement is to start working at Whelan Group next year."

The nurse walked in and fiddled with the pump around Annalee's ankle.

"I'm not usually a gossip, Annalee. I feel really bad about sharing that information. CJ should have the right to tell you in his own way."

Except that she hadn't let him speak to her. Then again, had she let him hang around while she cooked, he'd be in the same situation she was.

Chrissy rattled on, and the nurse fiddled with the equipment. But Annalee mulled over the other tidbit that she'd learned. At some point before, CJ said or did something to make Chrissy think he had feelings for Annalee. That was before he'd accused her of trying to burn down the center, of course. Had to be. How could he care anymore?

He knew his job. Protect the kids. They were his number one priority. Yet having watched that ambulance pull away had ripped out a piece of his heart.

Once the children had all been collected by their parents, the real struggle began. He needed to view the damage, make an assessment, plan. Yet, the gnawing at his heart and mind taunted him. After all this work to keep the center open, this accident would potentially close it for good.

None of that mattered at the moment, though. He'd urged Margo to go home and sleep, promising to give her a call when he learned anything. Steering his truck into the twilight streets toward Parkland, he resisted allowing his thoughts to have total sway. Instead, he reached out to His Father again and again, praying for total healing and protection on Annalee.

He found an empty space at the edge of one of the far lots and jogged toward the emergency entrance. The exercise felt good, and he picked up speed midway, darting between parked cars. He slowed and walked when he reached the building, mindful of others entering and exiting.

He spotted Annalee's father right away. He lifted his chin and headed toward the man, but Mr. Chambers shot him a withering glance and turned his back. The chauffeur that he'd met leaned toward his boss. Then his steely gaze landed on CJ.

This man didn't turn his back. He strode purposefully toward CJ, ignoring his offered hand, and not speaking until quite close. "The family asks politely that you leave."

"I just want to know how she is." CJ matched his hushed tone. Anyone watching would clearly recognize an altercation, but there was no need to draw unwanted attention.

"If necessary, we will call on security to have you removed, but Mr. Chambers doesn't want to take drastic measures if they can be avoided."

"Please, is Annalee all right?"

The man stood his ground and kept his tone low. "So, will you leave the easy way or make this hard?"

Oh, CJ could have stayed. With his dad's donations especially to the burn unit, security would have apologized deeply for even approaching him. Still, CJ didn't want a give any more pain to Annalee than he already had. He could wait to hear about her, perhaps even contact her.

So, he went home. Home to an upscale, million-dollar condo, the impossible situation with his father, and the image of blue eyes on a woman who used to trust him.

But sleep evaded CJ. After wrapping himself in the sheets several times he discarded them and stood at his window overlooking the uninhabited streets of downtown. Not really uninhabited, but the occupants crept into the dark recesses of the looming buildings where their secrets couldn't be exposed.

Like his secret had been exposed.

His thoughts whirled between assurance that Annalee hated him and equal conviction that she gave him no thought at all. Especially in the painful circumstances in which she found herself. If only her father had allowed him to stay at the hospital.

He paced to the kitchen twice before finally deciding to snatch a Pepsi out of the fridge. CJ popped the top and took a long swig. The caffeine wouldn't help him sleep, but the cold biting liquid stimulated him all the way down.

Bowing his head, he wiped his mouth with the back of his hand. Why did she have to go through all of this? Visions of her reddened face haunted him. His fault. If he hadn't upset her … hadn't kept up that stupid masquerade. Her anger distracted her in the kitchen. A fire like that would have only taken seconds to ignite. That must be the explanation.

The can in his hand began to crumple. Rivulets of dark liquid tracked over his fingers. He tightened his grip, reared back, and hurled it as hard as he could. The can cracked against metal sheeting behind the oven and poured the rest of its contents onto the ceramic stove.

CJ raked his fingers through his hair. There had to be something he could do. And yet he knew there was nothing.

Nothing for the children who needed the center. No chance of convincing his father to release him from his promise. And he had nothing to offer Annalee—nothing that mattered anyway.

He left the liquid dripping onto his kitchen tile and crossed the living room to go out on to the veranda. The chill of the night penetrated his lightweight pajama pants and a light mist stung his bare shoulders.

"God, I know I don't have to understand all that's going on. I know that this, like everything else, happened for a reason." He gripped the top rail on the balcony. "Everything in me wants to ask why, but why isn't important. Please just fix it."

The frigid rail stung his palms. He heaved a broken breath. He lowered to his knees, begging his Father for forgiveness and healing and resolution to so many issues, he couldn't recite them all.

A sob spilled out as he again envisioned her blistered face full of betrayal. He huddled on the cement until he began to shiver. Spent, he pushed to standing and shuffled into the living room. The stone clock that decorated the interior wall marked 4:37 AM. With a groan, he trudged back into his bedroom, straightened the balled-up sheets, and climbed back into bed.

God, have mercy on me. He shrugged his blanket over his shoulders and prayed for an hour of relief. A deliverance long enough to allow him a little sleep.

Marji Laine

Chapter 28

Annalee took another drag on her straw and let the cool water drift down her throat. Her doctor, thankfully she hadn't laid eyes on that Cantrell fellow again, made notes in her metal flip-book. "I like what I'm seeing. I can't explain it, but I like it."

Father stood from where he had perched on the arm of the squarish sofa. "We can take her home?"

Dr. Amry lightly touched Annalee's face and peered into her eyes. "It's remarkable, really." She made another note. "I'd expected the redness to remain, even possible swelling on her face and in her throat or lungs, but I'm not seeing any signs of it at all."

She closed the flip book and clicked her pen shut before tucking it into her left jacket pocket. "I'll go have the forms filled out for release. But …" She looked directly at Annalee. "Keep talking to a minimum for a while. Lots of cool water, no ice. No warm food or drinks. Rest. And if you feel the slightest discomfort in your chest or throat, breathing or swallowing, you come straight back here."

Annalee felt plenty discomfort, itching at the moment, but

none of it on her insides.

The only thing she felt there was the heartache of the damage done to the center. Was it repairable? Would the kids still be able to come while they made the repairs? What would happen to them if they couldn't?

She and her father drove in silence all the way home. Mother hadn't come to the hospital at all, though Parker said she'd called a couple of times for a status report.

When she'd gotten settled into her room, her father moved a platter of fruit to the bedside table next to her and popped a grape into his mouth. "I'll let you rest now." He leaned over to kiss her forehead.

"Father, I need to talk to you about something." Her voice was gravelly. She took a sip from her chilled glass of water.

"Of course, sweetheart. Whatever you need." He sat on the bed beside her.

"I need to find a new place for the children to have their afterschool program if the center is too damaged." With all the regulations for running the program, she knew, deep down, they wouldn't be able to stay on the Haskell property until it was fully repaired.

"I don't see how you should be the one to find a new location." Father popped another grape into his mouth.

"Think about it. Those children have nothing." A light breeze lifted her lace curtains where Corlia had opened the window to indulge in the fresh air and cooler temperatures. "Today is Tuesday. School ends, and there's nothing for them. We're talking little innocent kids here, Father. They have no place to go and no one to help them. Someone has to help them. Why shouldn't that be me?"

Her fervor had lifted her from against the incline of pillows at the head of her bed, but after her long discussion, she leaned back against them, partially spent.

Her father looked toward her window. "You're not responsible for the center, Annalee." He turned his eyes back toward her. "That director who played with your emotions is the responsible party."

"He didn't start the fire." She'd been the principal player in that catastrophe.

"Maybe not, but his reckless attitude in dealing with people, with you, had direct effects on this catastrophe." He looked back to the window. Her father's anger colored his normally rational mind.

"Your logic doesn't work. You're saying that the kid who ran his car into a mailbox wasn't to blame. It was his teacher who gave him a bad test grade."

The man shut his eyes and lowered his chin with a sigh. "The man broke my baby's heart."

"I don't think he intended to hurt me."

But CJ hadn't come by the hospital, hadn't called, obviously didn't care.

Father stood and paced to the sofa in her sitting area before turning. "But you were hurt, and his failure to reveal his true name … his attempt to hide something for his own purposes …"

"Isn't that what politicians and attorneys do all the time?" She didn't want to offend Father. And she still didn't understand why CJ felt he needed to hide his name and background from her. But she believed in him. Even though the purposeful distance he was now maintaining made it clear he didn't reciprocate those feelings.

"Do you really think so little of me, my dear?"

"No. Not at all. But I'm beginning to believe that there might be more to his secret than we know. He'd been trying to speak to me. I didn't have time. Maybe he had a good reason." Even a bad one that didn't involve him toying with her would be acceptable.

"I still say, you have no reason to feel you need to provide for these children. You aren't to blame for the fire."

Annalee blew out her frustration. "Technically I am. I mean, I did start the thing."

Father picked another grape, eyed it, and put it back on the platter, a frown pulling at the corners of his mouth. "You don't need to talk that way. Your lawyer is already screaming. If someone insinuates any hint of retribution or your discontentment at the center, your probation could be revoked."

"I wasn't discontent at the center. I love working with the children."

"Well, that chapter is closed regardless." Father moved to her amply filled bookshelves and fingered some of the spines. "I'm going to have your attorney press charges against the Intercede Foundation and against the director at the center for negligence."

"You can't." Annalee leaned forward and instantly regretted the motion as pain stabbed the inside of her elbows. She kept her face benign. The healing blisters that covered her chin and forehead pulled her skin taut and resisted any change of expression better than Botox.

"We have to take the offensive here." He returned to the side of her bed. "That way, the judge will think twice about any revocation should it come to that."

"But I don't want to sue the foundation. And we have no grounds to claim negligence." She wasn't exactly sure about that, but she had no intention of holding the center responsible for what she'd done to herself. "This was just an accident."

"That's a matter for the court to decide."

"Father, please …"

"I'm only doing this for you, sweetheart." He slowly lowered to sit beside her again. "We can't let anyone blame you for this tragedy."

Her mind whirled. What argument would stop his intentions? "You're jumping the gun. I haven't been blamed for anything, yet."

"The *yet* is what worries me. With a suit already in play, they'll think twice before attempting to lay the blame at your feet."

Father's expectation wasn't unreasonable. The fear had niggled at the back her mind since the fire. Especially with CJ's comment to her right afterward. *What were you thinking?* Still, throwing another mistake at the problem wouldn't solve anything. "Father, I won't sue the center."

"Rebellion doesn't favor you, Annalee. I can sue them on your behalf either way."

"I'm an adult. I won't allow it."

"You'd rather go to jail?"

The thought chilled her. Goosepimples popped out on her shoulders through her short-sleeved sweater. No, she didn't want to go to jail, but attacking the place that had given her such joy … And the man who had shared his faith with her?

She shut her eyes. Had all of the discussions about the Lord been only lies as well? No. Her heart knew the things she'd learned about Jesus were true.

And as far as CJ went … thoughts of the man still ignited her heart, even after his betrayal. Her cheeks heated as she remembered again her attempts to financially help the man she

413

thought was a manual laborer.

"I don't want to go to jail." She directed her gaze at her father. "But I will not sue the center or the foundation." She struggled to sit up straighter and laid a hand on his. "The children, Dad. They need a place, now."

"I don't remember the last time you called me Dad." He looked at her red blistered hand and sighed. "You have amazed me these past few months, my dear. The gala, your commitment to the center, even making time to attend my events." He shook his head. "And those paintings. I had no idea you were so talented. Your passion showed."

She kept steady eyes on him.

"This is what you really want?"

She nodded. *More than anything.*

He stood, kissed the top of her head, and moved to the door. "Let me make some calls."

CJ woke up way later than normal after his difficult night. The sky showed gray and overcast, like before dawn, but his clock read almost noon. He picked up his alarm and realized that he'd turned it off at some point during the night. He wanted to hurl it across the room but didn't want to waste another second of time.

As much as he wanted to see Annalee, he had to find a place for the kids. Bus pick-up was only hours away. He headed for downtown and put in a call to Margo as he drove.

"I knew you'd be calling, but I thought I'd hear from you

sooner than this."

"Rough night. What do you have?"

"I spoke to several managing groups. Mostly, the spaces that are available are too small."

"I thought maybe a grocery store?"

"I found one of those, no two." Her voice became distorted. CJ could picture her with the phone tucked under her chin. "I saw both of them. Not much to look at, but they might work. No privacy for the babies or toddlers. That'd be a nightmare."

For everyone. "Wait I'm getting another call." He clicked over to an unknown number. "This is CJ."

"My name is Darrell Hanson. I've gotten a contact from an anonymous donor with information that you need a place for a temporary, afterschool, childcare center."

Anonymous? "Yes, sir. We desperately need a place as soon as possible."

"I can open the doors for you right away. It's big, fairly clean, but not all that fancy."

CJ reeled. This guy was calling him, offering to solve his problem? Things didn't happen like that. But location meant everything right now. "Where is this building?"

"I'm sorry. Shoulda told you that right off. We're on Ross and Lemmon. Used to be a fitness place. Got a big yard attached, too."

He knew that place. Less than two blocks from the center. And before the exercise machines, the building housed a huge auto mechanic school. "The place sounds perfect. Can I meet you there in ten minutes?"

The man seemed nice. Though CJ stared at his phone for a second while he sat at a light. *You did this, didn't You, Lord?*

Margo was still waiting. He clicked the button. "Where are

you?"

"Hanging with Tony, why?"

CJ explained the call he'd received. She whooped.

She met him there. Darrell Hanson opened the door when they knocked. A big man with reddish hair tinged gray, CJ shook his hand and introduced Margo as he ushered them inside. "Just had the place cleaned out. I was about to put it back on the market when my Realtor called me. Seems she got a bite before I even had to post the sign."

Wonder of wonders. But he knew better than to ask who had been the benefactor. Darrell kept up the chatter as they did a walk-through. Margo pulled out a pad, sketching the layout and jotting notes. The loft would work great for art time or board games. Several dance rooms under the loft suited the needs of the babies and toddlers. The large center room worked perfectly for the older kids. Even if they would have to eat on the floor for a while.

"We don't have a kitchen per se. I mean there's a room, refrigerator and a sink, but that's about it."

Hm. He pointed to Margo and she noted the detail. Take-out would be costly. Sandwiches and such in warmer weather would be easy, but for the next month or so, until the center's kitchen could be restored, they'd need to find some ultra large crock pots or make friends with the managers of a few local restaurants.

Either way, they had a place for the kids. At least for today.

The new space for the center was a blessing that consumed CJ. The church pitched in, lending several rockers and cribs. The kids had a blast in their new surroundings. They didn't even seem to mind the smaller yard.

While Annalee had been on his thoughts throughout, he couldn't simply call her. He had to face her, probably her parents, as well, and make amends the best he knew how. Margo had learned she'd been released from the hospital, but it had only been a few hours. Maybe tomorrow, when she was well-rested.

That night, she filled his dreams. He awakened early with a determination to heal the breach between them as much as he could. After visiting Brimming Café to ask Tony for prayer, he headed north, stopping by a Kroger to pick up a flower arrangement.

He left the truck on the lane and burrowed through the heavy foliage to avoid the security guard at the head of the driveway. He didn't relish a trip to the fortified castle that she called home, but he had to broach this. Had to apologize. And for himself, he needed to see she was truly all right.

Parker was polishing a Bentley as he approached. The man instantly stiffened and fisted his rag. "What do you want?"

"I want to see Annalee." CJ paused, not wishing to instigate yet another issue.

"You haven't caused her enough pain?" He repositioned himself blocking the walkway to the front door.

"Yes, I have. I can't fix what I've done, but I've been trying to apologize since last weekend. And I feel awful about her accident on Monday."

"You should, but your lies were worse. She trusted you. How could you share the Truth with her on one hand and maintain your mask with the other?"

CJ stared at the ground. He'd wronged her on so many levels. "That's why I have to apologize. I don't want my failings to affect her new faith."

The man crossed his arms, a dark look washing over his face. "Kendra and I have wanted to talk to her about the Lord for some time, but the employer/employee thing always hindered our discussion. I guess I can appreciate you for that much." He released a pent-up exhale that sounded more like a growl then stepped aside.

Advancing closer to the entrance, CJ faced the man and held out his hand. "I'll do everything I can to make this right. Please pray that Annalee won't turn her back on what God has already shown her."

Parker nodded and took the hand after a hesitation. Probably not for CJ's benefit but for Annalee's that the man agreed.

He pressed a button near the door, sending long, low chimes resonated through the house.

An older woman with skin the color of coffee opened the door. Her welcoming smile faded as recognition hit her eyes. "You're young Mr. Whelan. I don't think you should be here right now, sir."

"Who is it, Winona?" A female voice that had to belong to Annalee's mother arrived before the woman actually appeared.

He held up his bouquet and straightened his shoulders. Nothing would be easy about this encounter.

The woman's blue eyes flashed as she recognized him. So much like Annalee's and yet not like them at all. "You. What are you doing here?"

"I came to speak to Annalee. I wanted to—"

She stepped in front of her housekeeper. "I don't care what you wanted. Get out." Her upswept blond hair shivered as she pointed down the drive that would take him out of the property.

"Please, I need to apologize to her for keeping my identity a secret."

She crossed her arms over a light salmon cardigan. "And

laughing at her behind her back with your girlfriend and the people at that horrible center. Absolutely not."

"That's not what happened. It was a stupid mis—"

She didn't let him finish but snapped her fingers. "Parker, escort Mr. Whelan off the grounds and do not let him return." She turned away.

"You don't understand." This hadn't gone at all like he'd imagined.

The ornate, lead crystal door closed without reply. CJ turned back toward the drive.

Parker fisted his hips. "Sorry, man."

CJ's head ached from lack of sleep and even more from lack of resolution over this whole thing. He strode toward the drive, pausing when he reached Parker and pressed the flowers against his chest. "Why don't you give these to your wife to enjoy? Might as well not go to waste in a trash bin."

"Okay." The chauffeur still sounded dubious but took the bouquet. "If I get the chance, I'll let Annalee know you came by."

His promise gave little comfort as CJ strolled down the drive. He'd vowed to do his best to make amends. He'd done that. At least for now.

He returned to the Brimming Café and found Margo, again chatting with Tony. This time perched on a stool and grinning.

"Hey, man." Tony's grin matched Margo's. CJ desperately wanted an about-face, but couldn't bring himself to turn his back on the happy couple. He tried to urge a half smile.

"You look like road-kill." Margo sipped from her mug.

He cocked his head toward the woman. "I had to try to make things right with Annalee."

"Thought you did that yesterday before you started trying to find a place for the kids?" She crossed her thin legs. "I didn't realize you put the center in front of your relationship with Annalee."

Something akin to a growl emanated from his throat. He didn't need this right now. "Lay off."

"I don't mean it like that. But I know you, CJ. That girl is important to you. Even more important than your work at the center. Don't you think?"

She had a point. If he'd not slept-in yesterday, gotten behind in finding a place for the kids, Annalee would have had first priority. Instead, she'd haunted him most of the night and robbed his sleep again. But after her mom refused to let him see her, what else could he do? "Doesn't matter anymore."

"I think you should stop fighting your feelings, CJ and tell her."

"If I could speak to her, I'd consider it, but she has a hedge growing around her."

"Sleeping Beauty?"

"Clever." He didn't want to discuss the futility of his relationship with Annalee.

Annalee fingered the magazine she'd tried to enjoy. The clock read two thirty. Time for her to be at the center. Yesterday had been hard to miss, though her weariness hardly let her think of it. Today, they didn't expect her, but she yearned to see the kids, to reassure them that she was all right.

At least she knew they were taken care of.

She tossed the paper aside and picked up the remote, flicking on some romance movie from Hallmark Channel. Maybe something light would settle her mind.

The phone rang and she struggled to her feet and stood, holding out her hands and willing the room to stop swaying. Dr. Amry had warned her of a lack of energy and possible dizziness or nausea to deal with, and she hadn't been lying.

She could hear her mother's voice rising in the next room and moved in that direction.

"You tell Melody Fairbanks that Mr. Chambers is behaving as any father who loves his daughter would behave. He's comforting her, viewing the circumstances with an objective eye, and encouraging her to take the steps necessary to protect herself from slanderous accusations."

Annalee cringed at her mother's proprietorial words. But then, Melody Fairbanks, the local investigative reporter for one of the networks would color it however she wanted, based on the political whim of the moment.

And it wasn't CJ calling.

"Hey, kiddo." Parker stole in from the kitchen hallway carrying a vase full of yellow and white roses interspersed with a few bright orange lilies.

"Those are gorgeous. Where did they come from?"

Parker put a conspiratorial finger to his lips and set the bouquet on a table next to the window overlooking the gardens. "Your friend, CJ, brought them."

Her deep inhale and the subsequent raising of her eyebrows made her flinch. "He did?"

He nodded. "Your mom ..." Parker leaned forward and

scanned the next room, but her mother's voice still chatted with the reporter on the phone. "… wouldn't allow him to come inside. He's worried about you, though. He came to the hospital, too."

The bands around her chest crumbled. "He was worried?"

He nodded. "I can't speak for him, but he did want to apologize and didn't want his secrets to affect your faith."

"Is he still here?" She took a few steps toward the front door.

"No, I waited to bring these up until your father went to play golf." He wiped the back of his hand across his forehead. "I hope I didn't do the wrong thing. CJ gave me the flowers for Kendra since he couldn't see you, but I thought he'd approve of me getting them to you."

"*I* approve." Oh boy, did she.

"Don't tell your father. I have a child coming, remember." He put his hands together, shaking them a little like a prayer.

A tiny smile crept out with great pain. Parker scooted out the way he came. She felt the energy wash away from her and sat on the couch behind her.

The phone rang again, but this time, her mother brought the handheld device to her. "A woman asking for you, Annalee. And if it's a reporter, treat her nicely. Your father intends to run again. He can't afford for you to make enemies of the press."

Annalee exhaled in a puff and took the phone. If this was a reporter, she had nothing to tell her anyway. "This is Annalee Chambers."

"Laurel Stewart."

Oh, this wouldn't be good. She leaned back against the cushions. "So nice of you to call and check up on me."

"Ahem. Besides the fire and the other mistakes you've made, your director has complained about your poor work ethic, your late habits, and the way you treat the children."

CJ? Complained about her? A few days before, she would never have believed that, but he'd kept so much from her. Now, she wasn't sure.

"And I notice that you've missed quite a lot of time over the last month—unexcused absences such as today's—"

"My absence today is hardly unexcused …"

"Arriving late. Leaving early."

She'd had permission for all of her comings and goings in advance, but Laurel Stewart didn't care about that. She wanted Annalee reassigned away from the center.

"Ms. Stewart, I only have a handful of hours left. Did it occur to you that letting me finish them might get me away from the center faster than legal action?"

"You thwarted my plans." Her voice lowered to a wolf-like tone. "I don't abide interference from anyone. Especially not in this case."

Vindictive. Reasoning with her would gain nothing. *Fine. Go ahead. It's not like I can't volunteer there on my own.*

"I've discussed all of these items with Judge Vaught, but your causing the fire alone is grounds for a new hearing. Same courtroom, Friday at two o'clock."

A hearing? Why did she need a whole new hearing? "For what? Can't she simply reassign me?"

The hideous titter that Annalee had heard before spewed over the line. "You're not being reassigned. After trying to burn the place down? Are you kidding? Your probation is being revoked, or it will be. Don't try to leave town." She ended the call with another laugh.

Annalee froze at the menacing sound. Jail? She couldn't go to jail. She'd almost finished. She swallowed and set down the receiver.

That was it. Laurel had won. Not only would she succeed in getting Annalee away from CJ, but she'd enjoy her vengeance on her for taking CJ's attention away. Or had that been another lie? She glanced at the flowers. Was he lying still?

Nothing in her wanted to believe that. She wanted to protest Laurel's accusations, but how did she know that CJ hadn't complained about her. He'd certainly blamed her. With or without flowers. She'd been such a fool.

CJ breathed easier. The kids had initiated the new venue for several days. None of the parents seemed to mind the switch. For many of them, this place was actually closer to home.

And Parker Reid's call yesterday, after the buses did their drop-off, lightened his heart considerably.

Annalee accepted his flowers and even smiled. He'd have to make sure he gave Parker and his wife a super nice baby gift, once their little one made an appearance.

Not to mention that he was doubly determined to resolve this situation completely. Parker promised to let him know when there was a good time for him to speak to Annalee. And if he needed to give his girl a little room, then he would.

His girl. He liked that thought.

He didn't expect the opportunity to come so quickly though. They'd only spoken two days before, but CJ was on alert when a limo pulled into the bus lane about the time he'd arrived. Timing must be good to see Annalee. Maybe she was even in the back? Leaving the center right before the kids arrived would be tricky, but he'd figure out a way.

"Is the timing right?" CJ held out his hand and strode toward him as he climbed out of the black limo.

"Perfect." Parker pulled his right fist back and landed it on CJ's jaw, knocking him to the pavement. He pointed his finger at CJ. "Stay down there, you snake. Where you belong."

"What are you talking about?" CJ rubbed his cheek and sat on his heels. His jaw wasn't broken, but he tasted blood.

"You got your wish. You broke her. I'd have smashed you earlier if I'd known about your report, but I only found out as I transported the family to the courthouse."

"Courthouse?" Had his punch fogged up CJ's brain?

Parker paced the length of the car and did an about-face. "You had me fooled, too. I really thought you cared about her."

"I do." He breathed deep. "I love her."

Love. Yeah. He did, even though he hadn't even let himself think that actual word. Speaking it out loud strengthened him, and he stood. "I've been waiting, like you told me to. I don't know anything about a report."

"Your notes to her probation officer?"

"I never sent anything to Laurel." He rubbed his jaw again. "You've got some power there."

The chauffeur advanced on him.

CJ threw up a block, expecting another punch. "I don't want to fight you, man."

Parker shoved a finger in his face. "You didn't blame the fire on Annalee? Didn't complain because she had to leave early for her father's election events?"

"No. She had permission to leave early. Told us all about them weeks in advance."

"Then why is she in the Frank Crowley Courts Building, waiting to stand before Judge Vaught to have her probation revoked?"

"Revoked?" CJ bolted for the front door. "Why am I only hearing about this, now?"

"You didn't know?" Parker followed him.

"Think I'd be sitting here?" He jogged into the makeshift office and slammed his hand on Margo's desk. "What do you know about a report to Laurel detailing complaints against Annalee?"

She flinched with his first word, but then drew her brows into a tuft. "Complaints?"

"From us. If Laurel gets her way, Annalee's going to jail." He grabbed a file out of the almost empty cabinet and flipped through pages.

Her eyes widened. "You've got to stop such a travesty, CJ. This isn't right."

He yanked a clipboard off of the desk. "I'm on it. Take over. This place will be yours soon anyway."

"I'll pass, thank you, but I got your six on this. Don't worry about us. We'll be fine." Margo hopped up and trotted into the main room.

CJ raced back out to the limo with Parker in his wake. "Can you take a passenger?"

Chapter 29

Annalee had to hand it to her mother. She kept her mouth shut during all of Laurel Stewart's rant about Annalee's behavior at the center. She sat behind the rail, harrumphing. Had the complaints not been so serious, Annalee might have giggled at her mother's attempts at silence and control.

But as it was, she had trouble maintaining her own composure. Laurel Stewart had official documents claiming that Annalee had caused immeasurable havoc at her assigned community service site and did not deserve to continue her probation. She'd even donned the proper facade of humility, admitting her failure to correct Annalee's poor behavior.

The document pile grew in direct coordinates to Annalee's stress levels. Reports from both CJ and Margo as well as complaints from parents had been compiled into Laurel's official report. When the judge asked her about personal testimony to verify the reports, she explained that being shorthanded, the center couldn't afford to lose either of its two best workers. Especially in the wake of Annalee's near-destruction of the center itself.

Through all of the complaints, Mr. Walbright remained silent. When the probation officer finally sat down, Malcolm Walbright patted Annalee's arm and whispered in her direction. "This is all for show, to make your father look bad. There's nothing here."

He stood. "Your honor I'd like to have all of these unverified reports thrown out. There is no foundation for any of this so-called evidence."

"I tend to disagree with you, Mr. Walbright. Miss Stewart appears before me on a regular basis. The official report is sworn to by Miss Stewart, and, as liaison for Miss Chambers, she must accept responsibility for the probationer's failure. Her own record is marked with this notation. Therefore, I will ignore your request."

"But your honor, obviously Miss Stewart has a desire to shame Miss Chambers, or, more likely, her father who is active in this city's political environment."

"Have you anything to substantiate such a claim?"

Walbright straightened. "It's common knowledge that her father, Todd Chambers was a candidate—."

"That election is over. And I will not hear innuendo in my court. If you have no evidence, then sit down."

Walbright hesitated. "This woman …" He held out his hand toward Laurel Stewart.

The judge tapped the top of her pen on a mahogany block in front of her and lifted her chin. "Sit."

Mr. Walbright sat next to Annalee.

She turned toward him. Was that it? Didn't he have anything to offer in her defense?

"Will the probationer please stand?"

It took a moment for Annalee to realize that the woman was talking to her. She pressed her palms on the table and rose.

"I want you to know, Miss Chambers, I believed assignment to this South Dallas children's center would give you a chance to find yourself while you served others. I hoped that working with the poorest children in our city and witnessing how they had such uninhibited joy and enthusiasm for everything good would inspire you."

She took off her glasses. "I saw in you potential when you stood before me several months ago and pleaded guilty. I was sure you could not only benefit from the assignment but find purpose when you proved valuable to the center.

"But you didn't prove valuable. Instead, you seem to have undermined every attempt that the leadership of the center made to help you be successful." She put her glasses back on and glanced at the file in front of her before looking over the tops of the readers toward Annalee. "Do you have anything to say for yourself?"

All through the experience, Annalee believed that Judge Vaught was out to get her. Hearing that she had believed in her and assigned her by hand in an effort to help her succeed and grow, made her feel bad all over again.

She cleared her throat. "I can't argue with the times I left early or didn't arrive at the center on the dates reported. I did get permission for all of those times. At least I thought I did. And I have no knowledge of undermining. I enjoyed working with the children, and I believed that I was doing exactly what was asked of me, even more ..." Her voice faded. She wasn't going to toot about the gala.

A society party on one hand, a fire-starter on the other. Even in her own mind, she came off as a crazy woman.

"As for the fire ..." She wiped her palms on her brown slacks. "I truly don't know how that started. I didn't think I did anything wrong, but it was the first time I'd worked in the kitchen alone, so I can't be sure." She'd thought through the events in the kitchen several times but couldn't contemplate any cause for the explosion.

"I know what started the fire, Your Honor." The voice came with a loud burst through the doors behind her. She spun around to find CJ walking toward the front. A murmur rumbled through the seats of the room.

The judge tapped her pin again. "Order. Exactly who are you, and why are you interrupting my hearing?"

"I'm Carlton James Whelan, Your Honor. I only just learned of these proceedings, but I have evidence in this case."

Annalee's chest had convulsed when she caught sight of CJ. His words brought her hope, but the red and purple that spread across his left cheek confused her. Had he been in a fight?

"You're the director of Intercede Foundation's afterschool center?" Judge Vaught sifted through some of her papers as CJ nodded. "I have here a notarized request for your presence in this court."

"I never saw that. I never heard anything about this hearing until a half hour ago." He rubbed his cheek.

The judge's eyebrows furrowed as she glanced toward Laurel Stewart. "Miss Stewart, can you explain this?"

She stood. "You'll notice that Mr. Whelan could not be found to offer the request, Your Honor."

CJ scowled at her. "You never had a problem calling me on my cell phone before."

Laurel Stewart ignored him. "I should think the notary seal and the official documents should take precedence." The officer's voice broke. "Obviously, Mr. Whelan is feeling unnecessarily guilty because his honest reports will result in Miss Chambers spending her full tenure in a jail cell.

CJ's jaw stiffened.

"That remains to be seen, Miss Stewart." The judge directed her gaze toward the defendant's table. Annalee held the woman's intense stare without flinching. When the judge gave her a short nod, she lowered back into her seat.

"Mr. Whelan, tell me about the reports you submitted about Miss Chamber's activities at the center."

"I submitted no reports to Miss Stewart or to anyone else."

"Of course, he did. He and his assistant had many conversations with me about Annalee. How else would I have gotten the information?"

"Did you discuss the defendant with her probation officer?" The judge clasped her hands in front of her and eyed CJ.

He rubbed his forehead. "As I recall, Laurel complained quite a bit at first. Then a few weeks ago, she declared that she'd have Annalee away from the center and in jail where she belonged. Something to that effect. I don't believe I ever spoke a negative word against Annalee. Though I should have shut down the things Laurel and my assistant gossiped about earlier."

"Your assistant has problems with the probationer, then."

"Only at first. Annalee proved herself to both of us."

"Now, wait just a minute. What about the way she almost let that child get injured? Or her insistence on parking in the bus lane? Her blatant disobedience, or the way she humiliated a councilman?"

"Sit down, Miss Stewart." Judge Vaught glared at the woman. "Mr. Whelan, tell me about Miss Chambers's activities and behavior at the center over the last few months."

He nodded. "When she first arrived, I confess, I didn't believe she would remain, but she proved me wrong. She embraced every challenge with a good attitude. She works hard and really cares about the children. And, she singlehandedly saved the center from closing."

"I beg your pardon?"

"She arranged every aspect of a fundraiser, succeeding in bringing in enough money to make the repairs to the center and keep it open and functioning for years to come." He turned toward her. His soft eyes made her breath catch. "She inspired the children … and she inspires me. I can't imagine the center continuing to run without her."

He faced the judge again and set a clipboard on her high desk. "But we will have to find a way."

What had he said? He was joining Laurel Stewart? Trying to get rid of her?

"You see, Judge, because of all of her extra time organizing the center's fundraiser, Annalee Chambers has completed all of her necessary hours of community service."

The judge examined the forms. "Many of these entries are initialed by you, Mr. Whelan."

"I can have each of them verified by my assistant."

She flipped through the pages. "It seems here that Miss Chambers arrived early and stayed late much of the time. How do you explain your reports to the contrary, Miss Stewart?"

Laurel stood. "I can't explain Mr. Whelan's change of heart, Your Honor."

"Hmph. Still, I should think, after practically burning down your center, that you'd want her to have some punitive damages?"

CJ laid another form on the judge's desk. "This is the report I received from the Investigator at Dallas Fire Station Three. This indicates a faulty gas hose, worn. Likely the cleaning we'd just completed moved the stove enough to make the breach. Not enough gas had seeped out to be detected."

"You're saying the fire was a simple matter of timing?" The judge gave him a dubious look.

"Yes, ma'am. Another twenty minutes, and we would have smelled the seepage."

"Hmm." She held up her pen. "Or Miss Chambers could have been killed in the explosion."

CJ's face paled. He cleared his throat. "Thankfully, that wasn't the case."

"Indeed." She closed the file. "I have every intention of letting this case drop, but I exhort Mr. Chambers to find better legal representation. Mr. Walbright, you should have at least had a conversation with Mr. Whelan before stepping into my court. Furthermore, Miss Stewart, I am terribly disappointed in your work. I'm directing my bailiff to hold you in contempt of court while I contact your superior at the probation office. If I find you have brought me falsified documents of any kind, I will have charges pressed to the full extent of the law."

Laurel stood, her chin up. "I have data supporting all of my reports."

"And a reasonable explanation why Mr. Whelan knew nothing of this hearing?"

The woman's shoulders lowered slightly. She followed the bailiff through a side door.

She pointed her pen at Annalee. "And as for you, Miss Chambers …"

Annalee stood, feeling like she'd lived through a dream.

"Your community service time is officially over. Another year of meeting with a new probation officer and your record will be clean. I declare this matter closed."

The pen popped on the block again. Annalee startled. The hearing was over. Successful. She'd finished.

And CJ had been there for her. She heard sighs of relief around her and her father began fussing at Mr. Walbright, but CJ closed the gap between them.

"You're here." She reached her hand to his blue jean jacket. Feeling the texture of the denim, smelling his woodsy cologne, was like a verification code.

"I'll always be here for you. If you'll have me." He stroked her hair away from her face, circled her waist with his other hand and tugged her toward him. "Please say you'll have me."

The compassion in his gentle eyes drew her in. His secrecy and the doubts she'd carried fell away. With unspoken words blocking her throat, she remained silent. But couldn't imagine anything she'd ever wanted more. A tear seeped from her eye and she nodded. "I love you." She really did, and the surprise shocked her.

His face broke into a grin. "I was hoping I wasn't the only one of us to fall in love."

"Annalee." Her mother's voice chided her. "Show some decorum." Her mother had completed her discussion with the reporters in the room and frowned in her direction.

Father had glanced at her after stern words with Malcolm Walbright. The furrowed brow relaxed, and he gave her a winsome smile and a slight nod. He held out his hand. "Young man, looks like we're again in your debt.

CJ released Annalee to accept the greeting.

"Why don't you and I chat a little?" Father put his arm around his shoulders. CJ glanced back toward her.

What was Father thinking?

She shrugged as she offered a prayer of divine leading.

A shiver ran across Annalee's shoulders as she parked her Mustang. A news truck, decked out with lights and manned with a reporter and cameraman, blocked her path to the hospital entrance. *Not again.*

She hadn't had to deal with the media since her hearing last month. She'd even made a statement: "I'm relieved that this situation is resolved, but Mr. Madison is still recuperating, so he remains in my prayers."

Even her mom had released a tight-lipped smile over that.

Yet here the reporters were again. Channel four from the look of the truck. Why now? What had she destroyed this time?

Whatever it was, they wouldn't stop her from visiting Kendra Reid. She shifted her package and emerged from the car. Rounding the van, she followed a stream of people. Maybe she could slip past.

A reporter called out, "Mrs. Ellis, will your daughter recover?

Annalee stumbled. She hadn't noticed the mayor's wife in the group ahead of her until the woman peeled away with a couple of people in her wake and moved toward the news van.

Poor woman. Dealing with her daughter's trouble, whatever that was, and reporters at the same time. How impossible to be coherent about her child's condition on live television. She sent up a prayer for little Camille Ellis.

Thank goodness, the people ignored Annalee. As it should be. For now, she delighted in new-found invisibility.

Two other media teams were in the lobby. A guy from channel eight caught her eye and lifted his hand. Nice sort, but he'd hounded her in the days following her accident. He approached as she waited for the elevators. "You here to see Ellis's daughter?"

At least the man didn't stick his microphone in her face. Obscurity had benefits.

She shook her head. "Just visiting a friend." She lifted the baby carrier. "It's a boy."

"Congratulations."

"What happened? To the mayor's daughter, I mean?" The elevator arrived and emptied.

"Looks like a drug overdose."

Dreadful news, but Annalee recognized conjecture and rumor when she heard it. She stepped into the box and pivoted. Her heart went out to the mom weaving her way through the lobby and forced to pause for questions and statements. Nightmare. Annalee lifted up another prayer for the girl and included the entire Ellis family.

Still stunned, she made her way to Baylor's sixth floor. Father met her in the waiting room. "Perfect timing. Little Titus just went to mom and dad." The man was downright giddy. He took the wrapped car seat box and led her down the hallway.

"The lobby is a madhouse."

"I heard about thirty seconds ago. Did you have any trouble?"

"No, but I feel bad for Mrs. Ellis."

"Sad time for them." Father paused, staring at the floor. He met Annalee's eyes. "You know, I don't say it very well, or very often, but I'm proud of you and Ramona. Proud of the women you've become. And I feel … well … blessed, I guess, that God gave you both to me."

His eyes were moist. She planted a kiss on his cheek. "I love you, too, Father." She tapped on room 608 and entered at the muffled greeting.

Baby Titus lay sleeping in Parker's arms. Her friend was going to make a great dad. Even though he looked like a six-year-old trying to master the art of waiting on tables.

"You'd think that child was a football with the way you're holding him." Annalee scooted closer for a better look.

"I'm doing fine."

Kendra giggled. "He's afraid he's going to break the boy."

Annalee examined the bundled infant. Weighing in at over ten pounds, that wasn't likely. She turned to Kendra and presented her with a Kit Kat bar. "You need a break, new momma."

Her friend offered a weary smile. "Indeed, I do. But I'll be needing an exercise partner before long, to get rid of this baby weight."

"I'm your girl."

Father found an empty corner for the car seat and goo-gooed at Titus.

"Don't wake him." Annalee pulled her phone out and took a few pictures.

"You're really enjoying the work at the center?"

"I love the kids. Love the purpose God has given me there."

Father's eyes crinkled. Like they had when he lost the election. A mix of acceptance and disappointment. What could he possibly be disappointed about? "Well, I'd better get back to the office." He patted Parker's shoulder and gave Kendra a half-hug.

Annalee kissed his cheek before his exit, then grabbed her phone again. "Let me get a family pic to show CJ."

"That's right." Parker moved closer to his wife. "The grand reopening of the center, today."

"Margo thought the last day before Christmas break would be the perfect time to do the official reopen. Paula's baked dozens of cookies, and Margo has little gifts for all of the kids. And I've heard there is a plan for a rip-roaring kickball game before sunset."

"Sounds like fun." Parker fairly whispered over his son's sleeping face. "So, you're having the reopening the day before the center closes until January?"

"No. We'll have all-day sessions for the kids who can walk there or get a drop-off, but we won't have any buses since school's not in session. And we'll be closing up entirely on the twenty-third."

Kendra smoothed the blanket around Titus's face. "Aren't you going to be late?"

Annalee checked the wall clock. "Oh, dear. I hadn't realized …" She placed a light kiss on Titus's head and gave one-armed hugs to his parents.

A little cry broke out. Parker bounced and sang a worship song in his low baritone. Yes, Titus was in excellent hands.

Chapter 30

CJ squinted at the picture he'd just received from Annalee. Kendra's delivery timing complicated matters. As much as he wanted to visit, he'd have to wait until tomorrow.

"I've got cranberry and white chocolate cookies in the oven and chocolate chip coolin' on the racks." Paula didn't need to sound off every item. He trusted her.

Then again … "What about the dressing. We don't want that to burn."

"Not gonna burn."

"She's the expert, remember?" Margo trotted in, carrying an empty ornament box. "Tree's done. Lights're hung. And gifts stacked up underneath." She set the box in the corner with several others and turned to lay a hand on CJ's shoulder. "I think we're ready, boss-man."

As ready as they could be. The contractors had done a great job on the kitchen. All signs of the fire had disappeared and the new appliances gleamed in the sparkling room.

Paula danced around her new haven. "I still can't believe we got back in here so fast."

"Thank Dad." Though CJ found it hard to believe the man had lifted a finger, he had. Contractors had been onsite before Annalee's hearing and had started their work the following Monday. He checked his phone again. "Annalee's on her way."

"Good. Buses should be here anytime."

The door opened with a whipped wind ushering in Scott Whelan. *Speak of the devil* poised on CJ's tongue, but he couldn't utter it. Not after Dad's help over and above any expectations.

The Intercede Foundation board followed Dad inside. All of them? In the same vehicle? That must have been an interesting ride, but they didn't look too worse for the wear.

Mrs. Moncrief wrapped her thin arms around CJ's neck. He had to stoop to let the diminutive woman complete her bear hug. "I'm so proud of you, CJ. You've done an amazing job here. I know the Lord is pleased."

She stepped back. Tears sparkled her eyes. CJ could only smile. What an enigma the woman was. Tough in the boardroom and business conferences all over the nation, yet she had such a tender spot for the children. And as for her mentioning him pleasing the Lord … he had to pick up his jaw on that comment.

She moved on, and he accepted a handshake from Dean Simons before Dad made his way over. "Well. Looks like you've made your mark here."

"With the funds we've raised, Margo will be able to hire a handyman if things break down. And Annalee has done well with the children. She'll make a good assistant to Margo."

"Still, she isn't a man." Dad cocked up one eyebrow.

A laugh blew out. No one could possibly accuse Annalee Chambers of looking like a man, even at her worst, which was still drop-dead gorgeous. "No. I plan to come over every evening, after work, I assure you. It will give me a chance to eat with the kids, be a role model for the boys, and give a little security. The men at the body shop next door will keep an eye on things here until they close at six."

"Sounds like you've taken great care in providing for this place." His eyes narrowed.

What was he getting at? Of course, CJ would make sure the center was protected and well-staffed. "These are my kids, Dad. My staff. I couldn't just leave them to fend for themselves."

"Hmm." He caught sight of the food table. "Indeed."

CJ shook his head as he studied Dad's back. He still hated the idea of being trapped at Whelan Group as the heir apparent. But, of course, he would follow through on his promise to the man. However stupid he'd been to make that promise. Lovesick puppy. But he treasured the picture he'd gotten in the bargain. Should look great on the wall of his coming cage.

Fresh from their last day of school before Christmas break, a mass of children rushed in through the front door. They hung backpacks on hooks and just as quickly evaporated to the back lot with the Tigh sisters and Margo.

"My, but they are quick." Mrs. Moncrief giggled.

"They only get a little time to play at this point. I usually have to drag them back inside. Yet tonight, I don't think that's going to be so much of a problem. Thank you all for the special activities."

"Happy to do it, CJ." Arthur Bench smiled and popped a peppermint candy in his mouth.

The front door opened and CJ spun around expecting his final guests. Not his guests. Councilman Adams and a petite woman entered. Dad detached himself from Alton Leon and Charles Davis to greet the man. He brought him toward CJ.

Mustering a smile he didn't feel toward the man, CJ offered his hand. The last time, the gesture had been ignored, but this time he received a hearty shake. "So nice to see you again, Mr. Whelan."

Ah. The name. Assuming he'd been a mere janitor before, Adams hadn't bothered with consideration. Still, he smiled at the man. "I'm happy to see you under better circumstances. I trust you're hearing good reports from Jamaysia."

"Excellent reports. The child is delighted to have other kids in the house, mostly younger and a girl her own age. She said to give this to Miss Annalee." He held up a paper. "Said this would be a perfect outfit for her during the winter."

A torn magazine page held the image of a model in a royal blue dress edged with black fur. Yes, Annalee would be striking in that. He chuckled. "If Jamaysia isn't the next Coco Chanel, I'll be surprised."

"Yes, she lives, eats, and breathes fashion design. Said Annalee encouraged her. Makes the way I attacked that lady all the more to my shame."

"She doesn't hold it against you, Councilman."

"No, but she was right about one thing. I owe her father an apology. My mouth starts running on adrenaline sometimes … I accused him of a ridiculous thing."

CJ pointed to the opening door. "Looks like you're going to get your chance.

Adams glanced in the direction, looked back at CJ with a nod, and made his way toward Todd Chambers, who had just entered with his wife and Ramona.

Abigail Chambers approached CJ. "Isn't Annalee here yet? I

should think she'd know better than to be late to such an important gathering."

"Mother, don't pick on him." Ramona had changed drastically since their interaction at the Brimming Café so many months ago. Though he suspected his identity revelation had caused much of her attitude adjustment.

"She has no idea about all of this. She thinks it's a regular Friday back at the old center with a taste of the holiday thrown in," CJ explained. "Not an early dismissal day for the students, and certainly not an event like this." And boy, would she be surprised.

Traffic shouldn't have been heavy so early on a Friday, yet the short hop from Baylor to the center on Haskell Avenue had taken almost twenty minutes. What were buses doing out already?

The tickle of concern broke out in sweat across her forehead as she pulled into her parking spot. A collection of cars bordered the bus lane, shortening the kickball field. But the kids had been playing in a yard less than a third the size of the one in back of the center. They probably didn't notice.

Flexible. Fun. Adoring. These kids had crawled into her heart and made life so full of joy. *Thank You, God.*

She climbed from her Mustang and halted. Kids' laughter. That was wrong. Not wrong, but too early. Had she missed a time change? Last day of school. Did it end early? "Oh no." She sprinted for the gate, slowing when a red-suited man carrying a large bag emerged from a taxi.

"May I help you?" Santa in a taxi? She stifled a giggle. CJ had planned well. She could just picture little faces full of excitement.

"Intercede Foundation afterschool center?"

"This is the place." She held out her hand. "I'm Annalee. Can I help you with your bag?"

He ho-ho'ed. "Sorta goes with the outfit."

She led him through the gate.

"And it isn't heavy." He leaned close, a sparkle in his eye. "I just stuff it with fluff for effect."

Good effect. He looked every bit the part of her impression of Santa from the boots to a realistic spare tire and natural whiskers of a white-blond color lying against his chest. He burst into the door with a loud Ho-Ho-Ho. A number of well-dressed adults turned their attention toward him.

Annalee stopped outside the doorway and looked down at her paint-stained sneakers. She hadn't considered that the center's reopening would be a grand event. She should have anticipated such a plan. Dressed for mingling with society, or at least do better than bleached jeans and an over-stretched, ugly, Christmas sweater.

"About time you got here." CJ passed Santa and slipped his hands around her waist. "Would hate to have to initiate the mistletoe with someone other than my best girl."

"You wouldn't dare." She matched the teasing that his eyes held. She stepped from his embrace and pulled off her winter coat, hanging it in the closet behind the door. "I'm so sorry I'm late. At least, I guess I'm late. I didn't know we started early today."

"No worries. First day at the new place. Dad and the board wanted to have a to-do with the kids."

"And Santa." She planted a kiss on CJ's cheek as she passed, heading for the kitchen. "The kids are going to explode over him."

"I think Dad is starting to warm up to the idea of keeping the center going."

"Good thing." She stopped, eyeing the stove. "You sure it's safe?" The scar on her forehead hadn't disappeared, but her burns were only memories. Bad ones that she didn't want to ever relive.

"Positive. Paula already baked a ton of cookies."

As if on cue, the timer buzzed and the baker came inside from the back porch. "Good. The gang's all here." She pulled the rack from the shiny new oven. "Works like a dream." She pointed to a large metal box with a glassed-in window. "And I love the new warmer. I've got brisket already sliced as well as green beans and mashed potatoes rarin' to go. No cold plates tonight."

Good thing. The kids were getting tired of crock pot soups and sandwiches.

Margo bustled in the back door. "The kids are coming in. Washing up."

"Already?" They usually played until dark when they adults had to haul them inside.

"One of them caught sight of Santa. Couldn't keep them out any longer when that rumor spread. He's going to have a time of it."

Before Santa had the chance to start, Scott Whelan stepped to the center of the room. Even the kids quieted with his formidable presence. A shame she couldn't find a way to bottle that essence for truly rowdy days.

"Could I have your attention, please?" With the quick silence, his volume changed to little more than a regular conversation level. "We at Intercede Foundation are grateful for the efforts of Annalee Chambers, who secured the continuation of the afterschool program with her gala last month."

Applause rose.

"And this program wouldn't exist at all without the hard work of the center's director, Carlton ... uh ... CJ Whelan."

Another round of applause and some of the kids broke into cheers.

"But my son has agreed to begin work with me at the Whelan Group with the new year. So, this will be his last month as director of this afterschool center."

Annalee already knew about this. CJ and she had discussed the repercussions. The stunned silence around her reported that most had no idea of the plan.

He looked at CJ. "My son loves this program. I almost had to twist his arm off. His behavior reminded me of the lengths I was willing to go to please my dear wife, Sharon, while she was still alive."

He glanced at Annalee. Why was he looking at her?

"So, I'm not taking Carlton into Whelan Group after all."

Annalee reeled. This changed everything. She caught the shock on CJ's face as he herded some rowdy boys on the other side of the room. Paula stepped over and took his place.

"The foundation's board ..." He indicated a few of the adults standing around. "... has analyzed the work done at the center and noted the exhaustive waiting list and the other areas of the city which have no childcare assistance available to them. For that reason, we will be opening a new center by this time next year and at least two others in the next few years after that."

A cheer arose.

"We have also sent plans to the zoning committee to expand this facility in order to double the occupancy of the program within the next two years."

That announcement was met with louder appreciation. Annalee glanced around. Several parents had joined the group, squeezing in from the entryway and kitchen.

"Because of the additions, we are adding a position." He raised his glass. "I'd like to toast our new Vice President of Children's Affairs, CJ Whelan."

A whoop rang out and clapping erupted. A couple of boys ran up to CJ, offering him a high five.

CJ's face shined. He stepped toward his dad who met him with an outstretched hand.

"I'm proud of you, Son."

"Thanks, Dad, for understanding."

The kids had waited all they could. Santa was demanded with organized chants. How Mr. Whelan worked the magic, Annalee couldn't tell. Not only did all of the kids get gifts, but each seemed to be exactly what they wanted for Christmas. Dolls, electronics, cameras, sports equipment. Every squeal of delight warmed Annalee's heart.

Even some of the adults received gifts. But when Tally's name was called out, Annalee gasped. How had she missed Tally's presence? The girl came from the open door of the dark nursery. Mr. Madison sat nearby with his wife beside him.

Tally grinned at Annalee as she passed. The gift was an envelope. A scholarship to a local art institute. Tally's eyes shone and Annalee struggled to hold back tears.

Then her own name was called. Santa handed her a small box, a ring box if she was any judge. Her spine iced as she took the gift and unwrapped it. Exactly as it appeared. She looked past Santa to where CJ had been standing near a table of boys. He wasn't there but to search further would be rather obvious. She opened the box.

Empty.

"Whoops." Santa pulled something from his pocket. "I think this must be meant for you." He handed her a ring-pop.

Annalee giggled. "I'll treasure it." She broke open the clear, plastic wrapper and slipped it on her forefinger then licked the top of the gem-shaped lollipop. "I love it. Thank you."

She moved to return to her previous spot. Her parents and Ramona stood beside the nursery door with the Madisons. They must have brought Tally.

CJ approached with a yellow rose. He stepped closer, peering down at her and offered the flower.

Her shoulders stiffened as she took it from his hand and lifted it to her nose to cover her confusion. And the redness that likely accompanied the heat in her cheeks and neck.

"I have an announcement." CJ's gaze locked with hers. "More like a request."

What was he doing? Her breath caught, and her mouth went dry.

"Since I'm staying on at Intercede Foundation, I'm going to need someone to help me. Someone I can count on."

Annalee eyed Margo, near the kitchen door. She'd be the best candidate for his replacement. The older woman beamed.

"Someone who understands me and is willing to stand by me during difficult times."

This was no longer sounding as much like a job assignment. Air fled as he lowered to one knee and held up the solitaire that doubtless matched the empty slot in that box she'd opened.

Annalee gasped.

"And I need someone I can lean on, love, and spend my life

with."

This was real. The forever she'd seen in his face was true.

"If you'll have me." He scanned her face. Worry crept into the expression.

She smiled. Such love seeping out of his eyes. No, adoration. And it was for her. Words caught in her throat as tears filled her eyes. All she could do was nod.

He stood, and she threw her arms around his neck, no longer caring about composure or decorum even in a room full of money and power.

With a yell, CJ lifted Annalee in a whirling spin. She giggled and held him tight. Her hero. Her inspiration.

Cheers resounded around them, as kids and adults alike pressed in. But only CJ mattered. And she mattered to him.

About the Author

Marji Laine is a "graduated" homeschooling mom of four who is grateful to her twins for not forcing her into the empty nest season just yet. She now spends more time in her role as executive editor for Write Integrity Press than she does crafting her own stories, but she loves both jobs.

When she's not wearing the publishing hat, she directs a children's choir, teaches 10th grade girls Sunday school, and sings in the adult choir at her church. She also leads a high school and college weekly Bible study and has a monthly radio talk show.

She and her husband of 30 years live in a suburb on the north side of Dallas with their twins and their own version of Hank the cow dog, a rescue mutt that rides herd on the entire household. Marji prefers mountains to beaches, dogs to cats, Alaska to the Caribbean, entrees to dessert, and white roses to most any other flower. Her favorites include "Live PD," the Hallmark channel, Hand and Foot Canasta, NASCAR, and worship music.

You can learn more about Marji and her books at her author pages on Amazon.com and WriteIntegrity.com and her website, MarjiLaine.com

Acknowledgements

As a new publisher, I've found insight into the meticulous nature of the publishing business and realize just what a huge job it is to critique and proofread with the expertise of the Write Integrity Press editors. I'm so indebted to Angela Maddox and Kathy Nickel for their eagle eyes. I'm especially grateful for my intern, Brittany Clubine (also my daughter) who has learned with much enthusiasm about the publishing business and made life so much easier for me!

I also want to thank Fay Lamb, an extraordinary freelance editor, for stepping in to bless me with an extra eye on my manuscript. Her expertise, not only in editing, but also within the legal realm was invaluable.

Some of the parts of this story have been inspired by the Good News Clubs that meet at schools all over Dallas (and the country). These programs are exceptional for spreading the gospel. You can learn more about the clubs at the Child Evangelism Fellowship website.

I want to thank my sweet husband and kids for taking up the slack when I engage in my passion of writing. The Lord has blessed me with such a compassionate and encouraging family. And they never let me give up.

As for the Lord, He has been so generous with His stories, time, and letting the events fall into place in order to allow this book into the hands of readers.

And I'm grateful for you, dear reader, for your notes, emails, and reviews that encourage me to keep writing.

Other books by Marji

COUNTER POINT Book 1 of Heath's Point Suspense

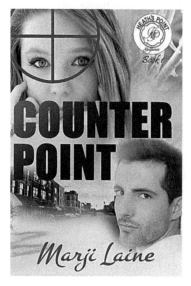

Someone is determined to finish a murdered hit man's final assignment.

Her father's gone. Her diner's closing. Her car's in the lake. Cat McPherson has nothing left to lose. Except her life. And a madman's bent on taking that away.

Her former boyfriend, Ray Alexander, returns as a hero from his foreign mission, bringing back souvenirs in the form of death threats. When several attempts are made on Cat's life, she must find a way to trust Ray, the man who broke her heart.

Keeping Cat safe from a fallen cartel leader might prove impossible for Ray, but after seeing his mission destroyed and several godly people killed, he knows better than to ignore the man's threats. Cat's resistance to his protection and the stirring of his long-denied feelings for her complicate his intentions, placing them both in a fight for their lives.

Can she survive when ultimate power wants her dead?

In print and e-book on Amazon.

GRIME FIGHTER MYSTERIES

Dani Foster has the perfect job for her neat-nick personality, but her inquisitive nature can't always be satisfied with merely cleaning up a crime scene. Especially when some of her friends become targets, suspects, and even victims.

Follow her entire saga, from her missing best friend to the intensity of her witness protection program. And watch for a coming bonus story!

Start with a free copy of *Grime Beat* e-book on Amazon. Also available in print.

Marji Laine

**Thank you
for reading our books!**

**Look for other books
published by**

**Write Integrity Press
www.WriteIntegrity.com**

CPSIA information can be obtained
at www.ICGtesting.com
Printed in the USA
LVHW081030231119
638270LV00028B/605/P